The Valiant Highlander

Highland Defender Series ~ Book Two

by

AMY JARECKI

Rapture Books
Copyright © 2016, Amy Jarecki
Jarecki, Amy
The Valiant Highlander

ISBN: 9781533098047

First Release: June, 2016

Book Cover Design by: Amy Jarecki
Edited by: Scott Moreland

To Maria. And to all lovers of Scottish historical romance. Thank you for sharing my passion for Scotland!

Chapter One

Castleton, Isle of Skye. June, 1695

With a deafening crack, the musket ball missed the target by a furlong. Mary cringed. Perhaps she'd exaggerated the distance of the miss, but after an hour of instruction she expected her little brother to show *some* improvement. With a sigh, she cast her gaze to the puffy, white clouds sailing above. Would the lad ever catch on?

She pulled the stopper from the powder horn with her teeth. "Give it to me," she said out of the corner of her mouth.

"Och, Mary." Rabbie inclined the musket her way. Goodness, the thing was longer than the nine-year-old was tall. "I lined up my sights just like you said."

She snatched the barrel and tilted it away from her face to ensure the gun didn't grow a mind of its own and misfire. "Aye? Then what went wrong?"

The lad rubbed his arm and winced. "Don't ken. But my shoulder feels like Florence stomped on it with one of her wooden heels."

"Then it's the kick. 'Tis forcing you off sights." Mary poured in the powder and jammed a lead musket ball down the barrel with the ramming rod. "You need to push your shoulder into the butt like so." She demonstrated, lifting the wooden stock and taking aim. "Then close your left eye and line up your sights with your right."

"I did all that." Rabbie clapped his hands over his ears as she pulled the trigger and fired.

The ball smacked straight through the center of the bullseye painted red on the straw target. Mary lowered the weapon and gave her little brother a nod. "Ready to give it another go?"

"Aye, and I'll top your shot this time for certain."

He'd been saying that since yesterday at the evening meal when they'd discussed doing some target practice. The lad was keen to prove himself with a musket. After all, before sunset this day every Jacobite chieftain in the Highlands would be arriving at Dunscaith Castle for the games—hosted by the MacDonalds of Castleton for the first time since the secret meetings had begun two years past.

"Just try to hit the target first." She again charged the barrel with powder.

Rabbie held out his hand. "Give me the ball. I'll ram it myself this time."

"Very well." After dropping the piece of lead in his palm, she passed him the musket. Then Mary stood back and folded her arms, saying a prayer he'd have some luck this go round.

Pulling back the cock, he lined up his sights. Then her ginger-haired, freckle-faced brother gave her a cheeky grin. Gracious, if Mary had been a lad, she would have looked just like him when she was a wee lass—though at one and twenty she was twelve years her brother's senior.

"Are you ready?" he asked.

She tipped up her chin. "The question is are *you* ready?"

"Och aye, sis."

She held her breath.

The musket fired and recoiled with a ferocious boom. The scrawny lad tottered backward while Mary waved her hand in front of her face to clear the smoke. "Merciful fairies, you hit it!"

Rabbie slung the musket over his shoulder and ran to the target. "I told you I'd do it."

She chuckled. At least he'd hit the outer edge of the target.

"Hey you pair," Lilas hollered, running over the hill with Florence in her wake. "A *birlinn* has landed and there are more sailing in behind it."

"So soon?" Mary regarded her attire. *I must slip in the postern gate afore anyone sees me.*

"I hit the target," Rabbie yelled, pointing.

Ignoring him, Mary eyed her younger sisters. "Do you ken what clan?"

"Nay." Florence caught up and planted her fists on her hips, giving Mary an exaggerated once-over. "Heaven's stars, why are you wearing trews?"

Mary had actually borrowed the whole get up from Da—bonnet and all. "I cannot very well teach Rabbie how to shoot wearing a kirtle and arisaid, now can I?" It was the same hunting costume Da had worn when teaching her how to handle a musket—in the years before the Battle of Dunkeld when he lost his leg.

"Why not?" The lad came up behind them. "You always wear a dress."

"Aye, but you couldn't see my feet. After the last disaster, I thought it would help some and it did." Mary glanced to her sisters and pointed to the target. "He hit it. Did you see?"

"I saw," an incredibly deep voice said from behind. "Having a bit of target practice afore the games are you?"

The nape of Mary's neck tingled while she spun on her heel. The guests were expected to begin arriving after the midday meal—three hours hence. She bit her bottom lip while her gaze swept down and then back up.

Holy Moses.

The voice belonged to a very tall man, grinning from ear to ear and carrying a musket under his arm. He wore a proper Highland bonnet covering tawny tresses, tied back with a ribbon. Goodness, the nearer he came, the girth of his shoulders grew ever so much wider. His sporran swung to and fro atop his dark plaid while he walked— sword sheathed in the belt across his shoulder, dirk at the front of his hip as if he were ready for battle. Mary's chin dropped. The muscles in his legs flexed like nothing she'd ever seen before.

At seven and ten, Lilas cleared her throat and nudged Mary's arm. "*Gracious,*" she whispered as if she were gazing upon a god.

Giving her sister a subtle elbow, Mary prayed she hadn't turned as red as Lilas. She threw her thumb over her shoulder in the direction of the target. "Teaching the lad how to shoot."

The big man gave Mary the most quizzical look. His stare was most unnerving. Aside from being perhaps the most handsome man she'd chanced to regard, his dark blue eyes made it difficult to breathe. Aye, as dark as midnight those eyes. His gaze started at her man's bonnet and meandered down to her trews before he looked to Rabbie. "Is that so?"

"Och aye. I'll be joining the rebellion soon." The lad never lacked in self-confidence for certain.

The man glanced behind as one eyebrow arched. "You'd best keep your voice down when uttering such fervent words."

Mary stepped in. "Why? Have you not come for the games?"

"Aye, lad." He studied her with a pinch to his brow, as if she posed a confounding sight. "But I spotted a camp of redcoats not fifty miles down the coast."

Mary pursed her lips with a brisk nod. "That would be Lieutenant Balfour MacLeod and his regiment of upstarts." She groaned with a huff. "He's a spineless weasel if you ask me." The officer always looked at her like a starved fox. Worse, he hated everything Jacobite, and insured everyone on her part of Skye suffered in the stocks if they were but a day late with their taxes.

"Aye, he's vile." Lilas batted her eyelashes at the Highlander like a harlot. The lass was incorrigible.

"Then I suggest you stay well away from the likes of him." The man raised his powder horn. Odd, he didn't give Mary's flirting sister a second glance. "Care for a wager?"

"With me?" Mary's jaw nearly hit the ground.

He again regarded her from head to toe. "Thought you said you were teaching the lad to shoot."

"Aye—since our da cannot." Mary took the gun from Rabbie. "A farthing?" Good heavens, she'd never placed a wager in her life.

Frowning, the big Highlander scratched his chin. Merciful fairies, his eyes were an intriguing shade of blue—not like the sky, but more like the sea made angry by a winter storm. "How about a crown?" he asked as if it were a trifle.

Her gaze shifted to the target. She'd hit the bullseye five times today—missed by an inch once. Odds were she'd win...and if she lost, she had a few crowns tucked away in the chest in her bedchamber. But those were intended for her future. No, she'd best not lose. She bit down on the cork and pulled it from the powder horn like she always did. "All right. You first."

Florence caught Mary's eye and mouthed, *a crown?*

Mary knit her eyebrows and batted her hand through the air. "Wheesht," she said so quietly, the shush was barely audible. "Go back to the keep and tell Da the guests are arriving." The last thing she needed was her two sisters giggling behind her and ogling the Highlander.

Nonetheless, Lilas made googly eyes at him. "Do we have to?"

"Aye. And now," Mary said, shooing them away.

"Best of three?" The man still appeared oblivious to her sister's antics.

Mary cringed considering his question. *Is that what men do when they place a wager?* "Certainly."

"Laddie, go fetch us a bit of charcoal. You can mark the shots so we will not lose track."

Rabbie's eyes sparkled as if he'd been commanded by King James himself. "Straight away, sir."

Aye, the man looked dapper with his hair the color of burnt honey neatly tied back with a bow at his nape—his silk waistcoat was of fine tailoring as well, but he couldn't be a chieftain. *Could he?* The man's laird must have alighted the birlinn and headed straight to the keep to greet their da.

By the time they charged their weapons, Rabbie returned, grinning from ear to ear. Mary wasn't sure if his excitement was because her brother wanted to see her bested or if he was happy to have a brawny man there to learn from.

"Do you mind if I fire off a practice shot?" he asked with a hypnotic burr. "I'm afraid my legs think they're still at sea."

Mary gave a polite nod. "By all means." Then a wicked grin spread across her lips. "But only one."

She swayed a bit, watching the man line up his sights. He planted his feet firm, closed one eye, his bold forehead angled down to the barrel. Dear Lord, his concentration was as impressive as his bonny countenance. A tic twitched above his eye just before his finger closed on the trigger. The blast cracked with a puff of smoke.

Mary hardly flinched. "Did you travel far?"

The man peered at her over the musket's stock. "Glasgow."

Goodness, he had come quite a long way. "Was the sea calm for your journey?"

He lowered his weapon. "Och, you're awful chatty for a lad." He squinted at her. "How old are you?"

Mr. Handsome thought her a lad? *Just as well.* Mary cast a thin-lipped glare at Rabbie, sending him a silent message to keep his mouth shut. "Forgive me for talking too much," she said, avoiding the question about her age. At one and twenty, she wasn't about to admit her advanced years to a stranger. She stole a downward glance. Ah yes, her breasts were concealed beneath her father's oversized waistcoat.

Mary hastily gestured to the target. "Carry on."

He again charged his musket and lined up his sights. This time she pursed her lips to prevent her mouth from distracting the man whilst he fired.

With a thunderous boom, his musket kicked more than hers ever had.

Mary's gaze snapped to the target. He hit the outer edge of the bullseye. "Nice shooting."

"My thanks." He grinned, seemingly satisfied with his mark.

Palms perspiring like never before, Mary stepped up to the line. Curses, even her hands shook a bit. She wiped them on her trews and took a deep breath. She wasn't about to lose a whole crown—a farthing mayhap, but not a crown. Positioning the butt against her shoulder, she eyed the bullseye. Confidence surged from her heart as her finger closed on the trigger.

When the smoke cleared, Rabbie was already running to the target. He marked both spots.

"Mine's a hair closer." Mary smiled.

The man squinted. "Perhaps, but there are two more to go."

After the second round, the contest was too close to call—even for Mary. The man had a keen eye for certain, but so did she. By the looks of his attire, losing an entire crown would make no difference to his purse. But it would mean a great deal to her.

His last shot hit the bullseye much like his first.

Mary blew on her palms. This was it. She had to win. Rabbie gave her a nod. With a subtle nod back, she raised the musket, lined up her sights and took a shallow breath. Before she blinked, her finger closed on the trigger.

"Lord in heaven," the man said. "Spot on the middle."

Grinning, Mary held out her palm. "Would you like another round?" Only the fairies knew what prompted her to say that. Holy Moses, she needed to hasten to her bedchamber and change into a kirtle. For heaven's sake, she was the lady of her father's keep. Thank goodness no one important had arrived as of yet. She'd be mortified to be discovered wearing a pair of trews by someone like the Baronet of Sleat.

He ignored her outstretched palm. Those hawkish eyes focused on her while he sauntered forward, rubbing his palm over the pommel of his dirk. "You have no other weapons?"

She took a wee step back. "N-no."

He smirked. "Are you ready to fight for *the cause* should you be called?"

She nodded.

His eyes shifted aside.

The hairs on the back of Mary's neck prickled.

With her next breath, the world reeled. Hands as powerful as a vise clamped on her shoulders and spun her around. Before she knew what happened, her arms were trapped, his dirk leveled at her neck. He pressed his lips to her ear. "Nay, laddie, you'll not be ready for battle until you build a bit o' muscle…can take on a man like me." The deep tenor of his voice rumbled through her entire body—made gooseflesh rise across every inch of skin.

Mary shook right down to the tips of her toes. Mercy, his body was warmer than a brazier and his arm clamped around her torso like iron. Lips parting, she chanced a glance over her shoulder. "Yes, s-sir."

I must not allow him to flummox my sensibilities.

Who was this man? And how dare he manhandle her, even if he thought her a lad?

With a rueful chuckle, he released his grip. "I suggest you wait until your beard comes in afore you join the wrestling competition."

"She's not going to wrestle." Throwing back his shoulders, Rabbie dashed forward and kicked the man in the shin. "Remove your hands from my sister!"

"Ow." The man's jaw dropped. "Sister?" His gaze snapped to Mary's face. "Bloody, miserable, bleating hell. You'd best don a proper gown afore you trick anyone else out of a crown."

Crossing her arms, Mary scooted away. "As I recall, you were the one who placed the wager."

"Aye," said Rabbie. "And I haven't seen your coin, mister."

The man looked at Rabbie as if he could shoot daggers through his eyes. With a growl, he dug in his sporran. "Do not tell me your father is John of Castleton?"

Mary's stomach turned over. Da wouldn't be happy if he found out she was wearing his trews, let alone placing wagers. But she raised her chin and held out her palm. "What if he is?"

"Good God." The man slapped the coin in her hand. "I would have thought more from his offspring."

Please, this cannot be someone important. "Pray tell, what is your name, Mr....?"

"MacDonald." He turned on his square-toed shoe and headed toward the keep.

She smoothed her fingers over the coin while studying his retreating form. Holy Moses, he posed a sight—tall, well-muscled, well-dressed. She bit her bottom lip. Aye, Mr. MacDonald had to be someone important for certain. *He called Da by the familiar.*

With luck, he'd soon forget this morning's events. Looking to the wispy clouds sailing above, Mary clapped her hands together and prayed it would be so.

Da had never allowed her to attend the games before—and growing up in Castleton on the Isle of Skye didn't give her much of an opportunity to meet anyone interesting. And goodness, nearly everyone in these parts was named MacDonald. Several of the clans who'd be here for the games were MacDonalds as well...and Camerons, and Grants, and MacDougalls. Her mind boggled. She'd best hurry. Dunscaith Castle kitchens would need oversight for certain—and she didn't want to be caught by any of the great men due to arrive this afternoon.

***

Marching toward the keep, Sir Donald MacDonald, the Baronet of Sleat, clutched his musket under his arm. Bloody oath, the castle looked as if it were crumbling.

And he'd just been bested by John of Castleton's *daughter*? Covered with freckles, a Highlander's bonnet pulled low over her forehead with her hair hidden, the lass looked more masculine than her little brother—aside from those heart-shaped buttocks. Damnation, he kent something was amiss when he wrestled her into his grip. Not only did she smell like a garden of lilacs, she weighed no more than seven stone. 'Tis why he asked his—rather—*her* age.

Don shook his head. He would have bested the wench if he hadn't been navigating a birlinn through the rough swells of the North Sea since dawn yesterday. He needed a good meal and a healthy tot of whisky to regain his land legs.

Bloody hell, he'd been looking forward to this jaunt to the Highlands. He didn't need a parcel of children in his way. He had serious matters to discuss with the Highland Defenders—the Jacobite chieftains who had pledged their fealty to *the cause*. Aye, one day they'd see King James returned to the throne and oust the usurper, William of Orange. To add insult, the false king's wife, posing as Queen Mary II, was James' very daughter. No greater backstabber hath ever worn a crown.

Chapter Two

Throughout the afternoon, galleys arrived with their chieftains, though there were only three impressive eighteen-oar galleys owned by the Baronet of Sleat, Cameron of Locheil and Stewart of Appin. Some came by land, like Sir Coll of Keppoch and his regiment of wily upstarts. Of all the Highland chieftains, Don felt Coll wielded the most powerful sword. But the young laird's strength would soon be tested. Och aye, this evening an impressive crowd of brawn amassed in Dunscaith Castle's great hall.

Sitting at the high table, Don reached for the ewer and poured himself a tankard of ale. "I haven't seen the Duke of Gordon or the Earl of Seaforth."

"Sent their apologies," said John of Castleton, their host. "That makes you our most esteemed guest, sir."

Don watched the froth of his ale bubble. "Aye? We need numbers—and a voice amongst the peers on the Privy Council."

"Agreed," said Hugh MacIain of Glencoe. The man had endured the worst of King William's ire against the Jacobites when his clan was decimated by that miserable Campbell lout of Glenlyon. "We'll never organize a rising with apathetic nobles who send their regrets."

"The time for battle will come." Ewen Cameron, the eldest chieftain in attendance, cracked his thumb knuckles. "Until then we must use other means to undermine the bastards."

"Aye, when English wares bear no taxes? I cannot sell a pound of packing salt anywhere throughout Europe." Donald took a healthy swallow of ale. 'Twas the main reason why he hadn't sent his regrets for this gathering. He'd traveled to Skye for two reasons. First, to partake in the games and secondly, to visit his salt pans. He had a meeting with a buyer from the Americas in a fortnight. All must be in order, for if that business transaction did not take place, the Baronetcy of Sleat could very well be forced into bankruptcy. *Then what will happen to my lands, my kin?*

"The bastards are trying to starve us out of existence," said Robert Stewart of Appin.

"But we will not let them." Ewen rapped his knuckles on the table. "Sir Donald, we must insure your meeting with the buyer from the Americas is successful."

"Bloody oath, I agree." Don tipped up his tankard and drank heartily. "And every last one of us must do our best to purchase Scottish wares—nothing from England. They want to destroy us? Well, two can play at that game."

"Slàinte," the cheers rose around the table. Every man there was in the same predicament. In fact, if Don's hunch was right, he was better off than most.

When three lasses stepped from the stairwell, the noise in the hall ebbed to a murmur.

Sir John pushed back his wheeled chair, his single, withered leg flopping sideways. "Mary, come," he hollered.

Don had to look twice before he recognized the lass from the shooting match. But still, he wasn't certain. Was it she, or did she have a bonny twin? Dear God, the woman's ginger tresses hung past her slender waist, gracefully swinging to and fro. The woman who moved toward the dais did so with such poise and grace, Don convinced himself she must be some other of John's offspring.

Miss Mary's smile radiated throughout the entire chamber and she walked like an angel floating over the floorboards. Petite, her figure reminded Don of an hourglass—incredibly feminine and delicate. As she climbed the steps to the dais, her freckles became more apparent, but the adorable splay across her nose only served to add to *this* woman's beauty. More freckles blended with the soft blush of her cheeks, with some hidden by the wisps of ginger ringlets surrounding her face.

It cannot be the same guttersnipe who pulled off her powder cork with her teeth.

Sir John gestured with a sweeping hand. "Please allow me to introduce my eldest, Miss Mary of Castleton."

Don stood. Hitting the table with his hips, his ale teetered and crashed sideways. His hands grappled blindly as the frothy liquid spilled. "P-pleased to meet you, miss."

As servants rushed to contain the mess, Sir Ewen stood and bowed, brushing Don's ale from his doublet with a kerchief. "Don't mind the clumsy Baronet of Sleat here. He's only come to douse us poor sops in ale."

Hands clapped and laughter rolled around the high table.

Miss Mary's red eyebrows arched while she drew a hand over her mouth. Her gaze trailed down to the mess, her cheeks turning from a lovely rose to ruby red. "Oh my. I do hope your doublet isn't ruined, Sir Cameron."

"Not at all." Ewen bowed his head.

"My daughters are looking forward to this night's dancing with fervent anticipation." Sir John beckoned Miss Mary to his side. "Though I hate to lose this bonny lass, I must make an alliance with her hand." The man gave Don a pointed look.

If a woman could die of blushing, it would be John of Castleton's daughter. Don had never seen anyone sustain such high color before—and he was the person who'd spilled the ale. But her father's inappropriate and untimely innuendo needed his attention more. Don frowned at the verbose chieftain. "I wish you well on your quest, sir."

"She runs this keep with the efficiency of a field marshal," Sir John blurted as if he had a prized heifer on the auction block.

"Och, you exaggerate, Da." Miss Mary kept her eyes downcast, refusing to meet Don's gaze—or regard anyone at the table for that matter.

Don shifted in his seat. The last thing he'd attended this gathering for was to discuss the future of any of Sir John of Castleton's daughters.

The old chieftain patted Miss Mary's hand. "Go join your wee brother and sisters. And I expect you to be on hand for the dancing—with so many lads about, they'll need partners for certain. And with a bit o' luck, I'll find husbands for the lot of you within a sennight."

Now the poor lass turned a shade of chartreuse. In fact, Don took pity upon the maid. Good God, her father not only embarrassed his daughter, but he also embarrassed himself carrying on so—and right in front of some of the most influential men in the Highlands. The man might be bound to his cripple chair, but he had three days to pull potential suitors aside and speak to them about possible matches with his daughters.

Mary maintained her downcast gaze and curtseyed. "Welcome guests. Please enjoy the fare."

"Och, Miss Mary," said Ewen Cameron. "Thanks to the baronet, I must change out of this ale-soaked kilt. Why not take my place at the high table? Surely, you're accustomed to sitting here with your father."

Her gaze shot to Don. Panic flashed across her azure eyes. Mercy, those blues captured the Highland sky on a summer's day.

Sir Ewen bowed. "Unless you object, sir?"

"Uh..." Don blinked dumbly. "Ah, of course, unless our conversation is a bit dry for a woman?" He addressed that to her father with a furrow to his brow. Don's sister, Barbara, would sooner keel over dead than join in a conversation about politics.

"Bah." Sir John swatted a hand through the air and pulled his rolling chair back to the table. "Miss Mary is as sharp as any man. Sit, dear. 'Tisn't often we have such company in our midst."

Don caught her subtle groan as she took the seat to his right.

He leaned toward her—searching for words to ease her embarrassment. "I daresay you are a mite more charming than that tomboy sister of yours."

"Oh?" Her back snapped straight as a board as she met his gaze.

"Aye." He smiled warmly. "Had I not poured ale all over Sir Ewen, we may not have had an opportunity to chat this eve." Craning his neck, Don looked to the table just below the dais where Sir John's children sat. "Where, pray tell, is your wayward sister?"

"Ahem, Miss Lilas and Miss Florence are seated with Rabbie..." Her eyes trailing aside, Miss Mary's face flushed scarlet, yet again. "Oh dear, you are referring to the sharpshooter, are you not?"

"Sharpshooter?" her father said with a belch. "Why, my Mary can hit a bullseye from two hundred paces."

Don reached for the ale, his gut clamping into a ball. Dear God, was he to put his foot in his mouth with his every word? This gathering couldn't end soon enough. "Is that so?" He poured for her, leaning close so only she could hear. "'Tis not a skill men find appealing in a maid, nor is placing wagers."

***

If Mary could have crawled under the table and slipped through a knot in the wooden floor, she would have turned herself into a mouse just to do so. Hells bells, she'd bested the Baronet of Sleat? Goodness, the man couldn't be more than five and twenty. Weren't baronets old? Curses, how daft could she be? And what could she say to exonerate herself? Or did she want to? The man appeared to be as arrogant as William of Orange himself.

She groaned under her breath. Blast it all, her father's hopes would be dashed if she didn't try to be nice—didn't show herself to be marriageable. Without instruction or a mother to guide her, she was failing miserably on that count. Why did she need a husband anyway? Da needed her to run the keep just as she'd done since the age of twelve.

Truth be told, Mary wanted a husband as much as she wanted a bad rash, but Da said it was her duty to help the clan. Things had grown troublesome since her father's paralyzing injury and the loss of his leg at the Battle of Dunkeld. To keep himself from financial ruination, Da needed to make an alliance with her hand—and fast.

Mary only hoped he wouldn't be so hasty with her younger sisters.

Unfortunately, she'd now ruined her chances with the Baronet of Sleat, not that such a man would ever look twice at a freckle-faced tomboy such as her. She surveyed the faces at the table. Sir Robert Stewart sitting across was still a candidate, as was Sir Ewen's son, Sir Kennan, though younger. And Sir Coll of Keppoch was impressive and he had red hair just like hers. Mary's stomach turned over as if she were about to squelch. The idea of making an alliance with her marriage bed made her want to don Da's trews and join the army. The only problem? Today's Government troops happened to be the enemy. If only the other eligible chieftains were half as alluring as the brawny man perched beside her.

Forget about him.

Sitting erect in his starched shirt, Mary didn't need a pompous baronet making her life miserable.

Taking a deep breath, she gave Sir Donald a weak smile. "Shooting is only a frivolous hobby, sir. Since my father is no longer able to address the target, someone must teach Rabbie to handle a musket."

He peered down his nose at her—it was a nice nose—masculine, but not too large for his face. "Perhaps the lad needs to be fostered."

She arched her eyebrows. "Are you volunteering?"

"Unfortunately, no. I've business in Glasgow that prevents me from such enjoyable exploits."

"You would exploit a lad of nine?"

He reached for the ewer and poured for her, then himself. "Of course not. You misunderstood my use of the word."

"Did I?" She sipped her ale and grinned behind her tankard. Why God had granted her with such a wicked tongue, she had no idea. But ribbing a nobleman was awfully fun—even more fun than vexing her father.

Sir Donald took a slice of bread and buttered it. "Why do I sense you are ribbing me?"

"Me?" She patted her chest giving him her most innocent wide-eyed stare—one that always worked with her father. "Why, I've no idea to what you are referring, sir."

Fyfe, one of the guards who posed as a servant this eve stepped between them. "Rack of lamb, sir?"

The baronet gestured toward Mary. "Please, serve the lady first."

"Thank you." She selected a tender looking morsel. She would expect a man like the Baronet of Sleat to have impeccable manners. He might even have some redeeming qualities aside from his good looks. "And how long do you intend to stay at Dunscaith, sir?"

"I'm heading north to my lands in Trotternish as soon as the games are over. I've a great many things to oversee afore I return to Glasgow."

"Aye," said Sir Robert. "If only your mine yielded gold rather than salt."

"Salt is white gold, Stewart. As long as there are no embargoes." Sir Donald cut his meat precisely, swirled it in gravy and slipped a bite into his mouth. "Mm. This is delicious. My compliments, Miss Mary."

"I shall inform the cook. He will be pleased you are agreeable."

The nice thing about food was it kept people's mouths busy so they didn't have to say much, which suited Mary just fine. In truth, she would have preferred to sit below with her siblings. Lilas cast frequent looks of longing toward Mary while at twelve, Florence waved and giggled. As usual, Rabbie paid more attention to pinching food from Florence's plate while his sister wasn't looking.

After dessert was served, the clansmen and women moved the tables to make room for the musicians and dancing. Mary clapped. "Do you enjoy a reel, Sir Donald?"

"I don't think it's a matter of enjoyment so much as a social obligation." He raised his tankard and sipped.

"Truly?" She chuckled and lowered her voice. "'Tis not quite like feeling the wind in your hair with the slow burn of a matchlock warming your cheek, is it?"

He snorted so loudly, ale could have frothed through his nose.

"You ken Sir Donald was decorated for his heroism in the Battle of Killiecrankie—called Sir Donald of the Wars—rode against the Government troops at the age of nineteen," said Mary's da.

Of course she knew the stories and respected the fact that she sat beside a war hero. And from the girth of his shoulders, it wasn't difficult to understand why. Still, were people to be revered all their lives because they fought valiantly in one or two battles? Why did men receive all the notoriety? Mary would ride into battle if they would allow her to do so. She'd lead her clan, too. But that wasn't the way of things. Until Da started planning this gathering of high-ranking Jacobites, Mary's lot in life was to stay in the castle and manage Dunscaith's affairs. No, they weren't wealthy, but they had a healthy flock of sheep, which brought in revenues from wool—and the crofters paid rent—when they had the coin.

The problem was no one had any coin at the moment—and that's exactly why her father volunteered to host the gathering this spring. Bring the Highlanders to Castleton so they can feast their eyes on my lovely daughters, he'd say.

The pipers filled their bladders with air, making a racket. Florence clapped her hands and squealed while the fiddlers tuned their instruments.

Sir Donald pushed back his chair and bowed deeply. "May I have this dance?"

Mary's hand flew to her chest. "With me?" she asked with incredulity. After all, the man had just admitted to his indifference for dancing.

"I'd wager the men outnumber the women at this gathering by three-to-one and I certainly do not aim to give the Chieftain of Appin a turn."

Shifting her gaze to Sir Robert, Mary agreed, "Thank you."

He took her palm in his—goodness it was warm and so much larger and more callused than Mary had imagined. Her small hand practically disappeared beneath his fingers. Sir Donald's tawny eyebrows drew together. "I thought you would rather enjoy a dance."

She chanced a glimpse of his face from beneath her red lashes. "Aye, just a wee bit surprised, all things considered."

Together they proceeded down the dais steps while the baronet sported a grin. "We are here for a gathering. Regardless if you'd rather be running around in your father's trews, a young lass who acts as lady of the keep should be the first to grace the dance floor."

Her cheeks grew warm for the umpteenth time. "Why is that, because you feel sorry for a spinster who cares for her father?"

"I hardly see you as a spinster—yet." His jaw twitched. "'Tis the way of things. I'm surprised you do not ken it."

Mary huffed. Decorum? How in heaven's name was she supposed to learn decorum when she'd never been to court—never been anywhere important? And why were her insides twisting about? This was but a silly dance. An interchange that meant naught but to make merry.

Arriving at the lady's line, Sir Donald released her hand, then stepped across and joined the men. Good heavens, he posed a picture. One tawny lock had slipped from his ponytail and curled down the side of his face. His cravat tied in a perfect knot with a lace collar peeking above his black-velvet doublet. Kilt, to hose, to square-toed ghillies tied with black ribbon, the Baronet of Sleat presented a picture of the ideal Highland chief. A descendant of the Lords of the Isles and heir to the most powerful clan in Scotland, with many septs and clans reporting to him, just as Mary's clan did, he alone was the most influential man on the Isle of Skye.

The introduction of a reel began.

Sir Donald bowed, but he didn't lower his head. Rather, he kept his gaze fixed on her—those dark eyes unwavering as if he were waiting for her to err, or challenging her to do so.

Mary curtseyed in kind. The man had already proved he enjoyed a good wager. Perhaps he aimed to best her with a high-stepping reel. Skipping toward him and locking arms, she couldn't help her burst of laughter with the image of Sir Donald leaping and kicking his legs higher and faster than anyone in the hall.

"Do you find the music humorous?" he asked.

"Not at all." Fortunately, the dance gave her an excuse to avoid an explanation when she locked elbows with the man to Donald's right and skipped in a circle.

Twirling back toward the baronet, her skirts billowed and brushed along his muscular calf. Mary could have sworn she saw something flash in the deep recesses of his eyes, but he soon covered any reaction with a calm and commanding presence. The Baronet of Sleat proved quite adept on his toes as he performed the steps to the reel with expert precision—with no exaggerated moves whatsoever. When they moved together, their palms met, but not too intimately. Sir Donald applied just the right amount of pressure and nothing more.

Mary's gaze meandered up to his face. His eyes focused on hers, his mouth forming a thin line. What on earth was the man thinking with a visage such as his?

"Does the music meet with your approval?" she asked.

"Aye, quite invigorating."

"And the hall?"

"Everything is very well appointed."

"Are you looking forward to the games on the morrow?"

"It shall be good sport, indeed." He took her hand and led her sashaying down the line so ably he could have passed for a statue in motion.

Mary mirrored his stately countenance, executing the steps as deftly as he. When at last her hand left his as she danced up the outside of the line, her fingers grew oddly cold and she balled her fist to ward off the uneasy sensation.

Stepping around the last woman, Mary again faced him. The music ended.

He offered a stately bow, and she a deep curtsey in return. "Thank you, sir. You are an accomplished dancer."

"'Tis kind of you to say so, but—"

The doors to the great hall burst open and in sauntered Lieutenant Balfour MacLeod, dressed in his red uniform—red like innocent blood. He sported his usual scowl, his gaze darting directly to Mary. "Exactly what is going on here and why was I not informed?"

Every man upon the dais stood—aside from Da, of course.

Mary hastened toward the boor. "Pardon me, lieutenant. Since when did it become a law for us to inform you when we have guests?"

"It is my duty to be apprised of all events in my territory."

"If you must ken, 'tis a clan gathering." She crossed her fingers behind her back. "The MacDonald Clans and guests from throughout the Highlands have come for feast and games."

Balfour squinted and swept his gaze to the high table. "MacDonalds," he spewed as if the name were vile. "Come to plan a rebellion, is that it?"

"I beg your pardon?" The Baronet of Sleat strolled forward, his palm resting atop the pommel of his dirk. "I believe the lady said this is a gathering. No more. Unless King William has suddenly written into law that kin are no longer allowed to meet?"

The lieutenant faced Sir Donald, looking him from head to toe with a sneer. "And who in God's name are you?"

Chapter Three

Sliding one foot forward, Don performed an exaggerated bow to mock the beslubbering codfish who'd interrupted their merriment. "Sir Donald MacDonald, Baronet of Sleat, at your service, lieutenant. And in the future you may address me as *Sir Donald.*"

"Aye?" The lieutenant pursed his lips, looking like he'd swallowed a bitter tonic. "So Sir John of Castleton finally managed to ferret you away from your dung hill in Glasgow?"

Don eyed the dozen redcoats standing behind the disrespectful officer. The Highlanders could take them for certain, but then word of action against Government troops would spread across Britain like a brushfire. No matter how much he wanted to teach the cur a lesson in treating one's betters, he folded his arms and meandered to within a hand's breadth of the spineless weasel. "We've arrived for the MacDonald gathering as Miss Mary has already said." He gestured toward the dance floor. "As you see, we are making merry. Have you an issue with that?"

The short and stocky officer craned his neck and met Don's gaze with beady, grey eyes. "I see the whisky is flowing abundantly. I wonder how Sir John ventured to afford such lavishness."

A crash erupted from the dais as their host banged the pommel of his dirk on the table. "By the saints, if I had use of my legs I'd come down and teach you a lesson. 'Tis no business of yours, you insolent pup."

"But it is my business." The lieutenant stepped around Don. "You've one too many eighteen-oar galleys moored in the bay. You're breaking the law for certain."

"Are you jesting?" Don asked, his blood beginning to thrum. He hated red-coated dragoons clear to the depths of his soul and this one epitomized the reason for his abhorrence. *Put a red coat on a man and give him some brass epaulets, and he thinks he's God Almighty.*

The lieutenant faced him with a thin-lipped grin. "Why jest when the law clearly states no more than two eighteen-oar galleys moored—'tis grounds for suspicion of a rising."

Don threw up his hands. "God's bones, we'll be on our way two days hence."

"You'd best be gone on the morrow."

"Or what?" He stepped in, refusing to let the man bully him.

MacLeod smirked. "I'm sure the crown would make good use of a sleek, new seafaring vessel."

"'Tis thievery." Don gripped his fingers around the hilt of his dirk, narrowing his eyes. "You place a hand on one of our galleys and I shall take it up with Colonel Hill in Fort William forthwith."

"You dare to directly disobey the edicts of our good king?" The nitwit's gaze drifted to Don's weapon—still sheathed but at the ready. "I'm sure the colonel would be interested to hear that Donald MacDonald of Sleat is a *Jacobite.*"

"Watch your tongue," Don seethed.

"Oh really?" The man swept his gaze across the crowd with an arrogant flare to his nostrils. "You'd best not think of placing one of your neatly manicured hands on a Government officer."

With one more step, Don growled, "Och, I wouldn't need to use my hands."

The Highland chieftains gathered behind him—no weapons drawn, but that could be remedied easily enough.

MacLeod took a wee step back—a sign of a coward. "What have you been doing since you lost the Battle of Dunkeld? Planning another revolution so we can boot your arse out of Scotland? You'd fare well heading to the Americas on a ship full of swine." The dragoons behind Balfour sniggered.

Gritting his teeth, Don thrust his finger toward the door. "My ship will sail after the games two days hence. Now I suggest you go find your flock. I can hear them bleating your name."

The lieutenant smirked and averted his attention to Mary. "How can you entertain guests who are so discourteous?" He tsked his tongue. "And you didn't think to invite me? I held you in higher esteem, Miss Mary."

"Forgive me if I've appraised poorly in your eyes," she said with a mocking edge in her voice.

"Did you not hear the lass when you first arrived?" asked Hugh MacIain. "This is a *Clan Donald* gathering. I believe I heard the lass refer to you as MacLeod—'tis no sept of ours."

"Too right," said Don before the piss-swilling cur had a chance to spurt a rebuke—or figure out that there were Stewarts, Camerons, MacDougalls and more in attendance. "Now we'd like to carry on with our celebrations."

The lieutenant inclined his head toward his men. "You haven't heard the last of this, mark me." Throwing back his shoulders, he stepped up to Miss Mary, took her hand and planted a vulgar kiss upon the back. It wasn't a proper light peck of a gentleman. The man hovered as if smelling a vat of mulled wine and then he took his bloody time pressing his lips to her flesh.

Don rubbed his palm around his dirk's pommel. If only he could challenge the lecherous cur here and now.

The lieutenant chuckled as he straightened. "As always, it has been a pleasure to see you again, Miss Mary."

The poor lass turned redder than beetroot. She snapped her hand away from the braggart and clasped it under her chin. "A sentiment which I do not return."

MacLeod snorted as he turned away. "You'd best watch your manners, else your guests will think ill of you."

Mary balled her fists like she was ready to take a swing at his head.

"I'll see you out." Don stepped between them. "I wish I could say it has been a pleasure." After he opened the big door, he leaned toward Balfour's ear so only the milk-livered swine could hear. "Keep your hands off the lass, else you'll answer to me."

"Are you threatening an officer of His Majesty's Army?"

"You'd best believe it." Before the lieutenant could come back with a sharp retort, Don slammed the door in his face. Then he spun on his heel. "Who the hell does that fat-kidneyed nitwit think he is?"

Mary gave her foot a good stamp. "He's reckons he owns the entire Isle of Skye."

"Aye," said Rabbie, moving in beside her. "And I do not like the way he ogles my sister."

Don didn't care for it, either. As a matter of fact, it had taken all of his self-control not to ask the officer to step outside. But an err like that could put his American contract in jeopardy—even if he wasn't thrown into the stocks. Damnation, Don would not allow William of Orange and the Government troops to stand in his way. He, his clan and the entire Jacobite cause depended on opening new lines of trade lest they be starved out of existence.

He grasped Mary by the shoulders. "Stay away from that despicable dragoon. A man like that would like nothing better than to pounce on a chance to break us."

Twisting away, she drew a hand to her chest. "Of course I would never do anything to put our cause in peril."

"Not knowingly."

Her brow furrowed. "Pardon me?"

Choosing not to pursue the conversation further, Don clapped his hands at the minstrels. "Why are you standing with your mouths agape? Our host has brought our clans together to make merry and that is what we shall do."

He looped his arm through Mary's elbow. "Dance with me."

"Very well," she said as if it were her bounden duty to do so. "As lady of the keep, I must see to the enjoyment of my father's guests."

He chuckled—aye, a lass who dressed in trews to teach her wee brother to shoot wouldn't let a visit from a red-coated buffoon spoil her evening. "You do have spirit, Miss Mary, I'll grant you that."

She stepped into the ladies line on the floor. "I would have thought there would be no doubt of my spirit after our wee shooting competition this morn."

A tic twitched at the corner of his eye. And she was growing more audacious by the minute. "Aye, but you caught me with my sea legs."

"Perhaps another match?" Her eyes twinkled with blue and mischief. "My coffers could use some fattening."

Och, I reckon I've allowed her to take her chiding a bit too far. No, he couldn't allow himself to play along with the vixen this time. God's teeth, a lass like Mary of Castleton could bring a man undone and that was the last thing Don could allow, given the circumstances. A dance or two he could manage, and that was all. He frowned. "As I said afore, 'tis not ladylike to place wagers with gentlemen."

"Och aye?" She rolled her eyes to the grand ceiling. "'Tis unfortunate my mother passed away afore she could teach me the finer qualities of being a lady. Not to mention my father succumbing to his wounds at Dunkeld." She skipped toward him and looped her arm through his elbow with a fair bit of force for such a small wisp. "I'll tell you, sir. A lass growing up on lands as remote as Castleton has no choice but to gird her loins and take every challenge as it comes."

Don pursed his lips together, forcing himself not to laugh. *Gird her loins? Good Lord, give the lass a wee compliment and she becomes insufferable.* "With such passionate fortitude, your father is fortunate to have you." *Because, with that fiery disposition, she'll likely remain a spinster for the rest of her days.*

Mary met him in the center of the line and pressed her palms against his. "Unfortunately, Da intends to sell me to the highest bidder."

His mouth twisted. "I thought all young maids looked forward to their betrothal."

"Not me." She twirled away.

A spinster—just as I thought. "Why ever not you?"

"As you see, I am needed here. Who will look after my father? Not to mention I have two sisters and a brother who rely on me."

Don glanced down the line at Mary's younger sister. "Perhaps 'tis time Miss Lilas took on responsibility for the keep?"

Her lips blew a raspberry. "You cannot be serious. I dearly love my sister, but she's as flighty as a finch. I daresay she'd run for her chamber the first time the cook disagreed with her menu choice."

"Aye? But isn't that how she'll learn? What will happen when she marries and must run a keep of her own?"

Mary rolled her eyes. "Heaven help her future husband."

Chuckling to himself, Don watched Mary out of the corner of his eye. Perhaps he'd judged her too harshly, but he rather doubted it. Indeed, with her mother gone and her father crippled, she'd been forced to step in and take charge. She was peculiarly attractive. Wholesomeness came to mind, though lacking in the finer skills of a cultured Glasgow woman. But where would a Highland lass like Mary find an opportunity to learn refinement? Lady MacLeod of Dunvegan to the north was out of the question. Aside from being a fire-breathing dragon, at every opportunity the woman's husband made it eminently clear he and the MacLeod Clan sided with the Williamite Government.

The music ended. After Mary curtseyed, she planted her fists on her hips. "Are you unwell, Sir Donald? You look dazed."

He blinked. "Forgive me. My mind is elsewhere."

"Blast the lieutenant," Mary said, evidently assuming Don was still thinking about the unpleasant visit from the dragoons. "How dare he come here and spoil everyone's merriment?"

Don offered his elbow and started toward the dais. "Och, our clans are of sturdy Highland ilk. We'll not allow such a miscreant to foul our good spirits."

"Miss Mary, may I have this dance?" interrupted Sir Robert.

Don glared at the Appin Chieftain.

"Of course, thank you." Mary curtseyed.

With no other recourse, Don relented and bowed. "Miss Mary." He turned on his heel. Why on earth it bothered him that young Stewart asked Mary for a turn on the floor, he had no idea. Sir Robert would be an ideal match for the lass. Damn it all, her father had been clear he intended to find a husband. No one needed to tell Don he was the last person in the hall to fulfill such a role. Let the maid spin her wiles around someone else's sensibilities for a while.

Uncouth, ginger-haired and freckled? He would be laughed out of every parlor in Glasgow with Miss Mary of Castleton on his arm.

Chapter Four

"Have you ever seen a more dapper gentleman?" Lilas said with a sigh, resting her elbows in a crenel notch atop Dunscaith Castle's bailey.

Leaning on the stone wall beside her sister, Mary smirked. "I'm not exactly sure that's the right word." True, she'd never seen a man who dressed in such well-appointed finery, but Sir Donald MacDonald's frame was large and solid, not *dapper*.

"What word would you use?" Lilas asked.

"Hmm…" If she said handsome or divine, her sisters would never let her live it down. "He's stately."

Lilas snorted. "You *are* entirely dull."

"I like him," said Florence.

"Oh?" Mary arched an eyebrow at her youngest sister. "Why, pray tell?"

"Because he stood up to Balfour MacLeod last eve." The twelve-year-old made an angry face, looking like a gargoyle. "I'd like to see the lieutenant receive his comeuppance one day. He always lurks about the castle acting like he's the most important man on the Isle of Skye."

"He thinks he is," said Mary.

Florence shook her finger. "I don't like the way he leers at you, either. Honestly, he looks like a hungry dog ready to pounce."

Mary shuddered. "He *is* a dog." She probably disliked the lieutenant more than her sisters did.

"A rabid dog," added Lilas. Her hips swayed in place as Sir Donald removed his waistcoat and took a sizable stone from the groomsman. "But Sir Donald MacDonald is *dreamy.*"

Heavens, Lilas lives in a world of fantasy.

Still, Mary's tongue slipped to the corner of her mouth as the baronet took his place for the stone put. All three sisters leaned through the crenel. Goodness, the baronet posed a sight dressed in his Highland garb, the folds of his kilt swishing against the backs of his muscular legs.

In two steps, Sir Donald hefted the stone with a deep bellow that resonated all the way up to the lasses at the top of the wall-walk.

Florence clapped her hands. "Farthest yet."

"See? Dreaaaaamy." Lilas harrumphed at Mary. "I have no idea why he turned his attentions to you during the entire feast last eve."

Mary crossed her eyes and groaned. "Oh please, father made me sit beside the poor man."

Tugging Mary's sleeve, Florence giggled. "Because he wants you to marry him."

Lilas crossed her arms and glared at their youngest sister. "Pardon me?" She pursed her lips, flushing apple red.

Clearly the lass is smitten.

Well, Mary wanted none of it. "Sir Donald has come for the games and that is all. Heavens, a man such as the Baronet of Sleat would have no interest in any of us. He resides in a townhouse in Glasgow, for goodness sakes.

Men like that attend the opera and keep company with all manner of dignitaries."

"Aye, but Glasgow?" Lilas swayed to and fro. "Imagine the dancing, the music, the society, gowns of silk."

"And delicious food," said Florence. Thank heavens Florence had her feet firmly on the ground.

Mary held up her palms and focused on the elder of the two. "I suggest you set your sights on a clan chieftain a wee bit closer to home."

Lilas threw her shoulders back. "I beg your pardon, the Baronet of Sleat owns lands in Trotternish, right here on the Isle of Skye."

How could Mary reason with the unreasonable? "Och, you are but a silly imp."

"I ken what I want in this life."

"I'm happy to hear one of us is so certain about the future." Mary moved to the next crenel. Goodness gracious, Sir Donald removed his shirt. Her knees turned to boneless mollusks. Mouth dry, she gaped at the undulating muscles bared for all to see. He didn't appear to have an ounce of fat anywhere—if only she were closer, surely the distance was playing tricks on her eyes.

"It appears there's been a tie for the stone put," said Florence.

Lilas clapped. "I hope the baronet wins."

Mary pursed her lips. Merciful fairies, her sister's foolish display of adoration was maddening. And why did the man have to remove his shirt? Could he not throw a blasted rock as far with it on? No man should be thusly appointed with banded muscles rippling across his back and chest. It was scandalous.

"Oh my," Lilas' voice resonated from the other crenel.

Unable to pull her gaze away, Mary's mouth dropped open. Sir Donald heaved the stone, sending it soaring until it landed with a thud.

"No one will be able to beat that," said Lilas.

Coll MacDonell, Chieftain of Clan MacDonell of Keppoch, stepped up to the line, removing his shirt as well. Unbelievable. He was built like the hindquarter of a hackney horse.

"Are all Highland chieftains made of iron?" asked Florence.

"I have died and gone to heaven," Lilas blubbered from her place on the wall-walk. "I'm certain of it."

"Just make sure you don't swoon and fall from the bailey." Mary clutched her hands to her chest while she watched Sir Donald take his shirt from his valet and pull it over his head. A long exhale slipped through her lips. Heaven forbid he spend the remainder of the afternoon half-naked. Lilas would have swooned and fallen to her death for certain.

Fortunately, one more day and the gathering would be over. In all likelihood everything would return to normal, except her father would be disappointed Mary hadn't made a braw chieftain fall in love with her. She straightened and brushed off her hands. "I'd best go see to Da's care."

"When there are games to be watched?" Lilas moved a hand to her hip. "Goodness, Mary, why are you always so serious?"

"Aye," Florence agreed. "Let Mrs. Watt look after him. He seems to like her."

"Mrs. Watt?" Knitting her eyebrows, Mary huffed. "What does she ken about taking care of Da's needs?"

Florence shrugged. "Not sure, but she's been spending more time in the library with him."

Mary's wee sister could be a snoop. "And how do you ken this?"

"Because I hide in the window embrasure and read..." Florence cringed like she expected a rebuke.

Mary gave her a stern frown. "You mustn't loiter about when our father is entertaining guests."

"Eew," said Lilas. "You're disgusting, Florence."

"But I always read in the window embrasure."

Mary started toward the stairwell. "Well, you had best find some other place to read—like your chamber. There's plenty of light there."

***

Mary hastened through the passageway to her father's chamber where he'd said he could watch the games from his window embrasure. Immobile, he spent his days either on the second floor in his solar or bedchamber and the men would carry him below stairs for each evening meal.

After knocking with her usual single rap, Mary opened the door. "Da, are you ready—?" Her jaw practically dropped open wide enough to hit the floor. Never in her life had she been assaulted with a scene so scandalous.

Da propped in the bed beside Mrs. Watt, both of their shoulders bare—a-and they were sipping sherry—at this hour.

Setting his glass on the bedside table, father tugged the bedclothes higher, thank goodness. "Don't just stand there like you're daft," he chided as if it were a daily occurrence for him to be abed, bare-shouldered, with a *woman*.

Slipping downward, Mrs. Watt all but disappeared.

Mary dropped her gaze to the floorboards. "Forgive me."

"Go on now—close the door, lassie." From the way Da grumbled, it sounded like he blamed her for the awkward situation.

Mary's stomach twisted in a knot—so did her shoulders—two painful, incredibly mortified knots. "W-when would you like me to return for your massages?"

Da took up his sherry and held it aloft in toast. "Mrs. Watt is assuming my care. Haste ye down to the games and smile at the chieftains. I want you to make a good impression on at least one of them. Time is growing short."

Drawing her hand over her eyes, Mary curtseyed. "Yes, Father."

"Now off with you."

Mary didn't need to be told again. She let the door slam and dashed for the stairwell.

Mrs. Watt is taking over Da's care? What on earth does that mean? Merciful fairies, it appeared like she was planning to take over a great deal more than that. A harlot in Da's bed! An evil, wicked, wanton harlot!

Tears welled in her eyes while she raced down the wheeled stairwell. No wonder her father had been overly anxious to marry her off. He'd already found a replacement—someone who provided services Mary never could. Worse, Da replaced her before she'd even been courted, let alone betrothed. No wonder he'd pushed her so.

I've done everything to see to it this gathering is perfect—to make my father proud, and what does he do before the games are over? How dare he behave this scandalously when so many guests are about?

Gulping, she tried to swallow back the burning in her throat. Not only was her father's behavior inconsiderate, he put her in a position to be completely humiliated. There was a clock on the mantel. He owned a pocket watch. Da knew she would be there for his mid-morning massage. She was never late. *Never.*

And why on earth didn't he bother to ask Mrs. Watt to lock the door? Did he want Mary to be shocked—scarred for the rest of her days?

How dare he do that to me?

Tears stung her eyes as she dashed through the great hall and out the front gate.

"Good morrow, Miss Mary," someone called from a group of clansmen.

"G-morrow," she croaked, trying to sound cheerful. Through bleary eyes, her gaze darted side-to-side, then ahead, looking for an escape. Curses, of all the days for the hall to be filled with clanspeople, it had to be today.

Tugging her arisaid around her shoulders, Mary held her head high as she slowed her pace and strode past her clansmen.

Fyfe walked in step beside her. "Are you unwell, Miss Mary?"

"I simply need a brisk walk and some Highland air." She tried to smile. "Please, leave me be."

"As you wish."

Fortunately, the guard did her bidding and allowed her pass through the gate alone. Once she crested the hill where the onlookers could no longer see, Mary broke into a run. She headed straight for the big sycamore—her place of solace when she was a young lass. Decorum had forced her to stop climbing trees after her fifteenth year, but today she would make an exception.

The giant tree sprawled with hundreds of welcoming green arms. 'Twas like returning to an old friend.

"You haven't changed much in the past six years," Mary said, placing her foot in the knot and hoisting herself up to the first branch. Hiking up her skirts above her knees, her entire body trembled with ire while she climbed until she was high enough not to be seen by passersby. She was so upset, her legs could hardly pull her up.

Tears streamed down her cheeks and her nose ran, but upward she went. No one need see her in such an overwrought state.

Finally high enough not to be noticed, she perched on good-sized branch and leaned her back against the tree's thick trunk. Mary closed her eyes and took in a deep, stuttering breath. Burying her face in the crook of her arm, she allowed the tears to come. Sobs wracked her body. Good gracious, Da usually consulted with her about everything. Ever since his accident, she'd kept the books, managed the servants, planned the menus, ordered the stores, and most of all, taken care of *him*. Yes, he had a groom who dressed him and tended to his bathing, but when it came to ministering to his health, Mary handled it alone in consultation with Doctor Murray.

When had he begun entertaining Mrs. Watt? Yes, they were both widowed—perhaps of similar age, but why hadn't Da told Mary about the woman's new role sooner? Did he want her to find out by walking in on them…in a bed…with bare shoulders? Lord only knew what they were wearing beneath the bedclothes.

Good heavens.

Mary cringed, trying to erase the image from her mind. How on earth was she supposed to return to the castle and carry on as if nothing had happened?

"No excuses," a deep voice said while muffled footsteps scuffed through the grass. "We need the shipment in Glasgow in a fortnight."

Craning her neck to peer through the foliage, Sir Donald, looking very serious, led a slightly smaller man beneath the tree.

"Bless it, brother, you're asking for the impossible," said the shorter one.

The baronet's brother? Is it William?

"I daresay I am entirely serious. You should be as well. Too much is riding on this—not just for our clan, but for *the cause*. Do you ken how many hours I've put into the transaction with the Americans? The contacts I've made? The glasses of sherry I've poured?"

"But you don't even like sherry."

"Precisely. Now hightail your arse to Trotternish and demand double shifts if you must. The damned Williamite Government will not push us out this time." The baronet planted his fists on his hips, totally unaware of Mary directly above them.

She slid forward on her branch, taking in every word. Goodness, is that why Sir Donald was residing in Glasgow? She'd assumed he preferred the city life over the archaic Duntulm Castle where he was born. But rumors were he was a snob—ignored his kin. She leaned further forward.

"I'll go straight away, but the clan kens you're here." William spread his hands wide. "They expect to see you as soon as these games are over."

"I'll be there," the baronet said, his voice deep with sincerity. "And you can tell them the same."

William started off.

"Wait." Sir Donald grasped his shoulder, then clasped him arm to arm. "I'm trusting you, brother."

"You will not be disappointed."

With a sigh, Mary rested her chin on her hand. Sir Donald seemed so in control of his life—so filled with purpose. Not that Mary's life didn't have purpose. She was just too isolated and sheltered. Yet she'd had to take on a great deal of responsibility at a very young age when her mother died giving birth to Rabbie. Her father's coffers might even be a bit healthier if she'd had an elder brother like the baronet. She couldn't imagine herself going to Glasgow and starting up trade for the clan.

The branch beneath her cracked.

Mary's heart flew to her throat.

Before she could move, the limb dropped from beneath her. With a squeal, she flung her arms out, grasping at branches and leaves. Something scraped her palm, breaking her fall. Stretching her feet downward, toes hit ground, her ankle twisted, sending her crashing to her backside.

Cringing, she clutched her sore hand against her stomach. "Ow."

"Miss Mary?" The exasperation in Sir Donald's voice made her out to be a snoop.

She curled into a heap and groaned.

Nothing like falling out of a tree to win a baronet's affections. If Da hears about this, Mrs. Watt might be moving into my chamber as well as taking over his care.

Hissing, she held up her palm and blew on it. Hells bells, the darned thing was bleeding—worse, the baronet hadn't moved. She glanced up. "Why on earth did you pick *my* tree for your conversation with your brother?"

"Forgive me. I had no idea this tree was taken." Sir Donald kneeled beside her, removing a kerchief from his top pocket. "Are you injured?"

He grasped her hand ever so gently and dabbed the blood.

Mary watched him, waiting for the pain to come, but his touch grew more soothing with every swirl of the linen. "I don't think so—at least nothing that won't come good in a day or two."

He leaned in for a closer look and blew on her palm. "What, may I ask, were you doing up a tree?"

Gooseflesh skittered up her skin. "You may not ask."

"Do you climb trees often?" His gaze drifted up and met hers.

Dear Lord, such beautiful eyes should never belong to a man. The gooseflesh proceeded to tingle down Mary's spine. "Not since the age of fifteen…but…but I needed to think."

"Isn't there anywhere less precarious to think?" he asked, still holding her hand and pressing the cloth firmly.

"Not after what I witnessed." A cry slid past her lips—not at the pressure of the kerchief but at how foolish she looked hiding in a tree at the age of one and twenty.

"I don't like the sound of that." His eyes squinted. "Was someone rude to you?"

She shook her head while her stomach clamped into a ball. If only Sir Donald would stop his questioning.

"Discourteous to your sisters?"

"No, nothing like that—'tis far worse." She bit her bottom lip and winced.

"Worse?" His gaze grew dark like a cloud had passed overhead. "You'd best tell me afore I start an inquisition."

"Oh, no, please." Her accursed stomach clamped even harder. "'Tis too dreadful to speak of."

He shook his fist. "I'll throw the miscreant in the stocks, I swear."

"No, no, no." Now she'd gone and made a mess of things. "Please do not do anything. I-I-I went to my father's chamber for his morning massage…and…a-a-and. Oh heavens, I cannot say it." Mary buried her face in her uninjured hand.

He removed the cloth and regarded her palm. "Is your father all right?"

She flung the hand from her face with an enraged gesture. "Oh yes, he's more than all right."

Again his penetrating gaze regarded her. "I don't understand."

"He's replacing me with Mrs. Watt. I found them…" Mary's shoulders wound like a spring, she shook her hands fumbling for the words. "In…in a *compromising* situation…in-in his *bedchamber.*"

"Oh." High color flooded the baronet's cheeks and he folded the kerchief clean side out, then replaced it in his pocket. "I see. That would be most disturbing."

"It was. And I hope you can now understand why I needed to spirit away from the castle, if not for but a moment."

"Apologies, and I interrupted your solace." He reached for her hand and regarded the cut. It didn't look so bad now the blood had been cleaned off. "Would you like me to leave you alone for a time?"

Mary bit her bottom lip and looked out to the bay. "No. I'd best be heading back."

He again blew on her hand and that same tingling sensation rendered her practically senseless. "You'd best put some ointment on this."

Her mouth dry, she licked her lips while her heart fluttered like a silly butterfly. "I-I think it's stopped bleeding."

"And the rest of you?" He grinned. Why on earth did he have to do that?

Now not one, but swarms of butterflies flitted about her insides. "Fine. I believe," she said, her voice far deeper than she'd ever heard.

"Then may I accompany you back to the gate?" He glanced over his shoulder. "There are many people here who are strangers to Castleton."

Goodness, the man did have an uncanny allure. "Thank you."

Dear Lord, why does the only man who makes my heart flutter at his accursed gathering have to be the Baronet of Sleat? He lives in Glasgow for goodness sakes. They ride in coaches there and attend the opera of all things. Sir Donald probably has his pick of any highborn woman for miles.

Grasping her elbow, he helped Mary to her feet. "How is that? Are you steady?"

"I'm fine." She took a step. Fire burned up her ankle. With the next step, her knee wobbled and she stumbled forward. She would have fallen in a heap if Sir Donald hadn't tightened his grip on her elbow.

"I beg your pardon, miss, but you are not fine."

She grimaced. "I think I twisted my ankle in the fall. Give me a moment and it will come good."

"Then allow me to carry you back to the keep."

"Oh noooo—"

Heavens, the man swept her into his arms as if she weighed no more than a wee lamb. Then he had the audacity to give her a saucy grin. "Not to worry, Miss Mary, I'll see you to your chamber in no time."

She glanced up with a feeble smile. Lord, his lips were but inches away, his scent even more intoxicating than it had been last eve. The arms surrounding her held her ever so securely. Her head inclined toward him as he started off. Then her eyes flashed wide as her body tensed. "What will everyone say? I think perhaps if you set me down, I will be fine."

Brawny arms tightened around her. "No. I shall see you to the comfort of your chamber where your ankle can be properly examined."

"No, no." Mary placed her palm on his chest. "It would be scandalous if you took me above stairs."

His lips formed a hard line. "Not if I summon a chambermaid."

When the thrum of his heart hammered beneath her fingers, she snapped her hand away. "Are you always this overbearing?"

"Always." He glanced at her while he continued to boldly stride nearer and nearer the castle. "My siblings forever chide me about it."

"Then 'tis pointless for me to insist you put me down this instant?"

"A complete and utter waste of breath, miss."

Astonishingly, by the time he'd carried her all the way back to the main gate, the baronet wasn't even breathing heavily. Was the man hewn of iron?

Fyfe dashed straight for them. "Miss Mary, whatever happened?"

"I fell—"

"We need a chambermaid in Miss Mary's chamber forthwith." Sir Donald didn't miss a step, marching across the great hall with purpose. "See to it she arrives there before I exit the stairwell."

Fyfe's brow furrowed. "But first I have to find a chambermaid."

Sir Donald stopped. "Are you saying you intend to keep me waiting with an injured woman in my arms? Fetch the chambermaid now before I order one of my men to kick you up the backside."

"Yes, sir." Fyfe bowed. "Straight away, sir."

Ducking his head, Sir Donald stepped into the stairwell, his feet resounding loudly.

Mary tried not to laugh. "Everyone in all of Castleton kens you're taking me above stairs."

"Aye, but they're also aware a chambermaid will be right on our heels." He hesitated at the first landing. "Where am I heading?"

"Up three more flights, down the passageway, first door on the left."

"Is that all?"

"Sorry." She placed her hand around his neck for balance. The movement drew them together all the more closely. His breath caressed her forehead like balmy steam. Realizing her folly, she snapped her fingers away. Good Lord, he was warm as a hearth. "You needn't carry me all the way."

He glanced down to her face. Long, feathery lashes shuttered his eyes, making him look far too desirous. "I do and I will. Now keep your head and feet tucked in so they don't graze the walls."

"Yes, sir."

A smile spread across his lips for the first time since she'd seen him that day. "That's better." He stepped out onto the fourth floor landing. "First on the left?"

Mary pointed. "Aye. Right there."

"My word," Lilas squealed from her doorway on the right. "Whatever happened?"

Mary waved her hand. "'Tis merely a twisted ankle."

Sir Donald kicked open the door. "Drag the chambermaid up here if you must, miss. I see she hasn't yet arrived."

"Straight away, sir," said Lilas—goodness gracious, it must have been the first time Mary's sister had ever obeyed anyone without giving them a bit of sass first.

"How on earth did you do that?" Mary asked.

He strode inside. "What?"

"Lilas obeyed you without issuing as much as one single objection."

His deep chuckle rumbled through Mary's body before he rested her atop the bed. "Not many people question me when I issue them an order."

She reclined against her feather-soft pillows. "Why do you think that is?"

His jaw twitched. Sir Donald mightn't outwardly display his emotions, but she'd seen that tic a few times now—a sure indication he wasn't hewn of iron. His gaze meandered down the length of her body. Mary shivered as if his stare had actually caressed her. "It has always been that way." Something in his voice changed, grew softer, deeper.

Something else deep inside her melted—a pleasant sensation, but one that left her wanting more. Mary looked him from head to toe, just as he'd done to her. "I think…" Her tongue slipped to the corner of her mouth. "Your size alone would intimidate some…and your station." *And the intensity of your eyes, and the way your mouth forms a bold line when you're not smiling…not to mention your smile. Yes, your smile could cause any woman to lose her senses.*

Sir Donald took her hand between his two warm palms. "My guess is that you are not often questioned at Dunscaith Castle as well."

"Mm," Mary said, praying he wouldn't release her hand too quickly—the comfort of his touch soothed. Besides, this man soon would be on his way and she might never see him again.

He bowed. "Rest whilst I go find out what is taking that chambermaid so long." His eyes locked with hers for a fleeting moment. A swirling current emanated from those fathomless blues, just like the undertow of the sea. Then one corner of his mouth ticked up. Long, tawny lashes again shuttered his eyes as he stooped lower. Hot breath skimmed the back of her hand.

Mary gasped.

As soft as a feather, he plied her hand with a kiss— not a brief peck, but his eyes closed and a sigh rumbled from his throat, so low, Mary wasn't certain she'd heard it. When he straightened, a faint grin turned up the corners of his mouth.

He's toying with me for certain.
"My lady," he said, turning and heading for the door.

Chapter Five

Mary's sister and the chambermaid nearly fell into Don when he opened the door. Flustered, both dipped into a curtsey.

"How is she?" asked Lilas.

Don glanced over his shoulder. "She's resting. Perhaps a healer should have a look at the ankle."

"No need to call for the healer." Mary lifted her foot slightly and rolled her ankle. "It feels better already."

Don frowned and lowered his voice. "I do not believe it for a minute. One of you must have a look and if there's any swelling, summon the healer."

"Yes, Sir Donald," said Lilas, grasping the servant by the arm and pushing past him with a daft smile on her face. "Janie will tend her—you mustn't worry."

Letting the door close behind him, Don adjusted his doublet and took a deep breath, thankful to pass Mary's care along to someone more capable than he. What in God's name did he know about twisted ankles, especially *female* twisted ankles?

"He carried you all the way from the old sycamore?" Miss Lilas' high-pitched voice resounded through to the stone passageway followed by a shrill giggle.

It was a stroke of mercy Don wasn't called upon to carry the younger sister above stairs. From what he'd seen at the gathering last eve, Miss Lilas was as flighty as a hen hatching an egg. He strode directly for the stairwell. Perhaps carrying Miss Mary to her chamber demonstrated a wee bit too much overzealousness. He realized that after he'd kissed her hand. The lass had gone glassy-eyed. Lord only knew what prompted him to linger when he kissed her. Thank God no one else saw.

But by the saints, he couldn't just pass her off to a guard. She was the lady of the keep, regardless if she had climbed a tree.

Grown women don't climb trees, blast it all. Miss Mary must be addled in the mind. Yesterday I found her wearing men's clothing, in public of all places, and today she ran away from her troubles and hid in a tree?

Truly it would have been disconcerting for the lass to find her father in such a compromising position, but running away for the solace of an old sycamore? In a castle as large as Dunscaith, there surely would be someplace quiet she could have gone—a place far less public, especially given the Castleton MacDonalds were hosting the gathering.

'Twasn't a wise decision on her part.

Don's conviction grew deeper. Indeed, Mary was the hostess of this fete, yet she had not the maturity to push her personal woes aside and hold her chin high. She should have been outside watching the games. In fact, Don had noticed her atop the wall-walk earlier. She should have stayed up there until they broke for their nooning.

When Don exited the stairwell, Narin, the Dunscaith henchman approached. "Laird John has requested an audience with you in his solar."

"Now?"

"Aye, Sir Donald. Unless you've other matters to attend?"

Don scratched his chin. "Do you ken what he wants? The afternoon games will commence soon."

"I'm sure he's aware of that, sir. Please, just a moment of your time."

Grumbling under his breath, Don followed the burly man. *Why in God's name did Miss Mary have to fall from the tree? And now Sir John wants a word? I should have let her limp back to the keep.*

Don rifled through the turn of events, clarifying the story in his mind. Because the lass was injured and walking clearly caused her pain, he'd carried her to her chamber, hollering for the chambermaid loud enough for everyone to hear. So not to risk impropriety, he didn't dare venture to examine her ankle. Thank God he'd had enough sense to tell the lasses to tend Miss Mary's leg when he met them in the passageway—else the chief might attempt to trap him.

By the time they arrived at the solar door, Don stood with confidence, tugging on his lapels. He had done nothing but act as a gentleman ought.

Narin pulled down on the latch. "Donald MacDonald of Sleat, m'laird."

Sitting at the head of the table in his wheeled chair, Sir John beckoned with his hand. "Come in, Sir Donald." He flicked his wrist at the henchman. "That will be all, Narin."

Don moved toward the table as the door closed.

Sir John smiled, though his appearance was rather withered for a man the age of one and fifty. He gestured toward the sideboard. "Will you pour us each a dram afore you sit?"

"By all means."

"Apologies for not serving you with my own hand. Being a peg-leg makes some things rather difficult."

"I can imagine how challenging things must be for you, especially living in a castle with so many stairs." Don pulled the stopper off the flagon, his thighs aching a bit from climbing up the stairwell with Mary in his arms. "I'll never forget your heroics at the Battle of Dunkeld."

"If only we had won."

Inhaling deeply through his nose, Don wished he could forget. "It was a debacle for us all—we completely lost our momentum."

"Aye, the clans disbanded—went home to lick their wounds."

"And the Government has been squeezing us ever since." Don placed a dram of whisky in front of the chieftain. "I'll never forgive William of Orange and the Campbells for their massacre at Glencoe."

Sir John frowned, a dark shadow passing across his face. "Nor will I."

After Don took a seat, the two men stared at their whisky for a moment. Whenever anyone mentioned the Government's horrendous actions at Glencoe, a moment of silence always ensued.

"Slàinte." John raised his cup.

Don returned the salutation and sipped. "Mm. 'Tis fine spirit."

"Indeed," the old chieftain agreed. "Sir Coll of Keppoch brought it as a gift—pure Speyside gold it is."

Don shifted in his seat. "I'll agree with you there." Having made the appropriate amount of small talk, Don looked the man in the eye. "To what do I owe the honor, sir?"

A grin twisted the corners of John's mouth. "With three daughters and one crippled leg to carry out my bidding, can you not guess?"

Sitting back, Don crossed his arms and his legs. "You ken I'm embroiled in negotiations to establish *Jacobite* trade in the Americas?" He whispered the word Jacobite—for though they were among loyalists, one never knew who might be listening. Furthermore, Donald never dared to utter the word in Glasgow.

"Aye." John smoothed his finger around the clan brooch at his shoulder. "But how does *the cause* preclude you from taking a wife?"

He cleared his throat. "I cannot possibly risk having my mind distracted from business matters. Besides, if I were to marry anyone, the poor lass would be ignored for God kens how long."

Sir John raised his cup and sipped, closing his eyes as if either enjoying the taste or collecting his thoughts—or both. "Miss Mary is a fine Highland lass. Had to grow up too fast on account of her mother's death after the birth of my only son—then had to play both mother and father after I fell at Dunkeld. She's tough as nails, mind you—runs the keep more efficiently than I ever did." He looked up. "And she's bonny—those wee freckles are as Scottish as the Highlands."

"Och, I have no doubt Miss Mary will make a fine wife, but not for me—not unless she wants to wait a decade." Perhaps by five and thirty Don might be ready to settle down.

The chieftain plucked a snuff box from his waistcoat pocket. "I can offer you lands south of Tokavaig."

Devil's breath, Don knew as well as anyone John could ill afford to lose the rents those lands brought in. "I wish I could humor you on this account, but timing prevents me doing so." He pushed back his chair and stood. "If there is nothing else, I must haste back to the games. I wouldn't want to miss the first round of the archery contest."

"Tell me." John's lips thinned while he pinched a bit of snuff and sniffed. "Was Mary too injured to make her own way back to the keep after her fall from the tree?"

Ah ha—now he asks. "In my opinion she was. When she tried to stand, she yelped and fell. I acted as any gentleman would have done given the circumstances." Lord, news traveled faster at Dunscaith than at Duntulm.

After a hearty sneeze into a white kerchief, the chieftain's face fell along with his shoulders. "I suppose I'll have to make an appeal to Sir Robert Stewart next. He would be my second choice for my daughter."

Don clenched his fist and bowed. "Do what you must," he said through gritted teeth. What else could he say? He'd told the man *the cause* came before his personal happiness. He should have known before he'd arrived Sir John would be looking for suitors for his eldest—mayhap he wanted to secure betrothals for all three lassies.

Excusing himself, he hastened away. Bloody Robert Stewart was a good man, though a bit too young to handle a spirited lass the likes of Mary of Castleton. A fiery woman such as Mary would give any man difficulty. She needed to be harnessed—to be introduced to society and trained in the art of feminine grace. Aye, she might run Dunscaith Castle with an iron fist, but she would be a duck out of water in Glasgow. Society would eat her alive—and then she'd go sulk in a tree. Such behavior simply wouldn't do for the wife of a baronet—or any man with important business connections and vast property.

No, no, Don must be ever mindful of the Jacobite cause. He must think of his clan. Thousands of people were depending on him—on his ability to build new trade routes so the clans in turn would have the means to rebuild their armies. He had been clear on his task when he sailed from Glasgow and, by God, he would not forget it now.

Chapter Six

Mary awoke before Janie came to add peat to the fire.
Last eve she'd had a wonderful excuse to stay away from
the festivities. Too embarrassed to see Sir Donald again,
she'd fallen asleep early. Goodness, the clan chiefs and
their retinues couldn't leave soon enough. Thank heavens
this was their last day.

She tested her ankle, slowly sliding out of bed and
transferring her weight to it. Still a little sore, she lifted her
shift and peered down. A little swelling—a bit purple.
Gingerly, she made her way to the hearth, stoked the fire
and used a twig to light the candles. The more she moved,
the better her ankle felt. Thank goodness. She didn't want
to be seen parading around Castleton with a limp when
most of the eligible Jacobite chieftains were present.
Honestly, she'd done nothing to encourage any of them
and doubted a one would give her a second look...

Aside from Sir Donald.

He might look twice and then race to his sea galley
and sail as far away from her as he could go. How poorly
she must have appraised in his eyes. There she was, a
grown woman, crashing out of a tree and nearly falling on
top of the poor man.

And, oh, how Father's hopes would be dashed. Not that he'd given her any instruction on how to be charming. Mary stepped up to the looking glass and examined the freckles dotting across the bridge of her nose. God certainly had a sense of humor when he made her. At least her red hair matched the spots. She swept her curls forward to cover her cheeks a bit and then gave herself a sideways look. *Better.*

But Mary couldn't fool herself. She was nothing like the portraits she'd seen of countesses and highborn ladies with their smooth skin. Why on earth did every woman in Scotland have to have porcelain skin except for her?

Groaning, she limped to the ewer and bowl, cleaned her teeth, splashed water on her face and dressed in a simple kirtle. She had best stop behaving like a silly gel and remember she was still the lady of this keep regardless of what Da was doing with Mrs. Watt.

Though the menu was set well before the games, Mary had stayed away from the kitchens long enough. After securing her hair in a plait, she headed for the smell of baking bread. Cook always set the bread to baking before daylight.

Fortunately, her ankle warmed as she moved and by the time she reached the great hall, it didn't bother her too much. Doubtless, it would be perfectly fine in a day or two.

"Good morrow, Raymond," she greeted the cook. "How are the preparations for the morning meal?"

"Och, Miss Mary, I'm glad you're here," the dear, rotund man said with a flabbergasted wheeze. He stopped stirring the big cast-iron pot suspended from the immense hearth and glanced back. "How's your leg?"

"Better, thank you." She moved toward him. "So, what's afoot? I ken that burdened tone when I hear it."

He nearly shook the bonnet off his head with his grumble. "Of all the sennights in a year, the blasted hens have decided to go on strike. We've but five dozen eggs and I need five bushels full."

"What about Mrs. Whyte? Have you sent anyone to fetch eggs from her?"

"Goodness, you are a hard task master. 'Tisn't even daylight yet."

Mary moved to the window and looked eastward. "There's a pink glow in the sky. Dawn is upon us."

"And so will be a few hundred hungry Highlanders in about an hour."

"That is a problem." She feigned a sigh. "No use stirring the lads. I'll fetch the eggs myself."

Raymond frowned. "But what about your ankle?"

Goodness, Mary yearned to jump at any opportunity to spirit away—even for a short jaunt to fetch some eggs. "I'll take the horse and cart. As you said, we must do something afore the guests start to rise." Mary took a plaid from the hook by the door and draped it over her head and shoulders. "Unless we miscalculated, we should be fine for bread, sausages and haggis?"

"Right you are."

"Good. If Mrs. Whyte's hens have also decided to mutiny we'll not starve."

"Haste ye."

Mary opened the door. "There you go, ordering me about." Laughing, she didn't wait for the cook's reply.

An expert horsewoman, Mary had her horse hitched to the wagon faster than the stable hand could have done. Good thing, because she had no time to waste and the stable hand was still abed.

Slapping the reins, she drove the horse at a trot out the gates and up the hill. At this pace, she'd return before their guests had even stirred. Cresting the hill, the horse sidestepped.

"Oh no, there's no time to head for the daisies for a snack." Mary made loud kissing sounds, tugging the gelding back on path and snapping the crop for added encouragement. But the horse whinnied and veered further off course.

Moving to the edge of her wooden bench, she raised up high enough to peer above the crest of the hill.

Then she wished she hadn't.

Followed by a band of redcoats, Lieutenant Balfour MacLeod ran toward her rig and latched on to the horse's bridle. "Whoa, laddie," he said before giving Mary a crooked grin. "What have we here? 'Tis a bit early for a morning ride, even for you, miss."

At least a dozen men surrounded the wagon—all on foot. Odd.

"Leave me be." Mary slapped the reins, but the lieutenant maintained his hold. "I'm off to fetch eggs from Mrs. Whyte. I've no time to waste. Release me and I'll be on my way."

"I think not." The officer smirked and regarded his men. "We cannot risk letting you return to the castle to sound the alarm."

"Pardon? What on earth are you talking about?" Mary didn't wait for an answer. Jerking back her crop, she slapped the horse's rear with all her might. "Haste ye!"

The horse reared. Throwing back her arm, Mary eyed her target as the lieutenant lost his grip. Before she could issue another slap, MacLeod launched himself into the wagon. His arm whipped around her midriff. Mary slammed him with her elbow and jerked aside, ready to jump. The lieutenant held fast.

"Help!" she screamed. "Hel—"

He clapped a hand over her mouth and tugged her off the wagon. Kicking her feet and slamming her elbows into his chest, she fought with every ounce of strength she had.

"Someone grab a rope afore the bitch pummels me half to death," MacLeod growled with cold indifference. He'd always been an unpleasant sort, but never disrespectful toward Mary.

The lieutenant barely removed his hand from her mouth when a cloth gagged her.

"Tie it firm," he commanded. "We want to spirit away afore the guests wake—and afore the sun's light peeks above the horizon. Mark me, they outnumber us by sixteen to one—and I do not recommend sailing with a barrage of musket balls piercing the hull."

Mary struggled while a dragoon tied her wrists behind her back, the hemp rope cutting into her wrists. They were stealing a galley? But Sir Donald had said they would sail this day—and Lieutenant MacLeod hadn't challenged him.

The dastard sauntered straight up to her face with a smug grin on his lips.

Mary jerked her arms against her bindings. "You won't get away with this," she garbled through her gag.

"You're wrong." MacLeod dropped his gaze to her breasts, the blackguard. "I'm fully within my rights to seize anything I like. Including you, Miss Mary." Bending down, the accursed officer hefted her over his shoulder and marched for the pier.

Mary bucked and squirmed, only to be met with Balfour's palm planted flush against her backside. "Remove your hand from my person," she seethed.

The cur had the audacity to laugh. "You'd best settle...ye wouldn't want to be violated, now would you, lass?"

Her blood pulsed like ice beneath her skin. *He wouldn't dare!*

***

Sleeping in the guest wing, Don awoke a bit bleary-eyed. Like anyone, he enjoyed fine whisky and rich ale, but there was nothing like a gathering of Highland clans to keep him up into the wee hours. When he'd finally found his bed, he'd toppled across the bedclothes and didn't move until someone entered his chamber to light the fire.

This morrow his head throbbed like he'd been hit over the skull with a mallet. After cleaning up, he took a sip of whisky from the wee flagon he kept in his sporran. Though he rarely imbibed during the day, he hoped the tot might benumb the merciless throbbing.

Foolish idea. He now added dizziness to his list of maladies.

Fastening his belt and weapons, Don bucked up and made his way to the great hall where most of his men camped for the night—the hapless sore-headed souls. Thank God this was the last day of the games else they'd all perish from overindulgence.

"Sir," a sentry bellowed, running toward Don with a slip of parchment in his fist. "Your galley has been seized."

Blinking while the pain from the man's ridiculously loud voice rattled in his head, Don grabbed the writ of seizure and read. Crumbling it in his palms, he growled. "Where in God's name were the guards?"

"Don't know, sir. My men and I started our rounds and found this first thing—thought we should bring it to you straight away."

"Men, follow me," Don said, racing for the postern gate. "I want words with the night guard afore they head to their pallets."

The sentry kept pace. "Are you going after them, sir?"

"Bloody oath I will—and I'll use John of Castleton's boat while I'm at it. If the laird cannot protect his keep from poaching Government troops, then he can very well lend us his galley." He flipped his wrist at the man. "Now fetch the night watch."

William met him on the beach, his face blanched. "I should have slept on the ship myself."

"Aye," Don growled, his stomach churning at the sight of the empty mooring where his boat had been tied. "The lot of us should have camped in the hull with our muskets loaded."

"I didn't think the bastard would seize the ship—not after you told him we'd be on our way."

"'Tis downright thievery." The pounding in Don's head threatened to burst his skull apart. "The milk-livered curs stole into the night like petty tinkers. Well, I'll not stand for it."

Sir Ewen Cameron strode to the beach, his men in his wake. "You cannot engage them in battle. All that we have built will be ruined." Why the hell hadn't the redcoats stolen Cameron or Stewart's boat? They both had eighteen oars.

"Aye?" Don faced the elder chieftain. "I cannot stand by while a sniveling maggot thieves my galley out from under my nose. Christ, there are two hundred Highland warriors here. Had he approached us in daylight, he wouldn't have taken a skiff without meeting his end."

"I urge you to exercise caution." Ewen raised his palms. "Think of the trade. We all need to feed our families come winter."

"Aye," William agreed. "And keep our men from being shipped to the American penal colony."

Don balled his fists. "You think me dull-witted? I'll retrieve my boat right out from under MacLeod's nose, just as he did to me."

Sir Ewen grasped Don's shoulder and squeezed. "I say you go straight to Fort William. Ask Colonel Hill to intervene. He's the only backstabber I trust."

"We cannot chance doing anything to cause Government suspicion." William nodded as well. "We'll sail at once then?"

Don cast his gaze down the coast. They'd lost a great deal of time—and he had no intention of wasting another minute. "I do not—"

"Sir Donald!" The stable hand ran toward them with the cook in his wake. "I fear they've taken Miss Mary as well."

Don's guts dropped to his toes. Dear God, only that bonny, redheaded lass could manage to get herself captured at a time like this. Unless she'd up and fallen out of another tree. "Pardon? The bastards ferreted their way into the keep?"

"No," said the cook, wheezing with exertion. "She went off to fetch some eggs from Mrs. Whyte but never returned."

"The horse and cart came back without a driver." The stable boy threw his thumb over his shoulder. "I galloped back to Mrs. Whyte's place and Miss Mary didn't even make it that far."

Devil's breath. Now he not only had to find his galley, but the blundering misfit of all Highland lasses had fallen victim to the redcoat's skullduggery? "Blast it all to hell," he cursed. Worse, her disappearance twisted his heartstrings far tighter than it should have. Damnation, the lass had found a way to confound him at every turn since his arrival.

William nudged Don's elbow. "What now?"

If things couldn't go from bad to worse. Now everyone looked to Don—*the Baronet of Sleat*. His title made him the commander of this gathering of Jacobites. It would be a hell of a lot easier to issue orders if Mary of Castleton weren't involved, but now all eyes focused on him for a decision—and her life hung in the balance. To make matters unbearable, for some reason, he felt responsible to find her. "Sir Robert—your lands aren't far from Fort William. Can you take my brother to lodge a formal complaint with Colonel Hill?"

"Aye," agreed the Stewart Chieftain.

"But what about the shipment?" William asked.

"After you've met with the colonel, take a transport to Trotternish. I'll meet you there." Don turned to his men. "I need a crew to come with me and three volunteers to accompany William. I hate dividing our forces, but it must be done."

"We'll back you up, sir," Sir Ewen gestured to the crowd that gathered. "We all will."

"My thanks." Don looked to the stable hand. "Where is this Balfour MacLeod stationed?"

"Around the Aird of Sleat at Teangue."

Don threw his hands to his sides. "Are you mad? It would be faster to ride. Why in God's name didn't someone say something sooner? Saddle the horses and we'll be off."

"But—"

"What is it now?" He glared at the lad.

"We only have three ponies fit enough to take the saddle."

Chapter Seven

Mary huddled in the rear of the galley with her mouth still gagged, her ankles and wrists bound. She refused to meet Balfour MacLeod's leery-eyed stare. Every time he'd caught her gaze, he'd grinned like he was flirting. Of all the twisted, nonsensical villains, this man had to be the worst. Not that she'd met many horrid people, but her father had told her numerous tales of the wars and the vile men who took up arms and turned evil.

What a predicament. The filthy redcoats had stolen Sir Donald's galley and kidnapped her. Thank God they hadn't taken Lilas or Florence. At least Mary could hold her own—especially with a musket in her hands. She eyed the cache of weapons in the bow, far out of her reach. Her fingers itched to snatch one.

And by the saints, she would escape at her very first opportunity. Balfour MacLeod thought he could bully her? Well, he would rue the day he forced her to board this galley. Either that or she would die trying to flee.

From his position at the bow, he continued to stare at her. Blast him. She had no intention of playing his games. Keeping her gaze focused on the timbers of the hull, she feigned ignorance. But make no bones about it; Mary could sense his every move in the periphery of her vision.

When he climbed over the rowing benches and headed toward her, her every muscle tensed. *If I had use of my hands I'd slap him and bear the consequences.*

His feet stopped in front of her. Big, fat, ugly black boots. She hated the uniform. It reminded her of everything wrong with the Government. The King's men continually attacked the Highlands with fire and sword. Their motive? To root out the Highland way of life. Didn't they know the clans would rather die than live like Londoners? Why did the redcoats have to march north to Scotland and enforce their will? Why couldn't her kin be allowed to live in peace among their clans as God intended?

The cur chuckled. "Miss Mary of Castleton, I daresay you look like a miserable rat."

Spittle seethed through her teeth. If he would remove her gag, she'd tell him who the rat was.

Then the swine had the gall to sit beside her. His hip touched Mary's hip, his arm pushed flush against hers. She tried to scoot away, but the hull and the bindings tying her legs to the bench would allow but a fraction of an inch.

"I suppose I'd be rather upset as well, given the circumstances." He ignored her discomfort and feigned friendliness. "But you must believe me when I say I mean you no harm."

Snapping her head around, Mary regarded the pompous braggart. The corners of his mouth seemed to always be turned up in a sneering grin, as if now that he'd attained the rank of lieutenant he thought he was lord of the land. Priggishness flickered in his grey eyes. Set too close together for his round face, his eyes were the most unpleasant part of his visage—aside from a nose that curved to the right as if it had been broken. Surely it had.

If Mary had use of her fists, she just might attempt to break it again.

When he reached up his hands, she shied, fearing he would deliver a slap, but he untied her gag. "Apologies for the muzzle. We couldn't risk being seen. The odds were too great that there would have been retaliation from the castle."

"Too right." Mary rubbed her jaw, clicking her tongue to moisten her arid mouth. "You never would have left Dunscaith Castle alive."

"You see?" He patted her thigh—touched her as if he had the right to be so shamelessly familiar. "A man tries to enforce the law and the cavalier Highlanders want to open fire." He tsked his tongue.

Mary squeezed her legs together and shoved her knees flush against the hull. "Pardon me? You *stole* the Baronet of Sleat's galley."

"Stole? Your father allowed there to be more than two eighteen-oar galleys in the bay—not to mention the plethora of smaller boats. The law clearly states that Highlanders who are suspected of aligning themselves with the Jacobite cause are threats to the crown, especially with a gathering of so many large vessels in one place."

If only she could slap that smug grin off his face. "I cannot believe you support such farcical laws. Do you not see 'tis just another ploy to take the livelihoods away from Highlanders and reward the English?"

"And you are naïve," he snapped. "But I would expect no less from a woman who has lived in an archaic castle on a remote peninsula all her life."

"Truly?" Clenching her fists, Mary stole a glance at the muskets—any one of them would do. "So a sheltered lass cannot develop common sense?"

"I didn't say that. But you cannot deny you've been shielded from the world—you've never been away from the Highlands. You have only been exposed to one side of the argument."

What was the problem with that? Mary had seen and heard plenty of the Government's rules. Almost their every action in Scotland demonstrated they had no care for the Highland way of life. "So you say your *thievery* is acting in line with your king—"

"Our king," he corrected.

Mary huffed—she wasn't about to bend to the lieutenant's will. "*Your* king's edicts." She held up her bound wrists. "What about abduction? I did not willfully set sail with you, nor did I do anything to warrant this barbaric treatment of my person."

"Finding you and your cart was a wee surprise but, I have to say, a fortuitous one." He threw his head back and laughed. The man had to be completely mad.

"To what on earth are you referring?" Mary squared her shoulders and raised her chin. This man wouldn't belittle her. "I demand you return me to Dunscaith Castle immediately. You have taken me against my will and I will file charges with the magistrate if you do not take me home at once."

"I'm afraid I cannot do that." His gaze drifted to her lips, then lower. The lecherous blackguard. "What chance did I have with so many Highland chieftains mulling about—men like the baronet and Coll of Keppoch? And don't think I was unaware of your father's plans to make a match."

Her jaw dropped. "You intended to kidnap me all along?"

"Not exactly." He rubbed his hand over his stubbled chin. "But I see my good fortune as destiny. You fell right into my hands."

"Pardon me?"

He gazed at her with far too much intensity in his beady eyes. "Do you not know? I have loved you since the very first moment when I set eyes on you but two years past."

Mary snorted and laughed out loud. The first time they'd met, he'd come to tell them he was the new law on the peninsula. Lorded it over her father like he was a stuffed-shirt general.

Balfour's face fell. The man actually looked crushed.

Mary felt absolutely no sympathy—not one thread. "You have a queer way of demonstrating your affections, lieutenant."

"Possibly, but I would prefer it if you saw my side for a change." He grasped her bound hands between his ice cold palms. "I know we would make a splendid match— me an officer and you the daughter of a laird. All of Skye would be astounded. Why, it would be a step toward harmony between the Government and the Highlanders."

She jerked her hands free. This man had completely lost his mind. He stole Sir Donald's galley. He supported policies meant to break Highland clan and kin. The worst thing? Mary could not hold her tongue. "*You* were in Glencoe. *You* were part of the massacre. *You* opened fire on innocent men, women and children."

He frowned, his face growing tempest grey. "I was ordered to do so."

"Do you think for a moment that an order as heinous as the one given by Glenlyon was in any way acceptable?" She again threw her shoulders back. "What? When you joined the army did they ask you to leave your ability to reason in your powder flask?"

He groaned and looked away. "Och, Mary. There are things in this world you cannot understand. A soldier must act on orders when given. There is no questioning. There is no refusing, else it is an act of treason."

"Even when committing murder against your own countrymen?"

He jerked up his palm while anger flashed through his grey eyes.

Mary flinched.

Clenching his fist, he lowered it to his side. "I see we have some differences. But I refuse to let that dissuade me. By the time we reach Invergarry, you will discover exactly what a suitable husband I will make."

She swallowed. Hard. *I sincerely doubt that. I'd rather die than marry this bombastic, sniveling blowfly.* "Invergarry?" Now she knew the lieutenant had to be insane.

"My family lands. Once we deliver the ship to the fort at Glenelg, I'll take you to meet my mother. She will adore you."

***

Cresting the hill, the wooden fort at Teangue came in to view. Don had brought the toughest men in the Highlands with him—Coll of Keppoch and Kennan Cameron of Locheil. Both men were solid as a horse's hindquarter. Kennan was especially talented with pistols and Coll, well, even Don wouldn't want to meet *him* in a narrow close after dark.

"Dammit. Your boat's not there," Coll grumbled.

Kennan pulled his horse to a stop behind Don. "Bloody hell, I kent we should have taken a galley."

"So now you're all the wiser?" Don patted the neck of the old garron gelding beneath him. True, it was his decision to ride rather than sail, but he wasn't yet convinced he'd erred. "Well, we've no recourse but to ride down and ask a few questions."

Coll leaned forward, resting his arm on the saddle's pommel. "You're serious?"

Spreading his palms, Don looked from one Highlander to the other. "You have a better idea?"

The big man shook his head. So did Kennan.

He'd rather go in with muskets in hand and swords at the ready, but the odds were a bit steep. Besides, if he laid low and played by the Government's rules, they just might be civil. The stakes were too high to throw caution to the wind. Prickles fired across Don's skin. Riding into a camp of redcoats always bore a risk.

He again glanced between the two men. "Keep your hands where they can see them."

"Aye," said Kennan. "I'll hold them in front of the pistol in me belt."

Coll sniggered. "I reckon we can take out half the camp afore they ken what hit."

"I'd like nothing more." Don jabbed his finger in the overzealous chieftain's shoulder. "But if we don't try to parley, we may never discover what they've done with *my* boat."

By the time they reached the bottom of the hill, a dozen dragoons stood in front of the gate, muskets raised to their shoulders.

"Such a welcome for the man who is lord of these lands," Coll growled under his breath, gesturing to Don.

"Aye," He had to agree. "The troops in Glasgow are far more subtle. Though I think I like this tack better. At least a man kens where he stands."

They pulled their horses to a halt not twenty paces from the black-holed barrels pointing their way. Dropping his reins, Don raised his palms. "You aim to shoot us afore we've had our say?"

An officer in a grenadier hat lowered his weapon and scowled. "You'd best state your business quickly, else we'll shoot you for suspicion of attack."

"Why is that?" Indeed they all had their hands visible as he'd instructed. "We've come peacefully, our weapons sheathed."

The officer stood his ground. "I ken who you are—the Baronet of Sleat."

Don chuckled, exchanging glances with Coll. "I had no idea I instilled this much fear into the hearts of dragoons." He gnashed his teeth together. Aye, he had a lot more to say, but such derogatory remarks wouldn't help him find his galley. Smoothing the reins through his fingers, Don looked the grenadier in the eye. "My galley went missing afore dawn this morn." He pulled the writ of seizure out from inside his doublet. "Lieutenant MacLeod took it—though he was fully aware I intended to sail for my lands in Trotternish this very day."

The officer glanced at the note, but didn't take it. "He thought you'd come begging. But you broke the law. Too many eighteen-oar galleys at one gathering. Now you'd best be on your way."

A dragoon sniggered, his finger twitching on his musket's trigger.

Don maintained a heated gaze on the soldier. God save him, he wanted to stuff that smirk down the blackguard's throat, but he needed that goddamned boat too much. "I only ask you tell me where the lieutenant has taken my ship so I may negotiate its release from impound."

"'Tis in his majesty's service now," said the soldier with the twitchy finger, all too joyfully.

Don paid the maggot no mind and glared at the grenadier. "If you please, sir. I have matters of business to attend. Business that will benefit all of Scotland."

"Benefit the thieving Jacobites," said twitchy.

"Silence," the officer sniped, then looked to Don. "Clearly, the lieutenant is not here."

"He didn't tell you where he was taking the baronet's galley?" Kennan asked.

"It is not my place to question my superior officer." That had to be the most cunning ruse the man could have used.

Don tightened his fist around his reins. "I've a crew heading to Fort William to lodge a formal complaint, but it would be far easier for all if I could settle this quarrel outside the courts."

The grenadier again lifted his musket to his shoulder. "Of course he didn't say, but I reckon Mr. MacLeod took that into account when he drew up the writ of seizure. Now off with you afore you force me to command my men to fire."

Bloody, filthy imbeciles. All of Britain had gone to hell when the backstabbers rebelled against King James.

Don motioned to his men. "It seems ignorance is rife among these dragoons. Come." Riding away, he refused to look back. Let the bastards stare at their horses' arses. No one in the Highlands would dare shoot a man in the back—unless they were in Glencoe.

Once out of earshot, Coll removed his bonnet and scratched his full head of auburn hair. "Now what?"

"I cannot think, I'm so bloody hungry," Don grumbled under his breath—not to mention his head still throbbed like the pounding from a smithy's shack. "We head for the alehouse for our nooning. If we cannot dig up a bit of gossip there, we've naught but to return to Castleton for reinforcements."

＊＊＊

The three Highlanders sat at a table toward the rear of the alehouse. Coll hadn't touched his tankard since the barmaid set it in front of him—quite out of character for a man who earned the bulk of his living from distilling Speyside whisky. "Devil's fire, you're lord of these lands. Since when does that mean nothing?"

"Too right," Kennan held up a wooden spoon. "Each one of us is the overseer of our lands and the bastards see fit to push us out at every turn."

"The times are changing, for certain." Don took a healthy swig of his ale. "But that doesn't mean we lay down and let them kick us like dogs."

Kennan shoved his spoon into his lamb pottage. "I'll never stand for a redcoat coming to Achnacarry and telling me how to manage my clan."

Though the ale did nothing to help his sore head, Don took another drink, then picked up his spoon and dug it into his bowl. "Mayhap we should hold all the gatherings in Achnacarry."

"You're bloody mad." Coll finally picked up his tankard. "Achnacarry is a stone's throw away from Fort William."

"Aye, but at least Colonel Hill understands us," Kennan said with a full mouth.

"Does he?" asked Coll. "Wasn't his signature on the order commanding Glenlyon to put innocent men, women and children to fire and sword? And even if he acted under duress, the man is older than Ben Nevis. What will happen when he's gone?" The big Highlander downed his ale with one long swig, then wiped his mouth with the back of his sleeve. "Mark me, never trust anyone who dons a red coat. If he's not a backstabber already, he'll become one in very short order."

Don couldn't disagree, but sitting in an alehouse talking about the injustices spewing from the man who currently sat on the throne did nothing to help him find his damned ship—or Mary of Castleton. "Do either of you have any idea where MacLeod may have sailed my galley after he left Castleton? And why the blazes did he take Miss Mary with him?"

"That's where he's crossed the line, for certain," said Kennan. "The law may allow him to seize your galley, but we can bring him up on charges for nabbing the lass."

"I hope he has the sense to keep his hands off her," Coll said.

Those words made a shudder creep up Don's spine. Of course he knew how much peril Mary was in, but he'd refused to think about it. His palm slipped down and encircled the pommel of his dirk. "If that bastard so much as lays a finger on her I'll—"

"Excuse me, sir," an elderly voice cackled behind him.

Don turned. A bent old man grinned, revealing a single tooth and long, stringy hair hanging in his face. "What is it, man?"

"Ye are the Baronet of Sleat are ye not?" The man pinched a piece of the Don's lace cuff, his fingers filthy, not to mention he smelled like a privy. "Dressed in such finery, I assumed as much."

"What business do you have with the Chief of all MacDonalds?" asked Coll, giving the man a menacing glare.

The beggar shirked away. "I-I…ah…only what I overheard the lieutenant say."

Don narrowed his gaze. "MacLeod?"

"Aye." The man regarded Don's doublet like a starved deerhound. "I reckon what I have to say would be worth a crown."

Coll raised his palm. "You miserable tinker, I ought to—"

Don caught his friend's wrist before he struck the old fella. He might be a bit unsavory, but the man looked brittle enough to shatter. "I'll need to hear what you have to say afore you see any coin from me."

Licking his lips, the codger nodded. "I reckon that's fair…Ye see, I might clean the chamber pots, but it sees me inside the fort—and in places most common folk cannot go."

By the pall, Don had no cause to doubt the man's occupation. "When was this?"

"Yesterday." The man swiped a dirty hand across his mouth. "The lieutenant was meeting with the corporal in his chamber—a secret meeting it was."

"Go on."

"He said he was going to strike a blow to the pompous Baronet of Sleat and his Jacobite renegades."

The baronet shook his head. "Did he say where he was taking my boat?"

"Nay. He mentioned nothing about a boat, but told the corporal to meet him in Glenelg across the sound."

"Rumor is they're planning to build a fort there," said Kennan.

Don nodded. "And Mary of Castleton. Did you overhear anything about Sir John's daughter?"

The man gasped. "Ye mean the redcoat bastards have Miss Mary?"

"Afraid so." Don should have known the lass would be popular with the locals.

"Bloody, fobbing, fly-bitten wagtails. Why didn't ye say they had Miss Mary? She's the kindest lass in all of Skye. Kept me from freezing winter last."

"And we had to ride ponies rather than take a boat," grumbled Coll.

Don ground his molars. The MacDonell Chief was right, of course. Had they sailed to Teangue, it would have taken a bit longer to navigate around the peninsula, but they'd be less than an hour from Glenelg. "Do you ken anyone who can ferry us across the sound?"

"I can take ye, but it'll cost a bob apiece."

Kennan looked the man from head to toe. "You have a seafaring vessel? What is it, a raft bound together with hemp?"

"Nay, my brother-in-law ferries people across all the time—even ferries the lieutenant."

Don looked to Coll. "It looks as if we're in luck."

"With the luck this day has brought?" The big man shook his head. "I'll give it no more than a thumbs up for improvement."

"Aye," Kennan agreed. "We haven't seen the sea vessel as of yet."

Chapter Eight

After Balfour finally left her side, Mary toiled, twisting her wrists, wrenching them back and forth against the coarse ropes. The more she tugged, the more the hemp cut through her skin, but she was too close to stop. With every agonizing twist, the bindings loosened slightly. Her lips trembled as she kept her countenance neutral, forcing herself not to grit her teeth, all the while blinking back tears of pain.

When the galley ran aground, Mary's heart surged with palpitations as her bindings dropped to the timbers. She watched the men while they secured the boat, resisting the urge to rub her burning wrists. If she bent down to untie her ankles, Balfour would catch her for certain.

By the time all of the crew members had climbed over the side, the lieutenant, once again, clambered over the benches and stood in front of her. "I have arranged an escort to Invergarry. The horses are waiting."

Mary met his gaze with the most heated glare she could muster. If she could shoot daggers through her eyes she wouldn't hesitate. "What makes you think I'll ride?"

"You will."

He kneeled and began untying her foot bindings.

Behind her back, Mary made a fist, patiently waiting until the ropes eased from her ankles. "Lieutenant," she said with more control than she felt.

He looked up with a grin. "Aye?" Holy Moses, she hated his smug, pinched features.

This was her chance.

Taking in a sharp inhale, Mary clenched her fist. With all her might she slammed a jab across his jaw. Following through with her shoulder, she grabbed his pistol and yanked it free.

Balfour stumbled back, his hand flying to his face, his eyes stunned.

Springing from the bench, she raced for the ladder. *Dear God, help me break free of this nightmare.*

"Damn it, Mary." The timbers clomped behind her.

She cocked the musket and pointed it at the cur. "Stay away."

He stopped and spread his hands to his sides. "You ken as well as I 'tis not charged."

Blast it all. She should have gone for his sword. "Aye?" Mary held her hand steady. "I can still strike you with it."

Stepping toward her he reached forward. "Come. Give it to me."

She shoved the weapon into her belt. She'd find a powder flask soon and a pebble would do if she hadn't a musket ball. Raising her chin, she silently dared him to come after it.

A villainous grin spread across his lips, his eyebrows angling down. "I'd like nothing more than to fetch the pistol myself."

She grabbed the rail and stepped onto the first rung of the ladder. "You wouldn't dare."

"Wouldn't I?" With his next step he lunged.

Shrieking, Mary leapt over the side. Feet smashing onto the stony beach, hot shards of pain shot through her knees.

No time to stop.

She forced her legs to pump beneath her. This might be her only chance to dash for freedom.

A blur of redcoats hastened from the left. Mary bolted to the right. Footsteps crunched the stones behind. Two saddled horses stood ahead with mounted soldiers behind them. Forcing her legs to run faster, she sprinted straight toward the nearest horse.

Stretching as far as she could, she reached for the reins.

A deep bellow roared, making the hair on the back of her neck stand on end.

Two more steps and she'd have hold of the leathers.

Burly arms wrapped around her.

Mary reached.

The reins slipped through her fingers as her body sailed downward.

Smacking the stones with her chin, her teeth bit so hard, sharp knifing pain shot through her face. The air whooshed from her lungs as Balfour's body slammed atop hers.

Vexed, Mary thrashed beneath him and sucked in life-giving air.

"Damnation," he cursed, wrenching her arm up behind her back. "Don't make me hurt you."

Crying out, stars darted through her vision as he twisted her wrist up her back. She tried to roll away from the force, but the more she fought the more the blackguard punished her.

"Stop fighting me, you feisty wench," he growled through clenched teeth.

If he pulled any harder, he'd break her arm. Panting, Mary stiffened. "I will not marry you and you cannot make me."

"Och, lass," his voice suddenly became buttery as he forced her arm down beneath his body while trapping her other hand. "In time you'll learn to like me—mayhap you'll even find love. Just give me a chance."

She bucked against him. "You're mad."

"Angry, yes." Sliding off her, he lashed a length of rope around one wrist. "Insane? I'd say not." Pushing her to her back, this time, he tied her wrists in front, but bound them so tight, her fingers throbbed.

Balfour may think himself sane, but on one thing Mary was certain. The lieutenant had lost all capacity for rational thought.

He examined her wrists and with a tsk of his tongue, he examined the raw skin peeking above her ropes. "This wouldn't have happened if you had trusted me."

"Truly? Trust a pig who abducts me from my home and then plans to force me into wedded misery?"

He drew back his hand, threatening to strike. But then he chuckled and let it drop to his side. "I figured you'd be hard to break. The best horses take the most time to train, but once they take to the bit, there's none better. Och aye, we shall be the most envied couple in the Highlands, mark me."

He speaks as if he's expecting to receive title and lands for his ill deeds. My father won't give him a penny of my dowry. How many times had he threatened to strike her? It was but a matter of time before he lost control and issued a slap or worse. Mary glared at him, lips pursed. Balfour MacLeod might have her in his clutches now, but there would come a time when he'd slip, and when that happed, she would be ready.

***

Donald paced around the clearing. After they'd spotted his galley on the shore by Glenelg, Don had instructed the ferryman to sail a half mile down the coast where they could alight with their ponies and not be seen. And since Kennan was the least likely to be recognized, Don had allowed the younger man to pose as a traveler and ride into the village. Still, such a move was risky. Glenelg had but a couple of cottages and a shack that looked as if it could be an alehouse. If a dragoon caught wind of a spy, their plan would be foiled.

"I reckon we should have waited for dark and gone in with guns a-blazin'," said Coll, pacing in opposition to Don. If only they had an eighteen-gun galleon at their disposal, the Chieftain of Keppoch would be raring to blast the entire regiment out of Scotland.

Honestly, Donald would be the first to hold a torch to a cannon's fuse, but carefully laid plans were not founded upon wishes. They were three men against a battalion of trained dragoons. "He'll be here," Don said, growing less convinced by the moment. Nonetheless, he wasn't about to hint to his misgivings to Coll. The cavalier chieftain would charge in with his musket and take the redcoats all on—and that would get the three of them killed faster than a dip in an ice-filled loch.

Regardless of the jittery prickles firing across his skin, Don would keep his head and act with maturity. He'd act with sharp judgement and his wits intact. Continuing to pace, he clenched his fists tighter with every step. "Blast it all, dusk is upon us."

"Bleeding, bloody, miserable hell." Coll stomped toward his horse. "I told you I should be the one to ride in there. Now we'll have to fight them all. You never should have sent Kennan. He's too bloody young."

"Haud yer wheesht." Don sliced his hand through the air. "The lad takes after his father. He has a good head on his shoulders. Damn it all, we'll give him until dark. If he's not back by then, we'll have no recourse but to spirit into the fort and find Miss Mary."

"God's bones, if their thievery wasn't bad enough, they had to snatch John of Castleton's daughter. I'll tell you, if she weren't behind those wooden ramparts, I'd blast my way—"

"Enough with the blasting." Don stopped pacing and grabbed Coll by the back of his collar. Damn, damn, damn. He owed a visit to his clan. They'd soon think he deserted them. But... He groaned. "Never forget she's kin. As much as I want to blast the redcoats to hell and sail my galley up to Trotternish, we have a responsibility to see Miss Mary back to Dunscaith Castle."

Coll's face fell. "Right. I didn't mean to imply—"

"I ken."

A twig snapped.

Both men silently drew their swords.

"'Tis just me, gentlemen," Kennan's voice came through the shadows. Thank God they wouldn't be forced to stage a rescue mission for him.

Don shoved his sword back in its scabbard. "We'd just about given up hope."

Dismounting, the lad led his pony into the clearing. "It took a few more than a couple tankards of ale to convince the townsfolk I wasn't a tinker, then a few more to find someone who'd seen Miss Mary."

"Don't tell me you're in your cups," Coll groused.

The young Cameron heir wobbled with a wry grin. "Aye, my liver is floating up near my teeth, I'd reckon."

Don's gut squeezed. "You didn't let on who you were?"

"That's what took me so bloody long." Kennan hiccupped. "A fisherman told me he watched Lieutenant

MacLeod chase after some ginger-haired lass. When he caught her, he threw her down and bound her wrists."

"My God." Coll yanked his dirk from its scabbard. "I'll kill the bastard."

"Too right," Kennan agreed, throwing his thumb over his shoulder. "Then he tossed her on the back of a horse and headed east."

Don's gut dropped clear to his toes. "You mean Miss Mary isn't in Glenelg?"

"Nope." Kennan shook his head as if the gravity of the situation hadn't hit.

Combing his fingers through his hair, Don scowled and looked to Coll. "Must this situation grow worse by the hour?"

MacDonell shrugged. "Bloody, miserable, bleeding…" The rest of his string of curses rolled together in one long mumble.

Don resumed his pacing, pushing the heels of his hands against his forehead. "Do you ken where the lieutenant was headed with Miss Mary?"

Kennan swayed in place and shrugged. "Just east."

"That makes no sense at all." He kicked a rock. "What, is he taking her to Inverness?"

Coll followed, kicking a rock the size of a large pinecone. He didn't flinch though his toe must have hurt like the devil. "Mayhap he'll turn south for Fort William."

"Damnation!" Don stomped his foot. All he needed was to embark on a lengthy pursuit, chasing a slippery officer through the Highlands. What a nightmare. Who knew what the man intended to do with Miss Mary. He'd attacked the poor lass and bound her wrists. She must be frightened out of her wits.

"You want me to haste after her?" asked Kennan, still swaying.

"No." *Nothing like the inept chasing the insidious.* "You look as if you'll fall off your mount if you ride fifty feet."

The young blighter belched. "But you told me to act like a traveler."

"I also bloody told you to find out where Miss Mary was, not to come back here and report that she's been absconded on horseback to the east. Bless it, now one of us will have to track them."

"I'll go." Coll raised his hand.

Don growled and jammed his fists into his hips. Why in God's name did Miss Mary have to continually be such a nuisance? Let Coll MacDonell chase after her? With her luck, the lass would likely be hit by one of the chieftain's stray musket balls. *Blast it all.* "She's my responsibility. I cannot, in good conscience, sail for Trotternish knowing John of Castleton's daughter is in peril." He pointed at each man. "I'll need the two of you to sail the galley north. Meet my brother, William, at Duntulm Castle and tell him it's up to him to have the cargo loaded and in Glasgow in a fortnight. I'll meet him there."

Coll stooped to pick up his musket, tucking it under his arm. "So are we off to take possession of your ship?"

"After dark—at high tide." Don looked to the Cameron heir. "You think you can sober up in a few hours."

The young man gave a nod. "I'll be right, no need to worry about me."

The cocky youth had Don worried since they'd alighted from the rickety old ferry. But there was nothing like war and danger to turn a lad of nineteen into a full-grown man. They mightn't be leading a regiment into battle like Don had done at the same age, but recapturing a galley out from under the noses of a hundred dragoons was every bit as dangerous. "Leave the ponies at the tree line. Spirit to the ship and, by all means, ensure the watch doesn't see you."

"I was born sailing a galley. We won't unfurl the sail until we're well out to sea." Kennan sounded like he was sobering already.

"Good lad," Don said, then he looked to Coll. "MacDonell, I'm putting you in charge of my boat. I don't need to tell you how much it cost or how important it is to our cause."

"Yes, sir."

"And be wary of their trickery—I'm sure the troops will be expecting us to react." Don secured his weapons and headed for his horse. "I'm trusting you with what could be the future of our kin. We need the trade with the Americas like we need our daily bread."

Coll tipped his bonnet. "You can count on me, Sir Donald. I'll see your cargo reaches Glasgow."

Kennan pounded his fist over his heart. "Me as well. Long live the king."

"Long live the king," Don responded. Everyone knew they meant the true king with the God-given birthright to rule.

Don mounted his horse and headed east. To where? Only the Almighty knew.

Chapter Nine

Mary huddled beneath her arisaid, clutching it closed as best she could with her bound wrists. The wind picked up with the setting of the sun. Cold and hungry, her hands were numb. She hadn't said a word since Lieutenant MacLeod had attacked her with such brutality and tossed her on the back of the horse. A dragoon rode on each side of her and there were two more in back. Ahead, Balfour towed her lead line, flanked by another pair. How on earth would she escape from seven redcoats? Seven ruthless varlets, including six who had all stood by and watched while their leader wrestled her to the ground and bound her wrists like a common criminal.

If she harbored any doubt of the depth of her hatred for the Government troops before, there was absolutely no question now. Swaying with the horse's movement, she stared at the lieutenant's back devising ways to retaliate. She could form her own Jacobite militia in Castleton. They could sabotage every Government ship that sailed past the Aird of Sleat. But more than that, she wanted Balfour to pay for his treatment of her person. And she wasn't so naïve to think lodging a complaint with the magistrate would get him anything more than a slap on the wrist.

As soon as she returned to Dunscaith Castle, she'd form her group of mercenaries and their first order would be to find a way to ensure Balfour MacLeod was dismissed from the army in disgrace. *I vow it on my very life.*

Mary's conviction infused her with strength. She sat surer in the saddle. "Pardon me, but I'm starving. Surely the lot of you are as well, unless you are some sort of bogles who need no sustenance."

"Aye," said one of the dragoons beside her. "The horses could do with a rest as well."

Balfour turned, the whites of his eyes piercing through the dusk. "There's a place to make camp ahead. I wanted to ensure we put good distance between us and MacDonald's galley. No doubt he'll make the mistake of coming after his ship." His steely-eyed gaze fixed on her. "And the lass. He'll find the first with a boatload of dragoons—then discover Miss Mary is nowhere to be found."

Mary's chest tightened like her stays had been cinched until she couldn't breathe. "You don't mean to kill him?"

The lieutenant flicked his wrist dismissively. "If he attempts to steal Government chattel and resists arrest, he'll meet his end."

Twisting in her saddle, she threw a sharp look over her shoulder. How could she send a message to Sir Donald? No doubt he and his men would want to retaliate, and they'd fall into the redcoat's trap for certain. "But the galley is *his* property," Mary argued.

"Not anymore. I obtained a legal writ of seizure. That galley will now serve His Majesty's Royal Navy."

One of the dragoons riding beside Balfour turned and regarded Mary, his gaze leery, devious. "I reckon the baronet will try to come after the lass soon—they'll not rest when one of their own has been abducted."

"I wish he would," said a deep voice behind her—the hiss of a dirk sliding from its scabbard was unmistakable. "It would be the last ride of his life."

Mary's face grew hot. These men thought it funny to make sport of treachery and outright murder?

"That's why I must marry the wee filly on the morrow," said Balfour. "Once she's my wife, there's nary a thing they can do about it."

Mary froze, her eyes round and unblinking.

The men around her laughed raucously.

She couldn't breathe.

On the morrow?

Then with a blink, her mind raced. How could she flee from these tyrants? Now? She must break away at her first opportunity—she couldn't let him get away with this. No, he could not and she would not allow him to see her pure terror. "I-I do believe I have a say in the matter— And. You. Will *never* hear me utter marriage vows."

"Ah, Miss Mary, you'd best reconsider." The lieutenant chuckled. "I'll wager I'll be able to persuade you."

Not in this lifetime. She ground her teeth and stared at his red-coated back. Red—the devil's color.

The dragoon riding beside her snorted. "It would be good sport to see Sir Donald MacDonald ride to her rescue."

"Can the man fire a musket?" The question from behind made Mary's blood boil. "I thought he moved to Glasgow where he attends the opera and sips fine port."

The laughter from the mob of vile dragoons swirled around her like ropes being drawn tighter and tighter. Mary wanted to hold her hands over her ears and scream. With their every word, their deceit, their skullduggery grew worse. Aye, they thought they were amusing, but Mary prayed they were wrong. She'd seen the nobleman shoot—had seen the great man win almost every game at the gathering. These soldiers severely underestimated the Baronet of Sleat. The only problem was there were seven redcoats and unless Sir Donald followed her with a regiment of men, he would be sorely outnumbered.

Again Mary slumped. *Who am I fooling? Sir Donald thinks I'm as feather-headed as an old woman with softening of the brain. His business transaction is far too important—far more important than I am.*

The lump swelling in Mary's throat made it difficult to swallow.

Who will Father send after me? The guard of Castleton, most likely.

Narin and Fyfe?
Holy Moses, I'm in trouble.

***

There was only one road leading east from Glenelg—the shadowy Military road, following the Glenmore River. But Don had lost precious time—at least a half a day in his estimation—with no chance to map an alternate route. Blast it all, if only he'd known MacLeod's plans, he wouldn't have sent his brother to Fort William. A complaint could be lodged any time. This whole sordid affair was wrought with errors.

Growing dark, thick clouds hung overhead making it impossible to see more than a few feet ahead. Spats of rain came and went with the wind blowing against his back. The well-traveled trail was thick with prints and wheel ruts, but the telltale signs of mud recently turned over by hooves were the tracks he needed to follow—tracks he could only see as he crossed over them.

The bad part? The damned lieutenant wasn't stupid enough to ride alone. It would have made the pursuit so much easier if Don only had to dispatch one man.

Now well past the evening meal, his stomach again rumbled and his head still throbbed. Thank God he'd had the wherewithal to order a meal at the alehouse in Teangue. At this pace, he mightn't see food for another day or two—or sleep for that matter. He clenched his teeth and bit back his hunger. He'd sleep in a fortnight after his packing salt had been loaded on a ship bound for the Americas.

Living in Glasgow had made him soft—but Don wouldn't give in to weakness. He'd led his clan's army into war and he could do it again at any time, if necessary. And Lieutenant Balfour MacLeod had declared war against his clan. Such an act would not go unpunished.

If only he had an army with him now.

But he didn't.

He must be stealthy and track them until he found his opportunity to pounce. Pushing his powder flask further under his cloak to ensure it stayed dry, Don considered his options. He had two shots—one from his musket and another from the pistol in his belt—then he'd fight them sword to sword. Aye, he'd make every movement count, dispatch them all, then he'd nab Mary and run like hell.

Mary of Castleton. Every time he mulled his plans over in his mind, her freckled face popped into his head. And then his damned chest tightened. What was it about the lass? She wasn't his type. Don preferred demure, full-figured women who enjoyed embroidery and music…and the wiles of the boudoir. True, by the quality of the minstrels she'd hired, Miss Mary likely enjoyed music, but all the same, she climbed trees and fired a musket like a sharpshooter. Hell, she'd bested him—Don of the Wars. Not a single man at the gathering had bested him in the contest, but Miss Mary charged her musket, pulled the stopper from her powder horn like a seasoned warrior and hit the bullseye square in the middle.

It just wasn't proper.

Besides, he doubted the lass had any clue what a bedchamber was used for aside from sleeping. His heart thrummed. He shouldn't berate the lass, not even to himself. She must have had an awful shock when she'd caught her father with the widow.

Regardless, Miss Mary needed to become a proper lady. When this business was over, he'd write to her father and suggest John of Castleton send her somewhere for instruction.

Don bit his bottom lip while he continued to watch the trail pass beneath him.

Where?

Of course his sister, Barbara, would welcome the opportunity to dote over someone like Miss Mary. Though Barbara would be beside herself with disbelief when presented with a Highland tomboy. Genteel, Barbara would never consider touching a musket, let alone becoming proficient with one. Don grinned. Imagining his sister flouncing through society with a redheaded apprentice in her wake amused him. Since the death of his parents, he'd been his sister's guardian. Barbara lived in the Glasgow townhouse and drove him mad at her every opportunity. Perhaps the lass needed a project.

Then his gut twisted.

In no way could he endure two strong-willed women in his domicile.

The lass cannot possibly go to Glasgow. Miss Mary would pose too much of a distraction in my household. Visions of the imp challenging houseguests to shooting contests made Don shudder.

No, no. Regardless that she'd attained her majority, Miss Mary needed to be fostered by a respected matron in the Highlands. Possibly Ewen Cameron's wife, Lady Isobel, would take her on.

Don's gut squeezed. If Mary were to stay at Achnacarry, young Kennan Cameron would be there, no doubt. The lad was hot blooded—liked the lassies for certain. And they liked him. What young maid wouldn't swoon over that youth's cocky grin? Devil's bones, Kennan's eyes even sparkled when he smiled. Why the hell would God make a man with eyes that sparkled? What if Kennan decided to court the lass whilst she was in Lady Cameron's care? It would be an abomination. Mary could not be courted by the son of her foster mother.

I would wring his neck.

Onward Don rode, wracking his brain for a solution, until the flicker of a flame caught his eye.

Chapter Ten

After eating a meager meal of bread and cheese while sitting on a soggy log in front of the fire, Mary watched the dragoons erect a tent. Balfour lifted the flap, his features made darker by the night's shadows. "'Tisn't anything like my cottage, but at least it will keep you dry, my love."

The man had made her eat with her wrists bound and yet he referred to her with such an inappropriate endearment? "I'm not your love," she hissed through clenched teeth.

"Yet."

The dragoons stood around the fire staring at her with blank expressions. Surely one of them had a conscience. Or did they all blindly follow orders regardless, even if they went against every moral code in the Highlands? Then she remembered the massacre at Glencoe and knew her answer.

No.

As she moved toward the tent, her gaze darted across each uncaring face, hoping she was wrong, hoping she'd find sympathy. One man looked away, then another. They all seemed more worried about spending the night in the drizzling rain.

Balfour made an exaggerated gesture with his palm, looking like an eager dog. "Stay atop the furs and you'll be toasty dry."

She met his feigned kindness with a scowl. "You sound like you care."

"Oh, but I do." He bowed. "I wouldn't want the mother of my heir to catch cold."

Mary winced. The mere thought of lying with the lieutenant made her stomach roil. The man had completely lost his hold on reality. "You will *never* touch me."

She bent down and started into the tent.

Stopped by his brutal hand grapping the nape of her neck, Mary jolted with a shriek. Jerking her up, the cur grasped her chin and forcefully twisted her face toward his. "I beg to differ."

She shivered to her toes. Heaven help her, his eyes were black and filled with hate.

With a surge of revulsion, Mary forced her bound wrists between them. But that only made him grip tighter. Scowling, he crushed his mouth over hers. Her stomach heaved as his tongue licked her lips, probing as if he wanted to stick the vile thing into her mouth.

Pushing as hard as she could, Mary finally broke his hold. Quickly shuffling to the tent, she ducked inside and regarded the blackguard over her shoulder. "*Never* try that again."

He chuckled—a sickly, ugly cackle. "That's a promise I cannot make." He bent down and poked his head inside. "Sleep well, for I want you to wake refreshed on the morrow."

Mary eyed the cutlass hanging from his right hip. "Would you release my hands? I would sleep more comfortably."

"I think not—at least not until I am lying beside you."
He shrugged. "Besides, once you drift off to sleep, those
bindings shouldn't be a worry."

Repulsed, Mary yanked the flap closed. At least
Balfour was right about one thing. The fur was dry and it
felt a wee bit warmer now that the canvas blocked then
wind and drizzle.

"We'll change watch every two hours," the
lieutenant's nasally voice came through the thin material.
"And keep an ear to the ground. I don't think Miss Mary's
kin will have caught wind of her whereabouts as of yet,
but one never kens."

"Aye," said another voice. "And she doesn't seem too
pleased with your wedding plans either, sir."

"She will be," Balfour snapped. "And that's none of
your concern. If you want your back pay, I suggest you lot
keep your opinions to yourselves. I will marry the lass and
she'll be well cared for. Once she realizes it is a fortuitous
match, she'll come around. Mark me."

The conversation beyond the tent did anything but
settle her nerves.

Lying on her side, Mary curled into a ball and tried to
think. It didn't matter if the lieutenant lived in a castle, she
wouldn't be happy. She hated him and everything he
stood for. Worse, he'd been collecting taxes and
intimidating every crofter on her peninsula for the past
two years. In no way would the man suddenly turn over a
new leaf and act as an upstanding, respectable husband.
Even if he playacted at being pleasant, it wouldn't last.
Aye, she had witnessed too much of his evil side.

Mary rolled to her knees. Holding her breath, she
peered through the gap in the tent. The fire had fizzled
with the increasing rain.

God save her. How on earth could she manage her
way out of this mess? Where was the Castleton guard

now? As Balfour had plainly said, her kin probably had no idea they were traveling inland to his home—and how many people on the peninsula knew he was from Invergarry? Mary hadn't a clue—not that she'd ever asked the lout. Who on earth would stop and drum up idle chat with their enemy?

Scrubbing her fingers across her lips, Mary wiped away the filth of the lieutenant's mouth. Gracious, his horrid lips had practically crushed hers. She wanted to spit and wash her mouth out with peppermint tonic. Why did her first kiss have to be the most vulgar experience imaginable? If she hadn't been so shocked by Balfour's actions, she would have bit him. How dare he force her? And in front of his men? Good heavens, that man was evil with a capital E.

Then Mary's blood turned icy cold. Surely he wouldn't force her to lie with him? Surely he was jesting? He couldn't marry her on the morrow. Could he?

But then, if he knew of a way to marry her without her consent, after the ceremony he'd be within his rights to force her.

And that's what he was laughing about.

Mother Mary, help me.

The lieutenant had no intention of pretending to be nice—to turn over a new leaf. He was the bully she knew him to be and he would feel not a lick of remorse when he took her, willing or nay, to his bed.

A flash of unwanted heat spread down her arms.

Oh God, if she didn't escape this night, there may be no other chance. She would be violated and ruined—and then she would have nowhere to go. Her life would be over. And if she didn't bow to Balfour's whims, only heaven knew what would happen. Mayhap Da would take her in, but she would be a burden to him for the rest of her days. No one would want her, even if she did find a way to escape from Balfour's clutches. Is that what he meant when he said she would learn to like him? She would realize how better off she would be, trapped in an unwanted marriage, bearing his hideous children?

She crawled to the back of the tent and carefully ran her hand down the rear canvas. Just her rotten luck, the thing had been lashed closed.

Of course, otherwise, Balfour would have posted a guard on this side as well. At least she hadn't heard anyone move back that way, nor had the lieutenant given an order to do so.

Not giving up, she sank her fingers down past the edge of the fur.

Wet moss.

Running her hand along the edge, the canvas was pulled taut, but beneath it was earth. Could she loosen the tension enough to slip under? Reaching to the corner, she found a metal spike. Would the tent collapse if she pulled it out?

Rocking back, Mary held her breath and listened. Rain pattered against the tent. The river rushed in the distance. Wind whistled and tossed the creaking branches overhead. Her heartbeat thundered in her ears so loudly, she feared everyone in the camp could hear it. Were the dragoons asleep yet? Should she wait a bit longer? If she stuck her head out the front flap, the guard would know she was up to something for certain.

Frozen in place, Mary took only shallow breaths, imagining the scene beyond. When her heart finally slowed enough to calm its deafening thrumming, she made her move. Carefully, she levered the spike back and forth until the tension eased a wee bit. Then she slid her hand under the canvas and lifted. It relaxed enough to create an opening no more than a foot, but perhaps enough for her to slip beneath without being noticed.

The rain pattered louder on the canvas.

Good, the noise would make her movement all the more unnoticeable. She had to be a ghost…slip out and tiptoe to the river and run. Taking one last deep inhale, Mary lay flat and slid out the back of the tent. With the rain, darkness shrouded everything. Once outside, she crouched, peering side to side. Rain splattered her face, but not a human sound came from the camp.

Picking up her skirts, she tiptoed over the mossy earth toward the rush of the river, looking back over her shoulder every few steps.

Mary's heart raced again. With every step, she feared a dragoon would lunge from behind a tree and capture her. Swallowing her fear, she pushed onward. By the time she reached the riverbank, her legs were pumping faster. But now she was far enough away not to worry as much about snapping twigs. Now she needed to run.

And run she did, as fast as her legs would carry her.

A stitch in her side cramped and she pushed her hand against the pain. She would drop of exhaustion before she stopped.

Somewhere there must be a boat, mayhap a horse. Anything to speed her flight.

With her next step, Mary's right foot sank into mud. Of all the miserable luck, the blasted thing stuck as she tried to pull it out. Bracing her left on the bank, she tugged hard.

With a loud sucking noise, the foot gave way as rainwater and mud poured toward the river. Falling, her bound wrists flew up and smacked her in the face. Trying not to cry out, her feet flew up and her backside landed, whisked to the raging torrent by unforgiving and slippery mud.

Mary closed her eyes and prayed. This was the end. She couldn't swim and with her hands bound, she had no chance.

The entire world went calm, serene. At least she would not be forced to marry Balfour MacLeod.

Ice cold water soaked her feet. Her legs.

She prepared herself for the end.

Fingers as hard as iron gauntlets gripped her arm. Mary's eyes flew open.

She'd not go back to the camp.

No. Chance.

Fighting with her entire body, her arms, her legs, she struggled to break away.

"Easy, lass," a deep voice grumbled.

Mary craned her neck and her heart launched into a myriad of fluttering palpitations. A familiar face grimaced with exertion as he pulled her from certain death.

Using her legs to help her ascent, he pulled her from the torrent.

God has sent me a savior.

Once on her feet, Sir Donald glowered. "I kent I'd find you in more peril than a MacGregor standing on the gallows with a rope around his neck."

Why on earth did his growl sound like the chimes of angel's bells?

***

"Keep quiet," Don growled in a low voice while he cut her wrists free.

"How did you find me?" she whispered.

"An old fisherman saw the lieutenant manhandle you in Glenelg—said you rode west with a retinue." He helped her stand and gestured to the pony. "Come, I'll give you a leg up. We must haste."

"Only one wee garron?" she asked, putting her foot in his interlaced palms. "Ragnar may be sturdy, but he's still only a pony."

"Quiet, I said." Don helped her onto the horse's back, then mounted behind her. "He'll have to do until we can find other transport."

She stroked the garron's neck as if greeting a long lost friend. "Did you see your galley moored in Glenelg?"

"Aye, and I tasked Sir Coll and Sir Kennan to recapture it and meet my brother in Trotternish." Reaching around her, he gathered the reins. Lord, she'd been beaten, bruised, slid down an embankment of mud and Mary's hair still managed to smell like a bouquet of lilacs in spring.

She leaned against him, turning that heart-shaped face to his, blinking as the raindrops sprinkled her eyes. Even in the dark, her lips enticed, ever so pouty and delicious. "Oh, no. Lieutenant MacLeod posted guards in your boat—said you'd be dead if you tried to ambush."

Don ground his molars as dread crept up his neck. He knew the redcoats wouldn't let the galley sit on the shore unguarded. Leaving the capture in the hands of a couple of Highlanders bore too much of a risk, yet he'd had no choice. Nonetheless, he'd never forgive himself if one of them was hurt. Thank God Coll MacDonell was the best man with a sword Don had ever seen. And Kennan wasn't far behind. Still, he should have told them to go for reinforcements first.

"Will they be all right?" she asked, her voice trembling.

"Aye," Don said with more surety than he felt. Even if he headed straight for Glenelg right now, the battle would be over. And Coll MacDonell was itching for a fight—no way would he have exercised the good sense to turn back—unless...

Don could only pray the chieftain didn't move too soon. If they listened and set up a watch like any well-trained Highlander, Coll and Kennan would have known the odds before they boarded the ship.

"You don't look so certain." Studying him in the darkness, Mary placed her fingers on his cheek. Fingers soft as petals plied his face—made him want to close his eyes and lean into her succor.

Don jerked his head away.

Damnation, he'd have a mob of redcoats on his arse by the time the sun rose and he was leaning into the lass' warm palm? "Mark me, they will not suffer at the Government's hand. And I will see to it they do not."

He grumbled under his breath. The kiss MacLeod had forced upon Miss Mary hadn't escaped his notice. At least it looked forced—and it was all he could do not to shoot the rutting weasel between the eyes right then and there.

Digging in his heels, he cantered the horse to the shallows and dashed across the river.

Mary leaned forward over the horse's neck and helped the gelding gain speed. At least she wasn't a simpering wench who cried for home. They needed to put as much distance between them and the dragoon's camp as they could before dawn. And the damn pony was already near exhaustion.

After they'd crossed the open lea and rode under cover of the forest, Don slowed the horse to a walk.

Mary settled against him, the softness of her bottom pushing right where it shouldn't. Don groaned and tried to shift his hips away but the curve of the saddle slid him right back flush against her bum. Heaven Almighty, what a wonderfully soft, well-formed pair of buttocks. He clenched his teeth, his eyes crossing while he tried to think of anything but the young maid's arse.

"Where are we headed?" she asked, using a normal speaking voice for the first time that night. It sounded a tad lower than most women's voices, sultry. The tone only served to stir his errant cock to life again. *Curses.* He clenched his every muscle taut. For God's sake, he was a war hero, not a ravisher of maidens.

Closing his eyes, Don drew in a deep inhale before he answered. Met with the heady scent of woman, the fire deep in his groin swept through his chest. How long had it been since he'd enjoyed the comfort of a woman's arms? Too bloody long. But he wasn't about to make a mistake with Mary of Castleton—one that could take his dreams and tear them to shreds. Besides, after MacLeod's manhandling, she may never want to kiss another man again.

"Cameron lands are due south," he replied. Perhaps his idea to leave Miss Mary with Lady Isobel was sound.

"South?"

"Aye. With luck, the lieutenant will think we're headed back to Castleton—tracking in the Highlands is a skill possessed by few. The only problem is the land between here and Achnacarry is nothing but rugged Highlands— filled with peaks and lochs. The going will be slow." Why on earth Don liked the idea of trekking through the mountains with Mary and one wee pony, he had no idea. Too many things required his attention. Too many things had to be pulled together to make this shipment and secure future trade with the American merchants—and he wouldn't be on hand to oversee a one of them.

As they rode on, one question had needled at the back of his mind since he'd started tracking the lieutenant and his retinue west. "Where was MacLeod taking you?"

Shaking her head, Mary shuddered between his arms. "To his family lands in Invergarry."

"Family? I figured he was headed to Fort William to put you up on contrived charges or some harebrained notion like that." Don refused to mention he'd feared the worst.

"I would have preferred to go to the gallows than endure what he had planned for me." She shuddered again. Miss Mary kept her gaze forward, her shoulders as tense as a rabbit snare.

No one had to tell him the woman was afraid for her life. Don glanced over his shoulder. He should have faced the bastard back at the camp when he'd had the chance. "Did he…ah…did he force you?"

She drew her hands over her face. "You mean, did he violate me?"

He gulped. "Aye."

"Nay, unless the vilest kiss imaginable is considered doing…uh…*that*."

"The bastard," Don cursed through clenched teeth. Pulsing rage coursed through his blood. He shouldn't have hesitated back at the camp. He'd had the swine in his sights. He should have taken the shot as soon as Mary ducked into the tent. But if something had happened to the lass…

"He was taking me to Invergarry to force me to marry him. 'Tis why I slipped out of the rear of the tent. Come morn I would have been Mrs. MacLeod—ruined for life." Crossing her arms, Mary curled against Don's chest, shaking furiously. "Please-please keep him away from me. I'd rather die than marry that man."

Don practically blew steam out his ears. The bastard forced Miss Mary to kiss him and then planned to wed her without consent? God's bones, no wonder the lass was shivering like a frightened kitten. Before he thought, Don pressed his lips to her temple and closed his eyes. Dear Lord, he needed to protect this lassie like he needed to breathe. "As long as you are with me, I'll not let anything harm you. That man will pay. One way or another, his misdeeds cannot be allowed to pass."

"Thank you." She smoothed her fingers over Don's arm. Even through his cloak and doublet, her touch drove him wild with longing. Again he growled through clenched teeth. He must block his inappropriate urges from his mind. Good God, the lass had been through a terrible ordeal and needed comforting, not a lusty rogue who hadn't bedded a woman in far too long. "I think he'll follow us. He's not one to give up," she said, her voice even deeper than before.

"Aye?" Don's gut clamped hard as stone. "I hope he does."

Chapter Eleven

Mary snuggled into the warmest pillow she'd ever had the pleasure to rest her head upon. How a pillow could be so warm, inviting, yet so incredibly firm, she had no idea. Something at the back of her mind told her she must open her eyes, but she couldn't. She was exhausted. Even the simple act of raising her eyelids was impossible.

With a sigh, she rubbed her cheek against the softness—like velvet. And the smell made her insides tremble. She liked the scent—somewhat spicy with a hint of danger. She could bury her face in that scent and lose herself. In fact, she did just that while the heavenly rocking motion beneath lulled her into a dreamy trance. Side to side, the rocking continued swinging her like a bairn in a cradle. But the motion clicked in time—more like a clock.

Mary sighed. *Or a horse.*

The pillow beneath her head flexed and hardened.

With a jolt of her heart, her eyes flew open.

A bit of spittle drooled from the corner of her mouth.

Swiping her hand across her face, Mary gasped. How on earth could she be such a muttonhead? Falling asleep and nestling into the Baronet of Sleat's chest? Holy Moses, it wasn't just any man she'd been all too familiar with, it was *a nobleman*—the most esteemed guest at her father's gathering. Could she be any more uncouth? The man must think her to be as insufferable as one of the guttersnipes from Glasgow she'd heard tale about.

When he cleared his throat, a warm rumble reverberated through her body. Goodness, her cheeks radiated with heat. "Forgive me," she said, making sure no more spittle stuck in the corner of her mouth and hoping to God he hadn't seen her drool. "I shouldn't have drifted off."

He flexed his fingers—she'd probably made his whole arm numb. "You needed the rest." Had Sir Donald's voice been that deep before?

"How long was I asleep?"

"An hour, mayhap two." He pointed eastward. "The sun will be up soon."

"Sunrise?" She looked toward the horizon—a hint of light gleamed cobalt blue. Wind tossed her hair and the moon shone bright above them. Though it was dark, she could see forever as if they had crested the summit of the entire world. "Where are we?"

"Not sure what this peak is called, but I'm fairly certain Loch Quoich is down below."

When she shifted her gaze down the steep incline, Mary's head swooned. Gasping, she grabbed the baronet's arm. The horse stomped with a loud snort, making them shift in the saddle. Good heavens, if the gelding moved another inch, they'd all dropped to their deaths.

Drawing his free hand to her abdomen, Sir Donald pulled her taut against his body. "Easy."

"Sorry."

He reined the horse to a stop a foot or two away from the precipice. "I didn't take you for the type to frighten at heights."

"I...ah...am not." Mary regarded the powerful arm in her clutches. Hard muscle pressed against the side of her breast. She should release him, but it felt too good, as if he'd awakened her bosoms with a tingling, swelling rush of desire. Curious, she raised her chin and regarded his eyes—fathomless and inky black like the loch below, his gaze connected with hers. And then he held her gaze as if they were pulled together by a powerful force. Something there, but unseen and unspoken.

Mary gasped.

His tongue slipped out and grazed the corner of his mouth, almost as if he wanted to kiss her—not a coarse and unmannerly kiss like Balfour had forced upon her. No, Mary couldn't imagine the baronet being crude. Sir Donald's lips shone with the moonlight, looking ever so delicious. She inclined her lips toward his mouth as if a magnet was pulling her closer. What would it be like to kiss him? The fluttering in her breasts swarmed lower, igniting a fire so deep inside, she thought she might burst into flames. His gaze dipped to her mouth, his lips parting slightly.

But then he blinked with a shake of his head. "Ah...we must find shelter. This old fella needs a rest."

Heat spread from the back of her neck and up her cheeks. How daft of her to think the Baronet of Sleat might actually like her enough to kiss her. Flustered, Mary released his arm. "Are you not feeling well?"

"I'm fine." He tapped his heels, his eyebrows pinching together. "Why would you ask?"

"Your voice sounds a wee bit hoarse. I'll wager you're tired as well."

He snapped his hand away from her waist. "I-I'm weary, I suppose." Goodness, he did sound gruff all of a sudden. But fatigue made bears out of everyone.

Regardless of what he said, she offered up a silent prayer for his good health. The last thing they needed was illness.

Neither of them spoke again while Don urged the garron down the path. Mary tried not to look down the steep incline and fixed her gaze on the sky as it turned from cobalt to violet to orange. Och aye, how Mother Nature could calm her nerves.

"'Tis beautiful," Sir Donald whispered behind her.

Tingles spread across her neck. "Aye. *Spectacular.*" Mary didn't want to say anything else—didn't want to think about the dragoons who would soon be waking to this very sun's rise—if Lieutenant MacLeod hadn't already realized she was gone. The warm body pressed against her back sheltered her from all evil. The baronet's braw arms surrounded her in a protective cocoon and the sight before them was the most breathtaking scenery she'd ever seen.

As the sun appeared like an orange ball on the horizon, Sir Donald gave the horse his head and allowed the gelding to pick his way down the slope into the trees. A bit further and they crossed a burn which led them to the entrance to a cave.

Sir Donald pulled the horse to a stop. "We can take our rest here." He dismounted and helped her down.

"Have you been here before?" she asked, noticing he held his hands on her waist a bit longer than necessary.

With a clear of his throat, he released her and looked away. "Not since I led my army to Killiecrankie. We camped here going down and coming back—'tis why I chose this path."

"'Tis amazing you found it in the dark of night."

He chuckled—goodness, Mary was growing accustomed to that deep rumble—she feared she enjoyed listening to it too much. "I recognized it as soon as we crossed the river. Otherwise, we'd just be heading south on a prayer that we'd run into Loch Arkaig."

"Cameron lands?"

"Aye."

Mary stretched her arms out. "And when do you think we'll arrive there?" Hopefully both of them would be able to rest and have a good meal once behind the walls of a fortress.

Sir Donald stooped to hobble the garron with a bit of rope. "That depends on how this fella holds up. My hopes are to be there afore dark."

"Oh, thank heavens. I fear once Lieutenant MacLeod discovers me missing, he'll pursue us mercilessly."

The baronet straightened. Merciful fairies, he was tall. Moreover, the way he looked at her made Mary swoon. *This lightheadedness is being caused from being overtired for certain. But, by the stars, he's fine to look upon.*

The man did, however, look as tired as she felt. "That's why I need to go back and cover our tracks."

"What?" She glanced to the cave with its dark, menacing opening, ready to swallow her in one big gulp. "I thought you said *we* needed to rest."

"You, aye." He brushed his forefinger across her cheek. "There's no need to worry. I'll not be long."

"No," she argued. What in heaven's name was he thinking? She'd just been abducted by dragoons and one threatened to ruin her life—would do so at his very next opportunity. Throwing decorum aside, Mary flung her arms around him. "You cannot leave me here alone."

Those enormous arms closed around Mary's back and tugged her into his warm chest. "Och, *mo leannan.* What happened to the fearless lass who pulls the powder horn cork with her teeth and shoots like a Highland sniper?"

Resting her head on his chest, she held him closer. If only he'd utter the Gaelic endearment one more time, her nerves might be calmed forever. But he'd most likely just made a mistake because he was so tired he couldn't think straight. Aye, he'd been right. She might put on the airs of a tough lass, but not today—not after she'd been abducted by those vile dragoons. For everything holy, she wanted to stay in Sir Donald's arms forever. How on earth his embrace felt better standing face to face rather than sitting a horse with her back against her, she never would have guessed. "That—that was before they took me," she stammered.

He smoothed his palm up and down her back. "I shan't be long. I give you my word."

"What should I do if they find me?"

"They won't."

She wanted to believe him. "But if they do?"

His hand continued to soothe her. "How about I leave you with my musket and powder flask?"

Mary started to pull away but this time Sir Donald held her close, cupping her cheek with a warm palm. She glanced up and met his gaze. His eyes weren't filled with anger like she expected. They were dark as midnight and stirred a hunger so deep within her, she couldn't quite understand the meaning of such overwhelming emotions—Mary sensed he liked her—mayhap, anyway. She bit her bottom lip as her gaze trailed to his lips— moist, full lips she thought might kiss her a while ago. The mere idea of his mouth pressed to hers made her heart nearly flit out of her chest.

"Would you...?" Holy Moses, she couldn't ask a baronet to kiss her. Licking her lips, she forced her gaze to shift to his eyes. His visage had grown even darker, hungrier. The corner of his mouth ticked up as he cradled the back of her head and threaded his fingers through her tresses.

"I reckon you need a proper kiss, lass," his voice rasped with the hum of a low growl.

Parting her lips, she gave a single nod. She watched as he bowed his head. His breath skimmed over her tingling skin. Then Mary's eyes closed as the gentlest lips imaginable met hers and kissed. He brushed his mouth across hers with the softness of a feather—not a brief peck like she'd receive from a family member, but a luscious kiss that lingered and made her heart thrum through every extremity of her body.

Just when she thought it couldn't get better, his low moan rumbled sending new waves of desire throughout Mary's insides. She'd never been so stimulated in her life—so alive—so filled with desire. If only this moment would last.

And then he fulfilled her wish. Rather than pull away, his tongue caressed her lips, coaxing them open. Craving friction, craving warmth, craving more of him, Mary tightened her embrace around his ever so masculine frame. After years of caring for her father, after being the stalwart strength for her family, a braw man surrounded her with powerful arms, a man who could protect her from vile dragoons and all the evil that existed beyond the walls of Dunscaith Castle.

Opening her mouth, Mary welcomed him in and allowed this nobleman to show her how lovers danced. His body moved against hers in a slow but sensual rhythm. Something hard and solid pressed low against her—something that heightened her desire all the more— made her want more, crave more, need more. Though tentative at first, she followed his lead and within a few swirls of her tongue, matched him stroke for stroke.

Taking in a deep breath, Sir Donald ended the kiss and rested his forehead against hers. "I...ah…"

"Yes?" she breathlessly replied.

"Forgive me. I shouldn't have taken liberties." His voice took on a gruff tone again. Was he upset with her? Had she been too willing? Had he not enjoyed the kiss as much as she?

Mary slid her hand up his back slowly, memorizing every thick band of muscle, afraid she'd never have Sir Donald MacDonald in her arms again. "I wanted you to—to show me…"

"Did you mean what you said?" Taking a step back, his tawny eyebrows slanted inward. "You've never had a proper kiss?"

"Nay. Never."

He looked aside. "Well, when your father makes a match, I'm certain your husband will ply you with something far more satisfying than a wee kiss in the wood."

Wee kiss? Why Mary's lips still thrummed from the pressure of their joining. She wanted to thread her fingers through his hair and draw him to her yet again. Did their wee kiss in the wood mean nothing to him? Was he only trying to make her feel better?

Most likely, aye.

He dropped his arms and cleared his throat. "I must go, else we'll have dragoons breathing down our necks for certain. Take my musket and powder horn and try to rest. I'll return anon and then we'll find something to eat." The moment had fled and the baronet had become more unflappable than ever.

He pulled his musket from the horse's saddle. "And by all means don't fire the damned thing unless you need it to defend yourself. The blast could lead the redcoats straight to you."

***

Don hated to leave the lass alone, but he was right. He'd learned the hard way that covering his tracks was necessary to keep him and his men alive. After they'd fought the battle of Dunkeld, his army had been ambushed by a mob of bloodthirsty dragoons. Two men had died and Mary's da had lost the use of his legs for the rest of his life. No, John of Castleton never blamed Don, but the baronet had blamed himself. The attack never would have happened if he'd been smart enough to send someone back with a branch. But at nineteen, a man oft needed to learn by fire. Don had been one of Scotland's reckless youths. He'd not err again.

Running to the crest of the mountain he continued down the other side a good two miles. Then he used a branch to etch out hoof prints. Fortunately, they had traveled over plenty of stone, making his task a bit easier.

Regardless, he needed to work fast and be meticulous. His head had been pounding since yesterday morn and going all night without rest didn't help matters. Being hungry and deprived of sleep marred his judgement beyond all reason. Good God, his cock had started telling his mind what to do rather than the other way around.

And no one had to tell the Baronet of Sleat he'd end up in more trouble than a heathen in the Vatican if he didn't force his head to take charge and never allow another slip.

What the hell was he thinking? He'd just wrapped his arms around Mary of Castleton and kissed her? Because she'd never had a proper kiss? That was the absolute last thing he should have done when met with a damsel in distress. Good God, he couldn't have acted more irresponsibly. The lass was in his care and his alone. He had a duty to protect her from lecherous swine like MacLeod and there he'd stood, the Baronet of Sleat, acting like a wet-eared lad who had never bedded a woman.

But for the love of God, Miss Mary had taken him by surprise when she flung her arms around him—molded those soft, succulent breasts into his chest. Regardless, he had to be stronger—had to resist the freckle-faced beauty. She wasn't supposed to act like a skittish lass. She had vim and fortitude. True, she might be a wee bit out of sorts after being abducted and nearly forced to marry MacLeod, but Don certainly didn't expect her to be so open with her fear.

His protective instincts must have taken over and marred his judgement. Now that Don knew she could have such an ardent effect on him, he'd be more guarded throughout the duration of their time together, which wouldn't be long. By this evening, he'd be at Achnacarry and he'd transfer Miss Mary's care into the hands of Lady Isobel Cameron.

Thank God.

As he worked, his stomach growled, making his aching head all the more agonizing. He hadn't eaten since he'd been at the alehouse in Teangue with Coll and Kennan. Good Lord, that seemed like a sennight ago, though it was just yesterday. Food was another thing he must force from his mind. There wasn't much chance of finding a meal between Loch Quoich and Loch Arkaig and wasting time hunting was out of the question. No. Balfour MacLeod struck Don as the type of bastard who enjoyed the pursuit—and his hankering for Miss Mary would make the swine more determined.

Don's stomach turned over with its next growl. He'd kill the lackwit if the lieutenant ever touched her again. MacLeod had sold his soul to wear a pair of brass epaulets on his shoulders—sold out the Highland ways and joined with the devil. He wasn't good enough to eat the crumbs beneath Miss Mary's table, let alone kiss her with his filthy mouth. God damn it, Don would see to her protection.

The Cameron Clan was one of the strongest in the Highlands—she'd be safe with Sir Ewen in charge—as long as she didn't venture away from the castle.

He'd see to this lassie's safety and let her father know she was safe. It was the least he could do. Och aye, Don must dispatch a missive to Mary's father at his first opportunity. John of Castleton had said he was looking for a suitor for the lass. Well, he'd best take it seriously and proceed with haste.

Don's chest tightened as he worked, covering tracks at a furious pace. He didn't want to think about Mary taking a husband and what that meant. The thought of her kissing another man or wrapping those fine-boned arms around *anyone* jarred his preserves. Of course, the recent chain of events had Don on edge as well. Defending instincts thrummed through his blood—through the blood of all the descendants of the Lord of the Iles. Mary of Castleton's clan was a sept to Clan Donald and, as such, she was under his protection just like every other member of the great and powerful Highland clan that once ruled the isles under Somerled.

Reaching the crest of the mountain, movement in the distance made the hair on the back of his neck stand on end.

God's teeth, the bastards must have realized Miss Mary had escaped well before dawn.

Chapter Twelve

"Mary," Don called, running for the horse. "We must haste!"

She stepped out of the cave lowering the musket from her shoulder, her finger still firm on the trigger. "How close are they?"

"Two—mayhap three miles back." He stooped to untie the hobbling rope. "With luck I've purchased time by covering our tracks."

She strode into the clearing. "But their horses have rested longer and have only one rider."

He didn't need to be reminded. Straightening, he gestured for her to come closer. "'Tis why I said we must haste."

Mary slid the musket into the leather harness on the saddle. "Will we reach Achnacarry afore they catch us?"

"On my life we will." Dammit, Donald didn't want to scare the lass, but if they didn't move quickly, the dragoons could easily spot them once the miserable sops reached the crest of the mountain. "If we make good time, we'll gain enough ground to elude them."

Without assistance she mounted the garron and sat like she ought. "Let's ride then." Giving the gelding a firm pat on the neck Mary leaned forward. "Come Ragnar, you must not fail us this day."

Don mounted behind her and took up the reins. "You seem in better spirits. Were you able to sleep?"

"Heavens, no." She glanced up. Lord, in daylight she had the most enticing eyes—blue as the summer's sky. "Every wee rustle of leaves made me jump. I'm just overjoyed to be moving again."

"Then that's what we shall do." Digging in his heels, he drove the garron hard—galloping when there was an opportunity, but still remaining beneath the canopy of trees so not to be seen.

Mary held tight to Don as they hastened down the slope and skirted around the western side of the loch. Having her curled under his chin, her arm around his back made his chest swell. By God, he would see her to safety. No amorous lieutenant would steal the lass away under Don's watch.

"Do you think they'll pick up our tracks?" she asked, leaning back and peering around his shoulder.

"Aye, 'tis a matter of time." He looked back as well. "I haven't seen them crest the mountain as of yet."

She rolled her eyes. "That's because we've been hidden in the trees."

He should have known he couldn't fool her into thinking they weren't in danger. "We're about to come to a clearing. Take a good look, ye ken?"

"Very well."

Don didn't slow the horse as they cantered through the opening.

Mary gasped. "Redcoats."

"How many?"

"Two, three." They dashed onto a game trail under thick scrub. "Could have been more."

"Did they see us?"

"I don't know."

"Did anyone point or look our way?"

"It was too hard to tell from such distance. If they weren't dressed in red I mightn't have seen them at all." She placed her hand atop his doublet—her dainty fingertips touched him, though gently, the sensation ignited a wildfire within him. Mercy, even his breathing sped. She met his gaze with trust filling her eyes. "Thank goodness neither of us is wearing red." Indeed, the black, blue and green plaids they wore were colors that blended well with the forest.

He tightened his grip on the reins. "Agreed, and thank goodness they've only just crested the mountain. We've purchased an hour or two for certain."

Again Mary leaned forward and patted the pony's neck. "Keep going old fella."

Don's heart squeezed, certain she'd just paid far more attention to Ragnar than she had to him since he returned from backtracking. If only he were covered with molting fur and had four legs.

For hours they rode onward up and down hills. White foam leeched from the gelding's coat, his snorts becoming more labored. Don had no choice but to restrict the animal's pace to a trot.

They'd leapt many a burn and splashed through rivers, and the little garron continued to power forward without complaint. Highland ponies mightn't be tall as the dragoon's hackneys, but they were sturdy stock—were as reliable as the mountains themselves.

Gathering the reins, Don leaned over Mary to jump another burn. Together they soared through the air while he eyed the footing on the other side of the babbling water.

His heart flew to his throat.

Mary squealed and clamped her arms taut around Don's waist.

When the pony's front hit the craggy rocks, the jolt flung them both from the saddle. Time slowed as Don twisted, trying to lever Mary's body above his. With a grunt, his shoulder hit first, sinking into mud in the bed of the burn. Again he grunted when Mary landed atop him. Cold water seeped through his boots, up his kilt and swept across his back.

Sprawled across his body, the lassie coughed, sucking in sharp gasps. "W-what happened?"

Don looked at her mud-splattered face, her long tresses tangled every which way and did his best not to grin. "Craggy rocks." Wrapping an arm around her, he sat up. "Are you all right?" Heaven help him, her petite frame felt good pressed over his. He slid his fingers down her back until it met the luscious curve of her hip.

"My knee hit something...You?"

Snapping his hand away, he pulled his kerchief from his amazingly dry top pocket and swiped the mud from her face. "The nice thing about having a sore head is a man doesn't notice other parts."

Mary cupped his face between her palms. "You have a sore head, Sir Donald?"

He stuffed the kerchief back in his pocket and forced all amorous thoughts from his mind. "'Tis nothing a bit of sleep won't cure."

"Goodness, you must be exhausted." And there was that sultry voice tempting him yet again.

"No more than you are, miss." Clearing his throat, he shook his head, lifted her up and set her on the edge of the burn. "Now let us have a wee peek at your knee."

Mary just spread her hands and ignored him. "Look at us, soaking wet and caked with mud."

"Fortunate for us the weather is fine, but I shall enjoy a warm bath when we reach Achnacarry."

She sighed.

Why must every sound emanating from her body sound entirely too sultry?

"My, that does sound luxurious."

Definitely too sultry.

Stepping out of the burn, he brushed the water away and wrung out his woolens. "Would you prefer to examine your knee whilst I turn my back?"

A darling blush blossomed in her cheeks. "Aye. If you please, sir."

Turning, he removed his doublet and wrung out more water while his entire body set to shivering. Ballocks, the last thing he needed was to be miserable and cold.

Behind him, Mary gasped.

Don spun around before he had a chance to think. God save him, the creamiest, most shapely leg he'd ever seen stretched out atop the grass—slender ankle tapering to a delicious calf—a calf worth savoring over dessert. But his gaze stopped at the blood oozing from a jagged cut just below Mary's kneecap.

He dropped beside her and applied pressure with his kerchief. "That looks nasty."

"It seems I'm making a habit of sullying your kerchiefs." She tugged her skirts down to his hand, but not before he'd glimpsed her thigh. Good God, at a time like this when the lass was in pain, all he could think about was shoving her kirtle back up so he could feast his eyes on her delectable flesh. Why a woman with legs as alluring as hers would want to hide them with layers of skirts was beyond him. Of course, decorum would be required, but only when Miss Mary was in public.

"I think it will be all right once the bleeding ebbs," she said, drawing him back to the task at hand.

Don nodded to the kerchief. "Hold this in place whilst I fashion a bandage." He pulled out his shirt and tore a length from the hem then tied it around her knee. "This should fix you up." Careful not to be overly familiar, he patted her calf. Smoother than satin beneath his fingertips, he rested his hand on her skin for a moment. If only he could slide his hand higher and sink his fingers into Mary's pillow-soft thigh. But that was absolutely out of the question.

Tucking her legs beneath her wet skirts, she looked down, her cheeks still red. "Thank you."

"Do you think you can stand?" Don offered his hand.

"Aye." When he pulled her up, she grimaced but took a few steps. "It should be like new in a day or two." Then she stopped dead in her tracks. "Ragnar!"

"Good God," Don swore. The damned horse was limping along the bank of the burn, tearing away at the grass. The mule's right front pastern was swollen all the way up past the cannon bone.

Mary flung her hands to her sides. "We cannot ride him like that."

Ballocks, what else could go wrong? He started for his musket. "We'll have to shoot him."

"No." Rushing forward, Mary grabbed his arm. "We can't kill Ragnar. He—he's part of the family."

"Aye?" Don frowned at her too-hopeful, too-angelic, too-goddamned-pretty face. "If you recall, we are on the run from a pack of mad dragoons, one of whom wants to force you into his bed." He used the word bed for added emphasis. Mary had seen her father. She had to know the root of MacLeod's intentions. Balfour MacLeod wanted to bed the lass for certain. God save him, so did Don. So would every man who took the time to really look at her—see the stunning beauty beneath the freckles. Holy hell, he'd soon start dreaming of freckles if he didn't soon pass the lass off onto Lady Isobel Cameron.

Mary crossed her arms. "Please. Let us try to lead the pony. Besides, a musket blast would alert the lieutenant of our location."

"I don't—"

She stamped her foot. "*I* hurt my knee and you wouldn't try to shoot me."

He glowered at her. "That's different."

"Is it?" Limping forward, she grabbed the garron's reins. "Come then. We've lost precious time."

Don growled as he watched them pass—looking like two injured feral animals limping in tandem—the horse still molting its winter coat and the woman wet and muddy. She crossed in front of him without giving him a look, sticking that mud-smudged nose into the air. Crossing his arms, he enjoyed the rear view, however. Though her skirts were wet to the waist, they surely did have a way of clinging to her maidenly form. By God, her hips swished when she walked—er—limped.

Holy bloody hell. He combed his fingers through his hair. *I'm in trouble.*

He didn't let the pair go far when his sense of decorum returned and he hastened forward to take charge of the lead. "How is your knee holding up?"

"Fine."

From her gimpy gait, she didn't appear to be too terribly fine. In fact, the horse ambled along a bit more sure footed than Miss Mary. "I could carry you on my back."

"I'm certain that is not necessary, sir." She clipped "sir" as if she were angry.

"You're upset with me?"

She stopped and pointed to the mangy pony. "If you dare try to fire your musket at Ragnar, I—I—I will *never* speak to you again."

A woman who swore to keep her mouth shut throughout eternity? Now that was tempting. "He's still alive is he not?" Don trudged forward. "Come along afore the redcoats pick up our trail."

His back prickled as she walked behind him. There was no need to glance over his shoulder. He could feel her eyes boring into him. "Damnation, I said I wouldn't shoot the beast. Why do I sense you are still angry?"

"Unfortunately for me, anger isn't an emotion from which I easily slip in and out. Besides, now you said it, I'll be worried about Ragnar until he heals."

"Well, if we don't keep up the pace, we all may end up filled with musket balls—excepting you *m'lady*. You'll be hearing wedding bells within the ranks of the Government troops."

"You're insufferable."

"My mother oft told me that when I was but a lad."

Finding sheer rock that wouldn't leave tracks, they plodded on while Mary's limp grew more pronounced and the pain in Don's back needled him with every jarring step. Perhaps he did hit a rock or something when he fell from the horse. And even Ragnar ambled along with his ears pinned. Nothing like a beautiful June day spent in agony, running from a mob of lusty dragoons to sour one's mood.

At least their clothes were drying.

"Do you think we would be able to stop and rest for a bit?" Mary's voice sounded strained.

Don's shoulders tensed. "The offer to carry you still holds."

"Bless it, I don't want to be carried." She stopped and jammed her fists into her hips. "I'm tired and I'm so hungry I could eat a leg of lamb all by myself. Pardon me, sir, I have never been one to complain, but neither of us can keep up this pace—especially without food."

Don glared back, his tongue twisting into a knot. The worst thing? Mary of Castleton was right and their nerves were fraying with every step.

He scratched his head and raked his gaze down the umpteenth slope they'd traversed. Surely they must be nearing Achnacarry by now. Then he blinked twice and wiped his eyes. Indeed, a bit of white shone through the trees. "Is that...?"

Mary stepped beside him. "I think 'tis a cottage."

Don hastened forward. To their fortune, a cottage and another stone structure came into view as well. "And a barn."

"Do you think anyone lives there?" Mary asked, peering around his shoulder.

"Not sure." Don didn't see anyone, but during these times who knew if the inhabitants would be friend or foe?

She grinned—a sweet, damned endearing grin. "I think mayhap the fairies of the Highlands have granted us a gift."

"Aye? If it's fairies you're counting on, they're more likely to play tricks than lend us a hand."

"Oh stop." She thwacked his arm. "You ken the fairy folk prefer Jacobites to Williamites."

"That I do." Without much other choice, Don led Mary to the cottage. "Let me do the talking."

"Yes, Sir Donald," she whispered, tiptoeing alongside him. "It looks abandoned."

Don urged her behind and drew his dirk. "Hello the cottage," he called in an assured voice.

They stood very still and heard not a thing.

Inching forward, Don pulled down on the latch and opened the door.

Something clicked, metallic like a trigger. "You'd best take not another step and return from whence you came," growled a threatening male voice.

Dammit all to hell, could nothing be easy? Don strengthened the grip on his dirk. "My wife is injured—horse too."

Mary snorted behind him.

Reaching back, he squeezed her wrist, demanding she keep quiet. The steel of the musket barrel glistened inside the dim chamber. Don lowered his weapon. "We seek shelter and a meal if it please you. I can pay you in coin."

"How much coin?"

"A crown for the night, with a meal and hay for our horse."

"A crown for all that? What? Are you a pair of tinkers or worse? I reckon our kind hospitality is worth—"

"Och, stop your wagering, Parlan," a woman's voice cackled. "Can you not see they're out of sorts?"

Don glanced down. His doublet was covered with mud and what he could see of his cravat wasn't much better. He bowed, happy to be taken as a commoner. "My thanks, madam."

The gun barrel lowered. "You're too trusting, Cadha."

"And when was the last time we had visitors?" The woman stepped into the light. "And such attractive young people you are. I'm Cadha and the old grumblebum is Parlan."

Bowing as was his habit, Don kept the introductions vague. "Donald and Mary at your service, m'lady."

The woman sputtered at the undue respect he gave her. "A strapping sort, is he not?" The old woman winked at Mary. "Welcome to A'chul Bothy Croft. Come inside and we'll serve you up a warm bowl of pottage. Parlan will take your pony to the stable and give him an extra ration of hay."

Mary moved alongside Don. "Thank you ever so much. We've been traveling for two days without rest."

"My heavens." Cadha gaped at Don. "You mean to tell me you've driven your poor young wife until she's nothing but skin and bone? From the looks of her, she hasn't eaten in a month. What, are you newlyweds?"

He cringed. Dear Lord, had they just stepped into the lair of Grandmother Cocksure? The sweet young thing was skin and bone by her own volition. And she wasn't *unduly* thin at that. The lass's rather shapely bottom had been riding in his lap which could certainly attest to the appropriateness of her figure. Thank God. If she'd been a heifer, Don would have been forced to take her back to the lieutenant.

Mary laced her fingers through his and smiled—not a pleasant, maidenly smile, but more like a grimace of annoyance with his wee fib. "Just wed."

"Oh, look at that, and what a lovely couple you make." Cadha flicked her wrist toward her husband. "Go stable the horse and give him a hearty ration of hay—oats, too." Knitting her brows at Don, she continued, "I reckon if this gentleman is as stingy with food for his wife as he is for his horse, the poor gelding probably has ribs showing beneath that saddle and blanket."

Ready to drag Mary and Ragnar onward to the next isolated cottage within fifty miles, Don squeezed Mary's hand. "They're both in good health," he managed through gritted teeth.

"Well, not to worry." Cadha ushered them inside. "I set a new pottage to simmering first thing this morn. 'Tis a good thing you arrived when you did, we were just about to take the evening meal."

Chapter Thirteen

Following Cadha's direction, Mary took a seat on the bench at the table. Don climbed beside her, his eyes darting to every nook and cranny like a mob of hairy bogles were about to spring from the shadows and attack. The old woman had marshalled him to the bench as soon as they'd stepped inside and the baronet appeared rather hot under the collar. His bamboozled expression made Mary want to laugh. Truly, she appreciated Sir Donald for his bravery—would put him on a pedestal for the rest of her days, but he had behaved a wee bit overbearing whilst they were running for their lives.

And Mary knew why. His head was sore not only from lack of food and sleep, but all of the men at the gathering had carried on into the wee hours the night before she was abducted. That's why no one was awake and Balfour was able to capture her as well as Sir Donald's galley. Indeed, the baronet needed sleep more than she.

The crofter's cottage was neatly kept. A peat fire burned against a masonry wall in an open hearth with a cast-iron pot hanging above the fire, suspended by a hook which was secured with a chain attached to the rafters. Smoke hung in the air and dissipated through the thatch.

Mary had seen the like in the cottages of the crofters around Castleton. The furnishings were modest. A table with two long benches, two rickety wooden chairs by the fire and on the far wall, a box bed with doors that closed to keep in warmth.

The thing that piqued Mary's interest the most were the white silk Jacobite roses sitting on a small table beside a spinning wheel, encircled by oak leaves and acorns. Doubtless, the fairies were with them. They had, indeed, arrived among allies. Thank heavens.

Cadha busied herself with setting the table. "Where are you from?"

Mary pointed. "Castle—"

"Up north," Sir Donald interrupted.

Inclining her head toward the white roses, Mary gave him a firm elbow—not that her efforts helped. He just scowled like he wanted to rip her head off.

"North? Up by Skye, would that be?" Cadha asked.

Sir Donald sat there like a lump. Again Mary poked the baronet in the ribs with her elbow, squeezing out a reluctant "Aye" from him.

"And where are you headed?"

"Achnacarry," Mary said before the baronet had a chance to blurt out something so vague it seemed rude. For goodness sakes, they hadn't eaten in a day and he was speaking to the matron as if he didn't trust her at all. Did Highland hospitality mean nothing to the baronet now he lived in a Glasgow townhouse?

The woman set a pitcher of ale on the table. "Are you on your way to see Laird Cameron?"

"No," said Sir Donald.

"Yes." Mary thwacked his arm.

He gave her a heated frown, lips turning white.

She overtly pointed to the darned flowers.

"How far is Achnacarry from here?" he asked as the door opened and Parlan strode inside, hanging his bonnet on a hook by the door.

"Fifteen miles due east," said the old man, scratching his balding head. "What business have you with Laird Cameron?"

By the hearth, Cadha ladled pottage into a bowl. "I asked the same thing."

"We're running from the redcoats," Mary blurted.

Sir Donald grasped her fingers under the table and squeezed.

Yanking her hand away, she again thrust her finger at the roses. "I cannot believe you haven't seen the white roses surrounded by oak leaves and acorns—plain as the nose on my face they are."

Silence filled the cottage as the couple exchanged knowing glances. "Och aye, there's nary a soul in these parts who trusts William of Orange especially after what he did in Glencoe—and don't you try to tell me he is innocent—he penned the order." Parlan held his fist over his heart. "Jacobus, the rightful king."

The baronet smoothed his hands over the tabletop. "'Tis good to hear. And aye, the redcoats stole my galley and tried to abduct my wife as well. We're en route to Achnacarry to enlist Sir Ewen's help to reclaim my boat." He gave Mary the evil eye, sending a clear message she wasn't to let anything else out of the bag. He'd lied to the couple about being married and if they found out he'd fibbed about that, they might hand them over to Lieutenant MacLeod. Oh no, no one lied about such serious matters in the Highlands. It just wasn't done.

"Oh, you poor dears," said Cadha while she set the bowls of pottage on the table. "Do you think we're in danger?"

Sir Donald reached for the ewer and poured for the womenfolk. "With luck, they've lost our trail." He then poured for Parlan and himself.

The old man broke the bread and dunked a piece in his pottage. "And if luck isn't on your side?"

"I'd be obliged if you didn't tell them you saw us." He looked to Mary. "We'll head off as soon as we've finished our meal."

Cadha picked up her spoon. "You cannot be serious. You've been riding all night and all day. You must be exhausted." She snorted with a blubber of her lips. "And I ken a tired man when I see it. Dark caverns have taken up residence under your eyes, sir."

"That might be so, but we cannot put you in danger." Don ladled a spoon of pottage into his mouth. "Och, this is delicious."

Cadha beamed, but Parlan ignored the compliment and pointed toward the door. "I reckon you should stay as well. I keep my musket by the door. If you had been one of those red-coated bastards, I would have shot a hole right through you."

"Parlan," Cadha chided.

"'Tis a relief to be amongst friends." Sir Donald gestured to the pot in the middle of the table. "Do you mind if I help myself to another serving?"

"By all means," said Cadha before she shifted her attention to Mary. "Did I hear Donald say you were abducted by those filthy redcoats?"

"Aye, took me just as the sun was rising. Bound my wrists and ankles and tossed me in the back of *his lordship's* galley as if I were a barrel of oats."

"His lordship?" Cadha's eyes nearly popped out of her head.

Across the table, Parlan sputtered and coughed. "You don't mean to say you pair are nobility?"

Sir Donald gave Mary an exasperated glare. "I've inherited a baronetcy, nothing more. Thus there's no need to refer to me as *his lordship*." He gripped her hand the table and squeezed hard like a smithy's vise. "Please accept my apologies. It has been imperative for me to conceal my identity."

"Och, you can trust us. We hardly ever receive visitors now our children are grown," said Cadha.

"Aye," Parlan agreed. "And now we have a nobleman in our wee cottage. I never would have guessed. Where are your lands? I'd think a baronet would live in a castle with a full regiment to protect him and his kin."

"We were at a gathering in Castleton." Mary yanked her hand away. "Sir Donald MacDonald is the Baronet of Sleat."

"Sleat?" Cadha said as if she'd been awestruck. "Why, you're descended from the Lords of the Isles."

Don's face turned red beneath the tawny stubble peppering his face. "Aye, but I would appreciate it if you would keep mum about my identity until this business is over."

"You can count on us, sir," Paden gushed with admiration. "I'll wager those dragoons are out to make an example of you to strike fear in the hearts of Jacobites."

Cadha fanned her face. "The gall of those soldiers, abducting a noblewoman. I wonder how William of Orange will respond to such brazenness."

Mary just about sank under the table. True, she was the daughter of a Highland chieftain, but far lower in society than the baronet.

Sir Donald wrapped his arm around Mary's shoulders. "'Tis exactly why I will be filing a formal complaint both for the abduction of my galley and the abominable act against *her ladyship*." He placed a tender kiss on her forehead, closed eyes and all. What a liar this man could be. "How are you feeling, my dearest?"

Mary smiled sweetly. "I'm gaining confidence by the moment. I'd like to take that musket and fire a hole through Lieutenant MacLeod's chest."

He gave her a squeeze, tightening his grip much harder than one would expect from an endearing hug. "That's my lassie."

Cadha stood and began picking up the empty bowls. "Well, you cannot possibly set out for Achnacarry now. You need a good rest."

"Aye, that garron of yours needs rest as well," said Paden. "I had a feel of his pastern and I doubt he'll be healed before a fortnight comes to pass."

"A fortnight?" Mary gasped.

Sir Donald raised his cup. "We'll leave the pony here in payment for your kind hospitality."

Cadha dropped the bowls on the table with a clatter. "A horse for a wee night's hospitality? My heavens, we cannot possibly accept such generosity."

Mary crossed her fingers. Leave Ragnar with these—albeit nice—strangers? She'd never see the pony again.

Shrugging, the baronet took a long drink of ale. "'Tis my pleasure. If you promise not to give us away to the redcoats, then you are welcome to the little fella."

Paden reached for his pipe and tapped it on a tray. "And as our esteemed guests, we insist you sleep in the box bed. I'm certain it is nothing close to the comfort to which you're accustomed, but it is soft and warm."

Mary's stomach flipped upside down. Sleep in a bed beside the Baronet of Sleat? "Oh no, we couldn't take your bed."

"Don't be silly," said Paden. "I'll fix up a pallet for the missus and me to sleep upon. And come morning, I'll hitch up the mule to the wagon and take you to

Achnacarry myself. I wouldn't have you stressing your injured knee, m'lady."

Placing his tankard on the table, Sir Donald regarded Mary as a thin-lipped grin spread across his face.

Mary's cheeks burned as if she'd held hot coals to it. "But you cannot give us your bed for the night. I am perfectly able—"

"No, no we'll not hear another word," said Cadha. "No one will say you pair came to visit and were asked to sleep on a pile of musty hay."

Goodness, the pottage continued to roil in Mary's stomach. Why on earth did Sir Donald have to tell the couple they were married? Now they had no choice but to sleep side by side? She turned around and regarded the box bed. Was it even big enough for two people? The baronet was a large man—a fact that hadn't escaped her thoughts since he'd first mounted Ragnar behind her. It was a wonder the garron didn't collapse from exhaustion sooner.

***

Don would have preferred a bath and a shave before he climbed into bed with a woman, but the two crofters had marshalled them into the box bed as if they were ushering a royal couple to their boudoir on their wedding night to ensure copulation took place. They'd even tried to convince him to leave his weapons beside the bed. Thank God the old man hadn't pressed him too hard there or else he would have had to put his foot down.

With the redcoats on their trail, Don stashed a dirk under his pillow, knives in his hose, and his sword beside him. The only thing outside the bed was his musket and it lay directly beneath, charged and ready to fire.

Mary lay beside him as stiff as a board—something seemed to be bothering her for certain. He'd only had to look at her face when Parlan had offered the bed to them.

If anyone had ever doubted Miss Mary's virginity, Don could vouch for her simply by watching her reaction. She was more frightened than a doe being chased by a fox.

It didn't matter. He had no intention of bedding the lass—not ever, and most assuredly not tonight.

He stretched his feet down and met with the wall at the foot of the bed. What? Was the bed made for an elf? Don hated to sleep with his knees bent and cramped. Rolling to his side, he angled his legs toward Mary. "I need a wee bit more space to stretch my knees," he whispered.

She wriggled away from him, but truly there was no other place for her to go. Her arm brushed his chest and she jerked it away. "I cannot believe you gave Ragnar to them without consulting me first," she said in a heated whisper.

Good God, the crofters had bedded down by the hearth only paces away. For all Don knew, they could hear their every word. "Oh?" He inclined his lips toward her ear to ensure only Mary would hear his low tone. Of course, her hair tangled across his nose—hair that still smelled sweeter than a mountain of heather in bloom. "Please. Did you expect us to drag the lame mule fifteen miles on the morrow?"

"I expected you to discuss it with me first."

"Forgive me." He crossed his arms, trying to pull his face from her voluminous tresses, but they seemed to grow a mind of their own and clung to his unshaven stubble. "I felt it little payment for their hospitality and their *loyalty*."

She huffed audibly. Through the darkness even her profile looked annoyed—darling, but annoyed. And how in God's name could a woman's profile be darling? Holy hell, Don had gone without sleep for so long, his mind was addled. He brushed her hair from his face. Little good that did. With another huff she rolled to her side—not putting her back to him, but she faced him. Why the bloody hell did she do that? Warm breath tickled his throat—sweet breath smoldering with a mixture of mint and succulent woman. There was a reason he'd never climbed into bed with a woman he didn't intend to swive. Within two blinks, his cock shot to rigid. In fact, the damned appendage was so hard it stiffened straight up to his belly.

Her fingers brushed his chest.

Don gasped.

"I'm sorry." The apology sent tendrils wrapping around his heart.

"Don't be." Good Lord, his mind couldn't focus on anything but the wispy breath caressing his skin. Her lips were only inches from his. All he needed to do was take his finger and incline her chin ever so slightly and he could steal another kiss. Och aye, he'd enjoyed the one he'd stolen in the forest—enjoyed it far too much. And so had she. Thank God he'd had the wherewithal to stop and act as if it meant nothing.

Don gulped, trying to ignore the hot breath driving him to the brink of madness.

That damned kiss will haunt me for sennights.

Of course it meant nothing. Kissing Mary of Castleton could *never* mean anything. Aye, she was the daughter of a chieftain, but she lived in a remote part of the Isle of Skye. He'd made his home in Glasgow…was supporting the Jacobite cause by entertaining dignitaries throughout the Americas and Europe and negotiating business transactions with them—fighting the murderous Government with trade rather than brawn. Fewer good men would die that way.

Good God, she sighed, sending a blast of heat radiating across his bare chest. Why on earth he'd

removed his shirt for bed, he had no idea. Not that he
ever slept in a shirt—or anything. It just seemed the right
thing to do. After all, he'd left his plaid belted around his
waist. He only had one bloody shirt at the moment and
sleeping in it…well, it didn't make sense when Mr. and
Mrs. Amorous marched them into the box bed and closed
the doors.

He could almost see Mary's face with the wee ray of
firelight that shone through the gap. Her eyes sparkled.
"You should sleep," he whispered.

"Mm hmm." Lithe fingers swirled around his chest
hair, sending shivers across his flesh.

His erection throbbed. Hell, a man could only take so
much. One wee kiss wouldn't kill him and he'd be free of
her allure come the morrow.

Ever so slowly, he inclined her chin with his pointer
finger. Her breath teased his face as if she were daring
him to kiss her. Sliding his hand to the back of her neck,
he lowered his mouth to hers. Silken, succulent lips that
begged to be kissed every time he looked at her, met his,
followed his lead and joined him in the most primal kiss
he'd ever experienced. What Miss Mary lacked in
expertise, she made up for with raw passion. Her body
writhed against him, rubbed him in all the right places.
Pert breasts connected with his bare chest. Christ, he
could even feel her nipples through her linen shift.

Closing his eyes, Don trailed his fingers down her
neck, lower and lower until he found what he wanted.
Stroking his thumb across her taut nipple, Mary moaned
into his mouth. His cock pulsed with a wee bit of
moisture oozing out the tip. He'd never been so hard in
his life. He kneaded her delicious breast as he pushed his
hips forward and connected with her mons. Oh yes, he
needed more. Just a wee tug of her skirts and he could slip
out from under his kilt and slide between her milky-white

thighs. Heaven help him, he'd wanted his hands, his lips, his cock, between those thighs since he'd seen them in the forest.

Panting, Mary stilled his hand between her palms. "You...you're not planning to *ravish* me? Not—not *here*?"

Every muscle in his body tensed. What the hell? What kind of monster ravished a virgin? And with strangers sleeping not twenty feet away? Good God, Don had plied her mouth for one wee kiss and now he had her breast in his hand and his cock flush against her body? He didn't ravish virgins. He didn't ravish anyone. Ever. No woman had ever crawled between the bed linens with him who wasn't willing and eager.

Clearing his throat, he forced his hips away. "Forgive me, lass. After our wee kiss in the forest I haven't been able to think of much but stealing another." It seemed Miss Mary was made for kissing—and a few other maneuvers he'd like to show her, but not this night. And blast it all, not ever. "Ah...If you'd roll to your other side, perhaps we'd both be comfortable enough to sleep."

Chapter Fourteen

When Mary opened her eyes, she realized she actually had slept. It didn't matter that she'd been exhausted beyond measure. Lying beside Sir Donald MacDonald was the most confounding, tantalizing, mind-muddling experience she'd ever encountered. Her skin tingled, her lips throbbed. Goodness, even after sleeping, she could still feel his kiss upon them.

Aye, last eve she'd wanted him to kiss her. Craved the feeling of his lips plying hers one more time before they reached Achnacarry and civilization. She doubted she would ever find herself again in such close proximity to the baronet. And he'd made it eminently clear he didn't intend to marry her. So, he'd said her future husband would be able to kiss her like Sir Donald MacDonald? Would he be as alluring as the baronet? Make her blood rush beneath her skin, her heart swell and yearn for him even though he was right there beside her?

If Mary grew any more amorous, she would burst out of her skin for certain. Had anyone ever burst from their skin whilst in the throes of passion? She'd never heard of such an affliction before. Mayhap she was different? Mayhap she was more amorous than other women? Could she be? She had no one to ask and no example to follow except the raging fire in the depths of her belly. Surely such heavy breathing, such anxious beating of her heart, such overwhelming awareness of the man beside her was unnatural.

The quite virile baronet emitted a low sigh, draping his arm across her waist.

Mary's eyes popped wider. Rolling to regard his face over her shoulder, her hips shifted back a fraction and met with something hard. Goodness gracious, it was the same thick column that had rubbed against her during their unbelievably amorous kiss. At least she knew enough about mating to realize what it was. A man was built for breeding—just like a fine stallion. That's why it was so imperative for her to marry well—to ensure the family survived into the future.

But why did the slightest friction make her crave more? With a low rumble, Sir Donald tugged her closer. "Och, *mo leannan.*"

Oh, how she loved to her him whisper the Gaelic endearment for sweetheart—though he was obviously dreaming.

She tensed when his hips rocked into her, pressing right between her buttocks. She wanted to move, to play along with his erotic dream, but that would be ever so wrong. Wouldn't it?

A loud pounding came from the cottage door.

Mary jerked up so fast, she hit her head on the wall.

Instantly awake, Sir Donald cracked the door to the box bed a fraction of an inch and held his finger to his lips.

The pounding pummeled again. "In the name of King William, I demand you open this door at once."

Dear God, it was Lieutenant MacLeod's voice.

"A moment," Parlan said with significant rustling coming from the direction of the hearth.

Sir Donald pulled his dirk from under his pillow and leaned forward, peering out the crack in the door and blocking Mary's view. Clutching the bedclothes to her chest, she squeezed herself into the far corner of the box, praying for a miracle and wishing she had a musket in her hands.

The hinges creaked. "What the devil?" Parlan cursed. "Isn't it awful early for a mob of redcoats to come to call?"

"We're chasing an escaped woman and a man. Lost their trail, then picked it up again at dawn. Led straight here." Mary could never mistake Balfour MacLeod's unpleasant, nasal tone.

"Escapees?" Parlan played along. "They sound dangerous."

"They are. Especially the woman—she's a sharp shooter—very, very dangerous."

"Och aye? What did she do?"

"Resisted arrest."

Good heavens, is that the best Balfour could come up with? I'd like to burst out of this box bed and show him just how good my aim is.

"You don't say? And the man?" asked Parlan.

"Not certain who he is. Seems he caught up with the lass after we abducted her."

"Abducted?" asked Parlan with skepticism in his voice.

"Have you seen them?" the lieutenant demanded.

"Aye, a couple like you described rode through yesterday. Said they were on their way to Fort William to file a complaint about a lieutenant who stole their boat."

Mary silently applauded. *Good for Parlan.*

"Blast. It *is* the damned baronet."

"Mind your vulgar tongue—you'll offend my missus." Feet shuffled. "You wouldn't be the culprit who took their galley, would you?"

"They broke the law. I did nothing wrong." Mary had heard Balfour say that before, the self-righteous measle. How dare he justify his lawlessness in the name of the Government?

"Then I suggest you hightail it to Fort William afore they have a chance to meet with the colonel." Parlan was thinking on his feet for certain. Mayhap it wasn't such a bad idea for Sir Donald to give him Ragnar.

"I need food for my men," said the lieutenant.

Mary tensed. Lord in heaven, he didn't intend to come inside?

"Wait there and I'll fetch you some bread—bloody hell, Fort William isn't far. With those hackneys you're riding, you'll be there within a few hours." The door slammed.

Don pushed open the box bed.

Parlan hastened to wrap a loaf of bread in a cloth and motioned for Don to hide.

The baronet glanced back to Mary, looking at her like he'd throttle her if she made a sound. Holy fairies, he'd been the one who moved, not Mary.

Again the latch clicked with the opening of the door.

"My corporal tells me there's a lame pony in the barn." Balfour sounded suspicious, the blackguard.

"Aye, 'tis the garron your escapees were riding—they took mine and left the old fella to heal—gave me a fair bit of coin for the trade as well."

Mary smiled to herself. Goodness, Parlan sounded convincing.

"Oh?" Curses, Balfour didn't sound swayed in the slightest. "I think you're telling tall tales. Why haven't you invited us inside?"

"At this hour of the morning? I've barely stepped out of bed and you come a pounding on my door demanding food."

The hinges creaked.

Don snatched Mary's wrist and pressed his lips to her ear. "Be ready." Words spoken so softly, he was barely audible.

But her heart flew to her throat while the hiss of a sword scraping from a scabbard turned her nerves ragged.

"Why were you sleeping on a pallet when you've a bed?" Footsteps crunched the dirt floor. "If I find out you're harboring my prisoners, I'll—"

In a blink, Sir Donald leapt from the bed, bellowing like a madman. Attacking the lieutenant, sword struck sword with screeching clangs.

Scrambling off the bed, Mary dove for the musket, training it on the fighting men, but Sir Donald's form was too large. The blades flickered with the firelight with every swing. The lieutenant was fast, but the baronet was faster, deadlier and far stronger.

Mary skirted around the perimeter, looking for her shot. Balfour MacLeod would not hurt Sir Donald and he most certainly would not capture her again. Her blood pulsed beneath her skin. She would never allow that miscreant to touch her, to force a vile kiss upon her. He wanted to marry? Well, she'd sooner *he* die first!

Out of the corner of her eye, Parlan, too, held his musket to his shoulder—and Cadha stood beside him with two pistols cocked and ready to fire.

Blood splattered to the floor.

Mary gasped, trying to make out who'd been cut.

With a forceful blow, Sir Donald pinned Balfour to the wall. "I'd like nothing better than to end this right now."

"Coward," Balfour spewed with blood drooling from the corner of his mouth.

"Mary, come behind." Sir Donald motioned with a nod of his head.

The door burst open, three muskets thrust inside. "Release him," demanded a dragoon.

Sir Donald wrenched Balfour against his body, using the lieutenant as a shield, angling the point of his sword to the blackguard's neck. "He's the first to die."

"And I don't like your chances," Mary added, making sure the soldiers saw her musket—and the others as well.

"Stand down," the corporal bellowed.

"Mary, behind me," Sir Donald commanded again, pushing out the door with Balfour in his clutches.

She obeyed with the crofters following, their muskets pointed at the line of dragoons outside.

How on earth would they escape this mess?

The lieutenant and five soldiers against a baronet, an elderly couple and Mary. She might be a good shot, but she only had one chance before they charged.

But Sir Donald didn't hesitate. He hauled the lieutenant straight for a hackney horse. "Mount up, Mary."

Bare feet, wearing only a shift, she complied, then quickly trained the musket on the others.

Using the pommel of his sword, Sir Donald smacked Balfour in the head. As the lieutenant dropped, the baronet leapt onto the back of another steed. With one slap of his reins, the young hackney burst into a gallop. Mary followed suit. Her musket misfired and the horse took off like a ball shot from a cannon.

A soldier howled.

A crack. Something whizzed over her head.

"Don't shoot at the woman," Balfour hollered.

"To your horses, men!" another bellow sounded behind.

Holding on for dear life, Mary's horse raced past Sir Donald. "Faster!" she shouted as she sped past.

***

Galloping his horse in Miss Mary's wake, Don had to grin, even with the redcoats close on their tail. The woman could handle her mount like she handled a musket. And why would that surprise him? For once, he thanked the stars she was talented at more masculine pursuits. He didn't doubt the soldiers were close behind, but the bastards were short two mounts and Don had ensured their leader suffered a severe ache to the head.

Barely an hour had passed when the stone walls of Achnacarry came into view. Don glanced behind. No redcoats moved through the trees. He pounded on the heavy wooden gate with the pommel of his dirk.

A man-at-arms appeared above, holding a musket to his shoulder. "Who goes there?"

Don fired off his name and title, then introduced Miss Mary. "Is Sir Ewen within?"

The guard lowered his weapon. "He hasn't returned from Dunscaith Castle as of yet."

"Fye. He should have been here a day ago." Don's stomach twisted. Had there been a problem securing his galley? Were Kennan and Coll in trouble? Bloody hell, he couldn't think about that now. "We've a mob of redcoats on our tail—I need a seafaring vessel to sail for Glasgow immediately."

"You'll have to ride to Corpach on Loch Eil—the laird moors his vessels there."

Blast. Another bloody setback. "Do you have a postern gate?"

"Aye, sir."

"Then show us through and man the battlements. A measly retinue of seven is no match for a fortress such as this."

The gates opened and they met the man-at-arms in the courtyard.

Don continued to ride toward the rear of the fortress. "We've no time to waste. Detain them by having a good yarn and, by all means, do not tell the soldiers we've ridden through. Suggest they ride to Fort William and enlist more forces if they want to take us on."

The man stood with a puzzled look on his face. "Fort William, sir?"

"I suspect if they ride for reinforcements, they'll meet with some resistance. My brother should have already lodged a complaint for the abduction of Miss Mary and the seizure of my galley." He looked toward the keep. "Is Lady Isobel within?"

"No, sir. She's visiting her sister in Inverness."

Pursing his lips, Don regarded Mary. "I'd hoped you could stay with her ladyship until we could arrange for a transport back to Castleton."

Mary blinked as if she hadn't considered what would happen to her—or that they must part. Then she regarded the dirty shift she was wearing—now only a mussed scrap of linen at that. "S-should I wait for her here?"

Dear God, a tear dribbled from the lassie's eye. "Fetch Miss Mary an arisaid forthwith." He regarded his own sweat-streaked, bare chest. "And I could do with a shirt of some sort as well. Quickly."

Don scrubbed his knuckles against his skull. If he left her there and MacLeod found out, the blackguard would try to abduct her for certain. And with half the Cameron guard still away, Don couldn't take the chance.

Damnation. The last thing he needed was a country lass following him all the way down the coast. But for the life of him he could think of no other solution.

He gave her a reassuring smile—at least he hoped it was reassuring. "Not to worry, Miss Mary. I'll secure you an escort and safe transport after we arrive in Glasgow."

Once he'd enlisted a pair of Cameron men who could help man the galley, they rode out the postern gate for Loch Eil.

Chapter Fifteen

Once Sir Ewen's small galley tacked into the Firth of Clyde, Mary stood at the bow in the crisp morning air. She watched the scenery pass while clutching her borrowed arisaid around her shoulders. She'd never been this far south—honestly, she'd only traveled off the Isle of Skye once and that was to Inverness. If only she could enjoy this voyage, but ever since they'd sailed from Corpach, she had replayed the scene from the Achnacarry courtyard over and over in her mind.

She'd been a fool to let Sir Donald kiss her—to harbor the remotest hope that he actually cared for her. She'd seen the disappointment on his face when he discovered Lady Isobel was away. Oh yes, his discontentment had been clear when he realized it would not be safe to leave Mary behind. It had been eminently obvious he intended to part ways once they reached the Cameron keep.

She felt like a leech—like an unwanted wastrel.

And now rather than sailing for the Isle of Skye, as sure as the brisk wind on her face, she was growing ever further away. Oh, how she missed Dunscaith Castle. There, people appreciated her, followed her direction. She ran the keep with efficiency. Mary had her family to look after—surely Lilas hadn't resumed Rabbie's lessons, or Florence's lessons for that matter. And only heaven knew what Mrs. Watt was up to with Da.

The sooner Mary hastened home, the better.

She glanced down at her bare feet. Goodness gracious, it was midsummer and her toes were blue. Though the guardsman had given her an arisaid of red and black plaid, there had been no time to search for a pair of shoes that would fit.

Sir Donald didn't seem to mind. He hopped around the galley working like a sailor as if he preferred bare feet.

Funny, Mary didn't take the Baronet of Sleat for a seafaring tar. Aye, the Highlands flowed through his blood, but when he was visiting Dunscaith Castle, he played the part of gentleman. His every movement had been like watching a choreographed ballet. Beneath his velvet doublet he wore shirts with neatly tied cravats and lace at his sleeves. True, he'd earned the moniker Don of the Wars after the Battle of Killiecrankie. Perhaps there was much more to this man than she initially thought.

Curses. She didn't want Sir Donald to have any other sides that might impress her. Mary was already impressed enough. Now that he'd kissed her, how was she to find a suitor who would live up to such lofty expectations? Was there another man in her future who could stir fire in her blood the way Sir Donald had in the box bed…and on the back of Ragnar?

And now they sailed through the Firth of Clyde with green hills rolling to the shores, the sun shining as if announcing a welcome. But no one need tell her there was nothing for Mary in a burgeoning town like Glasgow.

"Tack to portside," Sir Donald instructed, pulling on the rudder. "We'll be turning up the River Clyde soon. We're fortunate this galley is small enough to sail all the way to the city."

Mary nodded and turned her attention to the estuary ahead.

"Take the rudder," Donald barked. His feet pattered over the rowing benches. Mary knew who it was because the other crew members wore boots with heels that clomped. Goosebumps rose across her arms as he stepped behind her. Goodness, heat radiated off him— the same heat that had kept her warm the night before.

He rested his hand on her shoulder and pointed. "See the big rock with the castle on the far shore?"

"Aye."

"That's Dumbarton—a major stronghold for Scotland's west."

Mary had heard of Dumbarton, and the news hadn't been good. "Did they not fire cannons from her walls to celebrate when William of Orange forced King James into exile?"

Sir Donald gave her shoulder a firm pat. "Right you are, but one day the fortress will again revert to the hands of the true king. Mark me."

Mary eyed the enormous castle. From what she knew, it had stood on that rock for centuries. Goodness, stone battlements encircled the entire promontory for miles.

As the baronet resumed his place at the stern, the galley soon sailed past Dumbarton and up the river until the buildings of a city came into view. Grey smoke hung over the settlement and as they neared, the smells of humanity grew ever pungent. Not new smells for Mary, but stronger with a dead-fish overtone.

"Things are a bit unpleasant on the waterfront," Sir Donald hollered as if he could read her mind while he bore down on the rudder. "I'm certain you shall find the townhouse to your liking."

The mooring proceeded swiftly while Mary watched men on the shore pulling barrows of everything imaginable from newly caught fish, to whisky barrels, to hay and bolts of Holland cloth. Beyond the embankment, all manner of wagons waited to be loaded with wares while coaches rolled past, some pulled by magnificent horses and others pulled by mules. Merchants clad in rich silks and lace with long periwigs curling well beyond their shoulders conversed in groups. Swarming around them, people dressed in tattered rags carried on with their back-breaking labor, scarcely paying attention to the gentry as they pushed barrows or carried bushels on their backs.

Such a confounding scene. Why, in Castleton everyone pitched in to unload a galley of stores. They came so rarely, it was an exciting event.

Sir Donald affixed the wooden ladder and offered his hand. "I'll fetch us a coach quickly. And as soon as we arrive home, I'll order proper shoes and clothing."

She placed her fingers in his palm. Goodness, why did his touch have to make her insides flit about so? "I thank you for your kindness," she said as indifferently as possible.

"'Tis the least I can do."

Mary clutched the arisaid around her body, both excited and anxious about the prospect of her first ride in a coach.

Though it didn't take Sir Donald long, the coachman regarded their shabby attire warily, gaping at Mary's bare feet like she was a guttersnipe.

She couldn't allow his reproachful look to pass. "Forgive our appearance. We were set upon by thieves." Though not the complete truth it was easier than trying to explain all the details of the past few days.

Sir Donald sliced his hand through the air. "'Tis none of the coachman's concern." He regarded the driver. "Please take us to fifty Saltmarket."

"What dealings have *you* on Saltmarket, sir?"

"I beg your pardon?" Sir Donald said as if he'd been issued a personal affront. "I live there. Now climb aboard and give us a lift."

Looking very annoyed, the baronet offered Mary his hand and she clambered inside while glancing at his dirty feet. She smoothed her hand over the padded leather seat. It was quite luxurious compared to the wooden bench on the wagon at home. "We do look a wee bit out of sorts."

The baronet settled beside her. "Mayhap we do, but that's none of his concern. My coin is still the same."

"True." Letting it pass, Mary watched out the window while the coach began to amble along. The buildings were so different from Dunscaith Castle. Many were made of wood and they were all so very close together.

The sound of saws came from the timber yard. The stench in the air grew worse and Mary had to cover her nose with her arisaid. The source of the smell came clear when they passed a sign reading *Slaughter Yard*.

Sir Donald pointed. "We'll turn up Saltmarket now and the unpleasantness of the waterfront will soon fade."

True to his word, moments later, the entire scene had changed. All manner of folk strolled along the footpath. The buildings were all made of stone, but with no gaps between them. Some had shop fronts on their lower levels while others had bay windows from the first floor all the way up to the third—definitely looking like townhouses. Some even stood five stories high, just like a keep. They passed the coal warehouse and the cabinet maker's shop and a block later, the store fronts gave way to stately buildings with ornate doors with stained glass. It seemed every door they passed was more lavish than the last.

Sir Donald pounded his fist on the roof of the coach and the driver pulled the team to a stop.

Mary twisted her mouth. "We didn't travel far. Goodness, we could have walked."

"Oh no." The baronet hopped out, then offered his hand. "I'd not allow you to walk the streets of Glasgow wearing only a shift and a blanket."

After he paid the driver, Sir Donald pulled a skeleton key from his sporran and unlocked the leaded-glass door made more ornate by a relief of cast-iron. Stepping inside, Mary had never seen such modern splendor. Every furnishing in the entrance hall was polished to a sheen, the hardwood floor covered with a silk Oriental carpet swirling with reds and blues.

A man wearing trews, shirt and waistcoat pattered down the stairs. "Sir, we did not expect you for another few days. Is all well?" His hawkish gaze shot to Mary.

"We had a bit of unforeseen complications with the Government troops but, with luck, William should be on his way down the shore with our cargo."

"Donald!" said a beautiful woman, dressed in blue taffeta from the top of the stairway, seemingly to float all the way down. "I'm ever so glad you are home."

She took the baronet's hands and kissed both his cheeks. "How are things on Skye?"

"We had a few setbacks, but all is well, my dear."

The hackles on Mary's nape stood on end. *His dear? He never mentioned a wife. Who is this woman?*

The fair-haired beauty regarded Mary, her frown deepening as her gaze traveled from the arisaid to Mary's bare feet. "You've taken in a new servant?" Then she looked to Donald's bare feet and drew her hand to her chest. "My heavens, you both seem to have misplaced your shoes."

"Forgive me." Sir Donald gestured to Mary. "This is Miss Mary of Castleton, daughter of John, Chieftain of Castleton." Then he swung his palm toward the woman. "This is my sister, Barbara. She will see to your comfort."

Barbara offered a warm, if not quizzical smile and took Mary's hand. "You've brought me a companion from Skye? And how did you come to arrive in such a disheveled state, may I ask?"

Mary cringed. "'Tis a long story."

Barbara tugged her toward the staircase. "Oh, how I do love stories. And by my brother's shabby appearance, I am sure this one will bring more amusement than I've had in a very long time."

"Order shoes, gowns, cloak…whatever Miss Mary requires," Sir Donald called after them.

Barbara stopped, a spark of mischief flashing in her eyes. "Honestly? This will be fun. Mr. Kerr, please send up a tub and water to the guest chamber."

The trews-wearing valet bowed. "As you wish, Miss Barbara."

***

Don stood and watched the women ascend the stairs while he scratched his head.

"Shall I order a bath for you as well, sir?" asked Mr. Kerr.

"You'd better." He continued to stare after Mary. "Have there been any missives?"

"I've put all your correspondence on your writing desk, sir."

"Anything from William?"

"Not that I recall."

"Blast." Don started up the stairs.

Mr. Kerr followed. "If you don't mind my asking, what happened? Were you not to attend the gathering at Dunscaith Castle and then sail to Trotternish with William? 'Tis a wee bit baffling, your returning with the Laird of Castleton's daughter and not your brother."

"Baffling is right, along with confounding, maddening and downright frustrating." Don told him about the galley being seized, then continued up the stairs. "Please inform cook we have a guest."

"Yes, sir. How long will Miss Mary be staying with us?"

"Until I can secure safe transport home for the lass— which I'm finding is a lot easier said than done."

With that, he marched to the third landing and to his suite of rooms. By God, it felt good to be home. He crossed through the drawing room and straight for his bedchamber. Sorting through the missives on his writing desk, he found nothing from William. Curses, he hated not knowing. He opened another—the shipment for the Americas had been delayed by a fortnight. Thank God. That was the only shred of good news he'd had in what seemed like an age.

He sunk into his overstuffed chair, propped up his feet and started reading.

Perhaps an hour later, a knock came from the servant's entrance. "Your bath, sir."

"Come." Don normally made quick work of bathing, but the big wooden tub and buckets of hot water brought in by the servants looked incredibly inviting. Lowering his paper, his exhaustion hit full force.

Mr. Kerr set the bath salts, lye and drying towel on a stool beside the bath. "Is there anything else, sir?"

"No, thank you. I aim to enjoy a long soak free of interruption."

Mr. Kerr added coal to the fire and then bowed. "Very well, sir. I'll attend you before the evening meal as usual then."

"Ahhhh," Don sighed, lowering himself into the warm water. Sennights of pent up stress melted away as he leaned back and closed his eyes. Simply being home helped the tension melt from his shoulders. Though he did love Skye, his townhouse was equipped with modern conveniences—glass in the windows, no drafty chambers, hearths built to emit more heat. The worries of *the cause* faded in his quiet chamber which overlooked the rear courtyard and stables.

When the water started to cool, he sank down and soaked his hair, then worked up a lather, washing all the dirt away. He held the soap to his nose—lilac this time. Miss Mary's scent. He chuckled. Mr. Kerr had a fancy for sweet-smelling, flowery scents.

Mayhap the soap would make Miss Mary feel at home. Doubtless she would be bathing with the same scented soap a floor above—naked just like him. If only he could be the one to run the bar of soap over her lily-white shoulder, to massage it in with swirls of his fingers. Oh yes, he'd splay his fingers down her back, slowly moving his hands forward—beneath her arms until he cupped her breasts. Pert, ripe breasts, the same he'd filled his palm with when he'd kissed her in the box bed at the A'chul Bothy Croft.

If only Miss Mary weren't in his care. If only she were a nymph who'd come to tempt him, he might be able to act on his fantasies. But to take advantage of the lass would be akin to betraying the trust of the exiled King James, the trust of the Jacobites and the Highlanders he so dearly loved.

No. He couldn't ravish Miss Mary no matter how much his cods ached. And they ached plenty. He'd practically been hard for the past sennight and there was no respite in sight.

A howl came from the floor above—the guest chamber.

Sitting up, Don's eyes flashed wide.

Another howl sounded, followed by more muffled yelling.

Leaping from the bath, Don grabbed the drying cloth and wrapped it around his waist while he sprinted up the servant's stairs. What had happened now? Good God, would he ever enjoy a moment's peace?

Bursting through the guestroom door, he skidded to a stop.

Barbara looked up, her mouth agape as she stood beside Mary, sitting erect and bare naked in a wooden tub. "What on earth are you thinking, charging in here like a mad bull?"

Don glanced down at his bare chest, streaming with water that grew colder by the second. "I beg your pardon? You pair were the ones squealing as if you were being attacked by said bull. What was I to think?"

Crossing her arms over her breasts, Mary slid deeper into the tub, but not before Don got a good eyeful of sweet alabaster tipped by rose—a breast, not large, but round and so perfectly formed, merely the sight of it turned his knees to mush. Blinking away his lust, he clenched his drying cloth taut over his groin. Now was not the time to show Miss Mary exactly what her body did to him. Good God, his sister stood there gaping at him like he was some sort of lecherous swine.

He gave them both a good scowl. "What on earth were you doing?"

"Miss Mary was telling me about how you met—and the fact she won a crown in a shooting contest." Barbara laughed. "My heavens, if only I could have been there to see the look on your face."

Mary sank so low in the tub, only her head was visible. "Sorry," she mouthed with a cringe.

Moving toward him, Barbara took his shoulder and turned him back toward the door. "Miss Mary needs her privacy—and 'tis a bit awkward seeing my brother with only a wee cloth wrapped around his waist. Not a good style for a baronet, I'd say." She followed him into the servant's passageway.

Descending the stairs, Don shot an annoyed glance over his shoulder. "Mind your own affairs."

As usual, his sister ignored him. "You rescued Miss Mary from a retinue of dragoons all by yourself?"

"There were only seven." The fact that the lass had made his job easy with her escape out the back of the tent helped matters significantly as well, but repeating such to Barbara would be a waste of breath.

"Well, the lass is smitten."

"Hardly." Arriving at his door, he faced her. "Mary of Castleton has been sheltered all her life. How could she possibly ken what she wants?"

"You'd be surprised how much young maids know their own minds," Barbara said like she had a great deal of experience in the matter, but at the tender age of nineteen, Don sincerely doubted such wisdom. Possessed by some sort of deep-rooted feminine insight, Barbara shook her finger under his nose. "You'd best behave. I saw the look on your face when you glimpsed her in the tub—you're not as impervious to the lass as you may think."

"I beg your pardon?"

"You charged into her chamber with naught but a wee cloth around your hips. What would have happened if I hadn't been there?"

Don scowled. How dare his little sister challenge him so? "If you hadn't been attending Miss Mary, I would have been content to stay in my own bath—which is where I intend to return anon."

He pulled down on the latch, but Barbara moved forward as if she planned to enter *his* chamber. "How long do you plan to keep her here?"

He stopped, blocking the doorway. "Until the shipment bound for the Americas sails. Only then will I have the opportunity to take her back to Skye."

"You?" Barbara crossed her arms like an indignant waif—a knowing look fixed in place. "Why not let William do it?"

Well, he had a staunch reply to such a nonsensical barb. "If you haven't noticed, William isn't here."

"I meant when he returns."

"For your information, I believe Miss Mary is in danger. Presently, she's safer here with me. In the interim, take her on as your project. She can use a bit of city refinement before she traipses back to the Highlands."

Barbara rolled her eyes with a tsk of her tongue. "But she's delightful as she is. Besides, more women should become proficient with a musket." She covered her damned mouth when she laughed. "I still cannot believe she bested *you* of all people."

"Stop. Miss Mary's mother passed away when she was very young. I'm certain you understand what I mean when I say she can use your flair for refinement. Now, if you'll excuse me, I aim to return to the peace and tranquility of my bath while there's still some warmth left in the water."

Chapter Sixteen

Wearing a borrowed gown of yellow silk, Mary gave herself a once-over in the mirror before heading to the dining hall to break her fast. Though taller, Miss Barbara loaned Mary two sets of clothes until the tailor could pay a visit. The gowns and shifts were a very close fit, though they had to pad the slippers with lamb's wool. Nonetheless, Mary felt a bit out of sorts. Her kirtles and arisaids were always made of wool—very practical and necessary for the Highlands. In winter they helped stave off the bitter cold. Even then icy winters on the Isle of Skye could pierce through the woolen weave like a thousand knives.

She turned in place and watched her skirts billow. The silk rustled with her every move—made her ever so aware of how expensive the gown must be. She turned again and regarded her image in the mirror. Goodness, she looked so stylish she doubted anyone in Castleton would recognize her.

Though modern and grand, the guest chamber was a bit smaller than her chamber at Dunscaith Castle. They burnt coal rather than peat, which seemed to keep the room warmer, but the best thing was the feather mattress she'd slept upon. Had it not been for the chambermaid coming in to light the fire and lay out her clothes, Mary might have opted to sleep all day. After her ordeal, a night spent sleeping in sublime comfort had been exactly what she needed.

However, once awake and laced into her stays by Hattie, the efficient chambermaid who must haul buckets of water all day long to develop muscles large enough to corset Mary within an inch of her life, her growling stomach won out and she headed toward the smell of good cooking. Scarcely able to breathe, Mary wondered where she'd put any food whatsoever, but by the growling, she had to try.

"Miss Mary, how lovely to see you this morn," said Mr. Kerr as soon as she entered the hall, lavishly appointed with tapestries depicting pastoral scenes. The groomsman pulled out a chair and gestured toward it.

"Good morrow." At first Mary didn't recognize Sir Donald. Wearing a velvet doublet and a flaxen colored periwig that curled down past his shoulders, he was seated at the head of the table reading some sort of missive with a great deal of writing on both sides. Even more perplexing, the table had been prepared as if they were to eat a five-course meal, not a simple bowl of porridge and a few rashers of bacon.

Mary thanked Mr. Kerr and took her seat.

Sir Donald looked up. "Ah Miss Mary," he said as if she were merely an acquaintance come to call. "Did you sleep well?"

"Indeed, I slept like a bairn on your feather mattress—could have stayed there all day." She reached for a scone and buttered it.

Mr. Kerr presented her with a platter piled with food. "Blood pudding and eggs?"

Nodding, she pointed. "And I'll eat two of those fat sausages as well thank you."

Sir Donald, who had resumed his reading, peered over the parchment.

She tried to look pleasant, though she wondered who on earth the man at the head of the table was. His entire demeanor seemed nothing like the Baronet of Sleat who had ridden double with her through the rugged Highlands and who'd seemed as comfortable as a lad sailing a galley with bare feet.

"Where is Miss Barbara?" she asked.

"My sister hasn't arisen as of yet," he mumbled, reverting his gaze to his reading. "You'll find Barbara is more of a night owl. And she rarely takes the morning meal—says it always adds inches to her waistline."

Mary gulped down her mouthful of sausage and egg and studied the title of Sir Donald's document. *The Oxford Gazette*. "Why, pray tell, are you reading that rubbish?"

He folded the parchment and slapped it on the table. "'Tis full of information and the best way to beat your enemies is to ken what they're up to."

"Hmm," she snorted and took a drink of watered wine. "Is that why you're dressing like them? I think I prefer you without the pompous wig."

He patted the gauche curls. "But 'tis the style and what is expected from a man of my station."

"Well I don't care for it. I prefer not to put on airs and wear what is comfortable—what I've always worn."

"Aye? Though I daresay the frock you're wearing now is becoming." He sighed. "But when you're in a war, the one for *the cause* that are in at this very moment, sometimes it is imperative to behave as is expected rather than as one pleases."

Mary nudged her egg with her knife. "I suppose."

"'Tis why I asked Barbara to work with you on etiquette."

Jolting upright, Mary gaped. *How dare he?* She leveled her knife at him, a bit of egg flying across the table. "You think I am unmannerly?"

"Ladies, especially those who are first daughters of chieftains, do not go about pulling stoppers out of powder horns with their teeth and firing muskets."

"I beg your pardon?"

"Nor do they head off to borrow eggs afore dawn."

Mary's stomach churned. "Are you saying my abduction was *my* fault?"

He eyed her—and without amusement as if he'd never felt a shred of fondness for her. "I'm saying a young lassie doesn't set out alone—*ever.*"

"But we've never had outlaws and highwaymen around Dunscaith Castle. It has always been safe to wander about."

"You believe so? But what of the dragoons? I understand Lieutenant MacLeod had been stationed near Teangue for two years."

"The army is supposed to support and protect the citizens, not *kidnap* them and force them into marriage."

"Now you ken differently, do you not?"

She banged her knife beside her plate. "Is that what you think of me? I'm some sort of fool who has no common sense?"

"Not at all—'tis just that you didn't have the benefit of spending time with your mother at a tender age when all young lassies need an older, wiser woman to guide them. You were forced to become the lady of the castle at the age of twelve." Reaching out, he patted her hand as if she were a child. "Spend some time with my sister. The two of you seem amenable. And by all means, Barbara could use a companion."

Och, this man can muddle my mind like no other I've ever met. "Companion? But I thought you planned to send me home at your earliest opportunity."

"I shall pen a missive to your father and let him know you are safe and enjoying the company of my sister. Besides, in Glasgow you are well away from the lieutenant's clutches and where I can keep an eye on you."

Suddenly not hungry, Mary stared at her plate. Sir Donald intended to keep an eye on her while his sister imparted the wonders of modern etiquette? Who was this pompous baboon sitting at the head of the table? Did he think he could run her life? Of all the arrogance. Yes, she probably could benefit from Barbara's tutelage, but she wasn't about to let on that Sir Donald's idea had an iota of merit. If he didn't like her as she was, she wouldn't do *anything* to change for his sake. Curses to him. He'd used his good looks and charm to reel her in—to make her think he actually cared. And like a mindless imp she'd played right into his hand.

She pushed back her chair. "I would prefer to return to Dunscaith Castle immediately."

The baronet furrowed his brow beneath his ridiculous periwig. "To be kidnapped again?"

She clenched her fists and stood. "Whether or not you believe me, I can look after myself. Now I ken the lieutenant is a threat, I'll strengthen the guard."

Rushing for the door, Mary berated herself. She'd never forget Sir Donald's scowl when he saw her in the bath last eve. Shouldn't a man at least look embarrassed when presented with a naked maid in a tub of water? When they were alone in the wood, his heated stare had made gooseflesh rise across her skin. Clearly, she'd embarrassed him in front of his sister. Clearly, he didn't think she was good enough for him.

And why in heaven's name did he have to barge into her chamber wearing nothing but a wee cloth around his hips? Goodness gracious, no man should be thus endowed—especially a pompous, wig-wearing baronet like Sir Donald. Good Lord, he even had bands of muscle in his chest that had rippled all the way down his abdomen. Worse, she'd been made breathless by a wee line of tawny hair trailing from his naval down beneath his drying cloth.

His body was nothing but sinful.

Mary stomped up the stairs. He wanted her to learn manners? The baronet had best learn some as well.

A man who barrels into a woman's chamber without a stitch of clothing? And then pretends to be aloof, standing all but naked in front of his sister and the daughter of a chieftain? He should be as rife with embarrassment as I am.

***

As Mary stormed out of the hall, Don resisted the urge to comb his fingers through his hair—ah, periwig. He hated wearing bloody wigs as much as Miss Mary apparently hated their appearance. But men's wigs served a purpose. Aside from being fashionable, they were a part of a gentleman's costume—along with his attire, a well-groomed periwig set him apart from commoners. Not that Don gave a lick about his station in life, but his buyers did. He was able to negotiate and gain alliances because of his status and he used it not only to his advantage, but to the advantage of *the cause*.

He straightened his cravat. It would serve Miss Mary well to grow accustomed to the lines of society.

Mr. Kerr entered from the servant's door. "Whatever did you say to the young lady?"

Don reached for his cider. "I suggested she learn some etiquette from Miss Barbara whilst she's staying with us."

"Reeeeeally?" Mr. Kerr said as if he knew Mary would have such an adverse reaction. "Honestly, I find her Highland charm refreshing."

"Aye—for a lass who plans to remain on the Isle of Skye all her life."

"Don't tell me...are, are you planning to marry the lass?"

Don gave his valet a stern frown. "Of course not. God's bones, I try to help a maid learn the ways of society in the Lowlands and suddenly everyone thinks I'm bloody smitten."

"I beg your pardon, sir." Mr. Kerr reached for Don's plate. "Shall I order your coach?"

"Thank you. I've business on the waterfront. Thank heavens. It seems I'm completely ineffective at talking sense into Miss Mary—mayhap you and Miss Barbara will have more success."

"What sense is that, sir?"

"She needs to stay here. There's a deranged lieutenant up north who wants nothing but to enslave her as his wife."

"I've never quite heard holy matrimony described as slavery."

"Aside from stealing my galley, the idiot kidnapped her right from under our noses—intended to force her to marry him. I've dispatched a missive to Fort William requesting the man's dismissal. Until I'm satisfied he will no longer be a threat to Miss Mary, she is safer here."

"Yes, sir," Mr. Kerr said with an amused grin.

Don stood and tugged down his doublet. "You are aware her father is a cripple?"

"No. Such news had escaped me."

"Exactly." He made his point. "Miss Mary is not safe at Castleton. There is no one there who can protect her from that red-coated swine."

"Of course, sir." Arms laden with dishes, Mr. Kerr paused at the servant's door. "If it is any consolation, I'm happy to hear the lass will be staying with us for a time. I do like her spirit."

Chapter Seventeen

After spending half the day being poked and prodded by the tailor, Mary sat on the settee in the drawing room and watched Miss Barbara wield a fan. Goodness gracious, if only she'd known a fan properly wielded in a skilled woman's hand could be more effective than a dirk.

"There is a language to fan use," Barbara said, only her violet eyes appearing over the ruffled edge of her weapon. She blinked, looking rather like a doe flirting with a stag. "All women must carry fans—not only to cool themselves or to appear genteel, but a fan can be used to communicate when it is not appropriate to speak one's mind."

Mary chuckled. "Which seems to be the majority of the time."

"Exactly." Barbara closed her fan and slapped it in her palm. "Now pay attention. Your fan must be carried, opened, closed and fluttered with precision and reason."

Mary picked up one of Barbara's fans from the table, opened it, then fanned her face with rapid flicks of her wrist. "It doesn't seem too difficult."

"Aye, but fanning quickly like that means you are engaged."

Mary snapped the thing closed. "Hardly."

"See?" Barbara twirled and sat beside her. "You must always hold your fan with the pretty side facing out—and never cover your face with it...unless you're very serious about flirting."

With a cough, Mary rolled her eyes to the ceiling. "I don't flirt."

"No? We'll have to see about that." Barbara took her closed fan and shook it at Mary with pursed lips—of course the gesture must have meant something—most likely disbelief. She flicked the frilly thing partly open with her thumb. "For example, pressing a half-opened fan to your lips means *you may kiss me.*"

Mary drew a hand to her chest. "Shocking."

Barbara's shoulder shrugged. "Ladies must find ways to make their wishes known. If you hold your fan in your left hand in front of your face, you're telling a potential suitor you are desirous to make his acquaintance."

"My goodness, does Sir Donald know you're teaching me about fan language? I thought he wanted me to sit erect at the dining table, smile, curtsey deeper and keep my opinions to myself." *And stop pulling the powder cork with my teeth.*

Lowering her fan, Barbara grinned deviously. "He told me to introduce you to ladies' etiquette. Fans are an integral part of who we are when in public. No well-bred woman leaves her home without her fan. And you must not forget men as well as women are well acquainted with its language."

Mary lifted her fan and slowly spread it open, displaying a painting of a couple picnicking under a tree. "Sir Donald speaks fan?"

"Aye, *all* gentlemen speak fan." Barbara touched her fingers to Mary's shoulder. "Always remember you must be discrete. If you communicate with your fan, it is only for the eyes of the person with whom you are conversing—not an entire hall filled with dignitaries."

"Good heavens, how am I going to learn a new language?" With a sigh, Mary fanned herself slowly. "What does this mean?"

"You're married."

"Oh for heaven's sakes." She collapsed the fan and tossed it back on the table. "How do I cool myself and say I am completely disinterested in a relationship of any kind and I want to go home?"

"Unfortunately, that sentiment has not yet been invented." Barbara twirled her fan in a circle. "But I think returning to Skye at the moment would be rather dull. At the very least, we have to take you to a ball—you ken they are the most fashionable, most glorious and splendid way for your sponsor to introduce you to Scotland's eligible suitors."

"Like gatherings?"

"A bit. The idea comes from the French Court." Barbara sighed as if Hattie had cinched her stays too tight as well. "Royal balls are lavish displays of wealth and superb etiquette."

Mary squinted and pinched her eyebrows together. "How many royal balls have you been to?"

Barbara affected an exasperated expression. "I daresay only one."

Mary slapped her fan in her palm. "Well then, perhaps I needn't worry about adding ball etiquette to my retinue of expertise."

"'Twould be a folly, for every maid who understands the nuances of behavior at a ball can handle herself anywhere." Barbara took a bit of parchment she'd brought with her and smoothed it open on the table. It displayed a list of fan gestures together with a description of what each one meant.

Mary studied the document. "You mean silently flirt anywhere?"

Batting her eyelashes, Barbara nipped her bottom lip. "I mean, to be in control and to have the suitor of your dreams eating from the palm of your hand."

"Och, with Da being a cripple and a younger brother and two sisters to worry about, I'll most likely be a spinster the rest of my life."

"Is there no one who strikes your fancy?"

Mary crossed her arms. "No one." *Aside from a pompous baronet who thinks he needs to put on airs.*

"Then my brother is a larger nincompoop than I thought." Barbara tossed her fan on the table and stood. "While you're here, we must make the best of our alliance. Besides, 'tis summer. There will be endless opportunities for you to be introduced to society."

Mary eyed her. "You hardly look older than I. What is your age, pray tell?"

"I'll be twenty in September."

"Twenty? Goodness, I'm more than a year older." Mary stood and took Barbara's hands. "And you, is there a noble suitor in your sites?"

"Perhaps one." Barbara sighed—goodness, the lass certainly had perfected sighing. "But he's nay from Glasgow."

"Oh, that is good news, indeed, because the noblemen around Glasgow seem ridiculously pompous." Mary giggled. "Do I know him?"

Barbara shook her finger. "I'm not telling."

"Why ever not?" Spinning back to the settee, Mary wielded a fan, slashing it through the air like a dirk. "You're helping me...perhaps I can help you."

"'Tis only a fanciful dream." The lass' shoulders actually dropped. "Donald doesn't want me to marry a Highlander."

"Pardon me?" Mary planted her fists on her hips. "The baronet *is* a Highlander."

"You ken how brothers are—especially elder ones. They think they know what's best."

As the eldest, Mary could only imagine what it would be like to have the Baronet of Sleat ordering her about more than he already had. "Perhaps they're as opinionated as fathers."

***

Overhearing the lassies' conversation, Don stood by the door and rested his hand on the latch. Of course elder brothers were as opinionated as fathers—especially when a young lass had no father to look after her affairs. As the heir to the baronetcy, he'd had no choice but to become Barbara's guardian. And bless it, she was too young to marry.

He opened the door before he overheard anything else. "Good afternoon, ladies."

"Donald," Barbara said, dashing toward him and kissing his cheek.

Miss Mary flourished a fan from her perch on the settee. "Sir Donald, your sister has proved to be a wealth of information. She has thoroughly educated me in the art of fan language." She pressed the handle to her lips indicating she wanted a kiss.

Blinking rapidly, Donald's face burned as he shot a glower at his sister. "Fans?"

Barbara twirled one of her perfectly manicured curls around her finger. "No proper woman ever leaves her home without a fan in hand."

"What happened to your wig?" Miss Mary asked, touching her finger to the tip of her fan—a request for a private audience.

Don rolled his eyes to the ceiling and pretended not to notice. "I hate the damnable things. I only wear them when I've business dealings."

"I think you look rather dashing with all those curls cascading over your shoulders," Barbara said.

"I think they're ridiculous." Dropping the fan, Mary regarded it with a dour frown. Did she mean she wanted to be friends or had the damned thing slipped from her fingers?

Unable to just let the thing sit there, Don picked it up and tossed it on the table—atop a slip of paper with diagrams of fan language. "Where on earth did you find this?"

"The book shop has dozens of them." Barbara snatched it up, folded it, then tucked the accursed parchment into her stays. "How on earth do you expect ladies to learn anything if not for books and gazettes?"

He threw out his palms in exasperation. "When I suggested you instruct Miss Mary in etiquette, I meant things like table manners, how one behaves at the symphony—"

"Or a royal ball?" Barbara asked, with far too much mischief in her eyes.

"Precisely."

Snatching the fan, Miss Mary shook it at him, her eyebrows angling downward. "Then that's why I need to be aware of fan language. Goodness gracious, what if I did something like open the miserable thing too fast and some poor sop thought I wanted to marry him? I must know what I'm saying if I am forced to attend an event with a fan in my hand—as Miss Barbara stated, no self-respecting lady should be seen in society without one."

Don groaned. He wouldn't win such an argument with two strong-willed women combining against him. The only thing to do was to change the subject lest he succumb to death by fans. "I believe we are in for a bout of fine weather."

"Dear brother, you do ken when 'tis time to call a truce." Barbara winked at Mary. "'Tis a boon the weather has turned—I so love sunshine."

The tension that had mounted in Don's shoulders eased a bit. "Perhaps we should plan an outing."

"Perhaps we could do some target practice?" Mary slowly opened the fan in her left hand—an overtly provocative gesture for such an innocent lass. "Though I like the idea of using these lacy things as weapons." She looked up, her azure eyes taking on the darkness of the midnight sky. "They're much more subtle, are they not?"

Chapter Eighteen

It had taken Balfour a fortnight to gain an audience with Colonel Hill. Fort William's commanding officer had been away on a peacekeeping sortie while the lieutenant waited, pacing the wall-walk of the miserable fort. Christ, he could see Cameron lands across Loch Linnhe—just sitting there all peaceful-like. He could set his sights and fire the cannons—show them exactly what he would do to men who defied him.

Thank God Almighty he'd finally have his say this day. He'd be decorated for certain—given a new regiment to ride roughshod over anyone who crossed him.

Two dragoons accompanied him into the colonel's study. Holding his hat under his arm, Balfour saluted. "Sir, I come to you with grave news."

"Is that so?" The old man did not return the salute, but rested his quill in its holder and reclined in the chair behind his writing desk. "Come, lieutenant. I haven't all day."

Balfour stammered a bit. The colonel hadn't dismissed the soldiers, nor had he offered a seat. "I caught the Baronet of Sleat breaking the law. The miscreants held a gathering at Dunscaith Castle. A clandestine Jacobite meeting it was, with a number of galleys in the bay, including three with eighteen-oars, clearly breaking the law."

The colonel clasped his fingers atop his stomach. "And one of those boats belonged to Donald MacDonald."

"Aye—another to Ewen Cameron, and the last to Robert Stewart. And they told me it was a *MacDonald Clan* gathering."

"If there were so many chieftains at the gathering, why did you target Sir Donald's galley?"

Taking a step forward, Balfour placed his palms on the colonel's desk. "He's the leader of that band of upstarts—led his regiment into Killiecrankie and Dunkeld after that."

The old man issued such a heated frown, Balfour immediately straightened and drew his hands back to his sides. "True, but that was five years ago." The colonel tapped his chin. "Since, I've known the Baronet of Sleat to be a peace-loving businessman. One who has traded with the fort—brought in precious supplies in the midst of winter when others didn't dare."

Glancing between the two soldiers, Balfour spread his arms wide. "Are you daft?"

His gaze heated, the colonel pushed himself to the edge of his chair. "Mind your station, sir."

The corporal to his right moved his hand to the manacles suspended from his belt.

Blast it all, I must rein in my fervor. "Forgive me." Balfour bowed respectfully. "Regardless if the baronet is trying to portray airs of peace, I ken he's devious. I ken he's trying to organize the Jacobites against us."

"You, sir, are wrong." Colonel Hill pounded the desk with his fist. "There are absolutely no indications of Jacobite insurgence. For the love of God, Glencoe still has every chieftain in the Highlands quaking in his boots."

"I must respectfully disagree." Balfour's gut twisted in a knot. Regardless of the officer's lofty rank, the lieutenant had a responsibility to make him see what was going on beneath his very nose. "From my post on Skye, I've watched them. They're all rubbing their hands, waiting for a chance to strike."

"Is that so?" Hill folded his arms. "What have you done to bring them in to your confidence—encourage the Highlanders to trust you?"

A rueful snort blew through Balfour's nose. "Are you jesting? Jacobites *must* be controlled with a firm hand else they'll murder you in your sleep."

The colonel let out a long sigh, stood and faced the hearth with his hands clasped behind his back. "Too many people have the same view. Worse, the new trade embargoes against Scottish goods only make it more difficult for them to live. 'Tis setting us back—displacing all my work to bring peace to the Highlands."

Christ Almighty, the man is softer than a feather pillow. Balfour batted his hand through the air. "I think they deserve every embargo the king invokes."

Hill shot a hawkish gaze over his shoulder. "That's odd coming from you, a man bred in Invergarry, is it?"

"Aye, but I support the Government. You'll never find a more loyal soldier." He'd bend the fool to his way of thinking if he had to talk all afternoon.

The colonel turned, moving his fists to his hips. "What do you think will happen when the locals can no longer feed their families because their livelihoods are being choked from them?"

"They'll go to the Americas." Balfour smirked. "The sooner the better."

"Doubtless some will." With a sniff the old man scratched his chin. "I fear we will leave no choice to those who remain but to take up arms against us."

Balfour's chest swelled. Finally, the colonel appeared to be bending to his will. "We should confiscate their arms forthwith, just as King William did in Ireland."

Hill's eyes narrowed. "Meet them with an iron fist at every turn, is that what you think will endear their hearts to the Williamite Party, lieutenant?"

Clenching his fists at his sides, Balfour stood ramrod erect, showing his deep loyalty to the crown. "Yes, sir."

Frowning, the colonel sauntered forward and placed his knuckles on the desk. "I understand you kidnapped Mary of Castleton."

The lieutenant's spine slackened a bit. *I'm not being duped, am I?* Balfour glanced between the two soldiers who stood either side of him. Then he held fast to his stance. If nothing else, his intentions had been valorous. "I wish to marry her."

"And the woman was amenable to such a union?"

"She would have come around if Sir Donald hadn't stolen her from me." Tugging his lapels, Balfour tried to stand taller. "I request leave to take her back."

Hill's jaw dropped. "You're serious?"

"Absolutely. I want to introduce Miss Mary to my mother—show her the kindness of my family."

"Without her consent?" the colonel asked, throwing his hands up.

Balfour mimicked the old man's gesture. "I said she would come around."

"Dammit, man, seizing a galley is well within our rights, but you overstepped the very purpose of the King's Army when you captured Miss Mary." Hill's fist again slammed the desk.

The back of the lieutenant's neck flared with heat. "But she would have raised the alarm if I'd released her."

"And so you took her—with intent to force her into your bed?" The man's exasperated expression was unnerving.

"N-not before we were rightfully wed." *Dear God, can the officer not see reason?*

"I know exactly what you were planning." The old man shoved a piece of parchment toward him with Sir Donald's bold signature at the bottom. "I've pardoned the Baronet of Sleat, released his ship as well as the two Highland gentlemen who attempted to reclaim the galley in Glenelg." Hill gestured to the dragoons. "You, sir, are never to pose a threat to Mary of Castleton again. You are hereby reassigned to Fort William and for your first order of duty, you will spend an entire fortnight in the stocks."

"What? No. I am outraged!" Balfour struggled as hands clamped around his arms. "You support them, do you not? You hypocrite!"

Colonel Hill slapped his hand through the air. "Take him away."

While the cold steel of manacles closed around his wrists, Balfour glared at the colonel. "You're one of them. You've always been sympathetic toward the Jacobites. I'll wager you'd be thrilled to see King James reinstated to the throne." A soldier grasped his arm, but he yanked it away. "I am an ardent servant of the king and I vow I will see to your demise."

If his threat had struck a chord, the old man didn't show it. He nodded to one of the soldiers. "I'll need you to return and witness my statement, corporal."

"Yes, sir." The men forced Balfour outside, dragging him toward the bloody stocks—a place of humiliation meant for common filth—not for a lieutenant in the King's Army.

"I am innocent!" Balfour bellowed for all to hear.

***

Climbing the stairs to her chamber, Mary couldn't help but overhear the voices coming from Sir Donald's drawing room.

"I'll give you a sennight and if your shipment hasn't arrived by then, I will have no alternative but to go elsewhere," said a gruff man's voice.

"I assure you my brother will not fail me."

Mary stopped, grasping the bannister. William should have returned more than a fortnight ago. Had Balfour caused more problems? When the lieutenant and his men spent days chasing after her and Donald, she'd hoped their pursuit had given the baronet's men time to load the salt and be gone.

She'd convinced herself Coll and Kennan were successful in retrieving the baronet's galley. But what if they'd been caught? The clans wouldn't rest whilst a chieftain and an heir to a chieftainship were detained.

Is that why Sir Ewen had not yet returned to Achnacarry when they had passed through?

Moving to the landing, she snapped her hands to her cheeks. What could she do to help?

The door swung open. Sir Donald glared at her as if she'd been caught with her fingers in his strong box.

Lowering her hands, she curtseyed politely. "Good afternoon."

"Sir Donald," chortled an overstuffed man wearing a long, flaxen periwig. He raked his eyes down her body as if he were assessing a stallion on the auction block. "You didn't tell me you were entertaining guests of the female persuasion."

"Miss Mary of Castleton is spending time with my sister until my galley returns and I can ferry her back to Skye." He gestured toward the man. "May I introduce Mr. Smith, a business acquaintance."

The man took her hands between his, offering a licentious smile. "The pleasure is mine. I do hope you will still be in Glasgow for the Duke of Gordon's ball."

Mary shifted her gaze to Donald. "I'm—"

The baronet affected an exasperated roll of his eyes. "Good God, Walter, the invitation only arrived this afternoon and you're already plotting your dances."

"That is right, and if you're in attendance Miss Mary, I do hope you will reserve a dance for me."

The last thing she wanted to do was dance with the pasty codfish who still held her hand between his sweaty mitts. "I'm certain Mrs. Smith will have something to say about that?"

The man threw his head back and laughed. "She does have a sharp wit, does she not, Sir Donald?" He started down the stairs. "I'll wager Miss Mary is the cause of your lack of organization—anyone worth his salt can sail a galley down the coast of Scotland in summer."

Mary watched Mr. Smith's retreating form. "He's vulgar," she whispered.

"Mayhap, but he's financing the trade between Scotland and the Americas. *The cause* needs him." Sir Donald pushed past. "I'm going out for a bit."

Mary followed. She'd hardly seen Sir Donald in the past sennight and had spoken to him less. In fact, she was certain he was purposely avoiding her. "To where?"

"I need some air. I think I'll ride."

"Oh, that sounds delightful. Can you have a horse saddled for me?"

He threw an annoyed glance over his shoulder. "Do you not have lessons with Barbara?"

"I dearly love your sister, but we've been at it all day." Mary accompanied Sir Donald out the rear entry to the stables.

All the way to the tack room, he carried his shoulders high as if he were completely vexed with her. "Miss Mary and I are riding, please saddle my horse and one for the lady."

"Straight away sir," said the groomsman before he disappeared into the barn.

Sir Donald pushed his hands into his gloves with a fair bit of force.

Mary crossed her arms. Truly, she had enjoyed growing to know Miss Barbara, but the longer she remained at the townhouse, the more of a burden she posed. Sir Donald grew more distant by the day. Goodness, days ago when she'd touched her lips with her fan meaning to tease him about wanting a kiss, he'd practically blanched.

"I apologize if I have become a burden to you."

"Och, you're no burden."

"Is that so? I never would have guessed."

His shoulders fell. "Forgive me. I'm afraid I'm not in good humor today."

"You haven't been in good humor since we arrived in Glasgow."

"I've had a great many things on my mind."

"Aye, it seems everything except me."

He smacked his forehead with the heel of his hand. "I did receive a missive from Sir Hugh MacIain, Colonel Hill's son-in-law. It appears Lieutenant MacLeod has been reassigned to Fort William."

"Not imprisoned?" In her opinion, Balfour deserved greater punishment than a reassignment.

"At least he will not bother you once you return home, which I hope will be soon."

This time Mary's shoulders fell. "Are you anxious to be rid of me, sir?"

Shod horses clomped through the aisleway.

Sir Donald scraped his teeth across his bottom lip, then he met her gaze with a shadow passing across his face. "Mary, I—"

"Saddled and ready for a ride, sir," said the groomsman, handing Sir Donald the reins of a stallion.

The baronet balked at the roan mare. "You saddled Rosie for Miss Mary?"

The groom stopped short. "Miss Mary always rides him."

"That loony filly? She's hardly broke."

Mary snatched the reins. "Rosie just needs a gentle touch is all." She led the horse to the mounting block and mounted without assistance. Sir Donald didn't even try to help—bless him. Whatever she did to lose his affections, she certainly hoped to win them back before he took her home. Perhaps showing him how well she handled the mare would do the trick.

Chapter Nineteen

In no mood to humor a daft woman who insisted on riding a skittish mare, Don dug his spurs into his stallion's barrel and headed straight for Gallowgate Green. The wood at the southern end of the park would provide much sport—if Miss Mary could keep up.

He glanced over his shoulder to ensure he hadn't left her in his wake. No matter how much he tried to convince himself he didn't care, she was still his responsibility. God forbid something happen to her. He had no choice but to watch out for the lass. But then, she'd been riding Rosie and no one had told him? How many times had she taken the mare out? And where was Barbara when Miss Mary was riding? He'd dig to the bottom of that question for certain.

The woman gained on him, slapping her crop. With a groan he slowed a bit.

"Are you in a hurry?" Mary asked, reining her horse beside his.

"I like to ride hard after being cooped up in a business meeting for hours." He didn't need to apologize. Don wanted to be alone. He needed time to think, dammit, yet every time he turned around, Miss Mary was smiling at him with those confounded dimples—those incredibly shiny blue eyes, the little freckles that dotted across her nose like a nymph. Good God, how was a man to think whilst being distracted by such a woman?

The path narrowed as the wood grew denser. Taking the lead, Don jumped a fallen tree. He stole a backward glimpse. Mary cleared the log with room to spare. *Must the woman be adept at every imaginable masculine pursuit? And how confounding is such a notion?*

Of course, she sat a sidesaddle. Thank heavens, else Don would never allow her to venture beyond the courtyard at the rear of the townhouse. But he couldn't help but admire how the woman could handle her mount sitting aside. He doubted he'd be able to ride as well with such a handicap, though he'd never admit the fact to anyone, especially Miss Mary.

Demanding more speed, he galloped through the wood, ducking under branches and leaping over puddles. Don took this ride often. Still, his heart soared when he hit an open lea at breakneck speed. Crisp air filled his lungs. His head cleared of all the miserable business dealings. Aye, William would never let him down, no matter what transpired up north. His brother knew the odds and he wouldn't fail.

The horse beneath him sensed the release of Don's tension and bolted straight for the stone fence dividing the paddocks. Leaning forward, the stallion jumped. Together they soared, man and beast becoming one. Landing with barely a jolt, the horse continued to race up the hill. As they crested the top, Don tugged the reins and pulled the horse around.

Mary had fallen behind. She leaned forward, preparing for the jump.

But the mare paid no mind to the cue. The lackwit nag dipped her hindquarter and skidded for the stone wall. Joggling to a stop, Mary flew over the horse's head.

A shrill scream screeched in Don's ears before the lass thudded to the ground.

God no. His heart practically stopped. Slapping his reins, Don raced to her. Devil's breath, she lay in a heap, not moving. The damned mare trotted back into the paddock and began to graze. The senseless, mule-brained filly. Bloody hell, he should shoot the beast in the head. Mary had done everything right, but the stubborn mare decided the grass looked sweeter in the paddock behind her. God bless it, the damned filly had the mind of a mad cow.

His heart flying to his throat, Donald leapt from his horse and dropped to his knees beside Miss Mary. "Are you hurt?"

Blood swathed across her forehead. Her eyes flashed open. "I-I-I," she tried to speak, but her breath came in short gasps.

Gathering her into his arms, Don pressed his lips to her forehead. "I saw. The horse shied. You did nothing wrong." He closed his eyes holding the lass as tightly as he dared. "I never want to see you flung from a horse again."

Mary continued to wheeze. "I-do no'-ken-wha—"

"Wheesht, *mo leannan*." He gently rocked her back and forth, examining a gash beneath the hairline. "You've sustained a blow to the head."

Miss Mary reached up. With a gasp she regarded her bloody fingers.

Don pulled his kerchief from his pocket and dabbed the blood. "This looks bad."

"'Tis throbbing."

"Does anything else hurt? Your spine, your shoulders?"

"Not certain." She wriggled a bit. "I-I seem to be in one piece." Still, she cringed and hid her face in her hands.

"I'll take you home forthwith. I purchased that mare for breeding purposes. She's merely a brood mare—hasn't had the proper training to carry anyone, especially a woman as precious as you. Forgive me for allowing you to ride her." Damnation, he never should have challenged the lass so. Good God, he'd told himself he couldn't have ridden as well if he'd been riding in a ridiculous sidesaddle, and yet he went on testing Mary until she met her limits—or the blasted, doltish nag just decided she wanted an afternoon graze.

Gathering Mary in his arms, Don climbed aboard his steed and hastened for the townhouse at a fast trot. He posted with the motion and cradled the lass against his chest. The pain on Mary's face was palpable even with his efforts to shield her from the stallion's gait. It had taken them mere minutes to ride to Gallowgate, but it seemed like an eternity before Don rode through the close leading to the townhouse's stable.

Duff, the stable hand looked up from his raking. "What—?"

"Quickly, go fetch the mare. She's out the back of Gallowgate, grazing in one of Hamilton's paddocks."

The lad rested the rake against the wall. "What happened to Miss Mary?"

"She had a spill. Now off with you."

"I'm coming good. I just need a bit of sleep…" Mary's head bobbed against Don's chest.

She wasn't all right. She received a nasty blow to the head. He slid from the saddle, keeping Miss Mary steady, then strode toward the house.

Barbara opened the door, cringing at the blood that now covered them both. "Good gracious, what happened?"

Don figured about five more people would ask the same question before he reached Mary's bedchamber.

"That damned mare, Rosie. I should sell her to the butcher."

"Oh, no." Mary smoothed her fingers across his chest. "You cannot possibly do that. She shied is all and I wasn't fast enough to catch it."

Donald rolled his eyes at Barbara. "Miss Mary was riding like a cavalryman. Quickly, fetch Hattie and her medicine basket." He started up the stairs. "And call the physician."

Mary nestled into him. "I don't need a physician. I've already lost enough blood."

"You must have a diagnosis by someone who is properly trained. I'll not stand by while you succumb to a head injury—or worse."

Though the lass was light as a feather, by the time Don reached the fourth landing, he was breathing deeply. "Nearly there."

"I'm ever so tired."

He didn't like the listlessness in Mary's voice. In the sennights he'd known her, she'd always been anything but listless. Kicking through the door, he rested her on the bed. "Let me fluff the pillows behind you."

Leaning over her, Don forced himself to ignore the ridiculous palpitations of his heart. Her hair smelled of delicious lilacs and ginger curls tickled his nose. A stirring began deep and low—something he might have welcomed if he weren't worried half to death for Mary's health but, presently, his body's reactions were entirely inappropriate. He punched a pillow with his fist.

Then she kissed him. Planted a smooch right on his cheek. His goddamned heart hammered against his chest. Good God, if only he could wrap her in his arms and plunge his tongue into her mouth and taste her decadence.

But no, no, no.

Don placed his hand on the lass's fine-boned shoulder and kissed her forehead—just like he'd done a dozen times since collecting her in his arms. "We'll see you set to rights, Miss Mary," he said more to remind himself that this was a maiden who needed to be tended by a physician. Presently thinking of anything other than the lassie's wellbeing would not be tolerated—especially by him.

Mary's eyes fluttered open. "Can we attend the ball?"

"You're thinking about a fancy fete at a time like this?"

She grasped his hand, her fingers ever so soft and delicate. "I may never have another chance to go—you ken in Castleton we have gatherings—not balls."

Barbara hastened through the door with Hattie in her wake.

"Sir Donald," chided the older woman. "You must give Miss Mary a chance to breathe."

"Forgive me." Hopping to his feet, he tugged his lapels. "I was just fluffing the pillows."

"Did you hear?" Mary gave Barbara a wide, but glassy-eyed stare. "The Duke of Gordon is hosting a ball."

Barbara clapped like a wee child. "What marvelous news. You must simply spring from your bed as soon as you've been tended." She drew a hand to her hip and regarded her brother. "Donald, aren't the Gordon lands in Aberdeenshire?"

Don nodded. "Aye, though the duke recently purchased a manse across the bridge—where he'll stay when conducting business in Glasgow."

"Oh, my." Snapping open her fan, Barbara cooled her face. "A royal ball? How utterly exciting."

Don gestured to Mary. "Well, we've naught to think about until Miss Mary is back on her feet."

"I'm only abed because you haven't allowed me to touch my toes to the ground since I fell from the horse." At least Mary's willfulness was returning.

Hattie dabbed a cloth in the basin and cleansed Mary's forehead. "'Tis a good thing that gash is under the hairline, else you'd have a scar."

"Is it bad?" Don asked, craning his neck for a better view.

"I've seen worse." Hattie ran the cloth around Mary's face. "Are you tired, miss?"

Mary let out a long sigh. "Ever so much. And my head is pounding something fierce."

Hattie looked to Don and frowned. "We must keep her awake. At least until the physician arrives. I'll go prepare some willow bark tea."

"How could someone sleep when there's a ball for which to plan?" Barbara sat on the edge of the bed and clasped Mary's hands. "When is it?"

"The first of August." Don rolled his eyes to the ceiling. "We never should have mentioned it—now my sister will speak of nothing else."

Barbara laughed. "Oh, brother dear, you are so utterly dull. There's nothing like the anticipation of a ball to cure all ills." She smoothed Mary's hair away from her face. "As soon as you're out of this bed, we're off to the dressmaker. Then new fans, new slippers, new stays and petticoats. We will have the grandest time."

Don grumbled. *My new galley had best make a showing up the river soon, else next season the only thing new Miss Barbara will see will be the apples growing in the orchard at Duntulm Castle.*

A man cleared his voice from the doorway. "Sir Donald, I came straight away." Doctor Ellis clutched his black satchel with both hands. "I understand the young lady had quite a fall?"

"Yes, thank you for coming so quickly." Don explained what had happened and then the physician asked them to step into the corridor.

After the door closed, Barbara shoved Don's shoulder. "How could you have allowed her to ride Rosie through the wood?"

He furrowed his brow. "I thought you'd gone riding with her."

"Aye, at a stately walk in the company of Mr. Kerr, and definitely not through the wood. Goodness, Donald, we didn't even gait our horses at a trot."

"Miss Mary said she's ridden Rosie ever since she arrived. Is there a chance she's gone alone?"

Barbara huffed with a shrug of her shoulder. "Possibly. She awakes with the sun. You'd best have a word with Duff in the stables."

"I will, and she'll not be riding that mare again."

Doctor Ellis stepped into the hallway, closing the door behind him.

Donald regarded the man expectantly. "Will she be all right?"

"I think so. Though I'm worried she might develop dropsy of the brain. Someone will need to watch her through the night for certain. If she falls into fits I want to be notified straight away."

"Of course. Is there anything we can do to see to her comfort?" Don asked.

"Cool cloths applied to her forehead should ease the pain. Willow bark tea will help as well." The physician patted Don's shoulder. "My wager is she'll come good in a day or two. I doubt you have anything to worry about, sir."

"Thank goodness," said Barbara. "Miss Mary and I have far too much to do."

Don gave his sister a stern frown. "Please show Doctor Ellis out. I'll see to Miss Mary's care myself."

"You?" Barbara blinked as if his proposition was unheard of. "Why not Hattie?"

"Because if you haven't realized, I am *lord and master* of this house, and that should be the only thing that concerns you." He bowed to the physician, then offered his hand. "Forgive my sister's impertinence. Thank you for responding to our call. I am truly in your debt."

***

Don slipped back into Mary's chamber, careful to close the door without making a noise. The lass had already fallen asleep, looking like a vision with her luminous, red tresses sprawled across the pillows. He tiptoed to the bowl, doused a cloth and wrung it out with a cascade of droplets tinkling in the water.

Bending over her, he examined her forehead. A bruise discolored the skin, but the wound didn't look too bad now all the blood had been cleared away. Don had seen far worse on the battlefield. Though he'd earned the moniker Donald of the Wars, his tour with his regiment at Killiecrankie soured his taste for battle. Too many men cut down and bleeding lay in the damp grass, even though the Jacobites had been victorious. And then the following battle of Dunkeld had been a win for the Williamite Party, and the Jacobites headed home to the Highlands to lick their wounds—to breed new sons who could rise again.

And Miss Mary's father had borne the brunt of it.

Unfortunately, the exiled King James couldn't wait for a new crop of warriors to rise and join the ranks. That was precisely what drove Don's passion to fight the English through trade—providing higher quality at a fair price would help his people raise funds for so many things. This agreement he had struck with the American merchants was too important. It had to take precedence over everything including his own deep-seated desires.

Did he want the woman sleeping in his guestroom bed?

Don pulled up the chair and sat beside her. Watched her breathe ever so peacefully and his heart twisted so tight, he feared it would stop. Indeed, he wanted her with every fiber of his being. His feelings for Miss Mary were different than anything he'd ever experience before. God damn it, he wished times could be different. Perhaps if he asked her to wait for him—until he had things established—until his fortunes were where he wanted them. Aye, things were stable now, but it didn't take a seer to realize that King William's new policies were intended to make Scotland suffer and the bastards on the other side of the border prosper. It also didn't take a seer to understand that if things grew any worse, his crofters would not be able to pay him rents. God's teeth, so much hung on this damned shipment.

Miss Mary? Yes, she must wait too. She must.

For the time being, Don could do nothing but enjoy the woman's company. He chuckled. When he'd first seen her—first realized she was a woman, those darned freckles had thrown him. But now he adored the way they danced across the bridge of her saucy, little nose. They expressed her personality—told any admirer to tread lightly, for she was a woman to be reckoned with, a woman who knew her mind and spoke it—mayhap a bit too earnestly, but he liked that about her, too.

He'd never met a woman who could match his intellect, who was self-assured, athletic and, most certainly, too independent. But, oh, how quickly she could learn.

He chuckled about Miss Mary's quick study of fans. Lord, she'd only had the damned thing in her hand for minutes when she'd caught his attention with the subtle flicks of her wrist. God forbid she ever wield the thing around any other male. She would have them bending a knee with a proposal of marriage by the evening's end.

Though Don admitted she could practice her fan language on him any time she liked—as long as they were behind closed doors and his sister was nowhere in sight.

Don sighed and changed the cloth on Mary's forehead. Fortunately, Barbara soon moved on to more important etiquette—tools a maid with Mary's intellect needed in her arsenal. She might be a sharpshooter with a musket, but in these modern times a woman needed subtlety. Society expected a certain *je ne sais quoi* from nobility—an almost balletic air, every movement must be executed as if dancing to a symphony of violins—rather than reeling to a foot-stomping fiddle. True, if Don had a choice, he'd pick the fiddle and a Highland gathering every time, but such a societal misstep would not help him reach his goals.

Leaning forward, he kissed Mary's temple. The intoxicating fragrance of lilacs filled his senses and his heart. He grasped her fine-boned hand and held it between his much larger palms. Her touch calmed him. If only he weren't embroiled in the midst of the Jacobite cause. If his ruse were exposed, he'd be in trouble for certain. Through the ages, many a noble lost their lands and titles supporting the cause they believed in.

He could, too.

If that happened, he'd never want to pull the people he loved into purgatory as he fell from grace. The best he could hope for? Enjoy Miss Mary through the duration of her stay—and keep her virtue intact.

Aye, but such a challenge just might send him over the edge of his very sanity.

Chapter Twenty

Mary opened her eyes and rubbed her head. With a hiss, she snapped her hand away.

I suppose it will be tender for a time.

Placing her palm at her side, her fingers met with hair—velvety soft like spun silk. Before she thought, she threaded the tresses through her fingers, then regarded the person attached to such softness.

Her heart nearly stopped beating. Good Lord, the Baronet of Sleat, seated in a chair beside her, had fallen asleep. Resting on the edge of the bed, he cradled his head in his folded arms, breathing deeply. His face turned away, thick tawny tresses had slipped from the ribbon which rested precariously on his shoulder.

Sir Donald had spent the night at her bedside?

She swirled her hands into the mass of silk and massaged his scalp.

The man moaned—a deep, blood-stirring moan that reminded Mary too much of their kiss in the box bed. If only they could have stayed at the croft—or near the croft—or any place other than Glasgow. This town made Sir Donald so anxious. And the people were so false. Their display of controlled gestures was like watching a play, not real life. Sure, Mary could behave as they wished, but she preferred to be in Castleton with her family where she could just be Mary, lady of the keep. That in itself brought on a world of responsibility and plenty to keep her busy without putting on false airs.

She swirled her fingers again. The only problem with being tucked away at Dunscaith Castle was missing moments such as this—the chance to touch Sir Donald, to be close to him, the look upon his face when he approved of something she did—or even disapproved. At least she had his attention when he disapproved.

Yesterday, when they were riding, she'd convinced herself he didn't care for her. The kisses they'd shared had meant nothing. But why was he there beside her bed? Could she hope? Goodness gracious, she would put up with all the silly etiquette if it meant spending every night in Sir Donald's arms.

The big man rolled his shoulders then sat up with sleepy eyes. "You're awake."

"Aye." She drew her fingers to her nose. The musky scent of his hair lingered. If only she could bottle it.

His ribbon dropped to the ground and a lock of hair slid over his eye. "Forgive me. I must have drifted off."

"Not at all." She made a point of panning her gaze from his bonny face, shadowed with dark stubble down to—well, she could only see down to his lap, but that was delicious enough. Her tongue slipped out the corner of her mouth. Barbara had taught her the nuances of a lady's stare. It must have had an effect, because Sir Donald shifted in his chair.

Mary trained her gaze back to his face—something dark filled his eyes, rather dangerous, exciting. She grinned. "I like you a wee bit disheveled."

He picked up his ribbon. "I'd best go."

She grasped him by the wrist. "Must you?" Oh no, she wasn't ready to release him to the wiles of Glasgow. If only he'd kiss her again before he reverted back into a stiff merchant. "As a matter of fact..." She slowly drew the ribbon from his fingers—very seductive of her, even if such a move wasn't something Barbara had taught. "I like it when things are quiet. When we are alone."

"Aye?" his voice rasped. He either needed a drink or her antics were having some influence on his sensibilities.

"Yes, in fact, I'll be honest. I think you're happier when you're sailing a galley with bare feet and the wind in your hair." Mary leaned as close as she could without falling off the bed.

He touched her chin with the crook of his finger, but his gaze didn't fall to her lips, it strayed to the darned lump on her head. "How are you feeling this morrow?"

She licked her lips. Blast propriety. No one was there to catch them. Must she behave as a lady when the doors were closed? She mightn't ever have a chance again. "Well enough to be kissed," she dared to whisper. Her skin burned, but she'd blurted out the words she'd been holding in for sennights. Holy Moses, if Sir Donald didn't know how much she wanted him to court her, she'd now make sure he knew.

With a low chuckle, he pressed his lips to her forehead.

Curses to a wee peck.

Mary took his stubbly cheeks between her palms and looked him straight in the eyes—two dark, sensuous eyes that could melt a woman's resolve with a mere blink. "I mean this..."

Dipping her gaze to his lips, she slid her hands over his shoulders, trusting him to prevent her from falling. His big hands skimmed around her waist as their lips connected. Growling soft and low in his throat, he increased the pressure, his kiss as urgent as the blood thrumming beneath her skin. Mary's entire body ignited

with the fire that had been smoldering deep inside her.
Taking him deeper into her mouth, she combed her
fingers through his soft tresses.

Oh yes, yes, yes how much she'd longed for him to
kiss her again. With a pleasurable moan, he inclined her
back against the pillows and trailed kisses from her
earlobe down to the base of her neck. His hand worked
magic as it smoothed its way up and cupped her breast.
Lord in heaven, the sensation took her to a level of
rapture she never dreamed possible. Her breast grew
heavy, tingling with the kneading of his practiced fingers.
With her next heaving breath, he captured her nipple
between his pincers—taut, drawn to a point, his light
touch nearly drew her to the ragged edge of oblivion.

His kisses trailed lower as those deft fingers tugged
the neckline of her shift. The linen teased her sensitive
skin until he fully exposed her bosom. Hot lips closed
over her nipple, sending shudders of pleasure down
Mary's spine. Scarcely able to breathe, she threw back her
head and succumbed to the teasing licks of his tongue.
Restlessness thrummed through her blood as she arched
into his wicked mouth.

A rap came at the door. "Sir Donald?" Mr. Kerr's
voice.

Mary dropped to the pillows and yanked her neckline
back in place.

The baronet swiped a hand across his mouth. "Aye?"
Holy fairies, he sounded as composed as a lord justice.

"You've a message from the Court of Barony."

"Ballocks," he swore.

"What is it?" Mary asked. For the love of Moses,
could she not enjoy a moment of pure ecstasy with Sir
Donald without being interrupted?

"I'll be needed in Edinburgh for certain."

"May I go with you?" She'd never been to a big city like Edinburgh.

"I don't think it wise—I'll be attending to court business with all the barons and baronets in Scotland—no greater gossips in all the land. With luck, I'll not be away longer than a sennight."

"Will you return in time for the ball?"

"Aye, lass. The Duke of Gordon would be very upset if none of the barons attended his fancy-dress event."

"Good, because I wouldn't want to practice my fan language on a great hall full of strangers."

With a spark of ire in his midnight blue eyes, Sir Donald's expression wasn't half as composed as his tone.

***

A sennight later, Mary and Barbara strolled along the footpath toward the townhouse while Mr. Kerr carried an armload of parcels behind them.

"Your gown will be stunning," Barbara said.

Mary bit the inside of her cheek. "Are you certain?" She glanced down to her breasts, which weren't anywhere near as voluptuous as her friend's. "I'm not convinced a plunging neckline will suit my form."

"Oh, my sweeting, you have so much still to learn." Barbara looped her arm through Mary's elbow and grinned like a satisfied cat. "Do not forget I am the queen of fashion. You will be ravishing. Not a gentleman within twenty miles will be able to keep his eyes off you."

Mary knew that wouldn't be happening in a hundred years—not with her freckles. "You sound so sure of yourself."

"I am. Besides, that's why God invented stays." Barbara glanced over her shoulder at Mr. Kerr, then opened her hand and covered her mouth for secrecy. "With Hattie's strong arms, we'll have your lassies up for display and looking more radiant than the crown jewels."

Mary rapped the tart's arm with her fingers. "You are incorrigible."

Barbara waggled her shoulders. "I am practical."

Unconvinced, Mary's lips twisted. "Well, I'll say your gown will be the fairest at the ball, and with your fair coloring and blemish-free skin, my wager is all eyes will fall upon you."

Turning up the stairs to the townhouse, a polite giggle pealed through Barbara's lips—goodness, she had the whole society charade down to a science. "We *both* will be perfectly adorned and the envy of all the women who will pale in our shadows. I have no doubt."

Mary turned the knob and opened the door. Instantly sensing something was different, her gaze shot to Barbara.

She pointed to the table. "There's a satchel."

But it wasn't Sir Donald's, at least Mary hadn't seen it before.

"Don't just stand there, ladies," said Mr. Kerr from the rear, looking a bit red in the face.

Mary quickly stepped inside, while Barbara flounced ahead with balletic grace. "Please carry our things above stairs."

"Yes, miss."

As Mr. Kerr proceeded to the staircase, three men stepped into the entry from the parlor. Miss Barbara's face lit up like it was Christmas morn. "Sir Coll, where on earth did you come from?"

"Good to see you, too," said William, pulling his sister from her path toward the Chieftain of Keppoch and embracing her.

"'Tis a relief to see Miss Mary is safe," said Sir Kennan from the doorway, grinning like a wet-eared lad.

Mary curtseyed. "Sir Donald sent word to my father sennights ago. Did you not hear of my rescue?"

"Ah, no—" Sir Kennan looked to Sir Coll while rubbing his wrists. "We've been a bit tied up."

"Aye." William took Mary's hand and gave it a polite peck. "It seems you weren't the only one who needed rescue."

"Oh, my. That sounds dreadful." Barbara's gaze didn't stray from Coll MacDonell. "I'll order some refreshments and you can tell us all about it."

The Chieftain of Keppoch seemed equally smitten as he took Barbara's fingers in his palms and watched her eyes as he bowed and plied the back of her hand with a kiss that lasted far too long to be proper. "Miss Barbara, how long has it been?"

She blushed like a red rose. "Six months and five days." Tapping her fan to her lips, she giggled.

Blinking, Mary drew her hand to her chest with a stifled gasp.

She's flirting shamelessly.

"Will you be attending the Duke of Gordon's ball," Barbara asked.

Mary arched her eyebrows at William and accompanied them into the parlor. So, the love interest Barbara hadn't told Mary about was Sir Coll MacDonell of Keppoch? She liked it—though Sir Coll was as rugged as the Highlands and Barbara was anything but.

Regardless, the men's story should prove to be riveting.

Barbara sat beside Sir Coll, though not too close. Mary watched the lassie's fan for any inappropriate communication while William did most of the talking.

Did Sir Coll and the other gentlemen know fan language? Was Mary the only member of nobility in Scotland who hadn't the proper *education*?

William explained about his meeting with Colonel Hill and lodging a formal complaint about the capture of the galley and Miss Mary's abduction. It seemed the colonel mightn't have been spurred to action if the lieutenant had only seized the galley—but kidnapping the daughter of a chieftain had set a fire under his antiquated buttocks.

Sir Kennan told tale about their capture when he and Sir Coll had tried to take back the galley in Glenelg.

Barbara affected a sufficiently mortified expression, her fan coming to life and touching her heart. Good heavens, she was still *flirting*. Sir Coll's reaction was a subtle rise of his eyebrow and a white-toothed grin plastered from one ear to the other. All the while, Sir Kennan continued on, explaining how William had managed to secure a pardon from the colonel and spring the pair from the "pig's pen" in Glenelg where they were imprisoned.

The story finished with more antics dealt by the redcoats in Trotternish. Fortunately, through all their adversity, they still managed to arrive with a shipment of packing salt before the ship for the Americas sailed.

And to Barbara's obvious delight, in time to attend the ball.

"What happened with you, Miss Mary?" asked Sir Kennan. "I cannot tell you how relieved I am to see your bonny face."

Mary blinked. Goodness, the lad was smiling at her with unmistakable fondness etched across his features. But he wasn't yet twenty, was he? "Fortunately, Sir Donald came upon me when he did."

"Came in firing his musket, did he?" asked Sir Coll.

A fire flared in Mary's cheeks. "Actually, no. Late at night I slipped out the back of the tent and fled to the river. When I fell, Sir Donald caught my wrist just as I was about to be swept away by a swollen torrent."

"You escaped?" Kennan's eyes grew wide and full of awe. Perhaps someone appreciated her perseverance. "I'm impressed."

If only Sir Donald would be so moved.

"And how long will my brother be away in Edinburgh?" William reached for his cup of peppermint tea.

"Are you aware he was called to the Court of Barony—very untimely if you ask me." Barbara picked up the plate of cakes and offered it to Sir Coll. "But he promised to return in time for the ball."

A door slammed and footsteps clomped from the rear entry. Mary's stomach leapt. Only one person walked the halls of the townhouse with such a bold stride.

Stopping in the doorway, clad in a pair of trews, doublet, bonnet and looking as if he'd ridden like hellfire and brimstone, Sir Donald grinned at her with a smile that sent rays of sunlight streaking throughout the chamber. "Such a relief. Miss Mary is up and well, and the three men I've worried about for sennights are all gathered together at once. Good Lord, this sight was well worth spending an entire night riding the Glasgow-Edinburgh Road."

Mary clasped her hands tight in her lap to keep from springing from her seat, dashing across the floor and making a fool of herself. Breathless, heart hammering, she returned his smile. "Welcome home, Sir Donald. It is ever so good to see you."

There. Let no one say I am a brash Highland lass without proper manners.

Donald nodded, a glint of approval in his eyes as he crossed the floor, took up her hand and kissed it—hot breath, a hint of spice, gentle lips. "You are looking well, Miss Mary."

Their gazes locked.

Mary's mouth grew dry while her breasts swelled taut beneath her stays.

"We're nearly ready for the royal ball," said Barbara, breaking the crackle of energy. "You will simply love our gowns."

Releasing Mary's hand, Donald regarded his sister. "I trust they will be elegant yet modest."

Mary's face grew hot. "I can attest to the elegant part."

Chapter Twenty-One

Hattie untied the strips of rags and pulled them from Barbara's hair. Blonde curls sprang from the cocoons as the chambermaid unwrapped each one. She primped the ringlets framing the lass' face while Mary perched on the chair and practiced her fan language. She tried not to use the diagrams spread on the table before her, but checked her accuracy after each subtle movement. With practice, her movements had become more delicate—according to Barbara.

The young mentor inclined her head away from Hattie's comb. "If I were you, I'd just clonk my brother over the head with your fan. Sometimes Donald needs a good whack, I say."

Mary buried her face behind the darned thing and laughed. Goodness, Barbara could tickle her funny bone. The ironic thing was there was nothing Mary would rather do. Of course, Sir Donald had been congenial since his return two days past, but he'd been in meetings with everyone under the sun—had scarcely taken a meal with Mary and his guests, and when he did make an appearance in the dining hall, he was distracted by his gazette or missives, or anything rather than Mary. For all she knew, her fan would be better served used to shoo away the pigeons from the windowsill.

Barbara held up an ivory box. "You should apply a dusting of face powder 'Twill blend those freckles."

Mary's smile fell and her eyebrows pinched. "I thought you said you liked my freckles."

"I do, but for every day. This eve we are attending a *royal* ball." Barbara leaned over with the box and managed to place it on the table without falling off her perch. "Just a wee dusting so you do not appear like a harlot."

"I beg your pardon?" Mary tried to affect her most exasperated expression. *Easy for her to say.* Miss Barbara looked like she belonged in the king's court, and Mary? Well, if she were in London they might mistake her for a milkmaid—though a rather slender sort of milkmaid.

Taking the box, Mary moved to the mirror and examined the powder stuck to the underside of the puff.

"Put a cloth across your gown afore ye use it," said Hattie. "Ye wouldn't want to muss that fine pink taffeta, miss."

Mary did as instructed and gave her face a once-overonceover." Peering closely, the powder did make a significant difference. She could scarcely see the most prominent freckles crossing the bridge of her nose.

"Give us a look," said Barbara coming up behind.

Mary turned. "Well? Too much?"

Flicking her fingers across Mary's cheeks, Barbara gave an approving hmm. "'Tis just the most subtle application needed. And my pearls are perfect with your gown."

"Hopefully someone will notice."

"Donald will for certain…and if he doesn't I ken the duke will."

"Is he not married?"

Barbara fanned her face with her gloved hand. "He *was* married, but the duchess left him for a convent in Flanders. 'Tis well known Lord Gordon is a rake."

Mary nearly swooned, unsure if her reaction was from shock or that her stomacher was cutting into her abdomen making it difficult to breathe. "Truly? You're taking me to the manse of a rake?"

Tossing her curls, Barbara looked at Mary with a mischievous glint in her eyes. "His lustful reputation aside, he's a duke—though he'll notice every woman in the room, mind you."

"You've met him?"

"Once—at Edinburgh Castle when he was Governor. Fortunately I was very young at the time—nowhere near as…ah…*voluptuous* as I am now." The neckline of Barbara's silvery-blue gown dipped so low it amply displayed her breasts. In fact, the lace trim barely reached her shoulders, revealing so much flesh it was difficult not to stare.

Swiping a hand across her eyes, Mary averted her gaze. "You don't say?"

"Aye. He held the castle for King James as long as he could after William's *'Glorious Revolution'*." She spat the words as if they were served with a bitter tonic.

"Then what happened?" Mary asked.

The lass huffed. "Not sure—I suppose that's about the time the duchess left him."

"So then he's a Jacobite?" Mary quickly covered her mouth.

Barbara's gaze flicked to Hattie while she cleared her throat. "Mayhap. No one kens who's on what side anymore." She rapped Mary's shoulder with her fan. "Remember no one utters the word *Jacobite* south of the Great Divide—'tis treasonous."

Mary pursed her lips. A number of remarks came to the tip of her tongue. Though Hattie was loyal to the family, it was best not to speak of *the cause* around anyone in these parts.

Barbara regarded herself in the mirror and patted her ringlets. "I do believe we will be the two best dressed lassies at the ball."

Mary bit the corner of her mouth. Truly, her pink frock with its gold damask embroidery embellishing her stomacher and full, virago sleeves was splendid—made her feel pretty all the way down to her three silk petticoats and pink satin slippers. But in her eyes, she paled in comparison to Sir Donald's sister. "Your gown is simply stunning."

Barbara flicked one of the satin bows at Mary's elbow, sticking her tongue out the corner of her mouth. "I was thinking the same about yours, silly. I wish I had ginger tresses, too."

With a sigh, Mary ran her fingertips across the mounds of flesh swelling above her own bodice. "You don't think I'm a wee bit too *exposed?*" She wasn't quite as bare as Barbara, but still, she felt almost naked.

Barbara pushed against her stomacher, adjusting her own well-formed cleavage. "My dear, this is the best opportunity Glasgow has had in two seasons to find a suitable husband. Our wares must be properly, though discretely, presented—which I believe we have accomplished with utmost expertise and attention to detail."

"What about Sir Coll?"

The lass winked. "He'll be in attendance, will he not?"

Shocked, Mary stifled a giggle by clapping a hand over her mouth. Little good that did—she still snorted. Holy Moses, for a lass of nineteen, Barbara surely did seem wizened. Though Mary was beginning to wonder if her friend's bravado was more talk and show. That very morning when Sir Coll had appeared to break his fast, Barbara had turned into a blushing, tongue-tied nymph.

Regardless, Mary was relieved to have her companionship. She offered her elbow. "Shall we?"

Sipping sherry in the parlor with Sirs Coll and Kennan, Sir Donald had his pocket watch in hand when the two women arrived in the doorway. But when he looked up, it slipped from his palm and dangled from its chain.

Drop-jawed, his gaze swept down her body, then back up and met her stare, his eyes growing darker by the second. Had his brief once-over paused at Mary's cleavage? By the tingling, her breasts seemed to think so.

Holy Moses, Mary's knees wobbled. How on earth could the man grow more beautiful every time she laid eyes on him? Tall and exquisitely clad in a navy velvet cape lined with satin. Everything was perfect from his starched lace cravat, velvet doublet, satin breeches and hose secured just below the knee with ribbon of gold. Of course, he wore a ceremonial sword at his hip and a dirk angled across the front of his belt. He looked bonnier than a portrait. And this time, the long periwig of tawny curls cascading over his shoulders made him more masculine, more regal, and with the dark glint in his midnight eyes, more commanding.

Mary shivered right down to her toes.

"Sir Coll, Sir Kennan, you look as if your grooms spent an entire day on your costumes," said Barbara moving toward the other two men, but Mary couldn't pull her eyes away from Sir Donald if she'd wanted to.

Collecting his pocket watch and slipping it inside his doublet, Sir Donald's tongue moistened his bottom lip before he slid his foot forward and bowed deeply. "Miss Mary you are a vision to behold."

Me? Dear Lord, no man should be clad thus. How am I supposed to think when he is near? He took her hand, the midnight of his eyes growing darker still. "I hope you are planning to dance with me this eve."

She gulped and gave a single nod.

Again he bowed, though this time he pressed warm, moist lips to the back of her hand. She caught the delicious spiciness of his scent as his breath caressed her flesh. If only he would steal a kiss from her this night—one as passionate as the one he'd given her in the bedchamber a week past—his hand on her breast—

"Do you not agree, Miss Mary?" asked Barbara.

As if floating, Mary turned her attention to her friend's expression. "Ah, of course." How else could she respond?

Sir Kennan stepped forward, bowed and kissed Mary's hand as well. Though a practiced peck, the gesture from the younger man wasn't half as impassioned or welcomed as the kiss from Sir Donald.

"You look stunning," said the Cameron heir. "Both of you ladies are beautiful beyond all imagination."

Mary waited for Kennan to draw his hand away. Then Sir Donald moved in beside him and offered Mary his elbow. "The coach awaits. Shall we?"

Everything seemed so surreal, like a fairytale.

The coach ambled along the cobbled street while Mary's shoulder rubbed against Sir Donald's powerful arm. Even through the layers of taffeta and velvet, the strength in his arm felt like solid rock. On her other side, Sir Kennan sat with his hands folded, smiling at her.

Barbara and Sir Coll sat on the bench opposite, Don's sister looking like she'd just eaten the best plum tart ever. William sat on his sister's right, his arms crossed as he watched out the window.

Mary regarded the Cameron heir and wrung her hands. Why on earth was Sir Kennan smiling her way? He was two years younger for heaven's sake. "I do believe we should have had two more ladies in our party," Mary said, wishing Lilas was there—goodness, her younger sister would die if she knew Mary was in a coach sitting between two of the brawniest Highlanders in all of Scotland. Not to mention, Lilas would be an ideal dance partner for Sir Kennan—or mayhap she'd fancy William. Though quiet, Donald's younger brother certainly was comely to look upon.

The carriage's movement smoothed. "We're crossing the bridge." Sir Donald pointed out the big window in the door. "Can you see the river?"

The water sparkled like Mary's insides. "Aye, and thank heavens it isn't raining."

"My word," said Barbara unabashedly batting her eyelashes at Sir Coll. "It simply wouldn't do to rain on the eve of such a momentous occasion."

"Did you place a special order for fine weather on Sunday?" Sir Coll looked as rapt as the woman sitting beside him.

Barbara leaned a bit closer to him. "I most certainly did."

William shook his head. "Ah, my sister, Saint Barbara, summoner of sunshine and royal balls."

The lass shook her fan at her brother. "And you'd best thank me."

Mary chuckled, letting her shoulder ease into Donald's. Who cared about the ball? The coach ride was fun on its own and she hadn't been across the River Clyde yet.

But all too soon, the coach rolled to a stop outside a glorious stone manse. Though not fortified as an archaic castle, the manse seemed to sprawl forever. Mary counted four stories, innumerous leaded glass windows and two sandstone sculptures of lions at the foot of the stairs leading to the ornate front door.

"Don't worry about a thing," Barbara said as if she thought she needed to.

"Why would I worry?" Mary took Donald's hand and allowed him to help her from the coach. Though they both wore gloves, his touch infused her with confidence. "I am the daughter of a Highland chieftain."

"Aye, lassie, and never forget it." Sir Donald whispered in her ear in a deep rolling burr that took all her self-assured pomp and sent it swarming like butterflies in her stomach.

Everywhere she looked, people dressed in finery processed up the stairs to the great home. With her hand resting on Sir Donald's elbow, all she could do was move with the crowd. Ahead, a deep voice announced the guests as they entered. The Duke and Duchess of Hamilton and the Earl of Mar were titles she didn't miss.

Sir Donald handed his card to the attendant and soon they stood at the head of the reception line. "The Baronet of Sleat, his sister Miss Barbara, his brother Mr. MacDonald, Miss Mary of Castleton, Laird Coll MacDonell of Keppoch, and Sir Kennan Cameron of Locheil." Goodness, it sounded like a litany of Highlanders.

Dressed in a satin coat of gold and breeches with a chestnut periwig even more outrageous than Donald's with a cavernous part through the middle, the Duke of Gordon bowed and took Mary's hand. "Ever so charmed to make your acquaintance, Miss Mary. I kent your father in the wars…" His gaze met Sir Donald's as if he wanted to say more, but opted to remain silent. His two children, Anna and Alexander were introduced, but there was no woman beside His Grace.

Odd for a man who has a reputation of being a libertine.

Proceeding into the enormous hall, Mary realized the reason for the duke's brevity of conversation. Through the growing crowd, a group of a dozen or so red-coated officers stood beside the marble hearth, watching the guests arrive with feigned indifference. Though she knew better. Redcoats suspected all Highlanders of being Jacobites.

Mary froze. A gasp catching in the back of her throat, her fingers dug into Sir Donald's arms. *Is it? It couldn't be.*

As they moved toward the great hall, her line of sight was blocked. Rising to her toes, she strained for a better look, her heart hammering against her stomacher. Good heavens, her head swooned. *Curses, I wish Hattie wouldn't gird my stays so tight.*

"Is all well?" Sir Donald asked.

"No." Mary shook her finger in the direction of the group of officers. "I thought I saw Balfour MacLeod."

"That lout?" Sir Donald stretched and looked above the crowd. "Why on earth would he be in Glasgow?"

"My exact thoughts." She clutched his arm. "Do you see him?"

"Nay. Are you certain it was he?"

"No—only saw the man's profile. Perhaps it was someone else." Dear Lord, she prayed it was so.

Sir Donald patted her hand. "I'm sure after your ordeal, anyone wearing a Government uniform would make you nervous. I'm certain the lieutenant is far from here. Pay it not another thought."

Mary nodded, looking to the musicians who were playing a madrigal. *If only it were that easy.*

Sir Kennan touched Mary's arm. "Will you reserve the first dance with me?"

"Ah…" She looked to Sir Donald who indicated his approval with a nod—blast him. He'd given her no recourse but to accept. She bowed her head. "Thank you."

"Excellent."

Sir Donald inclined his lips to Mary's ear. "All I ask is that you save the last set for me."

Moving with balletic precision, she placed her fan over her heart—but only for a blink of an eye and only so Sir Donald could see.

Little good that did. The corner of his mouth ticking up, he bowed. "If you'll excuse me, I've a bit of business to tend."

Sir Kennan offered his elbow. "Shall we?"

Chapter Twenty-Two

Never looking at her straight on, Balfour watched Mary out of the corner of his eye, the harlot. It shouldn't surprise him to see her hanging on the arm of that snake, the Baronet of Sleat, or his crony, the young Cameron of Locheil. She'd been raised to believe Jacobites were gods. Even the host of this shameful gathering was a Jacobite parading around like a patriot. That the king hadn't rounded them all up and sent them to the gallows was beyond Balfour's understanding.

He smirked.

A mass execution on a much wider scale than Glencoe would certainly make room for loyal soldiers to become noblemen.

They could string up Colonel Hill while they were at it, too. The old man had kept Balfour in the stocks for an entire fortnight. The outrage! Balfour was one of the king's officers for Christ's sake. A loyal, servant of William and Mary, and he'd been maliciously thrown in the stocks for upholding the law.

Of course, taking Miss Mary away from those lawless Jacobites had not been received well by the colonel, but he, of all men, should realize that to tame the Highlands, drastic measures were necessary. Balfour had been willing—was still willing to tame Mary of Castleton. He would bend her to the new way of thinking and breed upstanding servants of the crown with her. Indeed, she would soon learn the error of the Highland ways. Chieftains were no longer the lords and masters of their lands. Chieftains could not send their armies to prey upon other clans no matter how long they had been feuding. Why didn't she understand that his way was the way of things to come? Times were changing and if Miss Mary did not embrace the new age, she would become extinct along with her people.

Thank God Colonel Hill had granted him leave once he'd been released—told him to go home and regain his strength with some of his mother's cooking afore taking up his new post in miserable Fort William. Balfour chuckled under his breath. A fortnight was a long time to think for a man as enterprising as he. And he'd guessed right. The damned baronet had taken Miss Mary to Glasgow to keep her safe.

What the colonel didn't realize was Miss Mary would never be safe until she was, again, reunited with Balfour. Only he could save her.

And men might have to die.

His stomach churned as the dance began with Kennan Cameron slobbering all over himself. Worse, Miss Mary didn't even look like herself. Her pink gown was so low cut, every man in the hall could see her milky white breasts rise and fall with her every breath.

Balfour rubbed his fingers together. Her skin was white as lilies—looked as soft as velvet. But only meant for his eyes and his alone. How dare the baronet allow her to be seen in society wearing something so disgraceful? There was no question. He must haste to ferret her away from MacDonald's clutches.

When she'd entered the hall and had been announced, Balfour exercised undue self-control and restrained himself from removing his coat and draping it over her shameful attire. *I'll wager MacDonald drooled all over that damned gown during the carriage ride. Dear God, if he has sullied her, I'll kill the bastard.*

Mary laughed while she locked elbows and skipped in a circle with the man opposite. And that bastard took a good eyeful of her breasts as well. Damn her. Balfour could watch no more.

He turned and headed to the door. *The Baronet of Sleat thinks he's going to aid the Highlanders by opening trade with the Americas?*

Aye, it hadn't taken the lieutenant long to figure out why Donald MacDonald was playing the gentleman in Glasgow. The pirate was a well-known Jacobite—Donald of the Wars would never be a true patriot—would always be someone operating beneath the letter of the law. Well, the bastard couldn't charm everyone he met into believing he was merely a merchant trying to earn an honest living.

The snake.

I'll ruin him.

***

After sealing his agreement with a handshake and a tot of whisky, Don left Mr. Smith to his pipe and headed for the great hall. The baronet may have been pushed to the brink of his tolerance, but William had pulled through, God bless him. On the morrow, MacDonald packing salt would be used to preserve the goods stored on three ships bound for the Americas. Salt mined by the hands of his clan on Trotternish. Salt that would ensure the comfort of Don's family for generations to come. At last, he'd gained a foothold that secured his place as a British merchant of substance.

Stepping into the great hall, happy violins further lifted his spirits. It didn't surprise him to find Mary dancing. Don chuckled to himself, now free to enjoy the evening as he wished. Dear God, the woman had nearly made him weak at the knees when she'd appeared in the parlor earlier that eve.

And now, she brightened the entire great hall like a rainbow glittering with the sun's rays. A smile stretched across her face as she gracefully placed her gloved palm against her partner's for the turn. Her movements were smooth and balletic as they should be. Funny, at Dunscaith Castle, Don never would have mistaken the trews-wearing sharpshooter for a swan. But somehow, the cygnet had transformed before his eyes.

When his gaze shifted to Mary's partner, Don's gut twisted. Sir Kennan left his fingers on the woman's waist a bit too long—and then his gaze lingered on her breasts.

The liberty-taking nitwit.

It didn't escape Don's observation that Sir Kennan had been overt about his attraction to Mary. What man wouldn't find the lass captivating? At first, Don had dismissed Kennan's adolescent ogling, but now he recognized the wolfish glint in the young man's eyes and it made him green with envy. Don clenched his fists, then splayed his fingers. The whelp might need a lesson afore he sailed home to his ma.

Have they been dancing together all evening?

It didn't matter that Sir Kennan was the heir to a chieftainship, he was too bloody young for Miss Mary. A match between the pair would never work.

Absolutely not. I cannot abide it.

The spirited lady would prove too much for the young whelp. Don glanced around the hall. There were plenty of young lassies waiting for a turn on the dance floor. At nineteen, young Cameron should be testing the waters, not spending the entire affair with Mary of Castleton.

God's teeth, why can he not keep his gaze on Miss Mary's face where it belongs? If that rabid dog looks at her breasts one more time, I'll gouge his bloody eyes out with my knuckles.

"Is all well, Sir Donald?" The Duke of Gordon tapped his shoulder.

Demonstrating a firm grasp of his composure, Don dragged his gaze away from Mary and made an exaggerated bow—one reserved for dukes and above. "Your Grace, I am simply anxious for this dance to end so that I might seize the opportunity to enjoy a turn myself."

The duke gave Don a sideways glance—a shrewd look, indeed. "Ah yes, I've been watching John of Castleton's daughter as well. Quite a delicate morsel she is, if you don't mind my saying."

Och, I bloody well mind you saying anything of the like about Miss Mary and you'll wish you'd never seen the lass if you so much as place your pinky finger on her.

With a deep inhale through his nostrils, Don smiled politely. "Miss Mary has been under the tutelage of my sister, Barbara. I daresay she has been an excellent student."

The duke's eyebrows arched. "Ah yes, I do believe you accompanied the two most fetching women to the ball this eve. You are a lucky man, indeed."

With such unfettered declaration of admiration, I hope the damned duke will be returning to Aberdeenshire soon. Very soon.

"And you?" Don asked with utmost decorum. "How are you faring without your duchess?"

Reaching for a glass of sherry from a passing servant, the duke subtly arched a single eyebrow. "Haven't you heard? Lady Elizabeth has left for a convent in Flanders and petitioned for a divorce of all things. I have sworn off women for the rest of my life."

The man made no sense at all. "Pardon?"

The duke clapped Don on the shoulder. "Let us just say you have nothing to fear from me. My philandering days are over."

Don stood dumbfounded as he watched Gordon's retreating form as he disappeared in the crowd. The most notorious rake in all of Scotland had sworn off women? Oh, how he'd like to hear that story.

The final chord of the allemande echoed between the walls. Spinning, Don focused on the applauding nymph across the floor. But the young man standing beside her with his hand around her waist made the hackles on Don's neck stand on end. In three strides, he pushed between the pair and glared directly at the young Cameron pup. "Be mindful of where you are placing your hands, sir."

The lad's face turned scarlet. "I—"

"I ken exactly what you were doing. Do not forget you are far too young to be courting Miss Mary. Now run along and cast your gaze on younger fare."

"I beg your pardon?" Mary shook her blasted fan under Don's nose. God's bones, he wished the damned flappers had never been invented. "At least Sir Kennan is here to enjoy himself rather than to make business alliances."

Don's gaze shifted to the lass. "Mind you, those business dealings are to benefit *the cause*—your family, the Camerons, as well as a host of other clans will profit from my work here this night."

A strathspey began and Mary spun into place with her fists on her hips. Damnation, she glared at him. At him! As if *he'd* done something wrong. Was she now smitten by the Cameron whelp?

The music demanded they moved together. Mary filled her chest with air, breasts heaving above her bodice, a defiant pout on her lips. Her beauty was as maddening as it was mind boggling. "I imagine your business dealings will profit the House of Sleat more than anything."

"Why should they not? I've done most of the work."

"I kent it."

"Pardon me?" The confounded lassie spun away. Pursing his lips, Don had no recourse but to dance with the next lady in line. Damnation, Mary could be cryptic. When finally their elbows looped together, he inclined his lips toward her ear. "What is this about? Surely you do not disapprove of my business dealings."

"Aye? So now your shipment has been arranged, you'll send me back to Castleton?" Though it was time to spin away, she stopped—right there in the middle of the dance floor. "And tonight your sister helped me dress in all this finery—hardly noticed by you—and now that the night is nearly at its end, you accuse poor Sir Kennan of being inappropriately familiar in front of all of these guests, embarrassing him to his toes, and you think I will bow down and parade around the dance floor with a smile on my face, pretending all is well?"

Don blinked.

Mary caught up with the other dancers and resumed her steps.

Good God, everyone in the room was staring at him as if he'd spilled port wine down his costume. With a low growl, it took but a moment to resume his place in the gentlemen's line. And when they again moved together, he spoke first. "This is your first ball."

"Oh?" Her blue eyes grew round, accusing. "Is that why you left me as soon as we entered the hall?"

"I said I had business dealings. Things that could not wait." How on earth could he make her understand? The lass dons a ball gown and suddenly behaves like a snotty princess? "Why are you being so vexing?"

"Me?"

The music stopped. Thank God.

She turned her back and fled toward the patio.

Oh no, she wasn't about to avoid him. Pushing through the crowd, he reached for Mary's hand.

"To the pier!" a loud voice boomed. "The entire waterfront is afire!"

Chapter Twenty-Three

The whisky Don had shared with Mr. Smith roiled in his gut and burned the base of his throat while a cold sweat broke out across his skin.

Fire?

"Heaven's no." Miss Mary grasped his arm. "What can I do to help?"

"Ah…" Craning his neck, his men and sister approached as the hall turned into a mass of pandemonium with people running everywhere. "Stay out of trouble," Don growled in her ear as his men approached.

"Coll, Kennan—see the women home. William, come with me."

With no alternative but to make haste, he left Mary and Barbara in his wake as he dashed outside. Just as he feared, with coaches vying for position, the tumult inside was nothing compared to the mishmash of horses and drivers and men yelling, practically causing a riot.

William pointed in the direction of the Clyde. "Look. You can see the flames against the sky."

He gulped against his horror. A deathly orange glow radiated above the trees. "There's no time to waste." Don beckoned with his hand as he started to run. "We'll travel faster on foot."

Why the devil he must be clad in his finery at this very moment added insult to the irony. If anything happened to his galley or his cargo, he might as well dive into the Clyde and let the current wash him out to sea—At least he was dressed for his funeral.

"Dear God," William cursed as they rounded the corner to the Glasgow Bridge. "The entire waterfront is ablaze."

Bright licks of fire and smoke leapt across the scene. His warehouse was ablaze, but so were the boats moored along the shore. If he lost his ship, he'd be ruined.

"The galley," Don shouted as flames leapt up her mast. "Haste!"

He sped his pace, leaving his brother in his wake. Thank the Almighty, the crew was already there with buckets. Sprinting, he couldn't cross the bridge fast enough, but as he neared the far shore, heat from the burning warehouses seared his face.

All cannot be lost.

Up and down the shore, moored galleys and skiffs were alight with their crews fighting to douse the flames. Everywhere Don looked, groups of men hauled buckets of water as tongues of fire teased them.

Drawing his arm across his face, the smoke burned his eyes as he rushed to his boat. "Reverse the siphon!" he bellowed, running up the gangway. No one seemed to hear while the men shouted and worked with buckets, throwing water at the threatening flames.

The fire had taken the sail and mast, and licked its way over the timbers. Don leaped through the blaze, rushing to the siphon he used for emptying the bilge. Levering it over the side he pumped with all his strength, using his foot to angle the hose toward the fire, but the thing grew a mind of its own. "Someone take charge of the blasted hose afore the galley goes down with us in it."

Having caught up, William hopped down from the gangway, his feet barely touching the deck as he dashed over benches to take up the hose. "Pump faster," he hollered, pointing it at the elusive flashes of fire leaping over the timbers.

Don pumped like a machine while river water gushed through the hose. Standing fast, William swept the stream back and forth across the base of the blaze.

In seconds they doused the fire while the crew stood, mouths agape, their buckets dangling.

"How the bloody hell...?"

"No time." Don pointed over his shoulder. "The boat behind is going down unless we help."

"The hose won't reach," said William.

"Put a plank across. Hurry!" Don's gaze shot to the warehouse—too far away for the pump to be of any good there.

Understanding flashed across William's face as he helped Don pull the pump across. By the time they doused the fire, the neighboring galley was listing in the river—taking water like a sieve.

But Don couldn't stop and survey the damages to either boat. "To the warehouse. Quickly."

Running from Saltmarket Street, Coll and Kennan met them in the midst of the mayhem.

"The galley?" Coll asked.

"Still afloat. Fire doused." Don pointed. "The warehouse needs us more. We must haste!"

But the line of buckets had stopped. Soot-faced men stood shoulder to shoulder, dumbly watching the inferno.

"What the hell?" Don barked. "You dimwits, the flames are growing higher. We cannot stand down."

"'Tis lost," said Kennan. "There's no use."

Don's ears rang. Ice pulsed through his blood.

No.

Don's hands shook with the rage coursing through his blood. Was everyone against him? His finery was blackened with char and smoke and the young pup standing beside him saying all was lost hadn't a strand of hair out of place.

His entire world was burning before his very eyes. His hopes, his dreams, his plan for *the cause*. In the span of an evening all was lost?

Over my dead body.

He glared at the Cameron heir with steam ready to burst out his ears, his nose, his eyes. The mule-brained lad had slavered all over Miss Mary at the ball. Placed his hands on her. Had behaved much too familiar than any young tom ought with a maiden. Good God, Kennan needed a lesson. A string of curses hurled to the tip of Don's tongue, but all he managed was a bellow that reverberated through his chest and roared out his mouth. His legs took over, launching his body at the unsuspecting whelp.

Kennan's eyes flashed wide before Don crashed into him.

Both men toppling over, Don swung back and crashed his fist into that pretty jaw as they hit the ground.

"Bastard," he spat, throwing another punch. By God, someone would pay for this night.

"You're mad." Kennan's eye's rolled like a raging bull as he slammed the heel of his hand into Don's nose.

Reeling back, the damned appendage felt like it had been shoved to the back of his brain. Eyes blurring with tears, Don threw a blind punch, grazing a cheek.

"Get off me, you crazed fiend," Kennan's voice ratcheted up to a shriek.

Fingers of iron clamped around each of Don's arms. "'Tis lost," William growled in one ear.

"Save your ire for someone who deserves it," came Coll's voice in the other.

Don's nostrils flared as he bore down, wrenching his arms to free himself. Back and forth he twisted but the two men refused to release their damned grips. "This is not over," Don growled. "I will kill anyone who had a hand in this."

Rising up, Kennan brushed himself off. "You think I did?"

Of course the Cameron heir had nothing to do with it. Tightness gripped Don's chest. He'd needed to hit something and that bonny face was the closest target in sight. "You look like shite."

The young man sauntered up. Cocking his head to one side and eying Don's nose, he let out a rueful chuckle. "I reckon I broke it. Serves you right. You're a bastard even if you are a baronet."

Don glanced down at his bloodstained shirt. His nose aching like a son-of-bitch. In the heat of the moment, he'd felt little pain, but now if the throbbing was any indication, his nose would soon be bigger than his face. "Lucky punch, you wee maggot."

Kennan rubbed his jaw, moving it side to side. "Yours, too."

"Come," said William, finally releasing Don's arm—now he'd stopped fighting. "'Tis late and there's naught we can do until morning."

"You go." Don stared at the flames, his face hot. "I need to think."

***

Wearing a dressing gown over her shift, Mary paced the bedchamber and wrung her hands.

*First he ignored me as soon as we arrived at the ball—
disappeared whist I danced with Sir Kennan for ages. Then he has
the gall to tell me to stay out of trouble?*

Is that what he thinks of me?

I'm a useless urchin he casts aside at the first sight of adversity?

I could have helped.

Right?

I could have carried buckets just like everyone else.

Mary hated being ordered to stay out of trouble like a
child—to be thrust into a coach with Barbara and hauled
to the townhouse on a circuitous route to ensure they
avoided the fire. While Sir Donald and his men ran into
peril.

Dear God, what if something happens to them?

She'd been pacing forever and yet the house remained
silent. How on earth would she be able to sleep knowing
the men were putting their lives in danger? She hadn't
seen much of the fire, but the glimpses she'd caught from
the coach were horrific. The entire street was lit bright as
day by the flames.

A door opened and closed on the floor below,
followed by footsteps.

Though she hadn't visited the baronet's chamber, she
knew it was right below hers. Just as she knew the
servant's door that Hattie used led straight to the den of
the man Mary wanted to know better, wanted to impress,
wanted something from—something she couldn't even
admit to herself. It seemed like ages ago when Sir Donald
had used the servant's stairs and had caught her in the
bath.

Tightening the sash on her robe, she took the candle
from her nightstand and opened the door to the
passageway. White-painted, stone walls curved, leading to
a stairwell—one similar to those in Dunscaith. Mary ran

one hand along the cold stone as she descended, holding her candle high.

She stepped out of the well at the first landing. The wooden door with blackened iron nail-heads looked ominous. Biting her bottom lip, Mary glanced back up the stairwell.

Why had she come?

Something banged loudly on the other side of the door accompanied by a curse.

Jolting, wax from her candle dribbled down Mary's fingers.

With a hiss, she steadied her nerves and knocked.

No sound came from within.

Her trembling fingers reached for the latch.

She really should turn around.

Wrapping her fingers tight, she pulled down the handle.

The door clicked.

Aye, she'd just step inside and ensure all was well.

"Sir Donald?"

Seated at an oblong table, the man looked up, his eyes red with dark bruises beneath, his periwig lying askew beside him, and next to that, a flagon of whisky and a glass. Mary hardly recognized Sir Donald's black stare. Sorrow, rage, and something even more dangerous oozed from his expression.

He turned the glass between his fingertips. "You shouldn't be here."

"W-what happened to your face?"

When he looked up, anger radiated from his gaze. "It met the wrong end of Kennan's hand."

"Oh, my heavens." She covered her mouth with her fingers. "Are you all right?"

He held up his glass and sipped. "I'll feel no pain after a few more of these."

She took a wee step closer. "I-I couldn't sleep without news..."

"Did you not see enough?" His eyes narrowed, almost as if he hated her—as if the whole disaster had been her fault. "Did you not see the flames of the warehouse licking the heavens?"

"'Tis grave?"

He tossed back the whisky and slammed the glass on the table. "I'm ruined, damn it. We *all* are ruined."

"Surely there is—"

"No, blast you!" he shouted, looking as if he might strike out with his fist. With a glower, he pushed back his chair, stood and started around the table. "How many ways do you want me to put it? A man is ruined and you want to dream up miracles?"

"I didn't say that." Mary slipped along the opposite side of the table, her gaze darting to the door. Truly the situation was weighty, but if only he'd allow her to speak.

"Oh? And did you fancy yourself falling in love with a dashing baronet and living a grand life in a fancy townhouse?"

"How can you be so crass? After we—"

"What? After you bewitched me into kissing you?"

Drawing her eyebrows together, she regarded him. "How much whisky have you consumed?"

"Enough to be dangerous." He sauntered after her.

Mary slipped to the head of the table and snatched the neck of the flagon. "Am I in peril, sir?"

"I said you shouldn't have come."

Unable to help herself, Mary's gaze slid from his disheveled mop of tawny locks, down his soot-stained satin shirt and breeches. Dear Lord, the man appeared more devilishly fetching than ever before.

But he's hurting.

Taking a deep breath, she acted on her instincts, though definitely against her better judgement. With one last look at his eyes, she turned. After steadying her hand, she set her candle down, took another glass from the sideboard and poured. "Since you were not gentlemanly enough to offer me a tot, I take it you'll not object if I help myself?"

"Ladies do not imbibe in spirit."

"Unless their lives are *ruined*." Keeping her back turned, she raised the glass to her lips and took a wee sip. Holy Moses, the liquid burned a fire from her mouth all the way down her throat. Eyes watering, Mary fought back her urge to cough and tapped the back of her hand to her lips.

The floorboards creaked behind her. And though she couldn't see him, she sensed his nearness, so close heat radiated from his body as if he'd brought the flames from the waterfront into his chamber.

A rush of hot anticipation thrummed through Mary's blood while his fingers brushed the curls away from her neck. Hot breath skimmed across her flesh. "Come," he uttered in a low growl. "I'll take you back to your chamber afore I do something we'll both regret."

Closing her eyes, Mary swooned into him. Heaven help her, how she wanted those full lips caressing the skin at her nape. Whenever she looked at the man, she'd craved his touch ever since the night they'd spent in the box bed. Dreamed of kissing him over and over again. Imagined his hard body pressed against hers. Wished she could spend an entire night in his arms. If only he felt something for her, felt the way she did, wanted her more than his blessed business transactions.

"Must you?" her voice rasped as if the sound came from outside her body.

***

Good God, could the woman make things more difficult? Merely her scent tantalized his aching nostrils and made his mind run amuck. Not that his mind wasn't already in a muddle. Don needed something—anything to take the pain away. But he couldn't use Miss Mary. No, not now when he had nothing to give her.

Damn it all. He should have sent the lady back to her father as soon as the galley arrived. Mary of Castleton was not Don's responsibility. He'd been a fool to bring her here, convincing himself that she needed to learn gentility from Barbara. Mary of Castleton was perfect as she was— musket and all.

The woman lifted the glass to her lips. Her gaze met his as she took the slightest of sips.

Then a rosy flush fled up her face and her eyes watered.

Chuckling, Don took the glass. "You're a swiller of spirit from the cradle, I see."

She patted her chest. "I find it quite—ah— invigorating."

He swallowed the contents with one smooth swig, relishing the rush as the whisky burned its way down to his empty stomach. Leaning closer to her intoxicating lilac scent, he twirled a lock of hair around his finger. Ever so soft, her tresses felt like spun silk. "Invigorating," he whispered, as he repeated her word—though his meaning was quite different. Moving the curl to his lips he plied it with a kiss.

Mary tightened the sash on her dressing gown. Dear God, she wasn't even dressed. Her shift peeked through the neckline of her red robe—a thin bit of linen. Not only had she come to his chamber, all he had to do was tug the sash around her waist and shove the damned robe from her shoulders. Were her nipples erect? With little effort, he could slip his hand inside her neckline and cup her breast, run his thumb over the rosy tips he ached to suckle.

But, God's teeth, he couldn't take advantage of her. Not a woman like Miss Mary. "Come," he said again, fighting every fiber in his body. Only steps away was the door to his bedchamber—a place he'd never taken any woman. But by the saints, he wanted to take Mary there now. Bury himself deep inside her core and forget this night. If only he could spread those lily white thighs and make love to her—take her to a place of ecstasy where she would cry his name over and over until her world shattered.

Her pink tongue slipped out and moistened her lips.

By the saints, did she have any idea how sensual she looked?

He took her hand and tugged.

Squeezing his fingers, she tugged back, her face rosy and ever so kissable. "Will you…?" Mary stepped into him, raising that damned beautiful face, her eyes dark and full of desire. He'd seen that look on a woman's face before. Aye, he knew what she wanted, and it took every thread of strength he could muster not to give it to her and more. Bloody oath, the look in her eyes made him hard. Worse, he'd been hard for a damned month.

"I'll see you to your chamber," he forced out in a tone much gruffer than he'd intended.

Her face fell, twisting his heart into a knot. He'd hurt her. The last person Don wanted to hurt was Mary of Castleton, but she had to understand. He hadn't wanted to be trapped before and, now, even if he wanted to court the lass, he couldn't. His entire life hung on a precipice and he just might lose everything on the morrow, including the townhouse in which they stood.

He needed to think, and with the lady's scent distracting him as well as the throbbing ache in his cock, he had to be free of her—had to polish off that flagon of whisky and drift into a drunken stupor.

Swallowing his self-loathing, he strode to the door and ushered her through.

Mary uttered not a word as she climbed, but at the top of the servant's stairs, she stopped and faced him, placing her palm over his heart.

Don gasped at her gentle touch. Every inch of his flesh tingled. His breath came in short bursts. His knees wobbled while he grasped her arm.

"My only wish is that the tenderness we shared when on the trail could have meant as much to you as it did to me," she said with a warbling voice.

Praying she wouldn't cry, a lump the size of the Isle of Skye formed in his throat. If only he could tell her how much she meant to him, how often he'd wanted to pull her into his arms and smother her with kisses. But all he did was gulp back declarations of adoration and nod.

Rising to her toes, Don's heart hammered as she kissed him. Pressed her delicious, petite lips to his warm lips—lips that could make his heart swell so goddamn enormously, the organ would burst from his very chest. His mind couldn't focus but for one thing. Pushing through those delectable lips with his tongue, all the restraint Don had exercised in the last month shattered into a thousand shards.

A wee moan escaped Mary's throat as she returned his kiss with a passion that burned hotter than the fire on the waterfront.

Running one hand up her slender spine, Don fumbled for the latch with the other.

Chapter Twenty-Four

Mary swooned while she held tight to Donald, kissing him as fervently as she possibly could—put all her emotion into the kiss, praying she had garnered enough experience to impart the depth of her affection. She followed his lead as he backed her into her chamber.

Clutching her arms around him, she took in a sharp inhale. "I don't want you to go."

A seductive grin spread across his lips—the dark shadows around his eyes making him look all the more devilish. "I've no intention of going anywhere," he growled, lifting her into his arms and carrying her toward the bed.

Mary's body trembled and she drew her hand over her mouth. "We mustn't," she forced herself to say, knowing she'd never be able to resist if he lay beside her.

Through the dim light cast by the fire, the seductive glint in his eyes made her heart flutter. "I mightn't be able to take your innocence, but I will show you pleasure…and then…"

"Then?" she asked breathlessly.

"Never mind." His breath became labored as he set Mary on her feet and held her at arm's length. "Forgive me. I would be no kind of gentleman if I didn't first ask you if you would prefer for me to go."

Mary's throat constricted. "I...uh." She glimpsed the bed, turned down by Hattie hours ago. Dear Lord, he couldn't leave. Not when a fire smoldered deep inside her core. "Stay."

His tongue slipped out and grazed his top lip. Pulling the sash from her robe, his hungry stare raked from her face down to her breasts. In one fluid motion, he pushed the dressing gown from her shoulders.

Heaven help her, she'd never felt so desired—and never felt so impassioned.

The man's lips parted as he cupped her breasts in his hands. His breath grew labored.

A rush of moist heat radiated between Mary's legs in the most sacred part of her entire being. Powerful longing took control of her body. Urgent need made her want to arch toward him while he untied the bow at her neckline.

"I've wanted to bare your breasts and suckle them ever since the day I wrestled you into my arms and realized you were a lass."

She crossed her arms over her chest. "Bare?"

He looked up. "Aye." Taking her wrists, he gently tugged her arms open. "Trust me."

Nodding, Mary couldn't speak. This man had ridden to her rescue and had taken her across the Highlands to ensure her safety. She would trust him with her life. She would follow him to the ends of the earth if he asked.

He pulled her shift from one shoulder, then the next, sending the last garment of modesty cascading to the floor. Mary wanted to cross her arms, but he held them open, and stared, his gaze drinking her in as if he were assessing a masterpiece.

A low moan rumbled from his throat. "God in heaven, you are more beautiful than my wildest imaginings."

He raked his gaze to her eyes and she smiled. "I..."

But his lips covered hers before she had a chance to refute his claims. The rush of longing grew stronger, begging for more as Mary wrapped her arms around him, kissing him with everything she had. Donald trailed kisses down her neck as gooseflesh pebbled across her skin. His hand again moved to her breast and kneaded.

Thrusting her hips forward, she craved friction as he ground his hard manhood against her. She nearly shattered when he moved to her side, his warm lips trailing lower until he covered her nipple with his mouth. Deft fingers swirled down to her navel, then to the triangle of red curls that thrummed with heat.

Oh God.

His finger slipped between her legs—lightly brushed the most intimate place on her body.

Mary's thighs shuddered. "What...?"

"Open."

"Here?"

"Aye, just a wee bit."

As she slightly parted her legs, Sir Donald slid his finger back and forth along her slick womanhood. Holy fairies, how on earth this could feel so exquisitely good, she had no idea. His fingers had to be magical. Just when Mary thought she couldn't possibly be more impassioned, he slipped a finger inside her—inside! The place where she craved for him to insert his manhood—to join with her as if they were husband and wife. Her entire body shuddered as her fingers grew a mind of her own and stroked him. Stroked the hard, long column of flesh that filled his breeches all the way up to his waistline.

In and out, his finger worked her into a writhing frenzy. "I cannot take anymore," she blurted breathlessly.

"Och aye, you can and you will." With a chuckle he straightened and lifted her onto the bed. "I want you."

Oh, God, was this really happening? She should pull the bedclothes over her naked body and insist he go. But doing so would cast her asunder. "What about your clothes?"

He glanced down at his soot-stained shirt and breeches—looking entirely desirous, but nothing like the polished baronet from earlier that evening. Opening the neck, he pulled the shirt from his head.

Good Lord, the man's abdomen and chest rippled with undulating muscles. His arms were nearly as big around as Mary's thighs. Who knew a man's body could be more beautiful than anything she'd ever seen in her life?

Her gaze dipped to his silk breeches. The tip of manhood now peeked above the thin fabric as if teasing her—a single eye winking at her. Licking her lips, she rubbed her finger across the tip. A deep moan rumbled from his throat. A moan filled with such longing, Mary knew he loved her. No matter what Sir Donald said or did, he loved her as much as she loved him.

Then he climbed onto the bed, a knee pushing against hers. With the force of his movement, Mary had no choice but to open for him. Oh Lord, he kneeled between her legs.

Her head buried in the pillows, Mary crossed her arms over her chest. "Sir Donald?" Yes, she wanted him more than life itself, but he'd scarcely uttered a word since her shift had fallen to the floor.

"Close your eyes and let me take you to the stars." For the love of holiness, such a voice could melt gold.

"But."

Leaning over her, he tapped her lips with his finger. "Wheesht, *mo leannan*. I'll not take your innocence, but I will show you passion."

First his breath caressed her womanhood, making Mary pant with unfettered abandon. Then his tongue licked—kissed her with sizzling hot moisture. Stars crossed her vision. Her hips couldn't stop rocking. She sank her fingers into his hair and worked her hips against him. "Donald, Donald, I want you so much." As the words escaped her lips, a high-pitched cry followed with a throbbing burst of euphoria.

Chuckling, Donald smoothed feathery kisses up her body, making the tremors within her body shudder all the more. "How do you feel?" he asked, ending his trail of kisses with a warm caress of her lips.

"Unbelievable."

"And your maidenhead is still intact."

He grinned—a devilishly sinful grin. "I didn't know it could be done—ah—with the mouth."

"I suspect there are a great many things you don't ken about love making."

She liked that he used the word love.

As he rolled to her side, the hard column of his manhood pushed into her hip. Donald's eyes rolled back with his groan.

Mary's gaze meandered downward. Oh dear, the passion that had released only moments ago returned full-force. "But I haven't given you pleasure."

"I am content with your release," he mumbled, nuzzling into her neck.

"Can I? Can the mouth be used similarly?"

Rising to his elbow, the man's jaw dropped. "I—ah. I could never ask a lady to do such a thing."

Mary grinned, her fingers trailing down his incredibly hard abdomen. "What of a Highland lass who pulls the stopper from the powder horn with her teeth?"

"But—"

She untied the cord securing his breeches and with that tug, he sprang forth in all his male glory. Goodness, he was hard and beautiful, and Mary couldn't stop herself from wrapping her fingers around him and stroking.

"Good God, woman, have you done this before?"

"Never." But no one need tell her what to do. She longed to taste him as he'd tasted her. She licked him. Donald's thighs trembled. Grinning, she tested different things, memorizing the strokes and kisses that made him shudder and moan the most.

Chapter Twenty-Five

A satisfied sigh rumbled in Mary's chest as she smoothed her hand over the bed linens. She could think of nothing more rapturous than spending this day abed and in Sir Donald's arms.

Feeling nothing but cool cloth, her sleepy eyes peeked open.

Mayhap I need to reach a bit farther.

But Sir Donald's warm body wasn't there either. She sat up and surveyed her empty chamber. The last thing she'd remembered, she'd fallen asleep spooned against his body, toasty warm as his arm draped around her waist and cuddled her.

Mary dropped back to the pillows and stretched her arms over her head. Though slightly disappointed not to wake to his bonny face, she knew Sir Donald would want an early start.

She closed her eyes and prayed all would go well for him this morrow. It simply had to. Most of the merchants in Glasgow would have been affected by the fire. And Sir Donald had saved his galley. Surely he would be able to renegotiate his terms.

Yes. He would weather this setback like any true Highlander.

And Mary would stand beside him doing everything she could to see to his success. Together, they would become the talk of Glasgow—mayhap eventually live in a grand manse like the Duke of Gordon's. Donald had been cynical about his state of affairs last night, but this morning Mary could imagine a silver lining in last night's dark clouds of smoke.

Her body felt like it was floating as she made her way to the bowl and ewer. As usual, Hattie must have been listening for her footsteps. No sooner had she washed her face and cleaned her teeth when the chambermaid came through the servant's entrance. The same passageway Mary had used last eve.

Had Hattie been aware of that, too?

"Good morrow, Miss Mary," Hattie said, picking up the tongs and adding a lump of coal to the fire.

Mary toweled off her face. "'Tis a wonderful morning, is it not?"

The chambermaid straightened and regarded her with a pinch to her brows. "I beg your pardon? Half the Glasgow waterfront succumbed to fire last eve and you're bright as a peony in sunshine?"

Mary slapped the cloth on the table. "I do not believe my positivity is your concern." Goodness, the maidservant had been growing more and more disrespectful with her offhanded comments and this one could not be allowed to slip.

The woman curtseyed. "Apologies. I must be overly distraught with the master's state of affairs."

Mary sighed. Perhaps she'd acted a bit too jovial. "I'm well aware of the gravity of Sir Donald's situation. But I'm an optimist. We aren't the only people affected by the fire, and if I were able to place a wager, I would bet on Sir Donald's ability to overcome in the face of adversity."

Hattie held up Mary's stays and shook her head. "I wish I had an ounce of your confidence, miss. But I fear we'll all see lean times ahead."

"That we may."

"But you shan't worry. You'll be able to return to your kin up north."

Holding her stays against her ribcage, Mary turned away—more to hide the ire heating her face than for Hattie to tie her into the contraption. She hadn't thought about returning to Dunscaith Castle in sennights. Surely Sir Donald would want her to stay. Especially after last eve. The glorious evening they'd spent in a cocoon of pleasure.

Wouldn't he?

Blast the chambermaid for planting doubt into her thoughts.

Mary couldn't dress fast enough and patter down to break her fast. She strode into the dining hall with a smile in place. She'd show Sir Donald that this was a new day— one they could face together and meet this setback head-on.

Stepping through the French doors, Mary's face fell.

"Good morrow, Miss Mary," said Sir Coll, standing with a bow.

Sir Kennan followed suit. "Ah, Miss Mary, I was wondering when you'd venture below stairs."

Barbara regarded her over her shoulder. "Goodness, I cannot believe I awoke before you, Mary."

She glanced to the mantel clock. At eight in the morning, Miss Barbara was usually still abed.

"And the baronet?" Mary asked, again searching the room, seeking the one face she wanted to see. "Has he already broken his fast?"

Sir Kennan grasped her hand and kissed it. "He and William have already left for the waterfront." He grinned and then winced, gingerly touching his jaw with the tips of his fingers.

"Dear Lord," said Mary, peering at a purple bruise swelling beneath his fingertips. "Whatever happened to you?"

"Compliments of our illustrious leader, I'm afraid."

"Sir Donald hit you?"

"Aye." Kennan shrugged and held the chair. "'Tis not a good idea to tell Sir Donald all is lost when…well, when all is truly lost."

Mary sat. "'Tis that grave?"

"We should ken more once he and William return," said Sir Coll.

Barbara spread jam over her toast. "There is not a cloud in the sky, yet I feel as if a tempest is roiling inside my breast."

Coll's gaze dipped to the maid's ample bosoms, swelling perfectly above her bodice. The admiration in his eyes was unmistakable. And Mary didn't need to be an experienced courtier to know the Highland laird was smitten.

Mary glanced to Sir Kennan. If he'd stolen a peek like Coll, he didn't show it. He simply smiled at her and passed the platter of sausages. "Are you hungry?"

Mary selected two and set them on her plate. "Famished."

"So, what do you two gentlemen have planned for the morning?" Barbara asked, clipping the smallest bit of toast with her teeth.

Sir Coll arched one eyebrow. "Mayhap I could accompany you on a stroll to the park whilst we await your brothers' return."

"That would be delightful. I imagine we wouldn't appear to be overly happy if we stepped out for a bit of air." Barbara glanced to Mary. "We'd need a chaperone."

Mary would have rather stayed at the townhouse and awaited news of Sir Donald.

Before she could answer, Sir Kennan placed his hand on her forearm. "Come, Miss Mary. I'll go, too."

Glancing down at Sir Kennan's much-too-familiar hand, she waited until he removed it.

"Yes, two couples would be ideal," Barbara said.

Brushing off her arm, Mary tried to smile. "As long as we won't be away long. I'm sure Sir Donald will be anxious when he returns."

Sir Kennan clapped his hands together. "Splendid."

Good heavens, Mary certainly hoped the Cameron heir wasn't flirting.

***

Sitting across the table from Mr. Smith, Don's cravat nearly choked him. "You mean to tell me the fire provided no setback for you in the slightest?" He ran his fingers around his collar, shooting an exasperated expression to William seated beside him.

"Obviously there have been setbacks, but Glasgow's merchants have more goods than my ships can hold," said Smith, his plump jowls jiggling beneath his robust periwig. "Thank God my two galleons are moored in the Firth of Clyde. And mark me, they will be sailing as planned."

"You honestly believe you'll replace your entire cargo within a sennight?" William asked.

The merchant scooped a bit of snuff with his fingernail and snorted it. "I reckon so, or very shortly thereafter. And I do need your packing salt—*if* you can have it to me in a sennight." Devil's breath, the gold snuff box on the table probably cost as much as Don's ship.

"My men are repairing my galley as we speak. We'll be able to set sail for the salt mine on the morrow. I cannot promise delivery within a sennight, but tack on a couple of days, and we'll have your salt here. On that I can give my word."

The man sneezed across the table. "I can allow you seven days. If you need longer, I'm afraid I must take my business elsewhere. My ship will sail in a sennight with or without your packing salt."

"Your cargo will sour in a fortnight without proper packing," said William.

"My cargo is my concern. My deadline is fixed." Smith shook his finger. "There happens to be a line of merchants waiting outside this door and if you cannot supply me what I need, there are plenty others to take your place."

Don swiped his brow with the heel of his hand. *I am ruined.* "Very well. We'll do our best to meet your terms."

William gasped. "But—"

Slicing his hand through the air, Don stifled his brother's retort. "What, pray tell, is your offering on future shipments?"

Mr. Smith ran his fingers down his lapels and stood. "I can offer no guarantees."

Rising to his feet, Don held out his hand. "You can count on the MacDonald Clan. There are no better sailors on the western seaboard of Scotland."

"So you say." Mr. Smith took Don's hand with a limp handshake—one that expressed no faith whatsoever in Don's ability to deliver. "Next time, might I suggest you store your wares in my warehouse in Newtown?"

Straightening his sword belt, Don gave the man a questioning look. "Why did you not tell me of this warehouse before?"

Smith shrugged. "'Tis not yet completed—but it shall be before the end of autumn."

"Stone walls?" William asked.

"Wood, though far away from the riffraff skulking around this pitiful town." Smith smirked. "What, pray tell, happened to your face?"

Don wondered when that question would arise. At least the rigors of last eve could easily explain a pair of black eyes. "A firefighting incident." Bowing, Don and his brother took their leave, pushing their way through the sea of merchants who, indeed, had gathered in Mr. Smith's antechamber.

Once outside, William inclined his head toward Don's ear. "Are you mad, promising him a delivery in a sennight?"

"We sail on the morrow. It is August—the finest month of the year. We've a better chance of making Smith's deadline now than ever. I expect you to see the repairs completed today. Work the men through the night if necessary."

"I don't know. It'll be tight."

Don stopped and grasped his brother's shoulders. "We have no choice. Replace the mast first. That's the only thing we cannot sail without."

"Very well. But do not blame me if we don't make Smith's ridiculous deadline."

"Have I ever blamed you for something beyond your control?"

"Plenty of times, just like you blamed Kennan for the fire last eve."

Don's face burned as he clenched his fists. He shouldn't have struck the lad, but he'd been so incensed. And Kennan needed to learn to hold his tongue. "We'll not fail, brother. Mark me."

"I wish I had your confidence." William turned and kicked a stone. "What of Miss Mary?"

Good God, would his brother ever stop asking maddening questions? A chunk of lead sank in Don's gut.

He never should have kept her in Glasgow so long. He'd practically seduced the woman last eve. *Practically?* He had done everything but take her maidenhead. Damnation, she was turning him into a lecherous debaucher of heiresses. He might have enjoyed a toss with a widow or a wench at the alehouse now and again, but Mary of Castleton needed to be strictly off limits. He couldn't chance a slip with her again lest he end up forced to marry the lass. "'Tis time to take her back to Dunscaith," he mumbled under his breath.

"Will there be time?"

"A detour to Castleton will only set us back a few hours at most." It was the right thing to do.

"I think she's rather enjoyed her time here," William said.

"Aye."

"I also think you've enjoyed having her in the guest chamber."

"She's a pleasant lass to have about for the most part—and she's been good company for our sister."

William guffawed. "You say that as if she were a pet deerhound."

"How else would you have me speak of her?"

"I've seen you steal glimpses of Miss Mary when she wasn't looking. You like her—in fact, I'll venture to say you're in love with her."

"Don't be preposterous. I cannot afford to be in love with her."

"So you'll take her back to Dunscaith Castle and applaud when her betrothal to some well-to-do, much-older laird is announced?"

Don's gut twisted tighter than the lock on a strongbox. "I didn't say that."

"But still, you're letting her go?"

"Have you lost your mind?" Don stopped at the corner of Saltmarket and Bridge. "In case you have, let me remind you that our situation is precarious. We must secure our place as a supplier to that vile Mr. Smith, else England will starve out not only us but all of the Highlands. We have pledged our lives and our swords to *the cause*. Never forget it."

William executed a pretentious bow. "Forgive me, *my lord*. With such enthusiasm I have no doubt you'll soon be declared the revered duke of Jacobinism."

"Mute your insolent tongue."

"Pardon me for stating the obvious. If you are hell-bent on breaking the young woman's heart, then by all means, I'll not stand in your way." William started toward the riverfront. "If you'll excuse me from your pig-headed presence, I have a galley in dire need of repair."

Don's blood boiled beneath his skin as he watched his brother cross the road. He ought to teach Willy a lesson, too. God knew the impertinent lout needed a good sparring session. How on earth could Don think of properly courting Mary at a time like this?

Besides, she'd be far better off with someone not so dedicated to *the cause*. Christ, if the Williamite Party uncovered his ardent loyalty to King James, he could very well be tried and hanged for treason.

Chapter Twenty-Six

Dressed as a chimney sweep, Balfour hid in the recesses of the close across the street from the Baronet of Sleat's townhouse. God, he hated this town. The streets were cluttered with beggars and filth. It hadn't been difficult to find his garb—flicked a bob at an urchin who gladly removed his shirt and bonnet, scampering after the coin like a dog. The only problem was it stank worse than a sewer.

Balfour nearly retched with every inhale. Christ, when he removed these tattered garments, he would burn them. But not yet. Licking his lips, he watched the windows and doors of the ritzy city home—a vile abode in truth. It lacked everything Balfour loved from the Highlands. But just like the Baronet of Sleat, it stood as a false façade. Behind its doors hid the evil of the Jacobite Party and their miserable code of clan law.

Not long after Balfour had slipped into his hiding place, he'd seen the baronet head out with his brother. He chuckled silently at the grave expressions on their faces. Last eve, he'd drawn a great deal of satisfaction when, from afar, he watched the warehouse burn to the ground—watched the guttersnipes battle the blaze in vain, throwing useless buckets of water onto the inferno.

Unfortunately, MacDonald had been too fast—cunning even—using the damned siphon to pump water onto the flames. But Balfour had hurt the man and he doubted Donald MacDonald's deep pockets would weather the setback.

Word on the street was Smith would give his business to whoever could fill his cargo hold and MacDonald's salt pans were too far away. Balfour laughed again. The baronet would also be forced to wait two seasons to shear his sheep again. His wool was lost and with luck, his clan would starve.

Balfour froze when Mary of Castleton exited the front door with Don's sister with those two Highland cads accompanying her. They all wore smiles on their faces as if nothing were amiss—all except Miss Mary. Something didn't seem quite right with her, though she opened her parasol and rested her hand on Sir Kennan's offered elbow. Christ, the slobbering maggot looked upon Miss Mary as if she were the only woman in the county.

What the devil? Balfour's gut turned upside down. The wench could be involved in all manner of immoral practices behind the doors of the baronet's townhouse. Was she whoring with every Jacobite laird in Scotland? *Ballocks to that.* Walking in front of Mary, Sir Donald's sister and Coll of Keppoch were fawning over each other like a pair of shameless dogs.

Balfour's knuckles turned white as he squeezed the handle of his chimney broom. He'd best do something fast or there would be no turning Miss Mary to his way of thinking. She was *his*, goddammit. No one else's.

***

"Come," Don responded to the light rap on the door. It could be only one person.

Miss Mary popped her head inside. "You sent for me?"

"Yes." He gestured to a chair then held it for her. "Please be seated."

"My thanks."

You'll not be thanking me after you've heard what I have to say. Don took the seat opposite. "I'm sure you're aware my cargo is lost."

White teeth scraped over her full bottom lip. "All of it?"

"Aye, even the wool. But William and the crew are hastily making repairs to my galley."

"Thank heavens."

"Regardless, there's little chance we'll make the next shipment to the Americas."

"But there's always the next one," she said, her eyes too bright and hopeful.

Don looked away, refusing to allow her optimism to sway his good judgement. "Possibly, but last eve's fire was a terrible setback, *terrible.*"

She nodded, her smile faltering a bit.

Taking a deep breath, he grasped the arms of his chair. "I sent for you because I wanted you to hear from me first that we are sailing north on the morrow."

The smile now gone, a hushed gasped slipped through her lips. "Oh? So soon?"

"We've not a moment to lose." He drummed his fingers. "I must retrieve another shipment from Trotternish, and I'd be remiss in my duty as the leader of the Defenders if I did not take you home to your father."

Mary's face blanched. "To Dunscaith?" she muttered as if forgetting her roots.

"I thought you'd be happy with the news. Are you not looking forward to being reunited with your family?"

She stared at him, mouth agape as if she were holding something inside. Though her eyes flashed with disbelief, the slight parting of her lips made her look more kissable than she'd ever been. Don swiped his hand over his sore eyes and tender nose. He could not be influenced by her wiles at a time like this.

"I beg your pardon, but after last eve, I thought…" She pressed those luscious lips into a thin line.

Don knew full well what she'd nearly uttered. But she'd silenced herself before voicing what would have been an embarrassment for both of them—improper as well. His fingernails bit into the armrests as he fought to remain impartial. His very existence was in peril. It was no time to allow a young woman to twist her desires around his heart, no matter how much the goddamned organ wanted her to do so. "You must ken I cannot make promises." He didn't need to give her an explanation, but for some reason, he felt he must explain. And she sat there looking like a puppy that had been left out alone in the snow on the coldest night imaginable. "God bless it, Mary, *the cause* is in crisis."

She squared her shoulders and looked him directly in the eye—the redheaded minx. "Och aye, *the cause*. 'Tis far more important than people's feelings, or families or…or *love*."

Jesus, she had to use that bleating four-letter word. "Mary, I—"

Shoving away her chair, she stood and backed toward the door. "What about Sir Coll and Sir Kennan?"

Don marched around the table, fists balled at his sides. "Why the devil are you bringing them up at a time like this?"

She tilted her defiant face up to him. "Are they sailing north as well?"

"Aye. They're returning to their clans. 'Tis time."

"Did *you* decide it was time? Did you discuss such inconvenient timing with your sister?"

He pinched the bridge of his nose. "Now you're speaking gibberish."

She took a daring step toward him. "Only because you are completely blind."

Don planted his fists on his hips, refusing to back down. "I beg your pardon?"

Mary snorted as if Don were a blasted numbskull. "Barbara is in love with Sir Coll of Keppoch."

Every muscle in his body clamped taut. His sister could not possibly be in love with anyone without Don's consent. "Preposterous! I'm her guardian and have heard nothing of the sort."

"That's because you've had your nose so deep in the *Oxford Gazette* you pay no attention to the world around you."

For the love of God, this woman could be so infuriating. And she was standing so damned close her scent had his mind completely flummoxed. Who could manage a rational thought with oil of lilac radiating around him while the most perfect heart-shaped face regarded him with such heated fury? Ruby lips, blue eyes the color of sky, hair as red as her temper. By God, Mary would bring any man to his knees with merely the arch of an eyebrow. Coughing out an exasperated growl, he grasped her face between his palms and devoured her mouth with the deepest, most probing kiss he'd ever imparted to a woman.

His ploy seemed to work because she moaned and melted like honey, sliding her lithe fingers around his waist. Dear God, he was harder than a stallion in a mating paddock filled with mares in heat. He'd hoped his release last eve would quell his hot-blooded desires. He'd never been more wrong in his life. The deeper he probed, the more his body demanded he pull her taut to his chest, feel those pliant breasts mold against his flesh. Mm, yes, just as he was doing now.

Mary pulled away breathless. Her kissable lips swollen and puckered. Her face flushed as if ready for a romp in the bedroom. "You see?" That damned look of defiance flashed through her eyes. "You cannot even face your own feelings. You kiss me like a rapturous suitor and yet you're planning to leave me in Castleton, hoping to never see me again."

Chapter Twenty-Seven

Mary dabbed her tears while Barbara blew her nose in her kerchief sounding like a blast from a trumpet. "My brother is ruining my life," the blonde beauty wailed.

A fresh bout of tears welled and streamed from Mary's eyes. "He's ruining mine, toooooo." She'd been crying ever since she fled to Barbara's chamber. Both of them had been bawling like a pair of mourners at a funeral. Mary couldn't even catch her breath, her head swooning with her short gasps. If only she could tell Barbara about how Sir Donald had behaved last eve. Merciful fairies, he'd stripped her bare—she'd lain prostrate on the bed for him while he had his way. Dear God in heaven, it was but a miracle the rake hadn't taken her maidenhead.

She still couldn't understand it. They'd been intimate together. Didn't that mean love? Mary had been so sure he loved her—he mightn't have spoken the words, but he'd shown it in so many ways. Her mind boggled. How could she live without him?

A wailing lament escaped her lips. How could he touch her like that and cast her aside with such callous indifference?

Barbara followed with a sobbing wail of her own. "With my luck, Sir Coll will be married before I ever see him agaaaaaaain."

Married? Mary's mind blanked. What would she do if Sir Donald took a wife? Holy Moses, she couldn't even imagine him showering another woman with attention—kissing her, touching her intimately, baring her breasts…Oh, Lord in heaven, the notion of losing him was enough to send her into a frenzy. She dropped onto the bed and curled into a ball, crying with abandon, not caring who heard, not caring what anyone thought. Especially the accursed Baronet of Sleat.

Barbara sat beside her and rubbed Mary's back. "You mightn't see it now, but my brother is doing you a favor. He has no capacity to care for anyone." She let out a high-pitched wail and hid her face in her kerchief. "Yoooooou can do so much better than Donald MacDonald."

"You're daft." Mary buried her face in the crux of her arm. "I'll be tucked away in Dunscaith Castle with no prospects."

"It couldn't be as bad as Duntulm on the north end of Skye. 'Tis absolutely desolate there."

"So is Castleton. There are no suitable matches within miles and miles." The image of Balfour MacLeod flashed through her mind. "Unless you want to be plundered by a vile dragoon."

Barbara removed the kerchief from her face. "Thank heavens that awful lieutenant will no longer be bothering you."

Mary shuddered. "I'd rather die than marry *him*."

Barbara dropped to her back and stared at the canopy above. Mary rolled and joined her while their tears slowly ebbed, followed by deep sighs and thoughts of gloom.

"How far is Dunscaith Castle from Sir Coll's lands in Glen Spean?" Barbara asked, her voice soft and dreamy.

"Not sure." Mary wiped the dregs of her tears. "Perhaps two days' ride, if not more."

Barbara groaned. "If only it were closer I might gain an opportunity to see him if I accompanied you home."

Mary rolled to her side and faced her friend, placing her head on her hand. "That would be fun, regardless. Though I'm afraid you might grow bored." She chuckled—at least it wasn't a wail. "What would your brother think if I taught you to shoot a musket?"

"Me?" she spouted through blubbering lips. "He'd be absolutely mortified."

Mary sat up. "Why should you not have an adventure? With or without Sir Coll—besides, he's a chieftain with a great many responsibilities. During the gathering, I heard he's in the midst of a feud with the MacIntosh Clan."

"You don't say?" Barbara looked almost like a normal person with her face all blotchy from crying. "He never mentioned that to me."

"Men." Mary threw up her hands. "They always think they need to protect us from the bad things."

"The bastards," Barbara swore.

"I beg your pardon?" Mary was, by far, more uncouth than the younger woman, yet she'd never uttered such a curse.

"Well, they are." Suddenly spry, Barbara hopped to her feet. "I will travel to Dunscaith Castle with you. If nothing else, it will give me a wee bit more time with Sir Coll, and even better, it will infuriate Donald."

This time Mary's belly shook with her laugh. "I do like how you think." Perhaps if Miss Barbara accompanied her home it would give Sir Donald a reason to pay a visit himself.

***

The black chimney sweep's costume had proved to be quite useful. Balfour had been a soldier for so long, he didn't realize how tight-lipped people were when he was in uniform. During the evening meal, he'd sat among the vilest characters in the alehouse, but the information he'd gathered had been invaluable.

MacDonald's men were scurrying to make repairs to the bastard's galley so they could sail to Skye on the morrow. Balfour had nearly fallen off his rickety wooden chair. He needed to act, and fast. Now he'd been reassigned to Fort William, he'd never find an opportunity to see Miss Mary once she returned home. And she would. Through his questions, he'd learned there had been no announcement of a betrothal. Not to mention it would be scandalous if the baronet kept Mary in Glasgow whilst he sailed right past her father's home. Och aye, he needed to seize his chance forthwith.

Once darkness had fallen, it hadn't been difficult to slip down the close leading to the back of MacDonald's townhouse. Not a soul had given him a second look. Now he stood in the shadows of the stable, looking up at the windows. Bloody hell, why one man needed so many windows was beyond him. The place looked even larger from the rear than it did from the front.

The windows illuminated by flickering candlelight caught most of his attention, though silhouettes on the lace curtains had been rare.

I'll not give up, God bless it. And I'll be damned if I'll stand idle while that milk-livered haggard traps her in his snare. She's mine.

A clank snapped Balfour from his thoughts. He ducked behind a stack of hay bales right before the stable hand pushed a barrow within inches of his nose.

Balfour lowered his face and held his breath. Then he laughed to himself. The dull-witted cad had no idea of his presence. The lad had just strode past, focusing on his barrow of shite. Christ, he could have run him through the back and the stable hand wouldn't have known who'd attacked.

Numbskull. No one suspects a thing. The bastard's men are all on the waterfront repairing the doomed galley—the sops.

When he again scanned the windows for movement, his heart froze. All the way up on the fourth floor, Miss Mary was holding the curtains aside. She stared beyond the stables, as if she were dreaming about something far away. Perhaps she missed home?

Perhaps she now realizes that I am the better match for her.

Such a thought emboldened him. He cared not if she was locked away in a tower with seven floors. He would slip inside and take what he wanted.

Quietly, Balfour moved to the flowerbed against the house and crouched between the bushes.

A servant burst through the rear entry with a bucket, heading toward the rear gate.

As quick as a cat, Balfour slipped inside before the door slammed closed. Now he only needed to hide until the witching hour when all would be asleep.

Dimly lit kitchens to his right, a dark stairwell ascended upward to his left.

How fortuitous.

Chapter Twenty-Eight

Mary's eyes popped open at the sound of a squeaking floorboard. Her breath caught as her heart flew to her throat. Had she dreamt it?

A shadow moved.

Clutching the bedclothes beneath her chin, she sat bolt upright. "S-sir Donald?"

"How can you utter that festering pustule's name?"

Mary shivered as if someone just walked over her grave. Mary would never forget that nasally voice. She scooted flush against the headboard. "L-lieutenant," she said in a tone far too shrill. "I insist you leave my chamber at once."

Balfour MacLeod stepped forward, the light from the coal burning in the hearth enough to illuminate his wretched smirk. "I'm disappointed you're not happier to see me, Mary."

Her stomach churned at his familiar use of her given name without the courtesy of "Miss" before it. Clenching her teeth, her gaze darted through the room. What could she use for a weapon? "I-I doubt it would *ever* please me to lay eyes on you."

"Still siding with the outlaws, are you?" He stepped a bit nearer.

Mary slid toward the far side of the bed. The servant's door was ajar. Could she make a run for it? "How did you spirit inside—how did you find my chamber?" Buying time, she moved closer to the edge of the bed with every word.

He wore a dirk sheathed on his belt—no other weapons, at least that she could see. "It wasn't all that difficult." In two steps he stood where she'd been laying. "You must realize the fire was for you. I've ruined Donald MacDonald because of you."

His words stunned. "*You* set fire to the waterfront?"

He laughed. "Aye, but 'tis you who made me do it."

"You're mad." Never would she accept blame for such abominable destruction. "I did no such thing. I would never intentionally hurt Sir Donald or any of the merchants."

With a feral growl, Balfour launched across the bed.

Shrieking, Mary sprang off the side and onto her feet. "Help!" she cried, dashing for the door.

"Shut up," he hissed.

Heart hammering in her chest, Mary ran.

A steely hand clamped around her wrist. Before she blinked, Balfour shoved her against the wall, forcing her arm up her back. "Dammit, I didn't want to have to do this."

Mary jerked, a sharp pain searing up the twisted limb. "Ow," she cried out.

"Blast you, hold still." He pinned her with his body. Though not a tall man, he was stocky and weighed considerably more than she.

He shoved a vile tasting rag into her mouth and gagged her, tying it tight around Mary's head.

Shrieking through the fabric, Mary thrust her body back and forth. With an elbow to his ribs, the lout jerked away enough for her to run.

"Oh no you don't," he growled, footsteps pounding behind her.

A chair clattered to the floorboards as he nabbed her wrist.

"Jesus Christ, you'll wake the dead," he growled, lunging for her elbow.

Before he could yank her away, Mary stretched for the tongs beside the hearth.

"Come, before that mongrel sets upon us." Balfour again yanked her arm behind her back, pulling a leather thong from his belt.

Oh, no. She wasn't about to let him bind her wrists. Not without a fight. Swinging around, Mary bashed the side of his head with the tongs.

Blood streaked from his temple, but the lieutenant only strengthened his iron grip on her wrist.

Noise clattered from the servant's stairs.

"Unhand her," Sir Donald roared from the doorway, brandishing a dirk.

The lieutenant leveled a knife at Mary's neck. "You take one more step and I'll slit her throat."

Freezing in a crouch, Donald's gaze snapped to Mary.

Dear Lord, everything shook. The sharp blade pressed against her neck so fiercely, it forced her to keep her chin held high. But the power of the baronet's gaze infused her with strength. All they needed was for Balfour to loosen his grip ever so slightly. Just one errant move.

The lieutenant dragged her with him as he backed toward the servant's stairs.

Mary's fingers clamped around the tongs while the knife at her neck drew blood. A hot trail of liquid streamed down, itchy until it met her shift. One misstep and she'd be dead.

Sir Donald crept after them, his gaze never leaving her face.

Balfour pulled her through the threshold.

Mary cringed.

Donald gave a nod.

Gnashing her teeth, she blindly hurled the tongs upward and stomped on the lieutenant's foot.

The knife jerked aside.

Mary ducked.

With a bloodcurdling roar, Donald attacked.

The two men met with flashes of steel and gnashing of teeth.

Blood spurted across the walls.

Clutching his arm, Balfour squawked like a rooster, scurrying for the stairs. "I'll see you *completely* ruined for this!"

Sir Coll ran into the passageway, sword in hand. "What happened?"

"Dragon's breath," William swore from behind.

Sir Kennan stepped though the doorway, a musket pistol in each hand. "Good God, you're bleeding, Miss Mary."

"'Twas MacLeod. Go after him," commanded Sir Donald, dropping to his knees beside her.

The three started down the stairs, but Donald caught William's coattails. "Go tend to our sister. Make sure she's aware the threat has passed."

William stopped and regarded the baronet, and then shifted a worried gaze to Mary. "Very well. I'm sure Barbara's frightened. No one could have slept through that racket. It sounded as if the battle of Dunkeld was being fought above stairs."

Pressing her hand against her bloody neck, Mary strained to lift her head. "There's something else you both should know."

Two pairs of midnight blue eyes regarded her, eyebrows slanted inward, though Sir Donald's still suffered the remnants of bruising.

Mary gulped. "Lieutenant MacLeod is responsible for last evening's arson."

Sir Donald growled through his teeth. "That diseased son of a pox-ridden whore."

"He's gone completely mad," seethed William.

"Aye, and we'll pay the magistrate a visit on the morrow." Sir Donald flicked his wrist at his brother. "Now off with you."

As soon as William turned away, Donald pulled his shirt over his head, then bent over Mary's neck. "Let me have a look."

She removed her fingers and he dabbed it with the cloth.

"Ssss," Mary hissed. She bit her tongue, though. In no way did she want Sir Donald to think her weak. "I'd nearly fought him off when you arrived."

"Aye, and that's how he ended up with a dagger at your throat." He dabbed some more.

"Has the bleeding stopped?" Mary turned her gaze to the wall, willing herself not to look at the muscles rippling in his bare chest. "Because if it has, you can return to your chamber."

He held the cloth firm. "I am the one who determines where I will go in my house."

She rolled her eyes. Even in the face of near death the man could be overbearing.

"Come." Slipping hands beneath her, he took her into his arms as he stood. Heavens, strong as Hercules, he lifted her as if she were no heavier than a bairn. "You'll be more comfortable resting on the bed whilst I clean your wound."

When he nestled her against the pillows, Mary crossed her arms over her chest. "I can take care of myself—or—or you can send Hattie in."

He strode to the bowl and ewer. "Would you prefer to be tended by the chambermaid?"

No. Mary shook away her inappropriate thoughts. "Yes, it is improper for you to still be in my chamber now the threat has passed."

With his back turned, Mary couldn't see his expression, though his shoulders tensed. "You didn't consider it improper last eve." Goodness, Sir Donald's voice had suddenly grown husky.

A swarm of butterflies danced low in Mary's belly. Clenching her fists, she fought to allay those ridiculous winged creatures. "Last eve you led me to believe you felt differently about…about…about us."

He turned. A dark, intense, tormented stare filled his eyes. "Forgive me. It was never my intention to mislead you. I'll see to your comfort and then I'll leave you in peace."

She wanted to crawl into a hole and hide for the rest of her life. Mary pursed her lips and fixated on the canopy above. How on earth had he just made her feel like a heel? For all holiness, she was the person who suffered an attack. And under Sir Donald's roof. As his guest, *he* had a responsibility to see to her safety.

The bed dipped quite a bit when he sat beside her.

Mary scooted away a little—not like she'd just done when Balfour had stalked her, but she certainly wasn't going to prove an easy mark for Donald MacDonald this eve. Not when he'd all but shattered her world.

Moving closer, he swathed her neck with a clean, damp cloth. "I cannot put to words how incensed I grew when I saw that monster with his hands upon you."

"And his knife at my neck." Mary dryly added.

Sir Donald again examined her wound—a fair bit too closely for Mary's taste. For the love of Moses, how was she to ignore the fact he wasn't wearing a shirt? How on earth was she to remain nonplussed when he accosted her with such muscular maleness? Furthermore, this eve, he managed to smell like cloves simmering in cider. Mary's head swooned.

"Are you all right?" He smoothed his palm against her face, so gently she had no choice but to close her eyes and lean into his warmth. "The bleeding has stopped and the wee cut doesn't appear to be deep."

Taking in a deep breath, she forced herself to draw away. "I'm certain I will be fine after I've had a good night's sleep."

"You're drowsy?"

"I didn't say that."

The corner of his mouth ticked up. Those too-blue-for-any-man's eyes grew darker as he lowered his eyelashes and regarded her mouth, his face growing nearer and nearer. "Och, Mary."

She parted her lips to speak, but he covered them so fast, Mary's bones melted like candle wax. Gracious, she wanted to push him away, but she could not manage to make her arms work.

Don hadn't intended to kiss her. But Mary's lips had been so close, so delightfully inviting. Besides, she was behaving with such pride, he'd had no recourse but to dip his chin and show her exactly what she had come to mean to him. He hadn't even realized how much until he saw her being manhandled by that fiend. In that moment, something inside him snapped. He never wanted to see another man place his hands upon the bonny lass. Not ever.

Hell, he didn't want to leave her at Dunscaith Castle with her da. Though it was the honorable thing to do. If only the fire hadn't happened, matters would be different. The arson had been caused by his ever-present nemesis. Ever since he'd met Mary, that bastard had plagued him.

He'd deal with MacLeod on the morrow. Presently, Mary returned his kiss with wanton sweeps of her tongue. A fast learner, lithe fingers swirled through the curls on his chest. Her breathing sped as he pulled her closer to his thrumming heart. With a shove, her hand stopped him. "Cease this amorous behavior. I will not allow you to seduce me. Not when you're planning to dump me at my father's gate never to see me again."

A lump the size of his fist took up residence in his throat. Damn it all, she was right, and Don felt like a rake, a lecherous rogue taking advantage of a young maid who'd done nothing but trust him. Removing his hand from around her shoulders, he sat straight. "Did I say I would never venture to see you again?"

"Not exactly, but what did you expect me to think? You mentioned nothing about courting me. You asserted *the cause* was more important than our very lives." Her gaze dipped to his crotch. "More important than what had occurred between us last eve," she whispered.

The heat of her gaze made him lengthen—no matter how inappropriate his desires, his cock was fully erect with his next blink. Damnation, he needed to think. "After I have words with the magistrate in the morning, we have no choice but to sail for Skye. And your father would be within his rights to take my head if I did not deliver you safely to him."

She folded her arms tight against her body. "So nothing's changed."

"Everything has changed." He hit the mattress. "If another man ever touches you again, he'll feel the cold steel of my sword."

She blinked as if in disbelief. "Won't that be a bit difficult when I'm in Castleton and you're in Glasgow?"

Don groaned. Making a commitment now could be a terrible folly. "How can I protect you when you're in Castleton?" he hedged—doing a very poor job of it.

"Are you planning to send for me?"

Why hadn't he thought to put it like that? "Of course that's my plan."

She stared at him for a moment as if expecting him to say more. Then she pinched her brows. "Then you're asking me to marry you?"

His tongue swelled in his mouth—felt like grit. "Ah." His heart twisted so taut, his head spun. Never in his life had he wanted to be tied down to any woman. A wife brought so much more responsibility...and children. As the heir of the baronetcy, he had a responsibility to produce a son. He looked into Mary's eyes. *A family?* "If you'll have me," he uttered, almost as if his soul commanded his mouth to speak.

Mary blinked again, followed by a sharp exhale. "W-w-why did you not say something earlier?"

"Because I am a dull-witted man." He shook his head. "You were right. I was too wrapped up in the needs of *the cause.*" He held up a finger. "Though it is and will continue to be the focus of my work until the true king returns to the throne."

She brushed his cheek with the tip of her finger, making him suck in a sharp gasp. "I like that you're committed to something in which we both believe." Then she swirled her fingers over the stubble along his jaw. A dainty pink tongue slipped out and tapped her top lip while her gaze slid down to his naked chest. "You must know that I am wholly committed to you, Sir Donald."

He grasped her hands and kissed them, staring into her eyes. Dear God, he loved this redheaded lass. "Please, call me Don."

"Aye," she muttered, sounding more like a sigh. The wispy tenor of her voice reignited the fire in his loins.

Gathering her into his arms he held her in a tight embrace. "Heaven help me, I worship you."

Mary raised her lips to his and joined with him, ravishing him with lips and teeth and tongue like she'd been bred for the pleasures of the bedchamber. Don plundered her mouth in kind, filling his palm with a luscious, unbound breast. "I want you," he growled.

Saying nothing, she slid down on the bed and pulled him atop her. "Show me how."

Dear God, no woman hath ever uttered more sensuous words.

He reached for the folds of her shift and tugged. "Wait."

Don stilled his hand. Passion he'd never known surged through him, threatening to burst.

Her eyes grew dark as she pushed his breeches. "I want to see you naked first."

Chuckling, he pushed himself to his knees, untied his waistband and let his silk drawers drop. Watching the lust building on her face as she stared at his member made him so hard the tip arched up and touched his stomach. "You do this to me." He stroked himself for her amusement, though only once. Good God, he'd nearly spurted his seed with the slightest friction.

She took in a stuttered breath. "I cannot believe something that size will fit inside me."

"It might hurt a bit the first time." He licked his lips. "We could—"

"No. I want you. I want to know what it feels like to join with you."

She tugged her shift high enough to reveal the nest of red curls at her apex. Merely the scent of her sex made his thighs quiver. But he had to make the first time good for her. Reaching down, he stroked the sensitive nub peeking through the curls.

Gasping, she bucked. "You drive me to madness."

"And I'll take you further," he growled, slipping his finger inside and stroking her as he captured her mouth. In and out he slid one then two fingers, reveling in the passion that made her entire body writhe with want.

"Please. I'm s-s-so close to coming undone."

Seed dribbled from the tip of his cock as he moved himself to her entrance. "Are you ready?"

She clamped her fingers into his buttocks and pulled him inside her. "Oh, God."

Her wee gasps took over his mind. With a deep thrust, he filled her.

Mary whimpered.

He froze.

Her hands tugged harder. "Don't stop!"

Exerting every ounce of control he could muster, he met her pace until she cried out and shattered around him. Blessed Jesus, he let everything go, his entire body shuddering until sweet euphoria left him panting and completely spent.

Chapter Twenty-Nine

Mr. Kerr held Don's doublet, waiting for him to slip his arms through. "Are you certain you don't want me to accompany you to the magistrate's office, sir?"

"There isn't time. Ensure Miss Mary is aboard my galley by ten o'clock." Don shrugged the jacket over his shoulders. "I'll file a complaint and head straight for the waterfront."

A rap sounded at the door. "May I come in?"

"Aye." Don looked twice as his sister stepped inside. He glanced to the mantel clock, reading seven in the morning. "What the devil are you doing up at this hour?"

With an exasperated cough, Barbara blinked consecutively. "Pardon me, but who in this household can honestly say they slept well last eve, what with all the excitement."

Don regarded her costume. She was fully dressed and wore an arisaid, of all things, over her gown. "Why are you dressed like a Highland lass?"

She smoothed her fingers over the MacDonald brooch at her neck. "I want to go to Castleton with Miss Mary."

"Impossible. We are sailing as soon as I've lodged a complaint with the magistrate, which will not take long, I assure you."

Barbara stamped her foot. "You cannot leave me here when there's a madman about."

Don raised his chin for Mr. Kerr to tie his cravat. "Mark me, he will be behind bars by the day's end."

"Are you certain? What if he is released before your return and comes to burn the house down with me in it?" She clenched her fists beneath her chin. "Worse, what if he tries to take *me*?"

"She has a point," said Mr. Kerr.

And she also has a propensity for exaggeration. Don crossed his arms and gave his sister a stern glare. Honestly, he would have to return to Dunscaith Castle in short order, lest Mary become distraught. "Quickly. Pack your things and if you are not at the pier precisely at ten, we'll sail without you."

"Oh, thank you." Barbara swept in and gave him a peck on his cheek. "I've only a few things left to pack. I've been at it since William visited my chamber last eve."

Don rolled his eyes to Mr. Kerr. "You'd best ensure she doesn't try to sink my boat, trying to bring along her entire wardrobe. One portmanteau—two at most."

"No chest?" she asked.

"Absolutely not." Don sliced his hand through the air. "You'd best ask Hattie to help you. I mean it. If you're not on the galley, we will set sail."

"Brothers," Barbara huffed, spinning on her heel. She opened the door and stopped short.

"Up here," a deep voice blared from the main staircase.

Don shot Mr. Kerr a questioning glance. "What on earth?"

"Here he is," bellowed a red-coated dragoon standing in the doorway and blocking Barbara's escape. She moved aside.

"What is the meaning of this?" Don demanded.

A lieutenant strode forward, musket in hand, a saber swinging from his hip. "Seize him!"

Don spun on his heel and dashed for the servant's door. A loud boom rattled his ears. A musket ball hit the door. He stretched for the latch. A flintlock clicked.

"If you try to run, I'll put a hole through your back," growled a menacing voice.

The odds were not good. Don turned as two soldiers grabbed his arms and pulled him to face the officer. Clenching his teeth, Don struggled to free himself, but the two miserable dragoons forced his arms behind his back, slapping manacles around his wrists.

"What are the charges?" he demanded.

"Attempted murder of one of the king's officers."

"Lieutenant MacLeod?" he asked, praying he hadn't been duped.

"The very same."

Don's empty stomach nearly heaved. That maniac had filed charges against him?

Dear God, the man will stop at nothing to ruin me and lay claim to Mary. "Are you out of your mind? The bastard broke into *my* house and assaulted *my* guest."

"Is that so? And from a man sporting two black eyes?" The lieutenant holstered his pistol, with an unconvinced frown. "You can plea your case to the magistrate. Word is you blamed the arson on him and then tried to kill him. And that doesn't bode well considering the Crown's suspicion that you are a Jacobite."

"These allegations are false." Don stumbled as a soldier pushed him in the back. "I have multiple witnesses in this household who can testify in my defense."

"Save your wind." The lieutenant motioned to the dragoons. "Take him to the Tolbooth."

"Donald!" Mary yelled as they wrestled him to the stairs.

He caught a glimpse of her red hair flickering from the stairs above. "Go with William. Set sail as planned. This is but a sham and I will have my name cleared by the end of this day, so help me God."

***

Staring out the window of the drawing room, Mary clasped her hands to her chest, trying to steady the erratic beat of her heart. Her entire life crumbled before her eyes—and just when she'd thought her luck had taken an enormous upswing. After an endless night turned from horror to rapture, the love of her life had been imprisoned in the Tolbooth and his galley and crew had sailed for Skye with Sir Coll and Sir Kennan at the helm.

William immediately took up the reins in his brother's absence, but he couldn't force Mary aboard the galley—not without breaking her legs and arms. She'd stood her ground, insisting her testimony would be needed while Barbara wept. The poor lass wanted to visit Dunscaith ever so much. Mary promised to make it up to her—though she believed Barbara's ploy was more to see Coll MacDonell than to be Mary's beloved companion.

And now, Mary of Castleton stood in the drawing room ever so anxious for William's return. He'd been gone for hours, meeting with the advocate, making all manner of inquiries. This was such unknown territory for Mary. She'd never spoken to an advocate—never been in a courtroom—never had been victimized until Lieutenant MacLeod abducted her.

She rubbed her outer arms and surveyed the street from east to west. Where was Balfour now? Plotting his next attack upon her person?

Dear God, no.

It was unbelievable they had seized Don without listening to a word of his story and yet the lieutenant had twisted the truth to implicate the baronet. A man of noble birth, for heaven's sake. Her hatred of the redcoats grew deeper by the moment. Their prejudice against Highlanders was unforgiveable.

No, Mary would not leave Glasgow whilst Donald suffered in the Tolbooth. Nor would she sit idle whilst a madman wrongly accused her betrothed of attempted murder.

By the time William entered the townhouse, Mary had insisted Mr. Kerr bring her every musket in the house for cleaning and inventory, including powder and lead balls. She picked up one of Donald's pistols and examined it. She would sleep with it under her pillow lest Balfour MacLeod steal into her chamber again—if he dared, he'd be leaving in a pine box.

Mary set down the pistol and dashed to the front door as soon as the handle clicked.

William entered with two men following, both wearing robes and wigs—very serious looking gentlemen, indeed. "I've brought Mr. Oliphant, our advocate, and Mr. Gunn, the court clerk, to hear your testimony."

After appropriate greetings, Mary gestured to the drawing room. "Thank goodness there is someone here willing to listen to the truth."

Mr. Oliphant took the chair closest to the hearth. They all sat, with Mary and William sharing the settee.

"When will the Baronet of Sleat be released?" she asked.

Mr. Oliphant situated his robes and frowned at Mr. Gunn. "If we can disprove the charges against him, I'd say a fortnight at best."

Mary clapped a hand over her heart. "For a nobleman?"

"The magistrate is sending a missive to Colonel Hill in Fort William and refuses to hear Sir Donald's plea until a reply is received."

"And that will take an entire fortnight?" Mary asked.

"Possibly longer, depending on the time it takes for missives to be scribed and delivered." The advocate tugged on his lace cravat and stretched his slender neck. "In the interim, it is our duty to collect as much evidence as possible."

Mary furrowed her brow and looked to William.

He gave her hand a pat. "Are you ready to answer Mr. Oliphant's questions?"

"Aye. I've been ready all day."

The man smiled—fortunately, his grin made his gaunt face look nearly pleasant. He gestured to the clerk, seated at the wee round table with quill at the ready. "Mr. Gunn is here to record your testament. It is imperative that you give an unbiased account of the events."

Mary nodded eagerly. "Of course."

"Now, first off, what is your relationship to Sir Donald and why are you residing in his home?"

She furrowed her brow. "Is that imperative to the inquisition?"

The advocate gave her the evil eye—a look so stern, she imagined he'd practiced it for hours in front of the looking glass. "Indeed, *everything* is imperative, miss."

Mary might be naïve about many things, but without a formal announcement of her betrothal to Donald, their relationship must not be made public. So, she started from the beginning and left nothing out from Balfour's threats at the gathering, to her abduction, her rescue and how they were forced to travel to Glasgow. She made it very clear Sir Donald fully intended to take her back to Castleton that very morning but his arrest had thwarted her chance to be rejoined with her father and siblings. She even managed to shed a tear with all the emotion coursing through her blood. It mattered not that her tears were more for her worries about Don's plight than her home—regardless, she worried all the same.

Mr. Oliphant held up his hand indicating for her to stop whilst Mr. Gunn dipped his quill and resumed writing. "I must say your recall is impressive for a woman."

Mary looked to the muskets she had sitting on the sideboard. "Do you think women to be dimwitted?"

"In my observation, they speak more from emotion than from reason."

Holy Moses, if only things weren't so grave, she'd invite the advocate to help her with a bit of target practice—using him as the target.

William must have sensed her unease and again patted her hand. "Please continue, Miss Mary. I'm sure they want to hear your account of last eve's plundering."

She blinked, snapping open her fan and pretending she'd nearly fainted. Why on earth did an image of what happened *after* Balfour fled come to mind? Her cheeks burned like they'd been held to a brazier.

"I know you must be terribly distraught," said Mr. Oliphant exhibiting a modicum of concern. "But, truly, your testimony must corroborate with that of Sir Donald."

Taking a deep breath, she closed her fan and gathered her thoughts. "I awoke when a floorboard creaked…" Mary left nothing out, removing the scarf from her neck and showing Mr. Oliphant where Balfour had cut her. She told them about the lieutenant's admission of his guilt in setting fire to the waterfront, which again made Mr. Oliphant hold up his palm.

"Mr. Gunn, please indicate you have recorded that the lieutenant confessed to the arson on the waterfront which led to the ruination of many of Glasgow's merchants."

The man stilled his quill and looked up from the table. "Recording it now, sir."

Mary sighed. Though the advocate seemed a bit rigid, he just might be on her side.

"You are aware the lieutenant blamed the arson on the baronet?" He again frowned, either in disbelief, or trying to make his case. Forever the optimist, Mary chose the latter.

"Twisting the facts to secure his own innocence, I'd wager," said William.

"He's a snake," Mary hissed. "Besides, how could Sir Donald have been responsible? He was dancing with me at the Duke of Gordon's ball when the alarm was raised."

Mr. Oliphant knit his brow. "Dancing? With you, miss? Are you certain you are not compromised—that you have no *amorous* affection for Sir Donald?"

William cringed.

Mary squared her shoulders. They weren't going to make a sham of her testimony. "As a matter of fact, I spent most of the evening dancing with Sir Kennan. Sir Donald only felt it his duty as my temporary guardian to grace me with one set, and due to the fire, our dance was cut short. After that, Sir Kennan and Sir Coll accompanied me and Miss Barbara to the townhouse whilst Sir Donald and Sir William raced into the flames." There. The old windbag could take that iron-clad testimony and see to it Don was released as soon as possible. Mary arched a brow at William who gave her a very subtle wink—one that would not be discernable by the party seated across the floor.

Mr. Oliphant patted his curly grey periwig. "Is there anything else to this testimony you have to add, miss?"

"I must say I'm very concerned for my safety." Mary wrung her hands for added effect. "Lieutenant MacLeod stole into the house through the servant's quarters and spirited into my chamber. What will be done to ensure that doesn't happen again?"

"I'm posting guards around the clock," said William.

She drew her hands beneath her chin. "You mean the true villain in this debacle is allowed to run free whilst Sir Donald, a member of the Court of Barony, is forced to remain in the Tolbooth?"

"Unfortunately, it is well known that Sir Donald rode against the king in the battle of Killiecrankie and, therefore, is under suspicion of being a Jacobite." Mr. Oliphant gave the clerk a stern frown. "Which I have on good order he is *not*. Regardless, had the lieutenant not been the first to file charges and had not been an officer in the King's Army, I believe due process would have been dispatched much more quickly."

Mary tapped her foot rapidly. Blast that confounded Balfour MacLeod. She never wanted to watch anyone swing from the gallows, but she'd make an exception for that yellow-bellied swine.

Chapter Thirty

Don sat on the edge of his pallet and hung his head. In the past fortnight he hadn't had a proper bath and his skin prickled with sweat. Naturally, they hadn't allowed him to use a razor. He ran his fingers over his beard— scraggly, no doubt. Fortunately, the itching from the growth had subsided.

He studied his filthy fingernails with disgust. Aye, they'd given him a gentleman's cell, but wouldn't allow him cutlery with which to eat—and no grooming utensils whatsoever.

If only Miss Mary would have sailed with the galley, she wouldn't have to see him in such a disgraceful state. But God bless her, she'd stayed to give her statement. Mr. Oliphant had said that with her testimony, he was sure once Colonel Hill's missive arrived, all charges would be dropped.

Then it would take every ounce of restraint in Don's body not to seek out Balfour MacLeod and dirk him in the dead of night. He'd had plenty of time to plan his revenge—think about all the satisfaction he'd gain from seeing the life flee from that bastard's eyes. But the Baronet of Sleat was no fool. Everyone knew he'd sided with the Jacobites in the Battle of Killiecrankie. Everyone knew he'd been born at Duntulm Castle, the once great stronghold of his ancestors, the Lords of the Isles. He'd been born to be a Jacobite, a supporter believing in Catholicism and the God given right of the Stuart's claim to the throne. Any action he took against the lieutenant would be seen as an act of treason. But that didn't mean he couldn't dream about the pox-ridden maggot's demise.

The lock to his door clicked. Don looked up with a flutter in his stomach. The brightest parts of his day were the moments when Mary came to call. He lumbered to his feet.

"Sir Donald." The lass used a formal address in front of the guard. Holding a basket between her hands, she moved inside and sat on the single wooden chair in the chamber. "I trust you are well?"

Sliding his foot forward, he performed a polite bow. "As well as can be expected, miss." He always gave the same reply.

With a boom, the guard closed the door, though continued to watch them through the barred viewing panel. *The swine.* Don stood a respectable distance from Mary, fighting every fiber in his body screaming for him to gather her in his arms and smother her with kisses. To feel her soft breasts pressed against him and hold her close for dear life. Damn the magistrate and the King's Army for taking MacLeod's side and ruining Don's reputation.

Mary smiled and removed the cloth from her basket, the ice around his heart always melted when she smiled. "I brought you a cake." She glanced at it with a wee snort. "It should still please your palette, though our friendly guardsman poked his finger in the middle to ensure I didn't conceal anything inside."

"Ever so fastidious of him." Don picked up the morsel and shoved the whole thing in his gob. Good heavens, his mouth watered. "Mm. 'Tis delicious."

"Miss Barbara and I asked the cook to show us how to bake it." She laughed. "You should have seen the pair of us covered with flour."

"I would have enjoyed that." Don would have enjoyed doing anything outside the four walls of his miserable cell.

She smoothed a hand over her skirts. "The missive from the colonel should arrive any day and this all will be over."

He nodded, regarding her hopeful eyes. Such a stunning shade of blue, he would never tire of staring into them. Don had almost given up hope that the colonel would support him. Once a man donned a red coat, he tended to be tarnished by the devil, but Mary's confidence had a way of infusing him with hope.

"And all has been safe at the townhouse?" Don asked, not wanting to trouble her with the mention of the lieutenant.

"Aye." She offered another smile—one that lit up the cell like sunshine. "Mr. Oliphant learned that Lieutenant MacLeod has been posted to Dumbarton Castle whilst awaiting the trial."

Don glanced at the guard. At least he'd turned his back. "'Tis less than twenty miles away. Do not grow overconfident."

"Not to worry. William has it in hand." That was code for: "*William has an army of Jacobite loyalists guarding the house.*"

"'Tis good to hear." He locked his gaze with hers. "I would never forgive myself if something happened to you whilst you're a guest in my home." He hoped she realized that was code for: "*I love you.*"

Maintaining her smile, Mary touched her fan to her heart. Indeed, she understood his meaning. Being in such close proximity to her and yet unable to touch her made a dark void fill his chest. "Mary, I—"

"Time's up," brayed the guard.

Standing, she grasped his hand. "I shall think of something wonderful to bring you on the morrow."

"I should like that very much." He kissed the back of her hand.

With a knowing wink, she moved her fan handle to her lips. Aye, he wanted to kiss her there, too. "Soon," he said as he took her to the door then listened to her footsteps fade as they pattered down the passageway.

***

When Mary walked into the townhouse entrance hall, an eerie awareness made the back of her neck prickle. To her utter shock, Fyfe, a guard from Dunscaith Castle stepped from the drawing room. "Miss Mary, 'tis ever so good to see you."

"Come in here, so I can see my daughter for myself."

Dear Lord, her father had come to Glasgow? Mary hastened into the drawing room. "Da? Is all well?"

"I should be asking you the same," he said from the chair by the hearth—the very one Mr. Oliphant had used a fortnight past. "News arrived the Baronet of Sleat has been incarcerated in the Tolbooth."

"Aye. 'Tis awful." Drawing a hand to her forehead, Mary's mind raced. "Lieutenant MacLeod forced his way into my chamber, and then blamed the fire on Sir Donald, and accused him of murder, and—"

"William has apprised me of all that has transpired." Da waved a dismissive hand. "And to be quite honest, I am irked that you refused to sail home to your family when Sir Donald commanded afore they led him to the Tolbooth."

The prickles on Mary's nape turned to a raging fire. "I beg your pardon? You *must* know I am the only witness who could testify to the lieutenant's trickery."

"You've given your statement."

"Aye." Mary glanced from her father to Fyfe. "B-but a missive should arrive from Colonel Hill of Fort William any day now, and then I'll be needed for the hearing."

"The only place you are needed is Dunscaith Castle."

"I am needed here and—"

Da slammed his fist on his armrest. "Do not take an insolent tone with me. There's nothing more you can do. Do you realize how scandalous this appears? You're sleeping beneath the roof of an incarcerated man— visiting him every day—taking him cakes and Lord knows what else."

Tears welled in her eyes. "Please, Da. Don't make me leave until Sir Donald's name is cleared."

"Has he spoken for you?" Da reached for his crutches. "I ken he has not because I have not received a request from him to court you. As your father, I forbid you to see the baronet again."

"But he—"

"My word is final." He motioned for Fyfe to help him to stand. "I have a coach waiting. I'll allow you five minutes to collect your things and then we are sailing home."

"I cannot." Mary stood dumbfounded, tears streaming from her eyes. If she told her father Don had asked her to marry him, it would only make him more incensed. "Please, Da."

"If you have nothing to collect, then we can leave this instant."

Mary thought of all the things she'd gathered since she'd been in Glasgow. Don had paid for everything, even the clothes she now wore. It would take ages to pack the lovely gowns, the gloves the corsets and petticoats.

A tear streaked from her eye and threatened to drip from her nose. "I have nothing."

Through bleary eyes, she regarded the faces of the guardsmen she'd known all her life, and the ones she'd come to know in the past two months. She had nowhere to run. William and Barbara stood in the entrance hall wringing their hands.

Barbara moved forward and kissed her. "I still want to visit."

Mary choked back a sob. "You're always welcome."

"As you are here. Any time," said William, kissing the back of her hand.

She curtseyed, pressing a calming hand to her chest. "Please give Sir Donald my apologies. I didn't want to leave this way."

"Come, Mary." Da passed with his crutches tapping the floorboards. "I'm anxious to set sail whilst we have a southern wind."

Chapter Thirty-One

One month and seven days since the dragoons stormed into his home and slapped manacles around his wrists for this farcical charade, Don's days had grown empty after William had paid a visit and told him Sir John had taken Mary back to Castleton. For the past sennights, he'd missed her with every fiber of his being. The only things he ever looked forward to were Mary's visits. After she left, the days droned on, as dreary as watching a snail climb a tree.

But her father was right. She needed to go home—to be as far away from Glasgow as possible and save what remained of her reputation.

Don looked up expectantly when Mr. Oliphant stepped into the antechamber where he awaited his trial. A hollow void expanded in Don's chest. "What news from Fort William?"

The old advocate shook his head, the grey wig jostling. "Still nothing, but the magistrate insists on proceeding." He patted Don's shoulder. "Have faith. I think we have enough to prove your innocence."

"Think?" Every muscle in Don's body tensed. "I *am* innocent. 'Tis my word against a fork-tongued whoreson who received punishment for his abduction of Mary of Castleton."

The bailiff pushed through the door. "'Tis time."

As he stood, Don closed his eyes and steadied his breathing. The only way to weather this farcical trial and prove his innocence was to project an image of calm. If he acted on his instincts and wrapped the chain between his manacles around the bailiff's neck and choked the life out of him, it would considerably reduce his chances of freedom. Oh no, this was no time to forget his breeding. He was born the heir to a baronetcy and he would ensure he behaved in a manner commensurate with his station.

Low murmurs filled the maple-paneled courtroom when they entered, the bailiff leading Don to the prisoner's platform. To add to his humiliation, like a commoner he would be forced to stand in his manacles through the duration of the trial. A smirk came from his right. Out of the corner of his eye, Don regarded the sniveling maggot—the lowlife he wanted to strangle. Balfour was a dirty liar. Don didn't give the bastard the satisfaction of a look, but he swore on his father's grave if justice didn't prevail this day, Balfour MacLeod would meet his end screaming. Don just hoped to God he would be there when the dirk slid into the whoreson's gut and slowly twisted.

The gallery of the courthouse was filled with commoners. How eager everyone seemed to watch the demise of one of Scotland's gentry. Don scanned their faces and saw not a sympathetic visage.

Once the magistrate had entered and took his seat at the board, he motioned for the bailiff to open a scroll. "Sir Donald MacDonald of Sleat, you have been accused of the attempted murder of one of the King's Army officers, Lieutenant Balfour MacLeod. And furthermore, the same lieutenant accuses you of arson which occurred on the first of August in the year of our Lord sixteen ninety-five."

The gallery erupted with rumbles of dissension.

"I am innocent," Don boomed loud enough to be heard over the crowd.

The magistrate hammered his gavel. "Silence."

Mr. Oliphant then proceeded to call the festering-pustule of a lieutenant to give testimony.

Don stood silently on his platform, clenching his fists as his wrists strained against his manacles. How the lieutenant could stand across from him and spew untruths sent Don's mind into a frenzy. Strangling was too easy a death for the maggot. Balfour spouted lies about how Don had accosted him in the alley, about how he'd seen Don set fire to the warehouse and to his own sea galley so he could collect on fire insurance marks.

Thank God Oliphant paused the litany of lies and turned to the baronet. "Sir Donald, did you take out fire insurance marks for your galley?"

A tic twitched in his jaw. "No, sir, I did not."

The advocate stroked his chin and returned his attention to the lieutenant. "Why would the Baronet of Sleat set fire to his property when he had no insurance marks placed against it?"

"You'd have to ask him, sir," said the lackwit.

Then MacLeod gave a similar response when questioned about the trail of blood on the floor leading down the servant's stairwell. "How on earth would I know how blood ended up in the baronet's servant's stairwell?"

The advocate sniffed. "But you alleged he stabbed you in the arm."

"In the close behind the stables," MacLeod lied.

"Hmm." Oliphant tapped his fingers together. "And why were you lurking behind the baronet's stables?"

"I was trying to gain an audience with Mary of Castleton."

"And what is your relationship with Miss Mary?"

"I…" He turned red as an apple.

"Haven't you, in fact, pursued the lady without her consent?"

"No, I have not."

"I have her testimony which purports the contrary." Mr. Oliphant handed a sheet of parchment to the magistrate, then turned for all the court to hear and relayed Mary's statement, as it was recorded and witnessed by the court clerk.

Oliphant then focused on MacLeod. "You, in fact, did take Miss Mary from her home in Castleton without her consent and with intent to force her into marriage, again without the lady's consent."

"I—"

The advocate held up his finger. "Do not deny the truth in this court, sir. You are infatuated with Mary of Castleton and abducted her from her home on the eighteenth of June, the year of our Lord sixteen ninety-five." He held up a missive. "I have in my hand a missive from Sir Hugh MacIain of Glencoe informing Sir Donald that Colonel Hill of Fort William locked the plaintiff in the stocks for a fortnight in punishment for said abduction. What say you, lieutenant? Were the stocks not enough to dissuade your lustful urges?"

"MacIain lies." Balfour scowled. "I should have dirked him in the Coe when I had the chance"

As the advocate continued, Don's confidence grew while MacLeod's face faded from red to pale.

After the lieutenant, William gave his testimony. Though Balfour had fled before William arrived in Mary's room that night, he had seen the blood, as well as Mary's injury. To Don's surprise, Oliphant called a chimney sweep to the stand who testified he'd sold his all-black costume to MacLeod for a bob the same day as the fire.

"Why did you need a chimney sweep's clothing?" the advocate again pointed to the plaintiff.

"Ah…" MacLeod's eyes shifted across the courtroom while a bead of sweat streaked from his brow. "So I wouldn't be seen whilst I was watching Miss Mary."

Oliphant leaned forward like a hawk on its perch. "So you admit to stalking the Castleton maid?"

"I love her."

Don cracked his knuckles, relishing what it would feel like to have that sniveling swine's neck in his grasp.

Love? The beast is obsessed. He knows nothing of love. And if he ever dares to place a finger on Miss Mary, it will be his last act on this earth.

Next, the advocate made a bold move and called the Duke of Gordon forward. If he won the trial, Don would ensure Oliphant received an additional quarter for his intestinal fortitude.

"Your Grace, can you testify that the Baronet of Sleat was attending a ball at your manse on the eve of the first of August?"

The duke arched an aristocratic eyebrow. "Indeed, I can. In fact, I spoke to Sir Donald only moments before my gala was interrupted with the announcement of the fire on the waterfront."

MacLeod sprang to his feet. "He is a Jacobite and a liar!"

"Sit down, lieutenant," said the magistrate, pounding his gavel. "How dare you speak ill of a peer of the realm? Your accusations are wearing thin and tolerance for your outbursts even thinner. I suggest you apologize to His Grace before he leaves this courtroom."

The lieutenant glowered at Donald as he resumed his seat.

Ignoring the flea-bitten boar, Don offered a subtle nod of thanks to the duke.

The door at the back of the courtroom burst open. "My lord," said a corporal, marching forward. "Forgive my tardiness. We were delayed en route from Fort William by a band of highwaymen who were looking for this." He held up a missive and placed it before the magistrate. "They caught us at a bend, demanding we hand over the mail. Fortunately, we were able to overpower the varlets."

Rumbles escalated from the crowd.

"Silence." The magistrate rapped his gavel. "I hope you brought the outlaws in. It will be my pleasure to oversee their trial."

"Aye, the survivors are in manacles and my sentinel is escorting them to a cell as we speak." The corporal pointed to the missive. "They admitted to being in Lieutenant MacLeod's regiment, m'lord."

"Good work, soldier," the magistrate said, glaring at MacLeod whilst he reached for the missive.

Don held his breath, watching the man ran his thumb under the red wax seal and read the contents.

"Mr. Oliphant." The justice placed the missive on the bar. "This corroborates MacIain's letter stating the lieutenant received punishment for kidnapping Miss Mary of Castleton. And combined with the evidence you have presented, I have no reason to believe any of Mr. MacLeod's testimony to be truthful."

Balfour's chair clattered over as he sprinted for the door.

"Seize him!" bellowed the magistrate. He hammered his gavel on the board. "This trial has been a sham. Sir Donald, you are free to go on one condition."

"What is that, sir?"

"You promise to avoid any and all activities organized by Jacobite supporters."

"Very well," he said, making eye contact with the Duke of Gordon and being very careful not to pledge an oath.

With one last thwack of his gavel, the magistrate pardoned him. The bailiff removed Don's manacles and in turn, slapped them on Balfour. Guards then ushered the lieutenant to the Tolbooth as he shouted curses about all Highlanders being Jacobites.

The Duke of Gordon shook Don's hand. "Isn't MacLeod a bloody Highlander?"

"Aye, he is."

"Well then, he must be one of the Jacobites of whom he is so vehemently shouting about."

"Indeed, he must."

Mr. Smith hastened toward them. "Sir Donald, congratulations on proving your innocence." He bowed deeply. "I am in grave need of your services. How soon can you have packing salt aboard my ship?"

William stepped beside them. "This very day." He grinned at Don. "Sir Coll and Sir Kennan arrived with a new shipment last eve."

"You never fail me, brother." Don clapped his brother on the back. "I'll enjoy sharing a tot you all."

William shook his head. "Unfortunately, they've gone. Sir Coll received word of a MacIntosh raid on his lands at Glen Spean."

"Dear God. Will we ever have peace?"

"I fear there are many battles left to fight before we see it." The duke cleared his throat. "This morn I dispatched my regiment to provide assistance to Coll of Keppoch. The young chieftain has always been a loyal ally to the Gordons."

Don bowed his head. "My thanks. I shall send troops at once."

"Only if this skirmish is not quickly resolved." The duke nudged Don with his elbow. "You are doing us a great service here in Glasgow."

"Aye, but I owe Sir Coll a debt of gratitude—Sir Kennan as well."

"I'm certain there will be many opportunities to express it. I'm leaving for Huntly on the morrow. I do hope to see you at the gathering next spring."

"You will. I wouldn't miss such an assembly of fine Highlanders for the world."

***

The voyage home took forever as Mary's father anchored the galley at every allied seaside castle along the way, introducing Mary as his eldest daughter for whom he was seeking a husband. She could have murdered him.

Finally walking through Dunscaith Castle's sea gate, Mary felt as hollow as a soap bubble.

"Welcome home, Miss Mary," piped Narin, holding the gate open. "We've missed you ever so much."

Gulping back her melancholy, Mary grasped his hands in greeting and smiled. "'Tis always good to see your face." She meant it, too. Seeing Narin reminded her of how comfortable and familiar home could be. And when she strode through the archway, it seemed the entire clan had gathered to welcome her with Rabbie, Florence and Lilas waving at the top of the path.

Regardless of her woes, it warmed Mary's insides to see so many happy faces. Dashing ahead, she opened her arms and welcomed her siblings into her embrace. "I have missed you three." She didn't realize how much until wrapped in a family hug.

"You simply must tell us everything," said Florence.

"Did you shoot any redcoats?" asked Rabbie.

"I want to hear about the Baronet of Sleat. Word came he rescued you from that vile lieutenant." Lilas drew the back of her hand to her forehead and feigned a swoon. "How utterly romantic."

"Aye," agreed Florence. "And the baronet is such a braw Highlander."

The two lasses looped their elbows through Mary's and led her into the keep with Rabbie trailing behind.

Once inside the keep, Mrs. Watt stood wringing her hands. "Welcome home, Miss Mary." The words came out as if sweetened with honey, but the woman's eyes regarded Mary like those of a moray eel.

Mary curtseyed. "Thank you." Then she hastened to the stairwell with her sisters.

"Mrs. Watt has been playing at being lady of the keep in your absence," whispered Lilas.

"Wheesht." Mary glanced over her shoulder before ducking into the stairwell. "Wait until we're above stairs."

"Da really cares for her," Florence whispered.

"Eew, you're disgusting." Lilas pushed ahead.

Florence gave her sister a shove. "But she's trying to be friendly."

"Aye...too friendly if you ask me."

The lasses giggled all the way up to the fourth floor landing—Rabbie evidently had been distracted because he hadn't followed. Just as well. Florence and Lilas proved enough to make Mary's head spin. Together they sat in front of Mary's hearth and yammered about everything that had happened in the past few months.

Of course, they insisted Mary relay the details of her adventure, which she did, leaving out all the romantic parts about Sir Donald. If father caught wind that the baronet had taken certain liberties, who knew what he'd do? Goodness, on the voyage to Skye when he wasn't talking about finding her a husband, he'd threatened to confront Sir Donald and demand to know if anything untoward had occurred…and if it had, he would demand to negotiate terms for a betrothal.

Deep down Mary prayed a demand wouldn't be necessary, but that a betrothal would, indeed, be negotiated. Though she dared not hope for herself. She focused all hope on Mr. Oliphant proving Sir Donald's innocence.

But still, the further they sailed away from Glasgow, Da's ramblings had Mary's insides twisted so tight she wanted to scream. How could her father ramble on about Sir Donald when he was being held in the Tolbooth for crimes for which he'd been falsely accused? All Da seemed to care about was Mary's virtue and reputation, and her waning prospects for a formidable marriage.

Lord, she was only one and twenty.

She couldn't bring herself to tell Da that Sir Donald had asked her to marry him. Not now. Not with his very life in peril. What if the baronet decided to renege? Goodness, such an admission on her part could start a feud between their clans.

Listening to Lilas and Florence prattle about their petty problems and ask her endless questions about the baronet only served to increase Mary's unease.

"You attended a ball?" Lilas asked, her eyes round as shillings.

Smoothing her skirts, Mary tried to feign excitement. "Aye. 'Twas nearly the most fantastical part of my adventure."

Florence fanned her face with her hands—as if she'd taken lessons on being flippant from Lilas. "I want every detail."

"Very well, but then that will be all. It took sennights to sail home and I'm ever so tired."

They eagerly agreed and Mary told them about Barbara and her exquisite gowns and fan language. Then she was careful to stress how much dancing she did with Sir Kennan so no one would suspect the depth of her affection for Sir Donald—Don—the man who could take her to the moon and send her back floating on the air like a feather.

Her voice was dry and sore by the time she'd finished, but after, Florence and Lilas left her alone as she'd asked. Rubbing her outer arms, the hollow feeling in her chest returned. While she'd sailed north, Mary's thoughts of how she could be reunited with Don consumed her mind. If only they could have stayed for the trial.

And there he sat, alone and suffering in that blasted Tolbooth.

Of course, it was completely improper for her to write to him, but she could pen a letter to Barbara.

Mary fetched her quill, ink well and a slip of parchment.

9th September, the year of our Lord 1695

Dear Miss Barbara,

I must apologize for leaving Glasgow so abruptly. It was quite a surprise to see my father. He hadn't traveled since the wars.

I must also enquire as to Sir Donald's hearing. Please do send word about the outcome as soon as possible. It would have been best if I'd been on hand to give my testament to the baronet's innocence. I only pray that justice will prevail. I, indeed, need to thank him and you for your kind hospitality, if you could please convey my sincere gratitude.

Though it is good to be home at Dunscaith Castle among my brother and sisters, I do miss you terribly. And how are you faring? Have Sir Coll and Sir Kennan returned with the new shipment?

Of course, I cannot forget how much you wanted to visit Castleton. Please know you are always welcome. I do hope you and

*your brothers can pay us a visit before winter sets in. Wouldn't it be
a boon for our families to spend Yule together?*

Do write soon.

Your dear friend,

Mary of Castleton

She sanded the parchment and re-read it to ensure she
hadn't made any unladylike mistakes. Holding a red wax
wafer to the candle, she sealed it closed with her brass seal
bearing the family crest. She'd been very careful not to
mention anything to indicate she and Donald had been
lovers. A missive could always fall into unwanted hands
and be read and resealed. Hopefully she'd shown enough
concern without being blatantly obvious that she was
desperately in love with Sir Donald MacDonald of Sleat.

Chapter Thirty-Two

One of the best things about returning home was that Mary could resume her daily routine. She'd missed her early morning meetings in the kitchens with Raymond. Today she awoke before sunrise like she always did, as if she'd never been gone.

Now late September, she was anxious to meet with the cook about the harvest and found him stirring the fire beneath the enormous iron pot suspended from a chain secured to the top of the hearth.

"Starting the oats to boil?" she asked.

"Mary," the old cook said with a big grin. "I was hoping you'd pay a visit this morn."

She gave him a squeeze. "And why wouldn't I?"

"Och, things haven't been much the same since you left."

"No?" She playfully batted her eyelashes. "Did you miss me, then?"

"Bloody oath I did." He glanced over his shoulder as if he thought someone might be listening. "Will you be resuming your duties in the kitchen?"

"I do not see why not." Mary stepped closer and lowered her voice. "What's happened whilst I've been away?"

The old cook shuddered. "Your da sent Mrs. Watt to oversee. I've been running this kitchen for thirty years. I worked for your grandmother and then your mother, and then you, and never had a problem."

Mary's back tensed. Why hadn't Da assigned Lilas to oversee the kitchen? Raymond had never needed much overseeing. Mary discussed the menu and the stores with him each morning, and then he was free to manage the meal preparation, and was quite efficient at it. She patted the cook's shoulder. "I daresay, with you at the helm, running the kitchens is one of the easiest, not to mention, most pleasurable tasks in this castle."

He grumbled under his breath. "Tell that to Mrs. Watt."

"For heaven's sakes, has she been unkind?"

"Overbearing is a better word—and she doesn't consult with me like a proper lady of the keep would do. She just makes decisions and when I tell her we don't have the stores for her menu, she'll hear none of it."

"My heavens." Mary drew her hand to her chest. She knew better than to speak ill of Mrs. Watt in front of the servant, but that didn't prevent her from digging deeper. "How have you been managing?"

"So far, I've scrambled to pull things together and meet her wishes." He shook his head. "We had to butcher two sheep whilst a side of beef hangs in the cellar. Dear me, I'm afeard it will go putrid if we don't eat it soon."

She gave his shoulder a pat. "Put it on the menu for the evening meal."

He shrank with a pinched brow. "Are you certain?"

"Do as I say." Mary inclined her head toward the passageway to the cellar. "And what about the harvest? Have the crofters brought in enough barrels of oats and barley?"

"I haven't had enough time to look. We've received a few deliveries, but 'tis a mess down there." Raymond leaned forward. "That is why I'm anxious to have you back, my dear."

"Miss Mary," Mrs. Watt said from the doorway. "I'm surprised to see you here this morn."

Whipping around, Mary grasped her hands behind her back while her heartbeat sped. Why on earth did she feel like she'd been caught stealing an apple tart? This was her home, for goodness sakes. She'd been the lady of the keep for nine years. Squaring her shoulders, she stood a bit straighter. "Why wouldn't I resume my duties now that I've returned?"

Mrs. Watt sauntered inside, giving Raymond the evil eye. "Didn't your father tell you? I'm in charge of the kitchens now."

Raymond busied himself by scooping a bucket of oats from the barrel and adding it to the pot.

Mary crossed her arms. "I thought you were taking over Da's care."

"Aye." The woman nodded, mirroring Mary's stance yet adding pursed lips that made her face look like a prune. "That, too. Your father has entrusted a great many tasks to me, bless him."

"And why on earth didn't he task my sisters with more responsibility? Heaven kens they need such experience."

Mrs. Watt pulled an apron from a peg on the wall and draped it over her head. Obviously, she planned to stay. "Perhaps you should to ask him." She folded her hands and pursed her lips. "I'm only doing his bidding. It wasn't easy for your father when you were away, but he realized his daughters will soon be wed and he needed to find a replacement."

Mary couldn't help but conjure a picture of the day she found them in Da's bed. Never in her life would she be able to think of that moment without shuddering. She paced in a circle around the usurper. "Pray tell, has my father made you an offer of marriage?"

The woman reached back and tied her apron strings. "Not as of yet, but I fail to see where that comes into it. The laird can appoint anyone he sees fit to his service and he has appointed me. The cook and I have things in hand. Might I suggest you tend to your embroidery?"

Mary hated embroidery. Da knew she hated embroidery. Everyone in the castle knew it as well—Mrs. Watt probably did, too. "I think not. I was just discussing the need to set the winter stores in order with Raymond."

"Aye," the cook said from his place at the fire. "Miss Mary always ensures we have enough put up come winter."

Mrs. Watt placed her hand on Mary's shoulder and ushered her toward the doorway. "Well, mayhap she has taken care of such things in years past, but I am here now. I will do it."

"But Raymond tells me the cellar is already in disarray." Sliding out from under the woman's heavy hand, Mary wasn't about to allow this pushy wench to buffalo her way onto her turf. She jammed her fists into her hips. "Tell me, how many barrels of oats do we need for the season? And how many meals can we expect a barrel to yield?"

"Ah," Mrs. Watt shot a panicked look to Raymond, who intently focused on stirring the oats.

Mary drummed her fingers against her chin. "What about barley? What about wheat and rye? Are the hens laying? Have we smoked enough meat? Have the apples been stowed in the cellar? What about cider?"

"Stop this. You are carrying on to make me look incompetent in the presence of the cook. I'll tell you right now, I raised six bairns and I shall manage just fine with Raymond's help."

Unconvinced, Mary strode toward the hearth. "How many mouths do we feed in this castle each meal, Raymond?"

"Sixty-six, last count."

"Six to sixty-six?" Mary arched her eyebrows at the widow. She might be overreacting, but goodness, she wouldn't allow her father to push her out the door. "Not quite the same is it?"

"Your da thinks I have done very well since you left." The woman's voice cracked.

I doubt my father has been out of his bedchamber now he has the enjoyment of the matron's company. "Can you read?"

"I fail to see where that matters." Mrs. Watt again made a sweeping gesture to the doorway. "Please, Miss Mary, go about your affairs and leave the running of the keep to me."

"So now you're overseeing everything?" Mary stamped her foot. "I beg your pardon, but *I* have always been the lady of the castle."

The woman thrust out her enormous bosoms as if she were the queen of blessed Scotland. "Well, no longer. I have assumed all your former tasks. Go on and ask your father."

Mary's fingers flexed. This old matron was insufferable, and worse, she had the wool pulled over Da's eyes. Never in her life had Mary wanted to show someone their place as she did right now. Her eyes narrowed and her lips thinned. "Would you care to venture up to the wall-walk for a shooting contest? I'm certain with all your newfound skills you would be an ace.

How about the first to drop four pigeons wins the right to be lady of *this* keep?" she spat with an acerbic edge.

The woman snorted. "I have never been met with such disrespect in my life."

"I find that hard to believe," Mary scoffed. She might have crossed the line, but she wouldn't be brushed aside without a fight.

"Of course I would never partake in such vulgar behavior. I ought to tell your father—"

Mary marched for the door. "Don't bother."

Of all the maddening confrontations she'd had, this one had to take the cake. Why did her father not tell her Mrs. Watt had been granted so much responsibility? Did he want her off his hands that badly?

True, he had an alliance to make with Mary's hand, but why did he have to be so overbearing about it? Were their coffers that thin? Why didn't he just ask for help rather than push her away like this?

And why in God's name hadn't she heard anything from Glasgow?

Dear Lord, Da will have me married off afore Donald's hearing.

***

The wind blew so hard, it whistled through the castle walls when Mary knocked on her father's solar door. After her confrontation with Mrs. Watt, she'd avoided him up until now.

"Come," Da's voice resounded from within like it had hundreds of times throughout her life at Dunscaith. Though, in the fortnight since her return, everything seemed different. The clansmen and women had carried on with their lives without her. Rabbie had grown taller, Florence and Lilas had become closer. The servants acted with more independence. Da no longer required her assistance with his massages. And no matter how she tried, the one person Mary hadn't been able to avoid at every turn was Mrs. Watt.

It seemed the widow wanted her gone more than Da.

She stepped inside, heading for the chair at her father's left—where she always sat when they discussed the running of the keep. "You asked to see me?"

"I did."

Mary's skin prickled while Da waited for her to sit. She'd always had an agreeable relationship with her father. But since he'd come to Glasgow and practically accused her of humiliating the family, she'd been guarded. So had he. And for some reason, every time he looked at her, she sensed the man judging her.

Had all the years she'd managed his care and his keep meant nothing?

Once seated, Mary looked to the ceiling and steeled her nerves.

Da crossed his arms. "Mrs. Watt has indicated you haven't been treating her respectfully."

So now the old battle-ax was spewing false accusations to her father? She had no doubt she'd been summoned because of her altercations with the widow, but having her father instantly side with the woman stuck in her craw. Besides, at least Mary hadn't strangled the woman…yet.

Affronted, Mary gaped. "I beg your pardon? I have done nothing but swallow my pride and endure the widow while she has supplanted me in nearly every endeavor."

"Aye? She told me you threatened her with a musket."

"Threatened? I challenged her to a shooting contest."

"Och, Mary. I rue the day your mother left us. What is to be done with you, challenging ladies with your musket? Bloody oath, you act as though you are a child."

"So you called me to your solar to issue a reprimand? Do you have any idea what Mrs. Watt is doing in the kitchens?"

"Aye, I've been told you tried to evict her from the kitchens as well."

"I wouldn't call it an eviction, but I will admit to flexing my muscles there." Since her altercation with the woman, Mary had been secretly meeting with Raymond to ensure the winter stores would be in order. "And why should I not? I have been in charge of the menu since the age of twelve. If she chose to step in and help during my absence, fine, but now I have returned, I expect to resume those duties previously assigned to me."

Da dragged his fingers through his hair. "Mrs. Watt has come to mean a great deal to me."

Mary pursed her lips, narrowed her gaze and looked him in the eye. She would not be made out to be the shrew, not even by her father. "I assure you it hasn't escaped my observation that she has become your *leman*."

"Pardon me?" He glared, sitting erect. "Such a statement is unduly insolent. You had best apologize, or I will have no recourse but to confine you to your chamber for an entire month."

"Forgive me. I'm still trying to come to grips with being dragged away from Glasgow when mine was the only testimony sure to prove Sir Donald's innocence. His fate could very well rest in my hands and if he is convicted, I will never forgive myself *or you!*" She pushed back her chair and stood. "Of course, I wouldn't expect you to understand. You want to confine me to quarters so things will revert to the way they were when I was away and out of your hair—so Mrs. Watt can run the keep without my meddling. Is that it?"

Da pounded his fist on the table. "Blast it Mary, you have become too overbearing."

"Become?" Clenching her fists, she turned and faced the wall. All of a sudden, she was too overbearing? She had to bite her tongue not to accuse the woman who warmed Da's bed of being the person who put that notion in his head.

"Sit down," Da said with an edge to his voice.

Biting back her groan, Mary faced him with crossed arms, but she didn't sit.

"I ken it must be difficult to have another woman step in, but I had a decision to make." His face softened while he opened his palms. "You will not be here forever and I need a companion with whom I can live out my days. Ye ken I love you and the lassies, but 'twas time for me to make a change, and as lord of this castle, I made the best decision available to me."

"But you're not—"

"Hear me." Da sliced a hand through the air. "As you are aware, I have decided 'tis time to select your suitor." He fingered a piece of parchment.

Her knees wobbled. Not at a time like this—and not when her own questions hadn't been answered. "Have you received word regarding the outcome of the trial?"

"Dear God, did you not hear me? Of course there has been no word from Glasgow, nor do I expect to hear from the baronet until he has cleared his name and is once again in charge of *the cause*. And that could take a very long time, indeed." Da thrust his finger at the chair. "Now sit."

Her skin hotter than hands held to a fire, Mary could no longer stand if she'd wanted to. Her back stiff as a board, she eased into the chair. "Please tell me you haven't gone off and promised my hand."

"If only it were that easy." Moving the slip of parchment in front of her, Da pointed. "I drew up a list of possible suitors from the gathering and our wee jaunt

up the coast—I've had words with each and every man on
this list and nary a one has been betrothed."

Mary's stomach churned with sickly bile.

"Och, *mo peata*." Da said with a gentle tone. "A
chieftain's eldest daughter must marry into her rank or
above, and an alliance with any one of these clans will
help our wool trade. Now tell me, who on that list should
I write first?"

Mary scanned the names, tears clouding her eyes. Of
course, Da had scratched a line through Sir Donald
MacDonald's name. "Why are you so anxious to be rid of
me?"

"Ye ken I would keep you here forever, but that
wouldn't be fair to you. Mayhap one day you'll
understand." Da leaned back and wrapped his fingers
around his armrests. "'Tis time for you to become a wife
and a mother, and my duty is to see to it you make a good
match—one that is respectable and increases our
influence."

She swiped a hand across her face. "And now you
think my reputation could be ruined because of Sir
Donald's incarceration?"

"Do not read more into this than what is plainly
before your eyes, lass. If things grow worse for the
baronet and word spreads through the Highlands you
were staying under his roof whilst he committed arson—"

"He did not commit arson."

Leaning forward, a fire blazed behind Da's eyes,
telling her to stop trifling. "Mayhap he did not. Many a
man has been sent to the gallows for crimes for which he
was innocent."

Mary's stomach convulsed. How could Da utter such
abominations? She picked up the parchment with a
trembling hand. Never in her life would she choose one
of the lairds on the list when her heart was already given.

A knock sounded at the door.

"I'm not to be disturbed," Da bellowed.

"A galley has sailed onto our beach, m'laird," Fyfe's voice resounded through the timbers.

"Bloody hell. Come in." Da pushed back his wheeled chair as Mary stood. "What standard are they flying?"

"Only the flag of Scotland, m'laird."

Mary's heart jolted as she snapped a hand to her chest. *Has word arrived?*

Wheeling up beside her, Da grabbed her wrist and squeezed. "Go to your chamber and remain there until I've sent for you."

"But I must greet—"

"Do as I say," Da slapped her backside as if she were a child. "Fyfe, bring the master to me and post a guard outside Miss Mary's door."

Mary stopped mid-stride. "That will not be necessary."

"Must you argue with my every word?" Da inclined his head toward the parchment. "Take the list with you, my dear. I want a name by the evening meal."

Chapter Thirty-Three

Don followed the Castleton guard up the stairwell to the chieftain's solar. Though a dreary day, he'd hoped for a jovial welcome. Upon his arrival there were no children practicing shooting, no spirited lass wearing trews, no tents and definitely no air of excitement.

And from the guard's cool welcome, he realized Miss Mary wouldn't be running to the galley to greet him with open arms. He should have known John of Castleton would require an audience first. Ascending the stairs, Don rifled through the things he needed to say to Mary's father. He only wished he knew what the chieftain thought of him. By Mr. Kerr's report, Don feared he appraised poorly in the chieftain's eyes, even if he was a baronet.

I swear on my father's grave I will not fail.

The guard opened the door. "Sir Donald MacDonald of Sleat, m'laird."

"Well, don't just stand in the passageway. Come in."

Don squared his shoulders and marched forward then executed a respectful bow—one far deeper than owed to a lesser chief. "Sir John. It is ever so good to see you."

"And it is ever so surprising to see you, sir." The man gestured to a chair. "Sit. I prefer to look a man in the eye."

Doing as asked, Don folded his hands atop the table. "I came as quickly as time would allow."

The lines on the old man's face etched deeper with his frown. "You must have, because the last I heard, you were imprisoned in Glasgow's Tolbooth."

"Accused of crimes I did not commit, sir. Fortunately the culprit is now behind bars."

"That would be Lieutenant Balfour MacLeod?"

"The same." Don shifted in his seat. "He's been stripped of his rank and I wouldn't be surprised if the magistrate sends him to the gallows—especially for arson. Many a merchant lost his livelihood in that fire."

"He was never well liked in these parts. I'll attest to that. 'Tis a relief to see he's received his comeuppance." Sir John stroked his fingers down his greying red beard. "And you? How are your coffers faring?"

"I did lose an entire shipment of packing salt and another of wool, but my galley has been repaired, and my men in Trotternish have supplied a ship bound for the Americas with ample packing salt."

"You're back in favor with the American merchant?" John asked, his tone becoming more respectful.

Don explained how he intended to introduce the clan chieftains to Mr. Smith and encourage him to purchase goods from Scotland. All the while, Mary's father sat eyeing him with an arch to his brow. "The Duke of Gordon is also arranging for American ships to sail to Aberdeen."

"The duke?"

"Aye. Were you not aware? His Grace has resumed his support of *the cause*."

"That is good news. And why am I just hearing of it now?"

"Because I have arrived faster than the mail carrier, sir." Don leaned forward. "Evidently the duke has sworn off women for life."

"You do not say?"

"I heard it from his very mouth. And the spring gathering will be at Huntly."

"Perhaps things are looking up for *the cause*."

"I believe so."

Sir John leaned forward and looked him in the eye. "But that isn't why you've come to Castleton, is it?"

Don made no outward indication of his jitters. Finally, the conversation had moved on to his reason for being there. He glanced over his shoulder as if he expected Miss Mary to burst through the door. Where was she? Why hadn't she even been atop the wall-walk and waved? He clenched his fists. Mr. Kerr had said Sir John had appeared angry when he'd come to Glasgow. If he'd unleashed his ire on Mary, the chieftain would have more than an amputated leg to worry about.

"No," Don answered. "I've come to discuss your daughter."

"I kent it." The chieftain rapped his knuckles on the table, snarling like he was about to commit murder. "You have debauched her. Dear God, I'll never be able to make a match with her hand."

"What the devil are you talking about?" Gulping, Don maintained his poise. Did Sir John force Mary to tell him about their interludes? But if she had, wouldn't Sir John be more condemning?

Is he fishing? Best get on with it.

"Sir, I must inform you that I only have the most honorable of intentions where Miss Mary is concerned."

"Honorable is it now?" Sir John boomed, his cringe growing more menacing. "Do you now think such a bold statement allays the fact that you, a bachelor, allowed a highborn, unmarried woman to reside under your roof for two months?"

"But my sister—"

The man slammed his fist onto the table. "I care not that your sister posed to cover up what could have been a humiliating scandal." He jutted out his chin, his face red as the coals in the hearth. "Do you have any idea how your actions could have tarnished my daughter's reputation?"

Thrusting himself to his feet, Don's chair toppled over behind him. "Sir. I assure you I acted with the utmost decorum." Don's gut twisted. Where Mary was concerned, he might have lost control a time or two, but he fully intended to make amends for his actions. "That aside, I've come to you this day to ask for Miss Mary's hand—not because you are backing me into a corner, conniving any manner of drivel to pin me into a suit of marriage, but because your daughter has won my heart. She is delightful and charming, and she brought a light into my life which I have never before experienced."

Sir John blinked, a confounded look spread across his face as if Don had taken him by surprise.

The air grew heavy while they both froze; a duel of unspoken emotion. Don gulped. "Damn it man, say something." Sir John may be Miss Mary's father, but by God, Don was his superior clan chief, and was due a fair bit more respect than he'd received since entering this blasted solar.

"I…you…ah?" John raked his fingers through his hair, a grin wider than the Firth of Forth stretched across his lips. "Och, Sir Donald, why didn't you state the true reason for your visit when you walked through the door?"

"You ken as well as I it wouldn't have been proper for me to do so."

"Aye? Well it would have saved this old man from a fair bit of worry. Fetch us some whisky." He motioned to the sideboard. "You say you've been cleared of all charges?"

Don was all too willing to pull the stopper off the flask and pour two tots—he even helped himself to a healthy swig and poured again. "I have, and the Duke of Gordon testified in my defense."

"His Grace *testified*?" Sir John asked. "My, that is impressive."

Don placed a glass in front of the gentleman, then resumed his seat. "I'm glad the whole pretense is over."

The man turned the glass between his fingers. "So, you've come to ask for Miss Mary's hand?" He sipped. "You are aware she means a great deal to this household."

Don expected there to be a negotiation. "And it goes without saying she will become Lady Mary, the Baronetess of Sleat."

Sipping his whisky, Sir John droned on and on, posturing to ferret out all he could from the arrangement. Don tolerated the negotiation with a lightness to his heart. On one side, he wanted to see Mary, pull her into his arms and shower her with kisses, but formalities had to come first, and he would be no Chieftain of Clan Donald if he sat back and allowed John of Castleton to swindle him out of more than his due.

After hours of negotiations and several tots of whisky, Sir John finally held out his hand. "Then we have an agreement."

Don shook it firmly. "Aye, if Miss Mary will have me."

***

Mary dabbed her eyes when, for the second time that day, Fyfe announced she was required in her father's solar. She hopped to her feet. "Is there news of the baronet?"

The guard's mouth twisted. "I'm not at liberty to say."

Mary eyed him. "There simply *must* be important news. Did the galley bring news?"

With a flick of his fingers, Fyfe beckoned her. "Come Miss Mary, I've been sworn to silence."

She picked up the parchment of names and shook it. "Da gave me until the evening meal."

Fyfe shrugged. "Perhaps he has something to say that will raise your spirits. Goodness, you've been melancholy since your return."

Dropping the paper, Mary moved to the wash basin and blotted her eyes. "You'd be upset if your life was ruined by an unfeeling ogre."

"Mm hmm," Fyfe said, again motioning for her to come.

She tossed the cloth beside the bowl and followed behind the guard, all the while praying good news had come about Sir Donald.

A hundred warring thoughts ratcheted up her fears. Why hadn't Da allowed her to stay and hear the news? And why had she been locked in her chamber for hours? Was she to be treated as a prisoner now she'd returned and Mrs. Watt had won so much favor with her father?

Her skin perspired uncomfortably. Mary had learned about the desires of the flesh—had become wizened to the impulses of passion. She closed her eyes tightly and shook her head. How dare she rationalize Da's relationship with Mrs. Watt? What kind of morals did his behavior impart to Lilas, Florence and, especially, Rabbie? At least Mary had been discrete—no one knew about her indiscretion and she intended to keep it that way…especially now her menses had shown.

Besides, she had far worse things to manage at the moment, the first being that abominable list. Holy Moses, she prayed Miss Barbara had already written with good news.

Fyfe opened the door. "Miss Mary of Castleton."

Still in the passageway, she gave him a questioning look. Fyfe never formally announced her to her father. "Really, Fyfe, I—" Her mouth dropped. Her heart thrummed. Her palms perspired and tingles of pure elation fired across her skin. She immediately dipped into a curtsey. "S-sir Donald?" This was no time for her mouth to go dry. She gulped, willing a wee bit of moisture to her arid tongue. "I-ah-you're…here?"

"I am." He grinned like it was the first day of spring. "Your testimony combined with that of the Duke of Gordon was enough to have the charges against me thrown out." He opened his arms.

From his chair Da cleared his throat.

Adjusting his posture, Don stepped forward, grasped Mary's hand and plied it with a proper kiss, careful not to linger too long. Mary's gaze darted to her father. He watched Sir Donald with the intensity of a peregrine falcon.

Mary cradled her kissed hand to her stomach, hoping not to wipe away the tingling sensation of Don's lips. Dear Lord, she may never wash the back of her hand again. "Have you come to Skye to replenish your supply of packing salt?"

"Ah…" A distinct flush filled the baronet's cheeks as he looked to Da. "I—um."

Da rolled his hand through the air. "Well, have out with it."

Sir Donald's Adam's apple bobbed. "Here, sir?"

Spreading his arms wide, Da looked from wall to wall. "Why ever not here?"

"Och." Don gave Mary an uncomfortable grimace. "Would you mind if we went for a stroll atop the wall-walk?"

Da eyed him again—goodness, what on earth was going on?

"If Fyfe chaperones us?" the baronet asked—sounding a wee bit obsequious, which wasn't like him in the least.

"What is this about?" Mary wrung her hands. Had Sir Donald come to apologize? To make amends and walk out of her life forever?

"Come," Sir Donald grasped her arm rather firmly and gave the poor guard a sharp glare. "We shan't be long and I do not need an armed escort." He shoved past, pulling Mary in his wake.

"Are you angry with me?" she asked in a sharp whisper.

"Not at all." He said not another word while they continued up the stairwell—three flights until they stepped out into a brisk wind.

They moved to her favorite vantage point—the one that overlooked the bay. Gannets called overhead, fishing for their midday meal.

Clutching her arms around her ribs, Mary chanced a look at Don. He'd been acting ever so peculiar. "I must apologize for leaving Glasgow so abruptly."

He brushed her cheek with coarse fingertips, a warm smile spreading across his face. "Och, lass, you had no recourse but to go with your father. I was remiss not to send you home sooner."

A lump the size of a cannonball sank to the pit of her stomach. He hadn't wanted her there all along. Their mutual attraction had always meant more to Mary than it had to Don. All manner of his plans must have altered during his incarceration. Curses, why did her eyes have to tear up? She blinked and looked out to sea. "I love to come up here ever so much. Please do not make this a memory that will crush my heart."

His lips thinned as if he might be suppressing a smile. "Forgive me. I truly hope what I have to say will be received with much happiness."

Her eyebrows drew together in question. "Sir?"

Taking her hand between his warm palms, the Baronet of Sleat lowered to his knee. Then his midnight blue eyes caught a ray of sunshine peeking through the dense clouds. They sparkled like magic. "Miss Mary, I have not always been the most well-mannered man when in your company and for that, I ask your forgiveness. Please ken that I intend to make up my shortcomings for the rest of my life." He released one of his hands and slipped it inside his sporran. "Ah—I have loved you since the moment we met and I realized you were the most beautiful, most wily woman in all of Scotland. My love for you grew every day we were together and the only thing that kept me sane while I sat in the Tolbooth was the memory of your smiling face with its adorable freckles, your scent, your red tresses that pick up the breeze and flicker like fire as they are doing now. And I love, I love, I love you from the depths of my heart."

Tears streamed from both Mary's eyes, her lips trembled, her throat constricted with so much happiness, she couldn't utter a sound.

He held up a ring set with a brilliant ruby. "Mary of Castleton, will you do me the honor of being my wife?"

Drawing a hand over her mouth, she didn't trust herself to speak. But she nodded in rapid succession while blinking her tears of happiness at bay.

"Will you?"

"Aye," she managed with a warble holding her hand out. "I will marry you and none other."

He slipped the ring over her finger. "This was my mother's and now it is yours."

Admiring the stone, a tear streaked from her eye. "'Tis beautiful."

After kissing the ring, Don stood and pulled her into an embrace, one filled with love and warmth and hope. "You have made my life complete. I do not ken what I would have done if you'd refused me."

She dabbed her nose as daintily as possible and gazed up at his bonny face. "I do not ken what I would have done if you had rejected me."

He pressed his lips to her forehead and held them there. "Dear God, I swear I will love you until the end of my days."

Epilogue

A year later

Sitting at her new dressing table, Mary ran her finger beneath the red wax seal of a letter from Lilas. She hadn't received a letter from Castleton in some time and her hands trembled a bit, anxious for news. It wasn't that Mary missed the old castle on the southern finger of the Isle of Skye, but she did pine for her family at times.

Don had seen to her comfort beyond her dreams and over the past year, they'd built a life in Glasgow—had even purchased an estate in Renfrewshire to allow for a growing family.

She unfolded the parchment.

Dearest Sister,

I am writing this on my nineteenth Saints day. As I awoke, I thought of all the things that have changed over the years and of all the things that I miss. Life in Castleton has grown ever so dreary without you.

But that will change, too.

You'll be happy to hear Mrs. Watt has mellowed since you left. Perhaps your talks with Da served to bring about the needed effect. She's behaved thoughtfully toward me and Florence, and especially Rabbie. Fortunately, she and Raymond are more amenable as of late, too. Moreover, Da has asked the widow to marry him and they

*plan to wed in midsummer. Has he written you of this news? I
rather doubt it. He has been otherwise occupied and in his solar less
often.*

*I will not be in Castleton for the wedding, as he has arranged
for me to be fostered by Lady Forbes in Aberdeenshire until I attain
the age of one and twenty. I'm looking forward to the change, though
a tad nervous since I haven't had the pleasure of meeting Lady
Forbes. I hear she has a son my age.*

Hmm.

Possibly Da is up to his scheming again?

I suppose time will tell.

*You'll be happy to hear Rabbie has become a true musketeer
and hits the target nearly every shot, and Florence has become quite
proficient at the pianoforte.*

*I do miss you and hope you can visit me at the Forbes estate.
Wouldn't that be a boon?*

Wishing you happiness,

Lilas

Sighing, Mary folded the missive just as Don opened
the door. "Good news?"

She held up the parchment. "A letter from Lilas. She
says she'll be fostered by Lady Forbes and Da plans to
marry Mrs. Watt midsummer."

Don leaned against the door jamb, looking relaxed
and very gallant in his kilt and waistcoat. "That is good
news on both counts."

"Yes, for Lilas." Mary pursed her lips and sighed.

"And your father—he'll be well cared for."

Alas, she had to give in. The widow would make Da
happy and that's what mattered for him. "True, I can
attest to that. Goodness, it seems things never do stay the
same." Mary watched her dashing husband take long
strides into the chamber. "That reminds me. How should
we go about making a match between Miss Barbara and
Sir Coll?"

Donald stopped short. "My sister—"

"Will be one and twenty in a year's time," Mary finished, eyeing him.

"But Sir Coll is too rough around the edges. Though I'd have no other clan chief beside me in battle, I'm afraid he's unsuitable for Barbara." Oh, how adorable he looked when a tad flummoxed.

Mary held up a finger. "Only the heart kens when a match is right."

"But they are so different," Don grumbled. "Barbara is enamored with new gowns and shopping and royal balls."

"Have you asked her what she wants?"

"Nay."

"Perhaps you should start there."

"I'll think on it. Mayhap I'll have a change of heart when she's nearer her twenty-first." Moving behind Mary, Don smoothed his hands over her swollen belly and regarded her in the mirror. "And how are you faring?"

Mary put her hands atop his so they both cradled their unborn. "Better now you're here."

"And our son?"

She giggled. "Or daughter." With her laughter came a hearty kick.

"Oh my." Don's eyes grew wide. "I felt that one, and with a boot as powerful as that, the bairn must be a lad for certain."

Mary leaned her head against Donald's arm and closed her eyes. "I care not, as long as the babe is healthy."

"With a mother as bonny and vigorous as you, I have no doubt our child will be of solid Highland stock." He drew her hand to his lips and kissed it. "I love you, Lady Mary, and I always will."

The End

Author's Note

Thank you for joining me for The Valiant Highlander. Though this is a work of fiction, Mary of Castleton was born and raised on the southernmost finger of the Isle of Skye near Tokavaig. She was the eldest daughter of John MacDonald, 2nd of Castleton, a laird owing fealty to the Baronet of Sleat.

Mary MacDonald of Castleton married Donald MacDonald, 4th Baronet of Sleat, chieftain of one of the largest clans in Scotland and a descendant of the Lords of the Isles. Sir Donald was the last in his line born at Duntulm Castle before the crumbling stronghold in Trotternish was abandoned. The date of Sir Donald and Lady Mary's marriage is not recorded.

The Baronet of Sleat was known by his clan as Sir Donald of the Wars (or in Gaelic, *Dòmhnall á Chogaidh*) for his heroism during the Battle of Killiecrankie, who at the age of nineteen raised the standard on behalf of his ailing father. From birth, Sir Donald was a staunch Jacobite supporter, though he resided in Glasgow all of his adult life.

***

I have many planned more books related to these early Jacobite supporters, though there are some upcoming changes I am excited to announce:

~ In 2017 Grand Central Publishing will release three books under their Forever imprint. The GCP books will be in a new series taking place in the same Jacobite era and you will recognize some of the supporting characters:

~ *The Highland Duke* ~ About the 1st Duke of Gordon and his involvement with the Jacobite cause and his steamy union with Akira Ayres, a Scottish healer, set to be released March, 2017

~ *The Highland Lord's Stolen Kiss* ~ The royal court at Whitehall comes into play with Jacobite spies and Whig plots embroiling Lord Aiden Murray and Lady Magdalen Keith in a tempestuous romance. To be set in 1708 with a release date of June, 2017

~ *The Highland Earl* ~ This is a working title, though the story will be about the Earl of Seaforth and his arranged marriage to Audrey Kennet, a Northumberland heiress. To be released October, 2017

~ *The Reckless Highlander* ~ I know everyone will be happy to know Coll and Barbara's story will be released thereafter.

~ Several more Highland Defender/Highland Lords novels have been planned for characters like Kennan Cameron and Robert Stewart as well as the MacRae Chieftain.

Excerpt from The Highland Duke

Chapter One

Hoord Moor, Scotland. 21ˢᵗ August, the year of our Lord 1703

The dead Highland soldier stared vacantly at the thick, low-hanging clouds. Akira clutched her basket tight to her stomach. This man needed no healing. Now only the minister could offer to redeem the hapless warrior's soul.

Death on the battlefield bore none of the heroics she'd heard from fireside tales. Death on the battlefield was but cold and lonely.

And for naught.

Gulping back her nausea, Akira turned away.

A deep moan came from the forest, the tree line not but ten paces away. She jolted, jostling the remedies in her basket. "Is s-someone there?"

When no answer came, she glanced over her shoulder. Unfortunate. Her companions had moved on—women from the village of Dunkeld had crossed the bridge over the River Tay to Hoord Moor where they tended the wounded before red-coated soldiers marshalled them into the back of a wagon.

The moan came again.

Akira tiptoed into the trees. Two black boots peeked from beneath a clump of broom. A telltale path of blood skimmed over the ground leading beneath the shrub. Had the man dragged himself off the battlefield?

"Are you injured?" she asked, her perspiring palms slipping on the basket's handle. Would he leap up and attack?

"My leg," said a strained burr.

"Goodness gracious," she whispered while she moved closer.

The poor man is hurt.

Dropping to her knees, she pulled away broom branches and debris. A man's vivid hazel eyes stared at her from beneath a layer of dirt. Wild as the Highlands and filled with pain, his gaze penetrated her defenses like attacking daggers. She'd never seen eyes that expressive—intense. They made her so...so *unnerved.*

"What happened?" she asked, ready to run like a rabbit.

He shuttered those eyes with a wince. "Shot."

Akira's gaze darted to his kilt, hitched up and exposing an enormous thigh. A mass of thick blood swathed across it with more congealed beneath.

"You a healer?" he asked, his Adam's apple bobbing.

"Aye," her voice croaked, didn't even sound like her. "It needs to come out."

She peered closer—puckered skin—a round hole. "A musket ball?"

His trembling fingers slid to the puncture wound. "'Tis still there—lodged in my thigh."

Care of musket wounds far exceeded her skill. "I-I'll fetch the physician."

"No," he said with an intense whisper. Before she moved, the man clasped her arm in a powerful grip. The strength of his huge hand hurt. Gasping, she tugged away, but his fingers clamped harder and those eyes grew more determined. "You do it."

She shook her head. "Sir, I cannot."

Releasing her arm, he pulled a knife from his sleeve. "Use my wee dagger." The blade glistened, honed sharp and shiny clean against his mud-encrusted doublet.

"But you could die," She shirked away from the weapon.

"Do it, I say." For a man on the brink of death, he spewed the command like a high-ranking officer.

Licking her lips, she stared at the wound, then pressed her fingers against it.

He hissed.

"Apologies." She snapped her hand away. "I was trying to feel for the musket ball."

"Whisky."

She glanced to her basket. "I've only herbs and tinctures."

"In my sporran."

The leather pouch rested askew, held in place by a belt around his hips. Merciful mercy, it covered his unmentionables. Moreover, he was armed like an outlaw with a dirk sheathed in one side of his belt, a flintlock pistol in the other—a gargantuan sword slung in its scabbard beside him. Who knew what other deadly weapons the imposing Highlander hid on his person?

Akira clenched her fists then reluctantly then pointed to the purse. "In there?"

"A wee flask, aye." His shaking fingers fumbled with the thong that cinched the sporran closed.

She licked her lips. "You expect me to reach inside?" Goodness, her voice sounded shrill.

"Och," he groaned, his hands dropping. "Give a wounded du—ah—scrapper a bit o' help, would you now?"

Akira scraped her teeth over her bottom lip. Merciful fairies, the Highlander did need something to ease his pain. Praying she wouldn't be seen and accused of stealing, she cringed, shoved inside the hideous thing and wrapped her fingers around a flask. She blinked twice as she pulled it out and held it up. *Silver?* Gracious, the flask alone could pay for Akira and her family to eat for a year or more.

She pulled the stopper and he raised his head, running his tongue across chapped lips. "Give me a good tot, lass."

He drank a healthy swig and coughed. "I'm ready," he said, his jaw muscles flexing as he bared his teeth—straight, white, contrasting with the dark stubble and dirt on his face. Lord in heaven, such a man could pass for the devil.

Remembering her gruesome task, Akira cringed. The faster she worked, the less he'd suffer. With a feather-light touch, she swirled her fingers over the puncture and located the hard lump not far beneath the skin. Thank heavens the musket ball had stopped in his flesh and hadn't shattered the bone. A few months ago, a man in Dunkeld was shot in the knee—the musket ball lodged in his bone and the physician was unable to remove it. A shudder slithered up her spine. She'd tended the poor soul through the duration of his slow decline and eventual death.

With a shake, she pushed the awful thoughts from her head.

This man could not die.

Please, not a man as bonny as he.

But she'd never removed a musket ball before. "Are you certain you want me to do this—n-not a physician?"

"Aye," he clipped as if growing impatient.

Steeling her nerves, she resumed her grip on the knife and willed her hand to steady. "Prepare yourself, sir."

Without another hesitation, she slid the small knife through the opening with one hand and pushed against the ball with the other. The Highlander's entire body quaked. A strained, but whispered wail pealed from his throat.

Blood gushed from the wound and soaked Akira's fingers. Gritting her teeth, she applied more pressure, pushing the knife until she hit lead.

I cannot fail.

Refusing to give up, she gritted her teeth and forced another flesh-carving twist of her wrist. The ball popped out. Blood flooded from the wound like an open spigot.

The man thrashed wildly. Akira dove for her basket and grabbed a cloth. Wadding it tight, she shoved it against the puncture with all her might. "Hold on. The worst is over."

Though he never cried out, the Highlander panted, sweat streaming from his brow. "Horse."

Akira pushed the cloth harder. "The soldiers took all the horses."

"Damnation," he swore through clenched teeth, his breathing still ragged. "I will pur-chase…yours."

Goodness, the man could die with his next breath, yet he still issued orders as if he were in charge of an entire battalion of cavalry.

"I can barely afford to feed my siblings. I have no horse. Not even a donkey—not that I'd let you have it if I did." There. She wasn't about to allow this Highlander to lord it over her as if he were the Marquess of Atholl.

His eyes rolled to the back of his head. "Buy one."

"I told you—""

"Spor—ran. Coin."

Akira glanced at the man's sporran again, dubious about what she'd find this time. Digging her hands into any man's purse was vile enough, but this one had to be resting atop the most unspeakable place imaginable. Though she might be poor, she was certainly no harlot.

Fishing in there was as nerve wracking as carving a musket ball out of the man's well-muscled thigh. With a cringe, she tried shifting his belt aside a wee bit. Curses, the sporran shifted not an inch.

And goodness, he was still bleeding like a stuck pig. "Even if I did purchase you a horse, you couldn't ride. I'd wager you'd travel no more than a mile afore you fell off and succumbed to your wound." Still holding the cloth in place, Akira reached for her basket. "Let me wrap this tight and I'll call the soldiers. They're helping the wounded into a cart."

"No." His eyes flashed wide as he gripped her wrist. "They must not know I'm here."

She gave him her most exasperated expression, the one she always used when infuriated with her surly sister, Annis. "But they can help you."

"The Government troops? They're *murderers*." He winced. "They'd slit my throat for certain."

Since the battle's end, she hadn't seen anyone slit a throat...but then she hadn't asked where the soldiers were taking the injured. She'd just assumed to the monastery to be tended by the monks. But something in this man's cold stare told her to do as he said. Further, something in his voice commanded she obey him.

The hairs on her nape stood on end as she twisted the bandage like a tourniquet and tied it. "Who are you?"

"Merely...merely a Highlander who needs to hightail it back to his lands..." he drew in a stuttering breath. "A-afore the backstabbers burn me out."

She narrowed her gaze. *A man of property?* Akira might be a Scot, but her Gypsy blood still told her to take advantage of a wager—especially when her mother's larder was bare. "I'll do it for a shilling."

"Done," he said as if such coin meant nothing. "Make haste—and tell no one I'm here."

Gulping, she glanced down to the sporran and cringed. But she'd been in there once before. And the Highlander was in no shape to do anything untoward. If it weren't for the care of her mother and three sisters, she'd call over the dragoons—let them see to this man's care. But for a shilling? Ma would be ever so happy.

Akira's fingers trembled.

Taking a deep breath, she reached inside. Goodness gracious, she pulled three silver shillings and two ten shilling pieces. She'd never seen so much money in her life. No, she should not feel badly about asking for payment. After dropping one shilling in her pocket and returning all but one of the other coins, she held up a ten shilling piece. *This ought to be enough.*

Standing, she hesitated. "What, may I ask is your name, sir?"

A deep crease formed between his brows. "'Tis no concern of yours."

He didn't trust her—not that she trusted him either. "I won't reveal it." she crossed herself. "I swear on my grandfather's grave."

His lips thinned. "You can call me Geordie…and you, miss?"

Using a familiar moniker? And Geordie is no given name I've ever heard. Odd.

She curtseyed. "Then you may call me Akira." Blast, she wasn't going to say Akie. Only her sisters referred to her thus. And "Ayres" would make him suspicious for certain. Her family might be descendants of Gypsy stock, but they'd given away their heathen practices for the most part. If Mr. Geordie wanted to hide his identity, she certainly would hide hers. With blue eyes, she hardly looked like a Gypsy, aside from her dark hair and olive skin.

***

After the healer left, George Gordon closed his eyes and prayed the woman had enough sense to keep her mouth shut. Jesus Christ, he wasn't supposed to end up shot. Yes, he'd agreed to stand by his cousin and challenge the Government troops with vengeance. Their timing was paramount. After Queen Anne rejected Scottish Parliament's Act of Security, the entire country was in an uproar—ready to strike at last.

Though, blast it all, they weren't supposed to fail. Thank God he hadn't worn anything to reveal his peerage. He'd even kept to the rear beside his cousin William. But someone had shot him. Be it a stray musket ball or the keen aim of a musketeer, he had no clue. After being thrown from his horse, the skirmish had raged on and the clan's men charged ahead, leaving Geordie for dead.

Once he'd dragged himself into the brush, he must have lost consciousness until that fiery wisp of a healer found him. He thanked the stars it had been she and not a redcoat. His lands would be forfeit if Queen Anne discovered he'd ridden against the English crown to support the Act of Security passed by parliament one month past.

Anne, not the true King James, entitled to the throne by birth and recognized as king by Louis XIV. James Francis Edward Stuart may be exiled, but he is the only king to whom I will pay fealty.

But alliances were the least of his worries. Geordie's leg throbbed—ached like someone stabbed him with a firebrand. Worse, he'd been bled within an inch of his life.

Holding up his head for the lass to pour a tot of whisky down his gullet had sapped every lick of strength he could muster.

He must have dozed again, because Akira returned in the blink of an eye. "Who saw you?" he demanded, forcing himself to sit. God's teeth, everything spun. The stabbing pain made his gut churn.

"Pardon?" she replied in a tone mirroring his own. Never in his life had he seen such a haughty expression come from a commoner. She thrust a fist against her hip. "'Tis a bit difficult to conceal a horse beneath my arisaid. Besides, I didn't *steal* the beast."

He eyed her sternly, as he would a servant. "Did the stable master ask questions?"

"He asked where I came up with that kind of coin."

Gordon licked his lips with an arid tongue. "How did you reply?"

Akira's fist slid down—a better stance for a wee maid. "I told him I'd received handsome payment from his lordship for tending his cousin."

"His lordship?"

"The Marquess of Atholl, of course."

Smart lass. "Do you ken the marquess?" Bloody hell, he hoped not.

"If you call paying him fealty, then aye. So does everyone around these parts. He's lord of these lands."

And he supports the Government troops, the bastard.

Geordie needed to mount that damned horse and ride like hellfire.

He leaned forward to stand. Jesus Christ, stars darted through his vision. Stifling his urge to bellow, he gritted his teeth.

The lass caught his arm. "Allow me to help."

His insides clamped taut. Geordie needed help from no one—usually. And holy hell, must she look at him with such innocent allure? He'd sworn off women for life. No bonny face could melt through the iron casing around his heart even if she did have blueberry eyes and incredible dimples.

He nodded, but only once. "My thanks."

Clutching both hands around his forearm, she gave him a firm tug, managing nothing. Och, he should have known a wisp of a lass couldn't help a man his size. Clenching his teeth, he slid his good foot beneath him. Akira tugged his arm while he pushed up with the other.

"Christ Almighty," bellowed from the depths of his gut before he had time to choke it back.

She slung his arm over her shoulder. "If they didn't ken you were here, they do now."

"Ballocks," he cursed. Then he looked at the damned nag. "No saddle?"

She held out a few copper farthings. "There wasn't enough."

"Damnation, this is why one should never send a lass on a man's errand." Bloody hell, he hadn't planned on buying a horse when he'd left Huntly—and there was no way he'd sign a note.

The urchin stamped her foot. "Pardon me, but I'm trying to help you and I'll not be cursed at like a doormat."

Geordie grumbled under his breath, removing his arm from her shoulder. "Lead the beast to the fallen tree, yonder."

She didn't budge. "Oh my," she said with a gasp. "Your leg is bleeding something awful."

He swayed on his feet. Good God, he couldn't lose his wits. Not until he rode to safety. "Can you staunch it?"

"Mayhap with the use of your belt."

He slid his hands to his buckle when a twig snapped behind them. Lead sank to Geordie's toes.

"Who goes there?" demanded a stern voice.

Akira's eyes popped wide.

The beat of Geordie's heart spiked. With a wave of strength, he grabbed the lassie's waist and threw her atop the horse. Taking charge of the reins, he urged the beast into a run, steering it beside the fallen tree. Agonizing pain stabbed his thigh, but the dire need to escape shot herculean energy through his limbs.

Haste.

In two leaps he landed astride the gelding right behind the lass. Slapping the reins, he kicked his heels into the horse's barrel. Stabbing torture in his thigh punished his every move.

Musket fire cracked from behind.

Geordie leaned forward, demanding more speed. He pressed lips to Akira's ear. "Hold on lass, for hell has just made chase."

Other Books by Amy Jarecki:

Highland Defender Series/Highland Lords Series:

The Fearless Highlander
The Highland Duke, March, 2017
The Highland Lord's Stolen Kiss, June, 2017
The Highland Earl's English Lass, October, 2017
The Reckless Highlander, 2018

Guardian of Scotland Time Travel Series
Rise of a Legend
In the Kingdom's Name

Highland Dynasty Series:
Knight in Highland Armor
A Highland Knight's Desire
A Highland Knight to Remember
Highland Knight of Rapture

Highland Force Series:
Captured by the Pirate Laird
The Highland Henchman
Beauty and the Barbarian
Return of the Highland Laird (A Highland Force Novella)

Pict/Roman Romances:
Rescued by the Celtic Warrior
Celtic Maid

If you enjoyed *In the Kingdom's Name*, we would be honored if you would consider leaving a review. *~Thank you!*

About the Author

A descendant of an ancient Lowland clan, Amy Jarecki adores Scotland. Though she now resides in southwest Utah, she received her MBA from Heriot-Watt University in Edinburgh. Winning multiple writing awards, she found her niche in the genre of Scottish historical romance. Amy loves hearing from her readers and can be contacted through her website at www.amyjarecki.com.

Visit Amy's web site & sign up to receive newsletter updates of new releases and giveaways exclusive to newsletter followers: www.amyjarecki.com
Follow on Facebook
Follow on Twitter: @amyjarecki

Made in the USA
Charleston, SC
30 June 2016